Literatures, Cultures, and the Environment

Ursula K. Heise, University of California, Los Angeles, USA

Literatures, Cultures, and the Environment focuses on new research in the Environmental Humanities, particularly work with a rhetorical or literary dimension. Books in this series seek to explore how ideas of nature and environmental concerns are expressed in different cultural contexts and at different historical moments. They investigate how cultural assumptions and practices as well as social structures and institutions shape conceptions of nature, the natural, species boundaries, uses of plants, animals and natural resources, the human body in its environmental dimensions, environmental health and illness, and relations between nature and technology. In turn, the series aims to make visible how concepts of nature and forms of environmentalist thought and representation arise from the confluence of a community's ecological and social conditions with its cultural assumptions, perceptions and institutions. Such assumptions and institutions help to make some environmental crises visible and conceal others, confer social and cultural significance on certain ecological changes and risk scenarios, and shape possible responses to them.

Across a wide range of historical moments and cultural communities, the verbal, visual and performing arts have helped to give expression to such concerns, but cultural assumptions also underlie legal, medical, religious, technological and media-based engagements with environmental issues. Books in this series will analyze how literatures and cultures of nature form and dissolve; how cultures map nature, literally and metaphorically; how cultures of nature rooted in particular places develop dimensions beyond that place (e.g. in the virtual realm); and what practical differences such literatures and cultures make for human uses of the environment and for historical reshapings of nature. The core of the series lies in literary and cultural studies, but it also embraces work that reaches out from that core to establish connections to related research in art history, anthropology, communication, history, philosophy, environmental psychology, media studies and cultural geography.

A great deal of work in the Environmental Humanities to date has focused on the United States and Britain and on the last two centuries. *Literatures, Cultures, and the Environment* seeks to build on new research in these areas, but also and in particular aims to make visible projects that address the relationship between culture and environmentalism from a comparative perspective, or that engage with regions, cultures or historical moments beyond the modern period in Britain and the US. The series also includes work that, reaching beyond national and majority cultures, focuses on emergent cultures, subcultures and minority cultures in their engagements with environmental issues. In some cases, such work was originally written in a language other than English and subsequently translated for publication in the series, so as to encourage multiple perspectives and intercultural dialogue on environmental issues and their representation.

Ecocriticism and Shakespeare: Reading Ecophobia
by Simon C. Estok

Ecofeminist Approaches to Early Modernity
Edited by Jennifer Munroe and Rebecca Laroche

Myths of Wilderness in Contemporary Narratives: Environmental Postcolonialism in Australia and Canada
by Kylie Crane

East Asian Ecocriticisms: A Critical Reader
Edited by Simon C. Estok and Won-Chung Kim

EAST ASIAN ECOCRITICISMS

A CRITICAL READER

Edited by
Simon C. Estok and
Won-Chung Kim

EAST ASIAN ECOCRITICISMS

First published in 2013 by
PALGRAVE MACMILLAN®
in the United States—a division of St. Martin's Press LLC,
175 Fifth Avenue, New York, NY 10010.

Where this book is distributed in the UK, Europe and the rest of the world,
this is by Palgrave Macmillan, a division of Macmillan Publishers Limited,
registered in England, company number 785998, of Houndmills,
Basingstoke, Hampshire RG21 6XS.

Palgrave Macmillan is the global academic imprint of the above companies
and has companies and representatives throughout the world.

Palgrave® and Macmillan® are registered trademarks in the United States,
the United Kingdom, Europe and other countries.

ISBN: 978–1–137–27431–1

Library of Congress Cataloging-in-Publication Data is available from the
Library of Congress.

A catalogue record of the book is available from the British Library.

Design by Newgen Imaging Systems (P) Ltd., Chennai, India.

First edition: March 2013

10 9 8 7 6 5 4 3 2 1

For Ferenc Estók
and
to the memory of Haengjin Kim and Jeongae Kwon

CONTENTS

Section III Taiwanese Section

Section IV Chinese Section

PREFACE

잎 지다	**Eep jeeda**
김 원 중	**Won-Chung Kim**

만해마을 언덕 기슭에   Manhae ma-eul ŏndŏk kee-seugay

작은 은행나무 한 그루   Jag-eun eun-heng namoo han keuroo

물바가지 엎듯 순식간   Mool ba-gajee ŏp-deut soon-she-găhn

잎을 다 쏟아 놓았다   Ip-eul da ssōd-a noh-adda

제 키보다 넓게 지름을 벌려   Jay kee-bōda neol-gay jee-reum-eul bŏl-yŏ

둥글게 노란 방석 펼치고 있다   Doon-geul-gay nōran bang-sŏk pyeol-chēgo itda.

평상시 눈길 한 번 주지 않았지만   Pyeong-sang-shee noon-gil han-bŏn joo-jee an-at jee-măn

잎 진 고운 자리 마음이 끌려   Eep jin goh-oon jăh-ree mah-eum-ee kkeul-yŏ

다가가 앉으려는데   Da-gaga anzleoneundae

나무는 앙상한 가지 흔들어   Namoo-neun ang-sang-han kăjee heun-deul-rŏ

잎들을 훑트려버린다   Eep-deu-reul heut-t-rŏ bŏ-rinda

어 내 자리가 아닌가,   Ŏh nae jăh-ree-ga a-nin-gă,

비로소 여기가 저 은행나무   Pee-rō-sō yŏ-gee-ga jŏ eun-heng namoo

살아서 한 번도 앉아보지 못할   Sal ăsŏ han-bŏn-dō ănjăh-bōjee mŏt-hăl

아니 죽어서도   Ănee jook-ŏsŏdō

몸 내리지 못할 자리,   Mom nae-ree-jee mŏht-hal jăh-ree

스스로를 지탱하는 비탈임이 보인다   Seu-seu-rō-reul jee-taeng-hă-neun
                            pee-tărimee bōinda.

잎 진 자리 당신이 뭉클하다   Eep jin jăh-ree dang-shin-ee
                            moong-keul-hădă.

August 2012[1]

NOTE

1. This is a poem entitled "Leaves Fall," by Won-Chung Kim. The English translation reads as follows:

> On the edge of a hill in Manhae Village
> a small ginkgo tree
> shed all its leaves in an instant,
> As the contents empty when one turns a dipper upside down.
> It has spread around a yellow cushion
> whose diameter is larger than its height.
> Normally, I don't even give it a glance.
> But when I, being attracted by the beauty of the spot with fallen leaves,
> try to come near and sit down,
> the tree shakes its bare boughs
> and scatters the leaves away.
> Oops, is this not the place for me?
> I didn't realize until then
> that this is the spot where the ginkgo tree
> will never sit down, not even once in its lifetime;
> nor will it lay its body down, even after death—
> the slope against which the tree supports its life.
>
> On the spot where the leaves fall, my tears fall also.
> (Translated by Won-Chung Kim and Simon C. Estok.)

ACKNOWLEDGMENTS

Like food once eaten becomes part of the body, all forms of help for a book once accepted become inextricable from the final material product. We have been lucky to have had good nourishment for this book.

We are indebted to the editorial staff at Palgrave Macmillan (particularly to Brigitte Shull, Ciara Vincent, and Naomi Tarlow) for their diligence and support, and to the copyediting and production team at Newgen Imaging Systems (particularly to Deepa John) for their patience and meticulous skill. We would also like to thank Rachel Nishan at Twin Oaks Indexing for her careful, impeccable, and scrupulous work.

Simon Estok would like to express his gratitude to Sungkyunkwan University (SKKU) for its generous funding and research incentives, and, in particular, to several SKKU faculty: to Dr. Hong Dauk Seon, Dean of the Humanities at SKKU; to Dr. Jun-Mo Cho, Provost of SKKU; and to Dr. Jun Young Kim, the President of SKKU—each of these people played a key role in making Simon a Junior Fellow, an honor that, to a large degree, helped make this book possible. Simon would also like to thank Dr. Won-Chung Kim for his active support over the years. Finally, Simon would like to express his deepest gratitude to the love of his life, Cho Yeon-hee and to their two little children, Sophia and Jonathan.

Won-Chung Kim would like to thank his wife Hyunsuk and his children Lily and John for supporting and encouraging him during this long project. Won-Chung would also like to express deep gratitude to his colleague and friend Dr. Simon C. Estok, with whom it was a real happiness to work. Finally, Won-Chung is grateful beyond words to the late Dr. Sherman Paul, for it is Paul who first led him down the path of ecocriticism.

We would both like to thank the unsung heroes of this book, the scholars who read and offered substantial and detailed comments on portions of this book: this kindness from Greta Gaard, Daniela Kato, and Iris Ralph, at a time when each was swamped with other work, has made this book better. Finally, we would also both like to thank each of the contributors for their extraordinary patience with sometimes snarky and always demanding editorial comments. With three exceptions (two expats—one Canadian, one American—and one American professor), all of the contributors have written in a language which is not their first—an accomplishment in itself, but more remarkable both for the calibre and content of this writing.

1

PARTIAL VIEWS

AN INTRODUCTION TO EAST ASIAN
ECOCRITICISMS

Simon C. Estok

"Translation is a form of civil disobedience," Yaofu Lin explained to me in late August 2012, over an afternoon coffee in Seattle. The father of the ASLE-T (the Taiwanese branch of the Association for the Study of Literature and Environment), Lin knows the potential power that rests in the hands of the translator. This book is about carryings-across. Partial carryings-across. We are partial to what we carry across, and what we choose *not* to translate is as much a form of resistance as what we *do* choose to translate.

In the evening of the last full day of the 2005 ASLE-US biennial conference in Eugene, Oregon, a panel session entitled "Modernization and Literary Environmentalism: Asian Perspectives" offered the first real focus in English on East Asian ecocriticisms. It was another three years before the first analytical retrospective appeared in English on East Asian ecocriticisms. Far from being in what some perceived as the rather marginal position of the tail-end of a conference, a November 2008 plenary speech (jointly delivered by three scholars—one Japanese, one an American expat living in Japan, and one Korean[1]) took center stage at the International Conference on Literature and Environment at the Central China Normal University in Wuhan, China. In between these two events was an ASLE-Japan/Korea Joint Symposium held in Kanazawa, an important event that was to become the first in a series—the second being at Sungkyunkwan University in Seoul in 2010, and the third at the National Taiwan University in Taipei, Taiwan, in December 2012. A growing consensus from these meetings has to do less with a rejection of Western environmental theory, ethics, and approaches than with addressing the one-sidedness of information flows, a one-sidedness that predictably and dangerously reiterates colonialist dynamics and structures. Central, then, to much of the concern within the East Asian environmental humanities is the question of carryings-across, translations. With so few people in Western scholarship able to understand Mandarin or Hangul or Japanese or Taiwanese, the onus has often been on the Asian scholar to translate for the Western scholar. This book performs precisely such a carrying-across. We proceed on the assumption that the work in East Asia is important and that we here in East Asia are in the best position to articulate the importance of our work for the larger ecocritical community.

It would be reductive and mistaken, though, to suggest that translation is the core concern of East Asian ecocriticisms. East Asian ecocriticisms address urgent problems (some unique to the region, others less so) regardless of whether the West listens or wants to listen. The rapid postwar industrialization currently progressing in the region poses perhaps the most immediate social and environmental challenges, but there are other matters very specific to parts of the region: the division of the Koreas, the continuing tensions between indigenous and non-indigenous land use in Taiwan, legacies of poison in Japan, the sheer size of China, the growing conflict within East Asia between community needs, on the one hand, and the relative position and value of the individual on the other. The field is enormous. It is impossible to see it all. Partial visions are bound to characterize any view of East Asian ecocriticism. Because we each see from our own biased eyes, there are also the important matters of distortion and of how we see.

I saw something I initially thought very disturbing where I live in Seoul, but, as I pushed the issue, it turned out that I really didn't see what was going on at all. I live beside a stream (on the twentieth floor of a condo) in Seoul, and I run along the stream every morning before sunrise. On several occasions, I have planted indigenous maple saplings illegally on public grounds along that stream. On a run once with Scott Slovic, who was in town for a talk, we planted a tree together. Not all have lived, but some are now 20 feet tall. Before dawn one morning in July 2007, I was running beside the stream and nodding to all of the other early runners in this dense city (it has a metro population of over 25 million). There was a man with a saw cutting down Acacia trees. I was astounded. There was a line of ten that he had already cut down along a hundred-meter stretch beside the stream. No one said anything. People tend to mind their own business in Seoul. Not me. I asked him angrily in Korean what he was doing.

He responded in fluent English that Japan had stripped the land of vegetation and seeded Acacia in many places as part of the colonizing process. Acacia, an invasive species, now dominates many mountains in Korea. It was early, and my brain wasn't working well enough for me to formulate a response, and I ran on, doubting that anyone would have seen his actions as wrong—indeed, doubting that it was wrong, doubting the applicability of the very notions of right and wrong. His actions were wound up with questions about history, national identity, ecological preservation, pride, fear, resistance, and many other things.

I have always considered the cutting of a tree as an act of violence, and violence is violence. A saw is a saw, and a tree is a tree. When Jane Bennett, discussing our bodily enmeshments with the material world, asks, "[W]ould we continue to produce and consume in the same violently reckless ways" if we took these enmeshments seriously,[2] we are forced to question with her the very meaning of the term "violence." In his Nobel Prize acceptance speech, Barack Obama commented that "[a] non-violent movement could not have halted Hitler's armies." Nor will smiling at pretty Acacias stop their spread. We all know what violence can result from indifference. One doesn't want to compare Acacia to Hitler, but there are obvious similarities.

As a longtime resident of South Korea, I have often wondered about the violence of indifference and about, by extension, the potential effects of Western indifference toward Korea—at least in terms of culture and scholarship. American culture and scholarship spread like Acacia. As a Canadian, it was hard for me not to notice while growing up what seemed a very different culture south of the 49th parallel, one that often seemed to me north of the 49th to lack the sense of humility that I was accustomed to seeing in Canada.

It was with questions about indifference and arrogance in mind that I attended a conference in Brussels in 2008 and spoke about similarities between Canada and Korea as each country looks in the enormous face of cultural power the United States presents. I asked, "What shall we do about the lack of humility, toward both human and nonhuman nature, when we see it? What shall we do? How can we make them interested in us? How can we make them want to listen to us?" These questions grew, both in me and in the communities where I worked and visited, and it was with these questions in mind that I suggested a book project to Won-Chung Kim. This volume is the result. With this volume, we will make it easier for them to listen.

While the field of ecocriticism began as an American academic pursuit, it is now a multinational, multivocal, multicultural area of scholarship. Within this context, *East Asian Ecocriticisms: A Critical Reader* presents 12 original essays from Japan, South Korea, Taiwan, and China that define and characterize trends in East Asian ecocriticism. Drawing on diverse theoretical perspectives and traditions of East Asian environmental thought, as well as on less theoretically oriented close readings of East Asian texts (especially those not commonly studied or even heard of in mainstream ecocriticism), the essays in this volume present a valuable and original contribution to an ongoing and increasingly global conversation within the environmental humanities. This work is needed, for mainstream ecocriticism has not been able to give a lot of attention to voices beyond the ken of Anglo-European intonations. It is far better for a community to speak for itself (even if in a different language than its own) than to let others subsume this voice either by speaking on behalf or in partial or complete ignorance of that community. This book modestly hopes to contribute enormously to the developing area of ecocritical studies by offering situated responses (that are neither singular nor unmediated) to environmental problems and crises that, in some senses, affect all people and defy boundaries of nation, creed, race, ideology, gender, sexuality, class, and so on, responses from East Asia targeted for a Western constituency, offering voices that need to be heard.

While the dimensions of the "environmental crisis" are clearly global, responses grow out of local systems with varying cultural valencies. What this means is that an American ecocriticism will differ significantly in its material implications from, say, a Korean or a Taiwanese ecocriticism. All of the essays in this book work within an understanding that the history of ecocriticism is a history of relatively one-way flows. Aware of the fact that American geographies tend to become matters of global interest, every essay in this book has nation front and center in its ecocritical discussion.

There are four sections that constitute the core of the book. Rather than dividing the contents thematically (which would effectively perform a kind of universalizing that this book is implicitly against), we organized the book according to the national contexts out of which the contributors wrote: one each for Japan, South Korea, Taiwan, and China.

Chapter 2 begins this book of carrying-across and is, in fact, literally a translation. It is the only previously published material in the book, a translation into English of an essay originally written and published only in Japanese and included in Masami Yuki's book *Mizu no oto no kioku* (*Remembering the Sound of Water: Essays in Ecocriticism*, 2010). Yuki seeks in the essay to show the logic that she sees as characterizing

Japanese writings and, to a certain extent, Japanese ecocriticism, and she carefully rejects the Western essay model in this chapter. Yuki explains that unlike written English, Japanese requires neither a demonstration of a thesis nor a deductive or inductive examination of a thesis: she proceeds on this basis to examine the literary contributions of poet and writer Kazue Morisaki (1927–) to Japan's growing ecological discourse.

This chapter demonstrates more than argues that Morisaki's work is keenly interested in radically questioning modern values of dualistic separations between life and death as well as between self and others. Yuki shows that Morisaki employs the idea of ecological identity as a theoretical framework and examines Morisaki's diasporic exploration of language and identity, delineating how Morisaki's (self-) critical reflection on identity and language highlights the significance of cultural and social factors in developing ecological identity.

The chapter concludes by showing that Morisaki's work demonstrates that what we call "ecological identity" does not simply concern human relationships with the natural world but should include more comprehensive issues of self and others.

In chapter 3, Bruce Allen discusses Michiko Ishimure's critique of modernity and her vision for creating a society that can foster reconciliation between humans and the nonhuman world. It outlines the central features of Ishimure's writing and social activism by examining their exposition in three of her major works: *Paradise in the Sea of Sorrow* (1969), *Story of the Sea of Camellias* (1976), and *Lake of Heaven* (1996). Focusing particularly on Ishimure's distinctive narrative methods, rooted in local traditions of storytelling, the chapter shows how her stories connect with her work to revitalize local culture, community, and environment. It touches on the trajectory that extends from Ishimure's activism and writing about the environmental pollution incident in Minamata to the more recent events of the Fukushima nuclear incident. Finally, it suggests some implications of Ishimure's writing for Japanese and global ecocritical thought.

Chapter 4, by Keitaro Morita, offers a radically different perspective and gives one of the only examples of queer green theorizing yet to come out of East Asian ecocriticism. Morita begins carefully in this chapter, contextualizing his position and arguing that Greta Gaard's 1997 paper "Toward a Queer Ecofeminism" was long-awaited by ecofeminists who were interested in queer theories and queer theorists who were interested in ecofeminist theories, and that Gaard's simultaneous focus on the emancipation of women, nature and the nonhuman, and queers signals a significant theoretical link that has only recently been much expanded.

This chapter continues the conversation Gaard began and notes that ecocriticism requires the queer ecofeminist perspective of Gaard (and of other more recent scholarship). Morita confirms Gaard's observation that straight ecofeminism has often lacked the variable of sexuality and that there is a continuing need to dismantle dualisms. Morita then examines Hiromi Ito's 1991 poem "Matsuri [Festival]" based on "queerings of the green" and shows the possibility of a utopia/ecotopia where women, the nonhuman, and queers are mutually liberated. This chapter shows that an ecocriticism committed to an activist stance connects powerfully with very important social theories.

Won-Chung Kim begins the Korean section with chapter 5. This essay provocatively observes that there are important matters of globalization within the environmental humanities that strongly warrant attention. Kim maintains that one of the most widely discussed issues in the field of ecocriticism today is how to get over the limitations of an ecocriticism that is gripped by a cultural cringing toward America and to thereby make it a more viable multicultural and transnational discourse.

This chapter shows that while countries have become more closely interconnected economically and culturally under the banner of "globalization," ecocriticism has been voicing predominantly Western viewpoints on literature and environment and thus limiting its scope. In order to truly globalize ecocriticism, Kim maintains, it is necessary to broaden its academic sphere to encompass literatures of non-English-speaking countries.

This chapter then goes on to argue that ecological literature of Korea obviously deserves more attention and that this attention can help to truly globalize ecocriticism by introducing fresh perspectives. Kim argues that many works of Korean literature carry poignant insights about rapid industrialization and a consumption-oriented society. Kim distinguishes two prominent characteristics of Korean environmental literature: the first trait is its investigation of the close relationship between the division of the Korean peninsula and environmental degradation. The second feature is Korean ecoliterature's emphasis on life, not only that of humans but also of nature. This chapter compellingly demonstrates a central position of the entire collection—namely, that twenty-first-century ecocriticism should transcend national and geographical boundaries and be enlarged to a multicultural and transnational discourse, which considers not only Western viewpoints but also elements about the politics, economies, and cultural subtleties of the non-Western world.

Dooho Shin's chapter is a logical follow-up to many of the issues raised in chapter 5. Shin looks at the intersection between development and conservation in South Korea, using the Cheongyecheon Restoration project of central Seoul as a point of entry into these discussions.

Shin argues that it is vital to understand the economic, social, and political circumstances of modern Korea that have produced environmental discourses as a kind of a dialectical struggle between preservation and development. Development is uneven globally, happening at different rates and under differ pressures in different places and times. The postwar, postcolonial Korean context, especially of the late twentieth and early twenty-first centuries, has seen enormous and rapid industrialization. It is within this context, Shin deftly shows, that Korean ecocriticism has defined itself, often through recourse to ideas of preservationism embedded within traditional East Asian philosophy. The result, Shin claims, is often to give less-than-complete or satisfactory consideration to the real social circumstances of modern times. Shin explains that this backward-looking attitude is simplistic and unrealistic in understanding modern Korean society and environmental issues, which require instead a perspective of environmental sustainability that combines both preservationist and developmentalist stances.

After making a case for broadening ecocritical visions, this chapter examines the Seoul Cheongyecheon Restoration project and its discourses from the perspectives of environmentally sustainable urban development and then proposes reconsideration and more serious evaluation of the Cheongyecheon novels than critics have yet been willing to offer.

In chapter 7, Chan-Je Wu directly addresses the ecological implications of the geopolitical division of the Korean peninsula. Wu argues that the long-standing and uneasy division of Korea has produced discourses about the loss and recovery of identity and that these have come in part to define a deeply problematic sense of Korean ecological identity—an identity defined by loss.

In the modern literature of the divided Korea, Wu claims, the demarcation line is one of the main reasons for the loss, and it is characteristic of Korean literature that the loss of ecological identity becomes a heavy burden. Yet, while Wu talks about how the division of Korea "has brought irrevocable destruction of the natural environment," we have also to recognize that the DMZ itself is an amazingly pristine and untouched swath of land. At 250 kilometers in length and 4 kilometers in breadth, it runs the width of Korea and (though studded with some two million landmines) is one of the most untouched nature reserves in the world.

Wu discusses three contemporary Korean novels—Choi In-hoon's *The Square* (1960), Park Sang-yeon's *DMZ* (1997), and Kang Hui-jin's *The Ghost* (2011)—and offers close readings of how these texts attempt to deal with the often tragic situations resulting from division. Wu reveals that these books examine the ecological circumstances and the characteristics of the division of Korea in the Cold War era, the post–Cold War era, and the digital era, respectively, through characters who struggle to reach for the "Blue Square," an archetypal state of ecological identity and harmony, but instead end up in failure, stuck with the real world.

Because the breadth of the material Wu discusses covers almost the entire history of postwar Korea (indeed right up to the present), one of the things Wu is able to do is to look at the growing importance of digital media as they relate with environmental ethics and problems. While by no means exhaustive, the sally into discussions about virtual realities and the environmental humanities is an important beginning of a conversation that is bound to continue for a very long time.

Chapter 8 begins the Taiwanese section with Peter I-min Huang's comparison of indigenous American writer Linda Hogan and Taiwanese writer Sheng Wu, each of whom share a concern about representing corporate globalization and the blurring between what is real and what is not.

Huang offers a close reading of each writer's work, beginning with Hogan's *People of the Whale*. Huang explains that the leaders of one Native American tribe in the novel use the ancient "tradition" of the whale hunt in an attempt to persuade their tribe to restore whale hunting. Highlighting the profound conflict that the novel portrays between local practices and an increasingly global corporate capitalism, Huang shows the profound disparity between commercial whaling and the sacred rituals of older hunting practices in North America and the effects this disparity has on people.

Huang compellingly describes the provocation of Hogan's novel for the readers, first, to consider the possibility of intrinsic value and authenticity and, second, to question the staged show, or "spectacle," of a whale hunt.

Noting similarities with Hogan, Huang discusses Taiwanese writer Sheng Wu's questioning of the loss of embodiment and embeddedness that results from corporate globalization. Wu protests the government's embrace of corporate globalization, an embrace that is performed at the expense of local environmental interests. If for

Hogan it is whales, for Wu it is dolphins. Huang shows Wu's passionate concern for saving the wetlands: it is a battle to save Taiwan's endangered pink dolphins and to protect farming and fishing traditions that have been passed down by Taiwanese people from generation to generation for hundreds of years. Connecting the concerns of these two writers is important work.

Huang finishes his argument with a gesture toward the materialist implications of Hogan and Wu, suggesting that they both support Stacy Alaimo's argument in *Bodily Natures* that we need to recultivate "a tangible sense of connection to the material world."

In chapter 9, Shiuhhuah Serena Chou examines the work of second-generation Taiwanese nature writer Mingyi Wu, who has received extensive scholarly attention for his attempt to localize the nature writing genre and thereby produce an authentic Taiwanese nature writing genre. Chou demonstrates how Wu attempts to localize the nature writing genre and turn this Western literary genre into a culturally nativized one.

Chou explains that much of what Wu is about is *balance* in his *A Fascination with Butterflies* (2000), *The Dao of Butterflies* (2003), and *So Much Water So Close to Home* (2007). Wu is vitally concerned with wild(er)ness experience, the science of ecology, and the representation of nature. Chou poses the question: What does the insistence on the wild reveal about Taiwanese nature writing at a time when Euro-American writers and critics shy away from "wilderness" and its associated white, heterosexual, middle/upper class, male values? Part of her answer is that in a highly developed and densely populated country such as Taiwan, we need also to ask to what extent Wu's conceptualization of the wild could be understood as being another Western import—a concern for ecology. These are complex and provocative questions, and Chou treads carefully here. For Taiwanese ecocritics, she explains, the "Taiwaneseness" of Wu's nature and essays is less the question than whether nature writing, as a subtle form of natural history, is capable of embodying nature's uncontaminated wildness or ecological order.

This chapter explores how Wu's fancy for wilderness and pristine nature is a borrowed utopian notion, yet it is a dream that could be compensated for and realized through the pursuit of wildness inherent in butterflies and water. Through a Taoist perspective, however, Wu's wilderness, characterized by transience and temporality, goes on to suggest an aesthetics of space where change and a sense of historicity constantly infringe upon ecological notions of nature as a community, orderly or disorderly. Wu's wilderness, Chou shows, constitutes an enduring record of and testimony to nature's passage of evolution and regeneration that urges the perceiving of nature beyond a scale of direct human experience.

Yalan Chang discusses in chapter 10 the sensational and famous Taiwanese novel *The Butcher's Wife* (*Shafu*), by Ang Li. Long viewed largely for the implicit and explicit feminist comment Li makes, this novel has also a heavy focus on food, animals, and space, and Chang argues that these various strands are best viewed not simply through a feminist lens but through an ecofeminist lens that accounts for connected concerns.

Chang provides an alternative way to see why the female protagonist of the novel butchers her husband and notes the structural similarity in the way he slaughters animals. Chang shows how the intricate relationships among sexism, misogyny, and ecophobia are highlighted in *Shafu* and how this analysis benefits and opens up the spectrum of Taiwanese ecoliterature. Given the international appeal of translations of *Shafu*, this, Chang maintains, is particularly important. Moreover, given the almost universal interest among ecocritics in maintaining an activist stance, Chang shows that the traumatized woman in Li's *Shafu*, far from being an outdated image of times long gone, is indeed very important within current Taiwanese society, with daily news often showing similar stories—ones that are not fiction.

Jincai Yang begins the Chinese section with chapter 11 and offers a broad summary of Chinese writing in the environmental humanities since the beginning of accelerated industrialization in China in the 1980s. Yang maintains that since that time, there has arisen a critical concern among Chinese intellectuals over the ruthless exploitation of land and natural resources, and over what has become steady environmental deterioration. This awareness of the ecological problems that grows with China's modernization, Yang argues, has urged Chinese literary critics to reflect on Chinese economic achievements and their consequent environmental problems, giving rise to an ecocritical trend in literary studies. Yang explores how such a critical change occurred and became a fashion in contemporary Chinese literary studies.

One of the things Yang insists on is the idea that Chinese literary critics have not only drawn inspiration from Western critics to shape their outlook but have also synthesized their own views into a distinctly Chinese ecocritical discourse. The Chinese expression of ecological aesthetics has displayed a significant understanding of the ecological-systemic holism, Yang maintains, and the theories that have developed reveal their influences, both traditional Chinese and contemporary Western. Yang argues for the need for continued development of Chinese ecocriticism and lays out a startlingly clear and provocative proposal for such development. In chapter 12, Lily Hong Chen takes us toward realization of such development. Focusing on Hubei writer Yingsong Chen's stories about people in or from the great forested mountains of Shen Nongjia (an area that includes a National Nature Reserve listed on UNESCO's World Network of Biosphere Reserves), Hong Chen proposes a Chinese version of "posthumanism" where the human connection with animals or machines exists as material facts in spite of ecological devastation. Chen's chapter focuses on the issue of posthumanism as it is explored in a number of Yingsong Chen's Shennongjia novelettes, where dehumanization is seen to be occurring when one is placed within harsh nature as well as when one is dislocated into the civilized and yet strange world of urban culture. By pointing out the interlinked fates of human and animal in times of survival struggles, the chapter argues that Yingsong Chen's posthumanist stories are actually proposing an environmental ethic that leaves little room for human privilege. Professor Chen shows us that the Shennongjia stories have as their focus both human and nonhuman subjects, with both the urban and the rural as backdrops and participants that offer substantial challenges to survival. The survival challenges confront all, despite species and location. Professor Chen shows that Chen's concern for and representations of both humans and animals confuse boundaries between human and nonhuman in productive ways that allow for an ethical rewriting of the human within a specific regional context in China.

Xiangzhan Cheng brings us into a different academic context and argues from the position of a philosopher in chapter 13 about ecological aesthetics. Cheng maintains that ecological appreciation consists of four key points. First, it abandons the traditional aesthetic model that is based on the oppositional dualism of subject and object, and replaces that with the model of aesthetic engagement that promotes the idea of unity between humans and the world. Second, an ecological appreciation is an activity predicated on biospherically based ecological ethics. It revises and strengthens the relationship between aesthetics and ethics in traditional aesthetics, and it takes ecological awareness as the premise of ecological appreciation. Third, ecological appreciation must inspire curiosity and association and stimulate imagination and feelings by means of ecological knowledge; without ecological knowledge, there will be no ecological appreciation. Fourth, the two guiding principles of ecological value for ecological aesthetic appreciation are biodiversity and ecological balance. Cheng argues that humanity must overcome and transcend anthropocentric value standards and human aesthetic preference, reflecting and criticizing anthropocentric aesthetic preferences and habits.

While it seems a mistake, though, to endorse Aldo Leopold's value for static integrity as a defining feature of ecosystemic health, Cheng's overall project of charting the parameters and contents of ecological aesthetic appreciation is an important one. It is work that until now has not really been done.

Finally, Harvard's Karen Thornber wraps it all up in an afterword, summarizing ecocriticism's rapid development into a diverse, interdisciplinary field and then laying out some of the substantial challenges that remain. Thornber identifies these challenges as being both *cultural* (linguistic and geographical) and *conceptual*, arguing that despite the rhetoric of inclusiveness, ecocritics have limited themselves almost exclusively to creative texts written in Western languages, and English-language American literature in particular. To be sure, she argues, pathbreaking scholarship on environmentalism and postcolonialism has surged in recent years, but it remains significantly hampered by its focus on Western-language writings, to the near exclusion of texts from postcolonial societies written in other tongues. Thornber reminds us of a key point that the entire collection addresses: the fact that the bulk of ecocritical scholarship has not taken into consideration writings from East Asia, a region with its own traumatic colonial past and one that is home to three of the world's largest economies and nearly one-fourth of its people. Thornber explains compellingly that East Asian and other non-Western literatures ultimately cannot be examined in isolation and that while cultures and environmental problems are distinctive, they are not unique, and the need to globalize ecocriticism remains acute. Precisely because damaged environments are a global phenomenon, literary treatments of ecodegradation regularly transcend their particular cultures of production and can be understood as together forming intercultural thematic and conceptual networks. Examining these networks will be an important part of our ecocritical, if not literary future.

Thornber works with the concept of environmental ambiguity—the multifaceted, contradictory interactions between people and the natural world—to describe the complexities we face in responding to the vexed issues raised by rapid ecological change and degradation and the multiple ways fiction and poetry highlight the absence of simple answers and the paucity of facile solutions to environmental problems. Ecocritical scholarship has yet to give sustained attention to these complex ambiguities, and it is one of the explicit goals of this book to investigate some of the many possibilities in this regard.

This book is truly the first of its kind: original essays from a group of motivated scholars speaking for themselves to a Western constituency. In this important sense, our book responds to the unidirectional flow of ecocritical readings and theory that has characterized the environmental humanities. Offering voices from the region,[3] this book is the first to challenge what in East Asia is often perceived as Western indifference to East Asian ecocritical scholarship, to insist on attention to these voices, to compel an audience to hear, to translate and carry-across, and to see with less partiality. In an age when globalization is trumpeted so loudly, this kind of work is profoundly important. Moreover, given the continued growth in the region, at a time when other economies are stagnating or shrinking, the active engagement in our book with questions about sustainable development speaks lucidly to concerns that promise only to grow more insistent in the foreseeable future.

NOTES

1. These are Dr. Masami Yuki, Bruce Allen, and Dr. Dooho Shin, respectively, each contributors to this volume.
2. Jane Bennett, *Vibrant Matter: A Political Ecology of Things*. Durham: Duke UP, 2010, 113.
3. To avoid confusion, we have followed the practice of writing given names first, followed by surnames—rather than using the practice common in East Asia and some parts of Europe (Hungary, for instance, where my father is from) of writing the surname first, followed by the given name(s). Our purpose is not to ignore or diminish the importance of the "different value system shared by those who have their identity based on their family name more so than [on] their given name" (to borrow Masami Yuki's words in our discussion of this matter); rather, our purpose to have consistency in the book so that readers don't become confused by which is the surname and which is the given name.

Section I

Japanese Section

2

TOWARD A LANGUAGE OF LIFE

ECOLOGICAL IDENTITY IN THE WORK OF KAZUE MORISAKI

Masami Yuki

The original form of the following essay was written in Japanese. In the process of translation, I made some stylistic changes so that the essay would be more readable to an English-speaking audience. I intended, however, to preserve the basic structure of the discussions as it unfolds in my book chapter, hoping to show the logic that usually characterizes Japanese writings and, to a certain extent, Japanese ecocriticism.

Unlike written English, Japanese requires neither a demonstration nor a deductive or inductive examination of a thesis. As the literary critic Shuichi Kato observes in his *A History of Japanese Literature*, the Japanese worldview—and the writing system based on it—is characterized by a lack of abstract and theoretical systems. This is true, Kato suggests, not only of literature but of thought and critical writings.

The following essay examines the diasporic explorations of identity and language in the work of Japanese poet and writer Kazue Morisaki (1927–). Morisaki writes at the intersection of poetry, creative nonfiction, oral history, women's studies, and nature writing, all of which share her critical perspective on conventional notions of life. In order to frame the discussion of Morisaki's inquiry into the idea of life, I have employed the concept of "ecological identity" as elaborated by educator and scholar Mitchell Thomashow, suggesting that Morisaki's (self-)critical reflection on identity and language highlights the significance of cultural and social factors in developing one's ecological identity. The essay begins with an introductory discussion on ecological identity, and then shifts focus to Morisaki's diasporic inquiry of language, which articulates an uninstitutionalized way of being as well as an all-inclusive sense of life.

ECOLOGICAL IDENTITY

Environmental crisis involves a crisis of imagination. This well-known maxim suggests that the fate of the environment is subject to how the human mind conceives of its surrounding world; as we all know, it is not easy to imagine something to which we cannot relate. All too frequent news reports of war and murder, for instance, do not stimulate our imagination unless these stories are perceived emphatically as being in relation to us. Likewise, individual and societal treatments of others—both human and nonhuman—are subject to our relationship with them. From global issues such as climate change to more local, everyday problems such as garbage disposal, environmental issues permeate our daily lives. This implies a limit and failure of utilitarian views of the environment, which separates the natural world from that of humans and sees it as simply a resource for human use.

The exploration of new relationships with the environment encompasses a wide spectrum from thorough inquiries into alternative worldviews based on radical transformations of modern values to the more practical and viable—or what deep ecologists may describe as *shallow*—efforts of trying to create environmentally friendly societies by means of policies and laws. It is not easy to determine what is effective and what is not, since different approaches seek different effects: a radical transformation in thinking may take a long time to be realized, but it is likely to attain greater effect in creating a more sound relationship with the environment, whereas legal manipulation is likely to bring a visible change more quickly, leaving aside whether it contributes to a durable transformation or not. One thing that is clear, though, is that the development of environmental discourses since the 1970s has created new concepts and terms, such as "deep ecology," "ecofeminism," and "environmental justice," all of which help illuminate different facets of the complex relationships between humans and the environment. The creation of new concepts gives linguistic expression to abstract ideas, which in turn enables such ideas to be shared by many, thereby providing new perspectives, unsettling given conceptual realms, and eventually helping to reform them. New concepts in environmental discourse play such a significant role that they are key in revisionist examinations of human attitudes on the environment.

"Ecological identity" is one such concept that attempts to disentangle utilitarian viewpoints from modern attitudes on the environment. Unlike the modern, conventional, self-sufficient, and self-contained sense of identity, an ecological identity stands for that which is (re)created in a process of negotiations between an individual and the environment in which that person exists. In *Ecological Identity* (1995), Mitchell Thomashow describes "ecological identity" as "[referring] to all the different ways people construe themselves in relationship to the earth as manifested in personality, values, actions, and sense of self" (3). He further explains that "ecological identity describes how we extend our sense of self in relationship to nature" (3). In brief, the idea is that ecological identity can work as a gauge of the extent of one's relationship to the environment, which, in turn, plays no small part in refashioning one's identity. Such a focus on a way of being *in relation to* others (human or nonhuman) presents a striking contrast to the conventional notion of identity based on difference and separation between self and others.

In a society in which technocratic rationality dominates and everyday life requires few interactions with—and therefore little sense of connection to—the nonhuman world, we cannot assume that an ecological identity could be attained naturally, but rather that it would necessitate a conscious and reflective effort. Being reflective is in fact a key concept in Thomashow's discussions; he claims that a "reflective capacity is the core of ecological identity work—the integrating capacity to make knowledge whole" (173). A number of the activities identified in his book as helping promote a reflective capacity are mostly designed as classwork for environment-oriented courses and classes; however, Thomashow suggests that there are many chances to animate a reflective capacity in our daily lives, and that such activities are not limited to taking place in the natural world but can include built environments as well. As an example of an event in a human-made environment stimulating the reflective capacity, Thomashow tells the story of how his Tanzanian colleague, to whom a megasupermarket in the United States is "a giant museum" exhibiting so many "strange artifacts" that he has never seen, made him conscious of what he usually ignores: "I should be aware of the amount of packaging that is used, whether the product is grown locally...But my Tanzanian friend showed me that my habits run even deeper...His 'beginner's eyes' were filled with a different kind of wisdom, allowing me to understand the extent to which I take material wealth and security for granted" (177). As this anecdote demonstrates, once perceived from a revisionist point of view, daily life can be the ground for a reconsideration of how one relates to the world.

There are many different activities and situations that could promote a more intricate understanding of how we relate to the world. Reading literature is certainly one of them. With its poetic capacity to give form to that which isn't often articulated in dominant discourse, literary works can often provide readers with a fresh look at our familiar environment: just as Thomashow's Tanzanian friend did for him, perhaps literature can offer "beginner's eyes," which radically illuminates how our perception is woven by our culture and society.

Among the many domestic and foreign writers whose works help modern readers reflect on human interactions with the environment, Kazue Morisaki, a Japanese contemporary writer and poet, has been exploring what can be termed "ecological identity." Morisaki's literary journey is rather convoluted, due to her cultural background and upbringing. A second-generation colonist, Morisaki expresses in many of her works her complex feelings about her relationships with Korea, whose natural and social environments "raised" her, as she recalls in her essay entitled "Two Languages, Two Souls." Accordingly, what I wish to examine as ecological identity in Morisaki's work does not necessarily focus on "nature." This is consistent with Thomashow's comment that "ecological identity describes how we extend our sense of self in relationship to nature" (3). What I wish to demonstrate as ecological identity in Morisaki's work is more like an inclusive sense of identity, which aims to reconcile the conventional gap between a sense of self and an understanding of others. In what follows, I will discuss how Morisaki's linguistic and theoretical pursuit for an inclusive sense of identity develops in her reflective considerations on ideas of self, woman, and home. Morisaki's literary exploration does not focus on nature per se; nonetheless, her perspective resonates with the idea of ecological identity unfolded by Thomashow in that it illustrates "how we extend our sense of self in relationship to" social, cultural, and natural environments.

A major characteristic of Morisaki's exploration of identity is that she keeps questioning given concepts and never allows herself to rely on any social or cultural frame of reference. Her literary stance involves what Thomashow calls "beginner's eyes," which offers a perspective from which to see ordinary life reflectively. But at the same time, "beginner's eyes" sounds too naïve to describe Morisaki's theoretical position of dismantling the social and cultural implications of nation and women, a position from which she radically questions country, woman, and self. As Brett de Bary suggests, Morisaki's work is characteristically not appropriated by institutionalized values (128). Such a refusal of institutionalized thinking does, in fact, function in a similar way to beginner's eyes, in that both provide a position to see underlying values of everyday life in a reflective way. However it is named, Morisaki's literary exploration of the uninstitutionalized, whole being accompanies a radical inquiry of an accepted conceptual and linguistic matrix.

UNINSTITUTIONALIZING LANGUAGE

Morisaki was born in 1927 in Korea during the period of Japanese colonial occupation. According to her essay entitled "Two Languages, Two Souls," the fact that she was born and brought up in the colony continues to complicate her understanding of who she is:

> To talk about Korea is a burden. It makes me feel so heavy-hearted, I hardly know how to begin. I was born in Mikasa-cho, Taegu, Kyongsangpukto, Korea.
>
> Sensing that your birth—not the way you lived your life, but the fact of having been born—was in itself a crime is not something you speak about easily... It does me just as little good to think that I was only a child, that I wasn't born in Korea because I wanted to be. It is the very fact that I was born in that land without having chosen to do so, that I absorbed its culture, which in turn gave shape to my being, that gives rise to my dilemma. I find it impossible to remain objective about Korea or the activities of Koreans; I lose my composure. The hair of my Korean mother and my Korean nanny who carried me on their backs sticks to my lips. It fills my month with memories I never would have had had we parted in a different way. Each strand is more filled with the contents of my soul than words will ever know. I have not the power to compromise. Words are shrunken, unable to contain the fullness. Korea raised me, fed me at its breast. (153)[1]

The description of her memory in Korea, which is so concrete that she could not think of the women whom she affectionately called her "Korean mother" and her "Korean nanny" without the feeling of their hair on her lips, demonstrates how people and the environment in Korea shaped and colored Morisaki's childhood. If we call the place of our childhood self-formation "home," Korea, where she "absorbed [the] culture which in turn gave shape to [her] being," is nothing but home. But Morisaki's sense of being "raised" by Korea never corresponds to her sense of who she is, because the historical fact of her being a second-generation colonist does not allow her to see Korea as her home. According to her autobiography *Keishu wa haha no yobigoe* [Gyeongju, The Call of Mother] (1984), Morisaki was brought up in a family that seemed unusually liberal at that time. It reflected her parents' liberal philosophy—especially that of her father, who was concerned about issues of ethnic minorities while working at a junior high school for Korean students in the colony. Morisaki's account illustrates how her father made continuous and occasionally life-threatening efforts to attain a genuine exchange between the Koreans and the Japanese. Morisaki was the oldest of their three children (two girls and one boy). That she was raised in a liberal, nuclear family seems to have helped her develop as an independent individual, which would have been difficult to attain in the more patriarchal society of Japan. Morisaki's mother, who died of cancer at the age of 36 when Morisaki was a high school student, is described as a gentle yet strong-willed woman, as is exemplified in the episode of her sneaking a bottle of wine into her daughter's suitcase as a token of freedom and responsibility when she moved to a boardinghouse near her high school. The family had a Korean nanny, who was more like a family member than a caretaker. Thus, Morisaki was brought up in an environment that did not necessarily follow Japan's cultural and social norms.

Free from these social pressures and nurtured by the people and environment of Korea, Morisaki expresses that when she realized the implications of her having lived in a colony, she became aware that "she had lived in a way that she fell in love with, without knowing anything and did not know what excuse to offer" (*Keishu* 240).[2] It is not difficult to imagine how such an awareness developed into an idea of her birth being a "crime," as is expressed at the beginning of "Two Languages, Two Souls." Instead of lamenting, Morisaki faces the fact of her not having a place either in Korea or Japan and accepts her diasporic being.

Far from being nostalgic, Morisaki's feelings about Korea involve a peculiar tension—peculiar due to her lack of foundation in her relations to Korea. In "Two Languages, Two Souls," she writes:

> Two different and overlapping cultures color my perception of "I." This is no self-protective subterfuge. "I" is innately a comprehensive expression of the historical structure of the individual. The word is thus composed of two appositive dynamics—the reductive dynamic that distinguishes between the individual self and other and the extensive

dynamic that encompasses the area of shared experience that exists between self and the other and that necessitates the inclusion within "I" of an indefinite number of others without whom "I" would have no meaning. Ordinarily, as it is used in everyday parlance in Japan, the latter function of the word is closer to the surface. Through it the range of responsibility the individual must accept for everyday life is more or less ambiguously defined.

I came to Japan after the war and learned that the Japanese used the word "I" around the axis of the latter function. In my life in Korea, my use of the word had been biased in favor of the former function. I thought to myself quizzically that the Japanese were a people unable to grasp the full functional range of "I." (154–55)

This passage illustrates where Morisaki culturally and linguistically locates herself: she sees Japan rather objectively without making herself conceptually assimilated as Japanese. Such a stance would be positively evaluated as cosmopolitan in the present culture of globalization, but a positive mood is incompatible to Morisaki's position from which she reflects on her past life as a second-generation colonist. Moreover, although the quoted passage shows that the Japanese usage of "I" appeared strange to Morisaki who "absorbed [Korean] culture, which in turn gave shape to [her] being," it does not imply that Morisaki's attitude is rooted in Korean culture. Rather, Morisaki forbids herself to rely on Korean values, as she claims that she "[has] simply lost the means to express what there is to say" (154). In other words, Morisaki suffers an absence of a language with which to articulate her thoughts, her feelings, and herself.

The awareness of the insufficiency of language and the resultant sense of a need for a new language permeate Morisaki's work. Rather than addressing epistemological questions of who she is, Morisaki looks for a language with which to express her diasporic identity. The writer and literary critic Kazuko Fujimoto, who also translated some short pieces of Morisaki, has touched upon this point, suggesting that Morisaki's thoughts have been revolving around an awareness of absence. Fujimoto says, "Morisaki has been conscious of an insufficient language of experiences and of the wholeness of being, developing such consciousness into a foundation on which she recognizes and expresses her life." Fujimoto continues that Morisaki sees such an absence of language "as the condition of her existence" and that she "lives her life without looking away from her existential abyss or abandoning the tensions at which she might be suspended in her wandering for a language that might enable her to express who she is" (147).

In addition to Morisaki's awareness of the linguistic insufficiency, Fujimoto observes, the death of her brother, who suffered a sense of homelessness, envying his sister's being able to attain connectedness to others due to her reproductive ability, drove Morisaki to explore who she is. Fujimoto explains,

> One of the reasons why Morisaki, using an awareness of absence as her strength, steps out onto terra incognita, instead of looking for a possibility of compromising with her situation, is found in her unsolved, entangled feelings about her brother Ken-ichi's killing himself when he was in his second-year at Waseda University in Tokyo...If her brother had not killed himself, it would have taken more time for Morisaki, who was trying to find her place as a woman with a child, to have a different perspective of life. (148)

Because Morisaki was establishing a happy household with her husband and baby daughter, when her brother visited her in 1953, she was understandably devastated with her brother's observation that a woman can attain a sense of connection by means of her reproductive ability. As a matter of fact, five years after her brother's suicide, Morisaki left home with her children and launched off on a journey to find what she calls "Japan-as-place."

Not so much coined but linguistically manipulated words such as "Japan-as-place" (in contrast to Japan) and "home-place" (in contrast to home) frequently appear in Morisaki's work, especially that written in the 1970s.[3] Differentiating "Japan-as-place" from Japan as a modern nation, as well as "home-place" from home, shows a part of Morisaki's attempt to unsettle given conceptual realms of language. However, in statements such as "I will make it a principle not to have a so-called home and try to explore home-place" (Morisaki "Ankoku," 61), for instance, it is not clear what Morisaki's deliberate differentiation between seemingly synonymous words such as "home" and "home-place" implies. As I will discuss in detail later, I would like to suggest that Morisaki's linguistic manipulation displays the peculiar position from which she gropes for a language to articulate herself while dismantling conventional conceptual understandings of self.

The following passage is a good example of Morisaki's linguistic attempt to objectively approach Japanese society by differentiating between "home-place" and home and between "Japan-as-place" and Japan:

> It would have been easy to allow myself to refuse Japan's authority by blaming the modern nation for its invasion of Korea. Neither

my brother nor I were able to feel at ease with the idea that...the traditional cultures of Japan-as-place still survive. Like rising sulfur smoke, exclusion and discrimination come out from people's everyday life in Japan-as-place after the war, expelling the Korea which raised and fed us. I decided not to complain about not having my home. I wanted to make myself home for my brother; moreover, I wanted to find a way to love with critical urgency Japan-as-place which internally constitutes Japan. (59–60)

The linguistic and conceptual difference between Japan and "Japan-as-place" is not intended to provide a means to criticize the modern nation from an ordinary person's point of view; Morisaki expresses her awkward feelings about "Japan-as-place" as well, implying that for her, home is not so much a place that exists as it is something that she should create anew. Yet, Morisaki's writings do not provide concrete descriptions of what home is like; this demonstrates that Morisaki's sense of home was not yet fully conceptualized, most likely because of a lack of language to embody the concept.

Morisaki's exploration of a new language, which parallels her inquiry into her identity, always takes place in marginalized areas, such as coal mining towns and coastal villages. Not being able to identify herself as Japanese, much less as Korean, she began a series of travels to places that are socially neglected by what an iconoclastic historian calls Japan's imperial, rice culture based ideology (cf. Amino).[4] In such travels she came across uninstitutionalized ways of being, ways that had survived imperial, patriarchal, centripetal ideologies as well as the succeeding technocratic modernization that swept through Japan.

Morisaki's first book, *Makkura* [Pitch Black] published in 1961, collects the oral stories of female ex-coal miners. Writing oral history is characteristic of Morisaki's early work; having suffered a loss of a way of understanding her diasporic being, Morisaki probably found in the female coal miners integrated beings, which were not severed into an erotic self and a social self. From the late 1950s till the mid-1970s, Morisaki's primary interest was in the "underground culture" of coal miners, which she depicts as being in stark contrast to the "above-ground culture" of Japan's imperial, agrarian, and mono-ethnic ideology.

When Morisaki moved to a coal mining town in the Chikuho region in the late 1950s, in order to look into finding a "home-place," the coal mining town was not so much a landscape of labor as a place of peculiar culture, which Morisaki would later define as "a spiritual history of coal mining" (she uses this as the subtitle of her 1974 book entitled *Naraku no Kamigami* [Gods of Abyss]). Such a peculiar culture of "spiritual history" is illustrated in her retelling of the stories that female ex-miners told to her:

> People believe that you shouldn't get in the pit during a period of red defilement (i.e., menstruation), but that's not true. Nothing happened to me. They say that you become impure due to red defilement or black defilement (i.e., someone's death), but that's a story of above-ground. You don't let your belief decide whether you should go in the pit or not; you let your will decide. Your will is everything.
>
> I found it no problem, and I just soiled myself in the pit during a period of red defilement, wearing only underwear as we usually did. Nobody knew since it's pitch black. Wetting myself with bloody stuff, blood stuck to my crotch as soon as it dried, making it difficult for me to work. Back then, nobody used a thing you put on your underwear. You don't put on but put in, balling it up like this and putting it in. When it was light, it was okay; but when it was heavy, blood spurted out. It's such heavy work. You pulled coal with your ass up, and it just spurted out.
>
> They say that you should go home when you see red ink, and leave the pit when you see a stain. Even the boss didn't say anything when you were in a period of red defilement. It actually wore you out and I wanted to take a day off. But if I didn't go work, the whole family would suffer...
>
> If you are thorough in your faith, that's good. But if your faith is superficial, it'd be better not to have one. A superficial faith does not do any good, just making you feel uneasy. It is not your faith but your will that makes you decide whether you should go in a pit or not. (*Makkura* 174–75)

This passage implied Morisaki's fascination with the underground world, in which "a story of above-ground" does not mean anything, as a place where the ideology-laden "Japanese" order cannot reach. The woman asserting that "[y]our will is the most important, [and] nothing else" materializes a way of being that is free from an institutionalized world of order. Later Morisaki would describe such female coal miners as those who "tried to live their love and labor together" (234). In other words, Morisaki sees in coal miners integrated beings in which the erotic self is the social self—no distinction between them.

The underground world of coal miners unfolds for Morisaki a world separate from the modern nation of Japan, but it does not mean that Morisaki sees it as an alternative viewpoint. While seeing the underground world as peculiar culture, Morisaki suffers a lack of language with which to articulate it: "Where the language of above-ground becomes useless and no accumulation of human experiences is at hand, how can one face such darkness? If the above-ground ideas are no use, how can one bear and overcome fear?" (*Naraku* 11). Morisaki's observation of an underground world echoes how she sees herself being "fed and raised by Korea" without being aware of the political history. In both cases, what Morisaki encounters is a lack of language with which to articulate an uninstitutionalized way of being. It should be noted that, although she was attracted by the underground "culture of spiritual history," Morisaki carefully avoids idealizing such culture, as is demonstrated by the fact that instead of writing *about* them, she chose to listen to them to "approach, reveal, and write down their reality or mental landscape" (Matsubara 129). In other words, Morisaki's listening to and transcribing of the stories of ex-miners represents her desire for a language of experience—a language with which the tough, bold women speak for themselves.

The treatment of female workers in coal mines changed drastically with the mechanization of coal mining. In *Makkura*, Morisaki describes a period of preindustrialized coal mining from the 1890s through the 1920s, during which tough, bold girls and women were not uncommonly found working underground (cf. Yamamoto). The mechanization of the work in the pits and the streamlining of the overall work structure, as well as a ban on employing "protected miners," brought major changes in the workforce, thus excluding female coal miners from the Chikuho coalfield where previously large numbers of women had worked in the pits (Tanaka 129). With mechanization and industrialization, an aboveground logic came down to and dominated the underground.

Morisaki sees a prototype of an uninstitutionalized way of being not only in coal miners but also in women abalone divers and *karayuki* (girls who were sold overseas from the late nineteenth to the early twentieth century). The 1976 publication of *Karayuki-san* [Sold Overseas] in fact marks Morisaki's literary transformation: her focus began to shift from the history of unknown people to the history of her own life, allowing her to voice an examination of the uinstitutionalized life of women in Japan and other countries in Asia. *Karayuki-san* is a hybrid text of oral history, literary and journalistic research, and creative writing, which opens with the story of Morisaki's acquaintance—who was the daughter of a former karayuki—showing the unspoken sense of life karayuki embodies by making Morisaki witness her abortion. Morisaki repeatedly told this story in slightly different versions until crystallizing it as a short story entitled "New Life" in 2001. I will discuss this story later; for now I would just like to suggest that perhaps the story of abortion, which questions the commonly shared opposition of life and death, gave form to what Morisaki seems to have been seeing: an all-inclusive sense of life and a language with which to talk about it. Also, Morisaki's resistance to the opposition between self and others shows the deep affection for one's fellow humans that Morisaki finds in karayuki, who were and still are labeled merely "prostitutes" and looked down on.

Whether working in a pit or overseas, those women epitomize a peculiar culture, which seems comparable to what Morisaki calls "home-place." But at the same time, their presence is almost always accompanied by an absence of language with which to speak of their values. In *Karayuki-san*, for instance, Morisaki observes how modern values misrepresent karayuki:

> Karayuki girls came into being in their home back then. In fact, they were embraced by their home; that's why they were called affectionately as *karayuki-don*. Outsiders called them "stowaways," "overseas prostitutes," "Amakusa girls," "a group of Japanese girls," "a national disgrace," and so forth...
>
> The naming of *karayuki-don* must have represented the compassionate feelings of the people of their home, so I thought while walking in the villages where, in the Meiji era, girls were given protection at Moji Port. If we see those girls only from present values, we may repeat the same mistake as the newspaper reporter who called them "stowaways." (47)

What is implied in this passage is that modern values fail to grasp how karayuki girls were perceived by the people of their home and how they perceived their home. As when she observes the peculiar "underground culture" among coal miners, Morisaki sees a unique value operating among those who were intimately called "karayuki-don" as well as those who called them so.

The value that karayuki as well as coal miners embody is not so much premodern as nonmodern because, while premodern values were being replaced by modernity, nonmodernity resists the modernization of conceptual reality.[5] As I have mentioned earlier, Morisaki's diasporic struggle for identity and language finds in Japan's premodern, rural, community-based value an exclusive mindset, which she implies parallels modernity's either-or logic of violence. A way of uninstitutionalized being and the language that articulates it is nonmodern by character, not appropriated by either the premodern or the modern, operating with its own peculiar value.

BIRTHING A LANGUAGE

Morisaki's literary exploration of a new language is demonstrated in the development of her idea of the continuation of life. Morisaki introduces an idea of birthing so as to disentangle the modern notion of a self-sufficient "I" and to reimagine a concept of life:

> We tend to think of our lifetime as being complete within one generation, beginning with birth and ending with death. This way of thinking underlies the conventional notion of "I."
>
> Such a way of thinking makes us feel that our life is complete by itself.
>
> But that's not the case. We are not simply born, live, and die; we give birth as well.
>
> A continuation of life is an important element of sex. Unless we see ourselves in a chain of life which involves birth, giving birth, and death, we cannot see a whole picture of life, let alone share a sense of history; but we don't have such a tradition. Perhaps life is so natural that people don't see it reflectively; consequently, our society or education are not operated with such a sense of life. (*Inochi hibikiau* 30–31)

This passage clearly illustrates the underlying philosophy of Morisaki's attempts to dismantle the conventional "I," question its self-sufficiency, and give linguistic as well as theoretical expression to "the continuation of life." All these attempts originate in the experiences of her mid-twenties, when she became pregnant and felt awkward in using the first-person pronoun "I" while chatting with her colleagues at the school where she was teaching art and Japanese. The awkward feeling was due to the gap she perceived between the conventional first-person pronoun and her reality of carrying life within her. Morisaki writes:

> Language is insufficient. The idea of life is not mature enough.
>
> ...
>
> It is perhaps because "giving birth" has only been a subjective experience, without being objectified as an important part of human life.
>
> I had used the pronoun "I" which is filled with a vivid sense of being an individual, or a sense of ego. That pronoun does not stimulate one's consciousness from inside of his/her own body as others do to us.
>
> ...
>
> But, I could not find any first-person pronoun which would articulate a woman carrying a life, simply realizing that there is no word which would express a whole being in which a mother giving birth and a child being born are not separated. (30–31)

What is at issue in this passage is the linguistic and philosophical immaturity of the conventional first-person pronoun that Morisaki sees cannot articulate a way of being in a continuation of life. I should note that Morisaki's idea of carrying life not only refers to the physical experience but also involves a theoretical examination. Theorizing the notion of birth and unsettling the conventional sense of "I," thereby dismantling the prevailing sense of binary oppositions such as woman and man, and those who give birth and those who do not, is a core element of Morisaki's exploration of identity.

Juxtaposed, life and death appear to be opposite, or even in conflict, and that is how they are usually perceived; life and death are generally seen as an either-or. Curiously, however, when introducing the idea of birthing, life and death no longer seem mutually exclusive. The following true story will help explain this.

A newspaper article featuring Japanese actor Konomi Mashita's experience of "birthing" illustrates a rather unconventional perception of life and death. The story goes like this. In the sixth month of her pregnancy, Mashita found her fetus dead within, having noticed that there were no fetal movements. The story continues:

> Three days later, with the help of an ecbolic, I gave "birth" to my child who had died inside me. I suffered a contraction, which seemed to me to continue for a long time...Unexpectedly, the baby was really beautiful—just a bit smaller than other babies. The baby "had the same eyes and nose as me, and the facial contours and legs were like my husband's." A smile broke out from me. It was strange since I had thought I would cry. ("Rokkagetsu tashikani ikita")

Mashita's encounter with her baby, her perception of the baby as beautiful, and her joyous recognition of the wonder of a new "life" are all strikingly similar to the responses of a mother to her newborn baby. Mashita smiled instead of mourned; she was fascinated with the beauty of life—or death—that her baby materialized. In the quoted passage, life and death are not contrasted but rather are situated in the same matrix of experience and knowledge.

In the continuation of life, life does not oppose death. Likewise, a language of life should be inclusive in a way that is able to talk about death and life without opposing either. Morisaki's short essay entitled "New Life" exemplifies this. This story begins with the episode of her friend insisting on her witnessing the abortion she is going to have, an episode that Morisaki has returned to many times in her writing. This episode describes her awkward feeling about the conventional pronoun "I" in her pregnancy. It touches upon the postwar landscape of a person selling a child and ends with her early poem that illustrates her confusion over the gulf between self and others. Interestingly, Morisaki writes this story in a manner that imagines livebirth and still-birth, or wanted life and unwanted life, without pitting one against the other or making moral judgments. As I touched upon in the translator's note of "New Life," the language of life is so encom-passing that it gives expressions to all life, including ones taken or unwanted: "Abortion and childbirth appear to be incompatible, yet in either case, the passage is the same—the birth canal" (Yuki 187). A language of "New Life" demonstrates a language that goes through a birth canal—in other words, a language of the process of life, or a language of the continuation of life. When "New Life" came out in 2001, Morisaki was 74 years old. Her exploration of a language of a whole being—which began with her awareness of a lack of identity as well as language in her twenties and has continued since then in her physical and spiritual journeys to marginal places—finally starts to take shape.

In concluding this essay, I wish to add that, although the works of Morisaki that I have discussed do not seem to directly show an envi-ronmental concern, they are intricately connected to issues of human relationships with the nonhuman world. Morisaki's primal interest in an inclusive vision of life is not confined to human society but encompasses the nonhuman world as well. Nature—both the exter-nal nature of a physical environment and the internal nature of the human body—serves as a point of reference for Morisaki's exploration of an integrated being. In "New Life," Morisaki's awareness of her unnatural sexual identity came in her recognition of a grapevine's natural and integrated way of being: "I saw grape vines climbing up to the balcony roof. On the vines were some grapes. Looking up at them, I shed tears. Vines and grapes, I envy you. Your leaves and fruit are all yourself" (185–86; I made minor changes to the original translation). Nature is always in flux, in process, and in continuation. A grapevine demonstrates a way of being whole in its progression from a young vine to a matured one laden with fruit. It is partly from her contact with and observations of the way of the natural world that Morisaki learns how to accept change, which is the major char-acteristic of a continuation of life. Morisaki's struggle for a way of whole, uninstitutionalized being and a language that gives form to it suggests how tightly and deeply cultural and social values determine one's perception of self, others, and life. It this way, Morisaki's work demonstrates that what we call "ecological identity" does not simply concern human relationships with the natural world but should include more comprehensive issues of self and others.

NOTES

This chapter is an English translation of the last chapter of my book *Mizu no oto no kioku* [Remembering the Sound of Water: Essays in Ecocirticism] (Suiseisha, 2010) with some revisions. The chapter's earliest form was published in English under the title of "New Life, New Language: Ecological Identity in the Work of Morisaki Kazue" (*Studies of Language and Culture* 13, 2009, 151–65), and the book chapter has the same title in Japanese. In order to avoid confusion, I have chosen a slightly different title for this essay, wishing to demonstrate that this essay, which is mostly based on the discussions I developed in the book, is a part of my continuous effort to examine Kazue Morisaki's idea of language and life in a context of literary environmentalism.

1. I changed "nanny" to "my Korean nanny" in the English version of the essay translated by Fujimoto Kazuko.
2. Except for those portions published in English translation, quoted passages of Morisaki's works in this chapter are my translation.
3. In Japanese, Morisaki employs different sets of Japanese syllabaries to demonstrate a difference between conventional concepts and her vision. For instance, she uses にほん instead of the conventional 日本 (both are pronounced the same), as well as differentiating ふるさと and ホーム, which are commonly regarded as synonyms.
4. Historian Yoshihiko Amino presents strikingly iconoclastic accounts about Japanese history. According to Amino, Japan's imperial ideology has been supported by the formation of an agrarian myth, which claims that Japan is traditionally a monoethnic rice-farming country with an emperor as its center; such a myth has marginalized and neglected diving/fishing culture (*Nihon no rekishi o yominaosu* 261, 267–68). Interestingly, Morisaki's interest in a "peculiar culture" extends to women abalone divers who maintain traditional diving methods—abalone divers as a symbol of a forgotten way of life. Paying attention to coastal societies, perhaps Morisaki's literary insight intuitively grabs what is systematically neglected by Japan's widespread ideology—neglected and yet not apparently victimized, a fact that fascinated Morisaki. She perceives the women abalone divers as materializations of an unconstrained, integrated being in their being independent of the social conventions of human relationships.
5. I owe the discussions of nonmodernity to Patrick Murphy's observations in his *Farther Afield in the Study of Nature-Oriented Literature* (2000), in which he claims that "[o]ne of the limitations of postmodernist critique is the reliance on binary oppositions as the fundamental mechanism of analysis...What is ignored by such opposition is the continuation of a nonmodernity—including various paramodern formations—that cannot be defined by the parameters of postmodernity" (90).

WORKS CITED

Amino, Yoshihiko. *Nihon no rekishi o yominaosu* [Revising a Japanese History]. 1991/1996. Tokyo: Chikuma, 2005.

de Bary, Brett. "Two Languages, Two Souls: Morisaki Kazue and the Politics of the Speech Act." Trans. Nagahara Yutaka. *Shiso* 886 (August 1996). 114–45.

Fujimoto, Kazuko. "Maru no mama eno kawaki, soshite ketsuraku no ishikika e" [Thirst for the Whole, and Awareness of Absence]. Morisaki Kazue, *Collected Poems by Morisaki Kazue*. 1984. Tokyo: Doyo bijutsha, 1990. 147–59.

Kato, Shuichi. *A History of Japanese Literature: The First Thousand Years*. Trans. David Chibbett. Tokyo: Kodansha International, 1979.

Matsubara, Shin-ichi. *Genei no commune* [A Visionary Commune: Examining Circle Village]. Osaka: Sogensha, 2001.

Morisaki, Kazue. "Ankoku to iu hikari ni mukatte" [Towards the Lights of Darkness], 1972. *Kaiho no shisou* (1974): 56–67.

———. *Inochi hibikiau* [Resonating Lives]. Tokyo: Fujiwara shoten, 1998.

———. *Karayuki-san* [Sold Overseas], 1976. Tokyo: Asahi Shimbunsha, 1980.

———. *Keishu wa haha no yobigoe* [Gyeongju, The Call of Mother], 1984. Tokyo: Yosensha, 2006.

———. *Makkura* [Pitch Black], 1961. Tokyo: San-ichi shobo, 1977.

———. *Naraku no kamigami* [Gods in the Abyss: History of Spiritual Labor in Coal Mines], 1974. Tokyo: Heibonsha, 1996.

———. "New Life." 2001. Trans. Yuki Masami (Raker). *ISLE* 13.1 (2006): 183–87.

———. "Two Languages, Two Souls." 1968. Trans. Fujimoto Kazuko. *Concerned Theatre Japan* 2. 3/4 (1978): 153–65.

Murphy, Patrick. *Farther Afield in the Study of Nature-Oriented Literature*. Charlottesville: UP of Virginia, 2000.

"Rokkagetsu tashikani ikita" [Living a Six-Month Life], *Asahi Shimbun*, February 6, 2007.

Tanaka, Naoki. *Kindai nihon tannkou rousoushi kenkyu* [History of Coal Miners in Modern Japan]. Tokyo: Sofukan, 1984.

Thomashow, Mitchell. *Ecological Identity: Becoming a Reflective Environmentalist*. Cambridge: MIT Press, 1995.

Yamamoto, Sakubei, ed. Morimoto Hiroyuki. Compiled. Tagawa City Coal-Mining Museum. *Chikuho tanko e-monogatari* [Pictorial Stories of Chikuho Coal Mines]. Fukuoka: Ashi shobo, 1998.

Yuki, Masami. "Translator's Note." Morisaki, "New Life." 187.

3

FIRST THERE WERE STORIES

MICHIKO ISHIMURE'S NARRATIVES OF RESISTANCE AND RECONCILIATION

Bruce Allen

It sometimes seems that story is approaching its end. Lest there be no more telling of stories at all, some of us out here...think we'd better start telling another one, which maybe people can go on with when the old one's finished.

—Ursula K. Le Guin (152)

In a 1998 interview, discussing the effects of modernization on the area around her home in Minamata, Michiko Ishimure claimed, "Destruction of language came first; this, I believe, lies at the core of modernization" ("Destruction" 128). Ishimure went on to describe at length the process through which the rich life steeped in connections to community and nature that she had known as a child unraveled in tandem with the rapid changes that occurred in the local language; in particular with the changes that accompanied the men who returned from World War II. In telling her story of the interrelated breakdowns of language, community, and environment, Ishimure touched on the central themes of her life's work as a writer and activist. Her story represents part of the larger history of the process of modernization that has played itself out in various scenarios in Japan, as well as in many other parts of the world. It is a story of the loss of language diversity and of the power of language to shape, rationalize, and modernize societies; often leaving not only traditional languages, but also local communities and nature fractured and impoverished.

Ishimure also stressed the fact that there has been a long and rich prologue to this modern story of breakdown. Throughout her career of writing and activism she has maintained that stories have come first in human civilization, and that they have nurtured both culture and nature. But when sudden incursions of powerful new forms of language replace native languages, dialects, and their associated myths and dreams, there almost inevitably follows a destructive, alienating force of modernization that leads to breakdowns. Hopefully, she suggests, we are still engaged in an ongoing and renewable story. And so, despite the apparently elegiac tone of the interview (published under the title "Destruction of Language Came First"), Ishimure's underlying message is that we can turn to old stories for inspiration, and we can create new ones that provide hope for a revival of culture, community, and nature.

What were the old stories? How and why did they become threatened? What happens when stories die out? Can there be, and must there be, new stories? How might we nurture a culture that fosters a rebirth of stories, language, culture, and nature? These questions have inspired Ishimure's lifework, and they provide the focus for this essay. Working from an attention to Ishimure's conception of stories, I will examine her related critique of modernity and her vision for creating a society that can foster reconciliation between humans and the nonhuman world. I will also touch on the trajectory that extends from Ishimure's activism and writing about the environmental pollution incident in Minamata to the more recent events of the Fukushima nuclear incident. Finally, I will suggest some implications of Ishimure's writing for Japanese and global ecocritical thought.

MICHIKO ISHIMURE: OBSERVER, ACTIVIST, STORYTELLER

Michiko Ishimure (b. 1927) is the author of more than 50 volumes of writing in a wide range of genres, including novels, poetry, essays, children's stories, autobiographical sketches, historical fiction, and Noh drama. As I will discuss later, her writing can be considered a pioneering genre that combines and transforms a range of styles. Ishimure is widely regarded as Japan's most influential and representative writer of environmental literature. Her best-known work is her trilogy based on the Minamata disease incident, which served as a powerful wake-up call to the Japanese and to people around the world regarding the dangers of industrial pollution. *Paradise in the Sea of Sorrow: Our Minamata Disease* (1969), the first volume in this trilogy, was a best seller for many years in Japan. It went through more than 30 reprintings and has been regarded as the "bible of the Japanese environmental movement" (Monnet, Preface to *Camellias* iii). Owing to the impact of her environmental activism, in conjunction with the beautiful literary quality of her writing, Ishimure has been known as the "Rachel Carson of Japan." For many years she has been at the forefront of the movement to establish the truth behind the Minamata incident and to provide relief to its victims, restore the damaged community and environment, and bring reconciliation among the parties involved.

The importance of Ishimure's work in support of the Minamata disease victims and her reference to this experience in many of her writings has led to her primary identification among many Japanese as an environmental writer-activist. But, although her experiences in Minamata constitute important aspects of her lifework, they represent only parts of it. Ishimure has expressed discomfort at being regarded primarily as an activist, social critic, or even a writer (Iwaoka, *Michiko Ishimure and Modernity* 2). At heart, she is a member of a community and a lover of stories; a person who listens to and records stories, retells and refashions them, and creates new ones. This work has been her sustaining passion, as well as her hope for contributing to change. Through this work, she has tried to bring about a rebirth of the "spirit of words," from which stories come. This spirit, she believes, once thrived in her community, as well as in communities around the world, but has been significantly weakened in the process of modernization.

Ishimure was brought up in, and has lived most of her life in or near Minamata, a small city of about 30,000 located on the southern coast of the island of Kyushu. She started her literary career by writing poetry, with no particular aim of becoming involved in a life of activism. But because she lived in Minamata, the site of the world's first recognized major incident of industrial environmental poisoning, she experienced the unfolding web of events connected with the Minamata disease incident. Witnessing this, she was moved to interview and listen to the stories of its victims—most of whom were fishermen, from the lowest ranks of society. She also listened to the stories of doctors and of civic and corporate leaders involved in the problem. She incorporated these stories into her writing, mixing them with her rich stock of childhood stories. Ishimure's childhood had given her an unusually close contact with nature and with the local community of poor, but richly cultured farmers, laborers, and fishermen. In Minamata she experienced herself intermingling and exchanging personas with other animals and plants—metamorphosing into foxes, crabs, snakes, and other creatures—as an entirely natural occurrence. Later, I will give several examples of these stories as they appear in her writing. With the industrial development of Minamata, eventually followed by World War II and the Minamata disease incident, the more peaceful, rural environment of Ishimure's town was sacrificed and the harsher realities of modernity struck her forcefully. In *Paradise*, she tells of her shock upon realizing the depth of this new reality, and how it transformed her life:

> Up to the time of my first visit to the hospital I'd been an incon-spicuous, self-effacing housewife; impractical, inclined to spend my time in useless reveries. I had a preference for old songs and ballads, and occasionally dabbled in poetry...On the day I saw Tsurumatsu [a Minamata disease patient], above all else, I despised myself unbearably for being a part of the despicable human race. From that day forward, the image of his pathetic blind body lying there like a piece of deadwood, and his restless, unforgiving spirit took up residence somewhere deep inside me. (139)

As a result of such encounters, Ishimure's life became radicalized and entwined with Minamata's now infamous incident, which included the destruction of local nature and culture. She was seized with a passion to penetrate the dark spirit that lay beneath the Minamata tragedy—to confront and to exorcise it. She writes,

> I know that the language of the victims of Minamata Disease—both that of the spirits of the dead who are unable to die, and that of the survivors who are little more than living ghosts—represents the pris-tine form of poetry before our societies were divided into classes. In order to preserve for posterity this language in which the historic sig-nificance of the Mercury Poisoning Incident is crudely branded, I must drink an infusion of my animism and "pre-animism" and become a sorceress cursing modern times forever. (60)

These were bitter, impassioned, necessary words. Words calling for resistance, even rebellion. But in the more than 40 years that have passed since writing them, Ishimure's writing has worked with, and through her outrage, and has created bridges to reconciliation. She has not only cursed, but has used her "sorcery" to repair relations between abusers and abused, humans and nonhumans, and society and nature.

Because of Ishimure's reluctance to be identified as an activist, and her preference for the world of stories, I am tempted to call her an accidental, or reluctant activist, yet I don't want to minimize this important aspect of her life work. Rather, I would like to foreground her attention to the transformative power of stories and language. These stories show how language can function to nurture—or, conversely, to unravel—culture and environment.

TRANSFORMATION BY LANGUAGE

In the interview referred to earlier, Ishimure relates her experience of how language played a decisive part in the breakdown of her community and its transition to modernity. For a period around the end of World War II, Ishimure worked as a substitute schoolteacher. It was a difficult role, and much of the pain she experienced came from witnessing the changes in the young people, especially the men, as they were affected by the power of a new kind of language. The language was still Japanese—not a foreign language forced on them by an occupation army—but to her it might as well have been. Gradually, this new language changed and supplanted the local language that had been so rich in dialect and imbued with local myths and culture. The formal, elitist, rational language of the soldiers impressed the people and won them over. She explains,

> When I think of it now, already the modernization of Japan had to some extent been effected…In the rural areas, the military way of speaking sounded so high class and fashionable. When the men came back home after getting out of the military, the men of the village would use…all kinds of military jargon…
>
> It shows how the modern is a sort of system that supplies words of resonance, or shall I say, commanding, manly words of grandeur. The men—especially the ones returning home after being in the service— used that sort of language without fail.…
>
> And next, before you knew it, that military jargon started to filter into the talk in the Chisso organization, and it became fashionable throughout the town. (124)

This change involved a subtle kind of warfare. It was one in which few people were aware of any attack—in fact most saw it as part of a desirable progression that was transforming and improving the economy and reputation of their rural area. Yet it spelled defeat for the older culture based on connections with stories, nature, and community. In this process, an elitist language—and a particularly male, militarized one—became a fashionable tool for advancing modernity. In this passage we can see Ishimure's close attention to the gendered aspects of words, showing the strong feminist sensibility that underlies her writing; although she does not particularly identify herself as a feminist writer.

The passage quoted earlier ends with a reference to the Chisso Corporation. Chisso is the company that built a petrochemical factory in the town of Minamata in the 1920s and gradually transformed the area's socioeconomic base from that of fishing and farming to modern industrial production. In this process of development, Chisso released the highly toxic methyl mercury effluent into Minamata Bay that caused Minamata disease. First recognized in 1953, Minamata disease affects the central nervous system, leading in severe cases to loss of neuromuscular control, paralysis, insanity, and death (George 3).

The language used by the Chisso management was akin to that of the military men, and in part derived from it. The use of this new elitist, abstract, rationalist language, along with the more physical and environmental changes that accompanied the change to modern manufacturing, played a major part in transforming the local culture. It helped to institutionalize a new mentality stressing class and rank. It facilitated both pulling some members of the lower class "up," if they adopted the modern language, and leaving others "behind," if they did not. For those who did not wish, or were not able to adopt the new language, their old language often became a source of discrimination. In her interview, Ishimure stresses how "we've thrown out the words of the country and come to speak in abstract, conceptual language" ("Destruction" 128).

DIALECT AND THE SPIRIT OF LANGUAGE

In attempting to revive a society that can nurture language and stories, Ishimure gives central importance in her writing to the use of dialect. Some of the dialect she uses appears strange even to Japanese readers, as it includes words that are normally only spoken and have never been put in writing. In using the dialect of the fishermen, farmers, laborers, and Minamata patients she has tried to preserve the richness of expression she feels has been largely washed out of standard modern Japanese. In her interview she explains why she has featured such dialect so strongly in her writing:

> I gave a lot of thought to what style I should write in. I reached the conclusion that I could not use the normal means of modern language and

literature to express the sense of my work. I found that the language produced where people are haggling, arguing, and grumbling was fascinating...The—what shall I call it—feelings of people who have lived by and with the sea; it's evident that those people have a far wider sensitivity. (129–30)

Thus, for Ishimure, facing the problems of modernity requires a restoration of language, stories, and dialect. Strong local dialects still exist in Japan today, but—like species of plants and animals—they are increasingly becoming endangered. Ishimure's writing calls for resistance to this extinction of language diversity. This diversity, she insists, is linked to diversity among the entire network of culture, biota, and the earth. As Masami Yuki explains, "Ishimure's strong attachment to Amakusa dialect, in particular, suggests the writer's belief that dialect is not such a human possession as a language created in and shared with a more-than-human world. While standard Japanese reflects an abstract national ideology, place-rooted dialects materialize lived interactions between people and their world" ("Aural" 138).

Working against the grain of modernity's relentless eroding of place-rooted language Ishimure explains,

> For a long time I have been thinking about the question of modernization, and where and how it is that humans come to change. The young leave their villages. It's a question of language...The children went off to Tokyo and made academic achievements and when they returned to their villages they no longer used the local village language at all. They spoke a language different from the villagers'—a kind of abstract, conceptual language. ("Destruction" 125)

Perhaps such a lament for loss of tradition and for the attraction of the city may sound like mere nostalgia for a pastoral past. But Ishimure's work not only serves as a documentary and elegy for disappearing things, it also suggests a possible pathway that may connect us to both past and future. It encourages an understanding of our relation to past and present that is recursive, rather than linear. Balancing an attention to what has been lost with a vision for reconciliation, Ishimure's writing suggests alternatives to modernity and a bridge to the future (Iwaoka, "Restoration" 12).

ALTERNATIVES TO MODERNITY, BRIDGES TO RECONCILIATION

At this point I'd like to outline some of the basic aspects of Ishimure's alternative vision for modernity and hope for reconciliation;

reconciliation both among humans, and with the nonhuman natural world. First is the need to restore the vital spirit of words. Ishimure believes that this quality, expressed in Japanese by the word "*koto-dama*," meaning "spirit, or soul of words," has been an important potential element in all world languages. It lies at the heart of our stories and is nurtured through our attentiveness to the sounds, sights, and other aspects of nature. But in the modern world this spirit has become endangered. In her 1996 novel *Lake of Heaven*, Ishimure deals at length with this problem of word spirit. The story connects her concern for language to the theme of dam construction and the problems of understanding between city and rural people. Although a novel, *Lake of Heaven* is based on actual events and stories from rural mountain villages near Ishimure's home.

The protagonist of *Lake of Heaven* is a young man from Tokyo named Masahiko who visits the countryside for the first time. Masahiko is hoping to become a music composer, but he finds his senses have become dulled, his imagination dried up, and his ears insensitive. He visits Amazoko, the ancestral hometown of his recently deceased grandfather, intending just to spread his ashes on a lake and then return to Tokyo. The area, and its people, however, induce him to stay on. Gradually, his experience radically changes his life. Amazoko has been sunk at the bottom of a new lake that was created by the construction of a dam. The villagers have seen their community and natural environment destroyed, yet are trying to revive it—in particular by restoring their stories, dreams, and local culture. At first, Masahiko undergoes a deep feeling of culture shock when he faces the gap between city and country ways, but gradually he adapts and becomes accepted into the community. In this process, he opens his senses to the natural and storied world. With this, he finds a way to heal his alienation and lack of inspiration. At the end of the novel, we are not told whether Masahiko will stay in the rural town or return to the city, but it seems likely he will return and try to bring his newfound awareness back to the city.

Early in *Lake of Heaven*, Masahiko questions the roots of his frustration about life and lack of inspiration in writing music. The rural setting and the sounds from nature—from animals, wind, and water, as well as the dialects and stories of the villagers—give him insight into what he is lacking, and how he might recover:

> Inspiration for a new piece of music—what is that?
>
> But even before that, I need to restore my ears. It seems they've been mostly destroyed...

Back in the time when the *true soul of language* still existed, the human voice and the sounds of things must have been bound together far more closely than they are today. (31–32; Emphasis mine)

Where does such "true soul of language" (kotodama) originate from, and can we still find it in modern times? For Ishimure, such spirited language cannot arise in a vacuum of experience with the natural world, or without the support of a community. Rather, it must be developed through close attentiveness to nature and enriched by the nurturing power of stories and community. Ishimure finds that most modern people have largely become deaf to the sounds of the natural world, and that this is a source of our alienation and destructive behaviors. *Lake of Heaven* narrates Masahiko's gradual transformation and recovery of his senses:

What was more, he found that he had been losing his ability to distinguish between good sounds and bad ones in his mind and body, and that he couldn't adjust his hearing…

But now…he was starting a healing process. It seems, he thought, I'm being healed by the soft moisture of the mountain mists that constantly flows from morning to night. (290)

This healing process, Ishimure suggests, is possible for all people, but it requires a rebirth of sensitivity to the "signs of life"—in Japanese "*kehai*," a key word that Ishimure uses in much of her writing. Kehai are all around us, but we usually ignore them. Masahiko develops a sensitivity to these signs of life during his stay at Amazoko and gains a visceral—not merely mental—connection to the world:

He was becoming bound up with all the signs of life in the mountains and valleys, from the buds of the quince and magnolia to the faint gurgling sounds of running water. All these trees, grasses, and flowers, whose names I hardly know—why have I never thought of their significance for the human world until now?…Even a lump of dirt—you can't look at it as something trivial. There isn't a single element that's not essential to the earth's make-up. (222)

Through healing and recovering his senses, Masahiko comes to adopt a new, nondualistic understanding of his connection to his surroundings. In overcoming his alienation from the world, Masahiko becomes bound up and connected to it.

Ishimure encourages us to start with basic things; by opening our ears, eyes, and all our senses. This, she believes, is where fundamental

environmental and social change originate. Without this, environmental
activism easily becomes rudderless and empty. Ishimure readily
acknowledges the need for top down projects to deal with environmental and social problems; in her activist work she has sometimes called
for concrete plans and laws. But her fundamental interest and contribution lie in bottom up work; in the grassroots work of experience.
Experience the kehai, she urges us; they are all around us, giving us
hints about how to be, and what to do. But most of us aren't listening,
or aren't even able to listen. Not, in most cases, because our ears are
physically damaged, but because of our lack of use, practice, and desire.
Our largely indoor lives, filled with competition and tension, deprive
us of the needed time and experience. Ishimure's work has been widely
noted as a wake-up call to the dangers of environmental pollution and
extinction of species (Huang, Iwaoka, Monnet, Murphy, Yuki). But
it also serves a wake-up call to the danger of what Robert Michael
Pyle has termed the "extinction of experience." Echoing Ishimure's
concerns he writes,

> The extinction of experience…implies a cycle of disaffection that can
> have disastrous consequences. As cities and metastasizing suburbs
> forsake their natural diversity, and their citizens grow more removed
> from personal contact with nature, awareness and appreciation retreat.
> This breeds apathy toward environmental concerns and, inevitably,
> further degradation of the common habitat.

Such degradation includes the Minamata incident and the destruction of the community and environment of Amazoko.
   Yet, Ishimure maintains, there is hope for restoration; as Masahiko
shows in Amazoko. And there are possibilities for reconciliation, as
has been shown in Minamata through the long years leading to the
restoration of Minamata Bay and the establishment of a more positive
relationship between the Chisso organization and the Minamata disease victims. For Ishimure, true reconciliation can only occur when
there is a reconciliation both among people and between people and
the nonhuman world of nature of which we are but a small part.

BEYOND DUALISMS: TRANSFORMATIONS, METAMORPHOSES, AND COEXISTENCE

The possibility of gaining a closer relationship between the body and
the world is a recurring theme in Ishimure's writing. Such a relationship both implies and necessitates a nondualistic; nonhierarchical
conception of the world. Her own childhood experiences in nature

provided the base for her ideas of coexistence between humans and nonhumans. Such coexistence implies not just a respectful, cerebral relationship, but a deeper participation, on both physical and imaginative levels, with the nonhuman world: a transformative imagination. Ishimure often writes about the transformations and metamorphoses that can take place between animals and humans. In *Story of the Sea of Camellias* (1976), an autobiographical account of her childhood, she describes one of the many times she imagined herself being changed into another animal:

> In that magical instant it wasn't difficult, it seemed to me, to become a white fox's cub; all I had to do was bend my hands inwards in imitation of the latter's forepaws and cry "*kon, kon*" and the metamorphosis would occur...Shall I become one of them or not? And if I become one, how shall I return to my former shape again? (189)

In such a world of interaction and metamorphosis there is no hierarchical ranking of species. In fact, Ishimure writes, often it may be preferable to live as another animal than as a human:

> The contradictions, mysteries, joys, and suffering that make up human existence seemed to me both inexplicable and disconcerting...How much more rewarding and unproblematic, by contrast, the metamorphoses, whether into plants or animals I would undergo whenever I despaired of the limits of human intellect! (241–42)

In such writing Ishimure suggests the possibility of a way of living that is free from the arrogance of speciesism. She allows readers to imagine how it might be to live a life of deep coexistence with the natural world.

In *Sea of Camellias*, she tells of her childhood efforts to become what she calls an "inseparable part" of the world of animals and plants, and to learn the "secret of their art of living:"

> Somehow wishing to mingle with them and to find an outlet for the unexpected burst of vitality within me, I started deliberately to chew some grass blades...It seemed to me that eating roots, grass and wild fruit, as young rabbits, monkeys and other animals did, made me an inseparable part of their world, that I was learning the secret of their art of living. (38)

Stemming in part from her legacy derived from the animist, Shinto, and Buddhist beliefs of her family and community, this nondualistic connection to the world extends beyond the realm of plants and animals to the supposedly inanimate world of things. Recounting a childhood scene involving her father and his boat, she writes,

> "This boat is pretty lonesome," I said.
>
> "Yes, I guess so," Father retorted sullenly and took out his pipe. "It may be lonesome all right, but it swarms with snails and crabs, and at night shooting stars flare up around it by the hundreds. I bet it never gets bored." ...
>
> "This boat will never move an inch from its position of transcending indifference, receiving with unaltered equanimity the rising and ebbing tide, day and night, calm and thunderstorm. But man...will never be able to endure that bravely the trials that come upon him."
> (51–52)

Whether we regard such belief in the life of all things as animism, Buddhism, pantheism, anthropomorphism, ecocentrism, or whatever, this belief represents the foundation—not spoken of in "-isms"—that grounds Ishimure's nondualistic worldview and her faith in the possibility of reconciliation and renewal.

COMMUNITY, DREAMS, MYTHS, AND THE GLOBAL NETWORK

Another essential element underlying Ishimure's alternative vision for modernity is her call for restoring the network of dreams and community. For Ishimure, dreams refer not only to those images and feelings we experience at night while sleeping, but also to those we share, during our waking times, with other people and other beings. Community refers not to an organizational principle of government, but to a cultural network rooted in living traditions of dances, songs, myths, stories, festivals, and dreams. Dreams and communities are mutually dependent and reinforcing. In *Lake*, Masahiko learns of this essential dream-community continuity that still exists in Amazoko. Ishimure suggests that modern society largely deprives us of such dreams and that this, in turn, deprives us of a sense of belonging to a community. In Amazoko, the community's underlying conception of time and being, which is rooted in dreams, is recursive. Its members return to, participate in, and learn from the past, rather than constantly striving for progression to a supposedly advanced future. During his stay in Amazoko, Masahiko gradually comes to understand such ideas and participate in this shared communal life: "Masahiko took great interest in how the waking dreams of the group were steeped in countless layers of experience, gained over the long passage of reality. He wondered if he was watching the workings of dreams in which each person was not merely a single being but a part of the greater body of a community" (280–81).

Although Ishimure does not use the term "bioregional" in her writing, her ideas of community share a common spirit with bioregional thinking, as I will discuss further in the concluding section. Her vision of local community, language, and economy encourages the sharing of resources—not only of material goods, but, just as importantly, of stories, dreams, time, and culture. Expressing little faith in national ideology and organization, she urges us, instead, to develop deeper identities rooted in local communities.

Similarly, Ishimure rarely writes directly about ecological or environmental theories, yet the spirit of her writing resonates deeply with an ecological understanding of the world. She prefers the vehicle of myths and stories to convey this understanding. In *Lake*, after going through a long period of doubt, Masahiko comes to understand such things:

> In his childhood Masahiko had thought of these tales of a far-off forgotten mountain village as merely the fragments of memories of an old man who had been separated from his hometown...Now he had come to realize that in order to see into the world that had been hidden in his grandfather's mind it wasn't necessary to resort to ideas from ethnology or recently fashionable ecological theories about saving the earth. All that was needed was to share in the feelings of these elders right here; these people who continued to return to Amazoko in their dreams. (275)

Although Ishimure writes mainly about her local region in the south of Kyushu, it is important to realize that her concerns are at the same time global. Preserving and renewing the web of stories and myths, she insists, is a worldwide responsibility: "All ethnic groups, all peoples when they are born, have their own myths. In the twentieth century we have been spending the entire legacy of that spirit. We're stamping it out and killing it off. In myth there is the wisdom of humans; the wisdom of every race and people is there" ("Destruction" 135). When we are working locally, creating stories and restoring community, we are also connecting to a global process and helping to restore a truer sense of reality. Our stories, she suggests, represent both our links to the past and our hopes for the future. Our responsibilities as keepers, tellers, and creators of stories, therefore, are great.

FROM MINAMATA TO FUKUSHIMA AND BEYOND

On March 11, 2011, Japan was shaken by another environmental catastrophe—one that at least partly involved human responsibility—the combined earthquake-tsunami-nuclear plant incident in Fukushima. A clear trajectory can be traced from the events in Minamata to those in Fukushima. Keeping in mind Ishimure's ideas about the connections between language, culture, and environment, I would like to briefly examine some of the broader links in this trajectory. Although the story is still unfolding, its outlines show some important points of similarity.

At the material level, the Minamata and Fukushima incidents involved the discharge of large amounts of highly toxic heavy metals; in particular, methyl mercury in Minamata and uranium and plutonium in Fukushima. Both of these "accidents" occurred under conditions of insufficient attention to the dangers, and despite repeated warnings. Both incidents have resulted in catastrophic, long-term damage to health and environment. These so-called accidents should rather be recognized as examples of what Charles Perrow terms "normal accidents" or "systems accidents." As he explains, "The odd term *normal accident* is meant to signal that, given the system characteristics, multiple and unexpected interactions of failures are inevitable" (qtd Heise 143). The Minamata and Fukushima incidents challenge us to make the necessary connections, realize the patterns that unite such events, and take steps to prevent future occurrences of such inevitable failures.

At the organizational and political levels, both incidents involved elite corporations—the Chisso Corporation in Minamata, and Tepco (Tokyo Electric Power Company) in Fukushima—that have long been granted special favored status by the government, including tax breaks, industry-favorable supervision, overlooking of accidents and cover-ups, and exemption from accounting for total costs, including costs for proper waste disposal and for damages to health and environment.

Both companies have operated under elitist relations and attitudes toward local citizens. The companies both encouraged and benefited from a culture of complacency in which they remained largely out of touch with local residents, as well as citizens nationwide. Their operations were regarded by the government, and by most citizens, as of such a high level and of such complicated nature that common people could not understand them and that they should, therefore, be entrusted to the companies. Questions regarding safety, arising from citizens and dissenting specialists, have consistently been met with condescension by company authorities. Being regarded as "too important to fail," these systems' frequent failings have been systematically overlooked or not reported. Ultimately, problems became too difficult for the companies and their specialists to control—clear evidence of "systems accidents." Finally, it took outsiders—including writers such as Ishimure and other independent critics—to investigate and establish the truth.

Considered from the perspective of language, both companies have been engaged—both consciously and unconsciously—in forms of linguistic hegemony. Their communications with the public have involved carefully managed messages, allowing little real dialogue, presented in the kind of abstract, technical language that Ishimure has criticized. Such language has served as a barrier to understanding, and often has stigmatized the users of local language and dialect; especially farmers, fishermen, and laborers. In April 2011, the Chisso Corporation adopted a new name, the nondescript letters JNC; likely representing a linguistic strategy to distance itself from associations of its former name.

Both Chisso and Tepco have been integrally connected to the military-industrial complex. Chisso was a major supplier of chemicals and materials for armaments during World War II. Although it has changed its focus to products such as liquid-crystal displays, the company continues to provide materials for the military-industrial complex. The nuclear industry in Japan, as in other countries, remains integrally tied to the military.

The victims of both incidents have, in most cases, been poor and from the lower class. In Minamata it was primarily the local fishermen who ate mercury-polluted fish who became affected by the disease. In Fukushima, it is still too early to assess the eventual casualties, but the workers who are going into the highly contaminated plants are mostly poor, risk-accepting contract workers, or military and fire department staff. The local farmers and fishermen living around Fukushima face uncertainty as to when, if ever, they will be allowed to return to their lands and sea.

Both incidents show examples of how intertwined problems of health and environment often remain long after the initial awareness of a crisis fades. The Minamata Bay was closed for fishing for over 40 years until the government judged that restoration projects had finally returned the water quality to a sufficiently safe level. Suffering and litigation related to Minamata disease continue even today, over 50 years since the original outbreak. Gradually, the oldest patients are dying out, and perhaps no new cases will emerge or be officially identified, but the damage to families and the environment continues. Ishimure and others continue to hold public lectures, exhibitions, and other events throughout the country to remind people that the Minamata incident has not yet been settled. In Fukushima, the future is even less clear, but it is certain that the nuclear incident will have continuing, severe long-term consequences.

Despite the severity of these incidents, there has been a common tendency for people to regard them as isolated events and not to connect them to larger patterns. This phenomenon represents an example of what Patrick Murphy has termed DIM or discrete incident mentality. Referring to the way "people treat every recurring event as a unique occurrence without precedence or prediction...DIM is employed to deny the cumulative effects of personal, cultural, and national behavior, [and represents] a denial of history and ecology" ("Consumption" 225). The application of this principle to toxic spills and to the practice of building toxin-producing plants in earthquake- and tsunami-prone areas should be clear—although, unfortunately, it rarely has been.

On the positive side, both the Minamata and Fukushima incidents have led to renewed public awareness about the dangers of industrial pollution, and to rethinking assumptions about modernity; in particular, regarding our use of energy and resources. These incidents have generated a renewal of volunteer and community cooperation, both locally and worldwide. This has led to renewed possibilities for reflection and change, including significant post-Fukushima decisions made by the German, Italian, Swiss, and Japanese governments and citizens to turn away from reliance on nuclear energy.

Amid these ongoing crises, Ishimure has held out hope for reconciliation and revival. Her fundamental hope is that we will create new stories—or "new myths"—to nourish and carry us forward:

> I believe that if we bring up new myths, they will become the nourishment that can bring up life in the 21st century...When we think about the interconnectedness of all life and ask how life should be brought about, naturally we need the trees and plants, and the water and oceans and earth—they are all indispensable. That is where the true myths are born. ("Destruction" 136)

The continuing challenge Ishimure leaves us is to listen to these voices, to connect them with our own voices, and to create new stories that may revitalize our own lives and the places in which we live.

ISHIMURE AND ECOCRITICISM

In this final section, I would like to suggest some of the implications of Ishimure's work for the development of ecocriticism and environmentally oriented writing. Important recent trends in this evolution have included an increased attention to issues of environmental justice, gender, feminism, ethnicity, urban nature, speciesism, transnational identity, and globalization (Buell, Estok, Garrard, Heise, Murphy, Yuki). Much of the debate regarding this process has been outlined by Ursula Heise in her influential book *Sense of Place and Sense of Planet: The Environmental Imagination of the Global* (2008). I would like to use some of the elements in Heise's outline to help situate Ishimure's work within this continuum and debate.

Heise argues that there has been, and needs to be, an expansion of ecocritical concern, moving from the traditional valorization of a more local sense of place to a greater recognition of the modern reality in which personal identity and sense of place is increasingly characterized as deterritorialized, diasporic, and nomadic (50–58). Her call is not for a rejection of the old concerns; rather it is for a widened concern, one that is more adequate in reflecting the recent globalized nature of many people's lives today. It calls for a new and positive sense of "eco-cosmopolitanism" (59). I take Heise's characterization of the range of outlooks not as one that claims a dualistic opposition between the local and the global, but as one that describes an ongoing dialectical process of transformation. Heise's is also a call for an increased recognition of international, intercultural, and global "varieties of environmentalism" (59). The following chart, based on Heise's overview, illustrates the wide span of these perspectives regarding sense of place and global identity. Although the elements in the two columns may appear to imply opposition, they indicate poles that exist within a continuum. The actual attitudes and orientations of most people involve considerable overlapping, ambivalence, and change among these elements.

Local and Global Perspectives

Local	Global
ties to local, bioregional community	ties to the planet as a whole
local sense of place, identity	transnational, global identity
valorization of the local, often rural	deterritorialization
traditional stories, culture	virtual communities, culture

(Continued)

Local	Global
direct experience with nature	indoor-centered experience
decentralized local organization	transnational connections
rootedness	rootlessness
reinhabitation of place	placed-nomadism, diasporic self
communication: face-to-face	communication: using social media

How can we situate Ishimure's work within this continuum and the dialectical process it involves? Viewed in this context, Ishimure's writing represents a more local, bioregional sense of place. It values local communities, face-to-face relations with humans and nonhumans, traditional cultures, and direct experience with nature, especially in rural places. Richard Evanoff has characterized the bioregional paradigm as calling for "the creation of economically self-sufficient and politically decentralized communities delinked from the global market but confederated at appropriate levels to address problems that transcend cultural borders" (1). The community of Amazoko in *Lake of Heaven*, the Minamata community in *Paradise in the Sea of Sorrow* and *Story of the Sea of Camellias*, and the communities depicted in most of Ishimure's other writings, meet many of these conditions for bioregional communities.

Ishimure's work gives less direct attention to such global issues as transnational identity, virtual communities, communication through social media, and the diasporic-self. And when it does treat such issues, it often does so in a critical way; such as in *Lake of Heaven*, where Ishimure negatively describes Masahiko's loss of his senses, his lack of connection to nature, and his isolation from community; or in *Paradise in the Sea of Sorrow* and *Sea of Camellias*, where she paints a damning portrait of the modern industrial society that led to the Minamata disease incident. Clearly, Ishimure's love is for the local dialects, myths, festivals, songs, dreams, and communities she has experienced in the rural areas of Kyushu where she has lived most of her life. Yet it would be a mistake to pigeonhole Ishimure's writing and regard it as dealing exclusively with local, rural, and traditional cultures and places. Her work also deals squarely with global problems such as toxicity, the media, and global economic and political trends.

Ishimure's long-standing attempt—developed both in her writing and activism—has been to work through the necessary stages in the cycle that extends from recognition of problems to confrontation, negotiation, and finally to the possibility for reconciliation.

Whether the incidents involve the local fishermen in Minamata facing corporate owners of polluting factories and national politicians, or the mountain villagers in Amazoko facing dam builders and their corporate and government sponsors, Ishimure reveals the global march of political and economic structures that underlies such events. Although she lives in one of the world's most developed industrial societies, Ishimure writes about the members of small, largely rural communities, the underprivileged, and the importance of traditional culture. Yet, paradoxically, her stories coming from these local communities have sparked the birth of the modern environmental movement in Japan and of a global awareness of the dangers of industrial pollution and toxic-related diseases. Ishimure's writing thus stands at the forefront of the necessary forms of contemporary literature that Heise refers to as "toxic discourse," "apocalyptic narratives," and "risk narratives" (136–42).

Second, I would like to position Ishimure's work within global literary efforts not only to prevent and overcome environmental tragedies, but also to achieve a reconciliation among opposing groups in this struggle. I should clarify, however, that for Ishimure reconciliation does not imply a mild form of compromise and appeasement between oppressors and oppressed. Rather, it means establishing a deeper, spiritual, imaginative level of awareness, understanding, and healing. This requires a major transformation and healing of the entire sociocultural base. This is the kind of process that the villagers of Amazoko in *Lake of Heaven* attempt after they find their town, culture, and environment destroyed by the construction of a dam. Like Rachel Carson, Ishimure leaves us not simply a distressing body of toxic discourse literature; rather, using poetic literary imagination, she suggests alternatives to alienation, apocalypse, and recrimination. As in Carson's *Sense of Wonder* and other writings, Ishimure highlights the condition of awareness as being central to our physical, mental, and spiritual well-being. And like Gary Snyder, she helps us to imagine the possibility of reinhabiting the places we live—whether rural or urban.

Ishimure also joins other environmentally conscious writers in suggesting how we might reconsider and revive the education of young people toward the natural world (Louv, Pyle, Orr, Thomashow). Her writing provides inspiration in facing problems such as the "extinction of experience," discussed earlier according to Pyle, and the increasing problems of "nature-deficit disorder" and "cultural autism" discussed by environmental education writer Richard Louv. The symptoms of cultural autism, he writes, are "tunneled senses, and feelings of isolation...atrophy of the senses" (64). These are precisely the kinds of problems that Masahiko experienced in Amazoko. Masahiko's recovery of his senses represents the kind of recovery process that Pyle and Louv prescribe. As Louv insists, "It takes time—unstructured dreamtime—to experience nature in a meaningful way" (117). Writing from her non-Western perspective and place, Ishimure suggests how we, like the villagers in Amazoko, might learn to reinhabit our places and discover our own dreamtime.

Finally, I would like to consider how Ishimure's work contributes to what Heise terms a "crosscultural literacy" that can support responsible global citizenship (159). In order to adequately comprehend Ishimure's writing, however, we may need to broaden and redefine some basic assumptions about the nature of literary genres and the role of writers. Ishimure's writing does not easily fit into classical Western, or even Japanese literary genres. It forcibly confronts readers with its otherness. While I have used the term "novel" to describe several of her works, in fact they are written in a unique style that combines elements of the novel with those of storytelling, reportage, dreams, poetry, autobiography, and Noh drama. Taken as a whole, Ishimure's work comprises a pioneering literary genre, which, as Livia Monnet writes, "seems to point to the literature of the future" (v).

Gary Snyder, too, has noted the distinctive quality of Ishimure's writing. He describes *Lake of Heaven* as "a remarkable text of mythopoetic quality—with a Noh flavor—that presents much of the ancient lore of Japan and the lore of the spirit world—and is in a way a kind of myth-drama, not a novel" (*Lake*, cover). Snyder's comprehensive description also holds valid for much of Ishimure's wide range of writing. The eclectic nature of her work, along with its characteristic method of narrating multiple stories using a nonlinear conception of time and plot development, has presented particular challenges for critics. But by developing this genre, Ishimure has contributed to a broadening of our understanding of narrative means. Her incisive criticism of modern thinking for its overreliance on the only-rational at the expense of a more adequate, more-than-rational imagination has both supported her creation of a new genre and suggested alternative ways of facing modernity.

Ishimure has provided a core of writing, coupled with a course of social activism, that has inspired the emergence and development of ecocriticism in Japan. In 1996 she was a keynote speaker at the First International Symposium on Environmental Literature, held in Hawaii, sponsored by ASLE-US and ASLE-Japan. In recent years her work has been featured at international symposia on environmental literature and ecocriticism held in Korea, China, Taiwan, the United States, and Japan. Ecocritical studies of Ishimure's writing have appeared regularly in international literary journals (Allen, Huang, Monnet, Murphy, Yuki). It would be beyond the scope of this chapter to present a comprehensive assessment of Japanese ecocriticism, but I will briefly outline some trends. After initially drawing considerable influence from American and British models, Japanese ecocriticism has been developing an increasingly native identity. While continuing to interact with Western influences, Japanese ecocritics and writers are also influenced by the older, native traditions of animism, Shinto, Buddhism, and Zen. These traditions share a sense of reverence for the power of nature, the presence of spirits in the natural world, and the unity of all things; both human and nonhuman. The Japanese narrative tradition presents rich possibilities for incorporating literary devices that may be unfamiliar to many Western readers, including nonlinear temporality, more-than rational thought, dreams, and other elements I have touched on in discussing Ishimure's writing. In modern times, native Japanese literary traditions have been considerably challenged and affected by contact with Western ideas, but there has been a growing effort to reintegrate native roots. In the wider East Asian region as well, similar efforts are being made to integrate native traditions with global, cross-cultural literary developments. Amid these changes, Ishimure's writing provides a particularly rich body of material in contributing to this ongoing dialogue, transformation, and growth.

Ishimure's work holds the radical promise that in stories—living stories rooted in living communities and cultures—there is hope for positively redirecting our course through the modern, increasingly globalized and environmentally challenged world. Her voice (coming from the rural communities of Japan) represents but one among many needed voices, but it provides a particularly strong imagination that may help us to better consider our task and our direction as we chart and enact our ways forward—individually and collectively, locally and globally.

WORKS CITED

Allen, Bruce. "Bridges to Reconciliation: The Restorative Vision of Ishimure Michiko." In *Proceedings of International Conference on Literature and Environment, Wuhan 2008.* Ed. Zhenzhao Nie and Hong Chen. Wuhan, China: Huazhong Normal UP, 2011. 483–96.
———. "Facing the True Costs of Living: Arundhati Roy and Ishimure Michiko on Dams and Writing." In *Coming into Contact: Explorations in*

Ecocritical Theory and Practice. Ed. Annie Merrill Ingram, Ian Marshall, Daniel J. Philippon, and Adam W. Sweeting, Athens: U of Georgia P, 2007. 154–67.

———. "Translator's Introduction." *Lake of Heaven,* by Michiko Ishimure, Trans. Bruce Allen. Lanham: Lexington Books, 2008.

Allen, Bruce and Michiko Ishimure. "*Lake of Heaven,* Dams, and Japan's Transformation." *Japan Focus* (online journal) #533, February 21, 2006.

Buell, Lawrence. *The Future of Environmental Criticism: Environmental Crisis and Literary Imagination.* Oxford: Blackwell, 2005.

Carson, Rachel. *The Sense of Wonder.* New York: Harper and Row, 1965.

———. *Silent Spring.* Boston: Houghton Mifflin, 1962.

Estok, Simon. "Theorizing in a Space of Ambivalent Openness: Ecocriticism and Ecophobia." *ISLE: Interdisciplinary Studies in Literature and Environment* 16.2 (Spring 2009): 213–25.

Evanoff, Richard. *Bioregionalism and Global Ethics: A Transactional Approach to Achieving Ecological Sustainability, Social Justice, and Human Well-being.* New York: Routledge, 2011.

Garrard, Greg. *Ecocriticism.* London: Routledge, 2004.

George, Timothy S. *Minamata: Pollution and the Struggle for Democracy in Postwar Japan.* Cambridge: Harvard UP, 2001.

Heise, Ursula. *Sense of Place and Sense of Planet: The Environmental Imagination of the Global.* New York: Oxford UP, 2008.

Huang, Peter I-min. "The Politics of Place in *Solar Storms, Lake of Heaven, and Spider Lilies.*" *Literature and Environment: The Journal of the Association for the Study of Literature and Environment in Japan* 13.13 (2010): 37–45.

Ishimure, Michiko. "*Kotoba kara mazu kowareta*" ["Destruction of Language Came First"; all translations from this article are mine]. *Folio a,* 5, February 15, 1999, 118–38.

———. *Lake of Heaven.* Trans. Bruce Allen. Lanham, NJ: Lexington Books, 2008. Original Japanese version, 1996.

———. *Paradise in the Sea of Sorrow: Our Minamata Disease.* Trans. Livia Monnet. Kyoto: Yamaguchi Publishing House, 1990. Original Japanese version, 1969.

———. *Story of the Sea of Camellias.* Trans. Livia Monnet. Kyoto: Yamaguchi Publishing House, 1983. Original Japanese version, 1976.

Iwaoka, Nakamasa. "*Ishimure Michiko ni okeru sonzai no kaifuku: tairitsu kara wakai e*" ["Restoration of 'Being' in Michiko Ishimure's Thought: From Antagonism to Reconciliation"]. *Kumamoto hogaku* 115, December 2008, 1–26.

———. "*Ishimure Michiko to gendai*" ["Michiko Ishimure and Modernity"]. In *Ishimure Michiko no sekai.* Fukuoka: Gen Shobo, 2006. 7–26.

Le Guin, Ursula K. "The Carrier Bag theory of Fiction." In *The Ecocriticism Reader; Landmarks in Literary Ecology.* Ed. Cheryll Glotfelty and Harold Fromm. Athens: U of Georgia P. 149–54.

Louv, Richard. *Last Child in the Woods: Saving our Children from Nature-Deficit Disorder.* Chapel Hill: Algonquin Books, 2008.

Monnet, Livia. "Translator's Introduction." Ishimure Michiko: *Paradise in the Sea of Sorrow: Our Minamata Disease.* Trans. Livia Monnet. Kyoto: Yamaguchi Publishing House, 1990.

Murphy, Patrick D. "Consumption as Addiction, Sustainability as Recovery." *Ecology, Consumption, and Otherness.* Publication of papers delivered at the 2nd ASLE-Korea and ASLE-Japan Joint Symposium on Literature and Environment, 2010. 217–30.

———. "Ishimure Michiko: The Price of Pollution and the Presence of the Past." In *Farther Afield in the Study of Nature-Oriented Literature.* Charlottesville: U of Virginia P, 2000. 146–58.

———. "The Writer as Activist, the Artist as Defender: The Work of Ishmure Michiko in Translation." *Transformations: The Journal of Inclusive Scholarship and Pedagogy* XXI.1 (2010): 163–68.

Orr, David W. *Earth in Mind: On Education, Environment, and the Human Prospect.* Washington, DC: Island Press, 1994.

Orr, David W. Ecological *Literacy: Education and Transition to a Postmodern World.* Albany, NY: SUNY, 1992.

Pyle, Robert Michael. "Thunder Tree: Lessons from the Urban Wildland," 1993. http://www.morning-earth.org/DE6103/Read%20DE/Extinction%20of%20Experience.pdf.

Snyder, Gary. Email communication, June 13, 2003 (also on back cover of *Lake of Heaven*).

———. "Reinhabitation." *A Place in Space: Ethics, Aesthetics, and Watersheds.* Washington, DC: Counterpoint, 1995. 183–91.

Thomashow, Mitchell. *Ecological Identity: Becoming a Reflective Environmentalist.* Cambridge, MA: MIT Press, 1996.

Yuki, Masami, R. "The Aural Imagination in the Work of Michiko Ishimure: An Ecocritical Approach to Literary Soundscapes." ASCA Conference Sonic Interventions: Pushing the Boundaries of Cultural Analysis, Amsterdam, March 29–31, 2005. 136–41.

———. *Mizu no oto no kioku* [Remembering the Sound of Water]. Tokyo: Suiseisha, 2010.

4

A QUEER ECOFEMINIST READING OF "MATSURI [FESTIVAL]" BY HIROMI ITO

Keitaro Morita

Greta Gaard's 1997 paper "Toward a Queer Ecofeminism" was long awaited by ecofeminists who were interested in queer theories, and queer theorists who were interested in ecofeminist theories, in part, perhaps, because it addresses the simultaneous emancipation of women, nonhuman-nature, and queers. Gaard signals a significant connection among the three agencies by incorporating a queer perspective into ecofeminism, noting that conventional ecofeminism has lacked the variable of sexuality. She argues that from a queer ecofeminist perspective, it becomes clear that liberating women requires liberating nonhuman-nature and queers. Alongside ecofeminist Val Plumwood, Gaard sees a necessity for dismantling the dualisms of male/female, human/nonhuman-nature, and heterosexual/queer as integral to the project, for the right sides of such dualisms are all conceptually linked and have historically been oppressed (see also Estok; Morton). This is to incorporate a perspective of nonhuman-nature into the claim of British literary scholar Eve Kosofsky Sedgwick that society is constructed based on the trilogy of homosociality, gender discrimination, and heterosexism. Simply put, queer ecofeminism is the enterprise to voice nature, women, and queers.

One of the foundations of queer ecofeminism is queer ecology, which dates back to 1994 when the journal *UnderCurrents: Critical Environmental Studies* published by York University ran a special issue on "queer nature."[1] Since then, several queer ecological books and papers have come out. *New Perspectives on Environmental Justice: Gender, Sexuality, and Activism* (2004) edited by Rachel Stein

is an important contribution to this evolving field, with several
of the chapters revealing an intersection between environmental
justice and sexuality and devoted to queer ecofeminism and ecology,
including Beth Berila's "Toxic Bodies? ACT UP's Disruption of
the Heteronormative Landscape of the Nation" and Catriona
Sandilands' "Sexual Politics and Environmental Justice: Lesbian
Separatists in Rural Oregon." Another significant contribution to
the field is *Queer Ecologies: Sex, Nature, Politics, Desire* edited by
Catriona Mortimer-Sandilands and Bruce Erickson. It is a theoretical, political, and cultural contribution to the intersection of
ecological and queer studies; in addition to queer ecofeminist
Catriona Mortimer-Sandilands's 2005 paper "Unnatural Passions?:
Notes toward a Queer Ecology," in which she points out that heterosexism is part of oppressive power relations where humans construct
relations to nature. Both queer ecofeminism and queer ecology
emphasize a queer perspective in ecologies.[2]

Based on Gaard's paper presenting the original intent of queer
ecofeminism, this chapter discusses Hiromi Ito's "Matsuri [Festival],"
from the book *Noro to Saniwa* [Noro and Saniwa] penned by Hiromi
Ito and Chizuko Ueno. My main purpose is to illustrate the ways
in which we might see the poem as an embodiment of Gaard's
queer ecofeminism, by showing us an ecotopia where women,
nonhuman-nature, and queers are emancipated and liberated.[3] Hence,
the key variables of this chapter are gender, nature, and queer sexuality. Although the definition of "queer" varies, this chapter classifies
it under the broad definition of engagement in and/or orientation
toward a nonheteronormative sexuality, based on queer studies
scholar Kazuya Kawaguchi (iii–iv).

*   *   *

Hiromi Ito, one of the most widely recognized contemporary female
poets in Japan, was born in 1955 and made her writing debut in
1978.[4] After having divorced twice, Ito moved to California in 1997
and has lived there ever since with her British husband and children.

Ito has said that during puberty, she suffered from anorexia
and wished to become androgynous—"I was a transvestite, had
anorexia, and wanted to remove my breasts and stop menstruat-
ing" ("Sen-Kyûhyaku" 28). Being a nontraditional Japanese woman,
she once created a sensation by having provocatively stated that "[a]
fetus is feces" ("Yoi Oppai" 43). She was greatly influenced by feminism and has been a trailblazer among women poets since the 1980s

in that she is "a 'poetess' who writes about female sensibility in an absolutely skillful manner" (Sasaki, "Hanmo Hanshoku" 131) and her poems "radically express life and Eros based on her physiological sense" (Ayukawa, Oooka, and Kitagawa 144). Ito, a prolific and successful writer of poems, novels, and essays, has produced several ecologically orientated writings, which overflow with passages and images of both outer and inner nature. *Kawara Arekusa* [Wild Grass Upon a Riverbank] (2005) and *Koyôte Songu* [Coyote Song] (2007) are two such examples, in which feminist and queer themes are also dealt with. She has received some of Japan's most prestigious literary awards, including the Takami Jun Award for *Kawara Arekusa*.

* * *

Hiromi Ito's poem "Matsuri," the focus of this chapter, is included in *Noro to Saniwa*, a book published in 1991 and coauthored by Ito and feminist scholar Chizuko Ueno. "*Noro*" is a term referring to an Okinawan shamaness, and "*saniwa*" means an interpreter of the noro's words; in the book, Ito plays the role of noro, being an intermediary between the natural and supernatural worlds and producing words about them in the form of a poem. Ueno plays the role of saniwa, interpreting Ito's words in the form of an essay. The book is divided into the following 12 provocatively, mostly queer-ish titled chapters: "Language," "Intercourse," "Hole," "Men," "Masturbation," "Defecation," "Daughter," "Middle Age," "Masochism," "Desire," "Lesbianism," and "Exile." Each chapter is one poem by Ito, followed by an interpretative essay by Ueno; the poem "Matsuri" is in the chapter "Defecation." The matsuri obviously alludes to a festival in Kumamoto, Ito's one-time hometown. Prior to its name change to a more politically correct one due to protest from the "Zainichi" (ethnic Korean Japanese), it was commonly called "Boshita Matsuri," literally meaning "Festival of Ruining," which celebrated the ruining of old Korea by a daimyo (Japanese feudal lord), in reality based in historical misrecognition. One of the currently used names is "Umaoi-Matsuri"—meaning "horse-chasing festival." The poem opens with the following stanza where such a chased horse is destined to be transformed into *sashimi* (slices of raw meat):

> After the festival the horse is sliced up to be sashimi
> Soy sauce
> Ginger garlic

Onion slices rinsed in water
The horse fat is transparent and elastic
Chewing it to shreds requires strength
Chewing it up requires deserved strength
Inside the mouth it
Becomes lukewarm mucus
Becomes lukewarm breast milk
Sticks to the throat lining
I hear some choke on it, and
The meat of a violent horse is strong
The meat of a horse that dies in rage is stronger. (76–77)

The five-day Japanese festival is held at the Shinto shrine Fujisaki-Hachimangu annually in mid-September, where horse sashimi used to be eaten after the horse had been paraded around. The festival is both heterosexist and unabashedly androcentric in that the horse is symbolically dedicated to the shrine's god in order to pray for fertility and that men lead and proceed with the festival duties, though recently, women have begun to participate. Accordingly, in the stanza cited here, the subjects eating the horse sashimi with strength after the festival appear to be men.

However, at the festival, it is not only the men who eat the horse-meat; it is eaten for luck by others, too. The rest of the first stanza vividly illustrates such a landscape:

Usually we don't eat this kind of thing but as it's a good luck charm
They say that to each other and share it
And rejoice at and laud
And eat it
This year as one person was
Kicked by the horse and critically injured and fell unconscious and
    remains so
All the more
All ate
All ate the horse
The horsemeat and the strings and the fat and the blood
Ate up
The meat and the strings and the fat were mixed up
And chewed up
The festival horse is completely gone
Until a while ago peeing into the street
Excreting
Excited and rampaging around and exciting the crowd
And kicking up the unlucky man was the horse. (77–78)

A charm becomes a charm only when something extraordinary or supernatural is associated with it. Hence, one interpretation based on Ueno's "Kannibarizumu" is that the festival horse is an embodiment of a god. Indeed, worldwide, the horse is a symbol of the god of fertility, which is prayed for at the horse-chasing festival. Thus, when people eat horse meat at the festival, they simultaneously eat the god, being in communion with and identifying with the god. According to Ueno's "Kannibarizumu," this can be considered as a form of cannibalism, because cannibalism is a queer act of consuming the flesh of a human or human-like other.[5] And yet, another interpretation is possible, namely, that the horse sashimi functions as a rite of passage for entry to the male-dominated, homosocial community: the festival. By eating the natural and raw horse sashimi, the eater becomes a member of the culture and community of male-bonding, becoming a contubernal, stable mate of the heterosexual world.

However, the agent of the poem, who is revealed later to be female, does not fall into the trap of the men's game of eating the horse at the gay (lively), carnivalesque festival. When a carnival is to sublimate death and dispel the fear of death (Bakhtin 51), the horse-chasing festival is to sublimate death and dispel the fear of death most probably by killing the horse. Yet the agent does not engage in creophagy, or meat-eating, and, instead, rescues and leads the horse out of the androcentric sphere and withdraws to wilderness; more precisely, she and the horse, marginalized in the culturally constructed festival, leave for the wilderness.[6]

Here, the importance of links between food and gender cannot be overstated. As vegetarian ecofeminist Carol Adams argues,

> We cannot tell the truth about women's lives if we do not take seriously their dietary choices which were at odds with dominant culture. Vegetarianism spoke to women; they would not have adopted it, maintained it, proselytized for it, if vegetarianism were not a positive influence on their lives. This is a historical fact that needs to be accepted and then responded to by scholars studying women's lives and texts. (184)

The sociological qualitative survey that I conducted, within the context of different study, in 2009 ("Ecological Reflection") among 29 staff members at an environmental NGO in Japan also indicates the differentiated proximities of women and men to food choices. Elaborating on my previous considerations, with regard to the woman and the horse (keeping in mind that the horse represents nonhuman-nature),

the Japanese culture sees the two agencies as abject and impure based
on sociologist Kokichiro Miura, both being alienated and excluded
from the androcentric sphere of culture, the festival in this case,
and being in a kind of heterotopia. The festival is a system that
maintains the border of a particular group (Ueno, "Matsuri to
Kyôdôtai" 54), or a group of men here. The above is poignantly told
in the first half of the second stanza:

> Today for the first time
> Pilot the horse
> And run in wilderness at the charging pace so could I
> The destination I was headed for was the autumn wilderness where
> There was no cloud
> Until recently until my butt was by a person
> Spanked I could not run at the charging pace
> Today I run so and the horseback jumps
> Grasses flow
> The horse butt is heavy
> The horse weight is heavy
> The heavy horse carries me and runs in the sky
> I don't need a person anymore
> I don't need a person who urges it forward to run
>   at the charging pace
> I don't need a person anymore
> The autumn wilderness is hairline all over and silver. (78–79)

In this wilderness, the agent and speaker "I" as a woman and the
horse as nonhuman-nature, both oppressed entities in the modern,
mainstream culture, are emancipated, coexisting with each other, not
that the agent eats up the horse as the men at the festival do.

Cultures have structurally associated the male and the female with
Thanatos and Eros, respectively; along that line, in the poem, the
female agent is not involved in the Thanatos, or meat-eating. Here,
the wilderness is a queer space, a space of difference and the possibility of liberation, allowing the agent to be herself and a queer relationship to form between her and the horse, promoting sexual diversity
and suggesting alternative forms of relationship. On the other hand,
it is worth recalling at this juncture that comparative literary scholar
Noriko Mizuta regards forests, lakes, rivers, seas, and sky as metaphors for both the internal landscape of women and the destinations
they choose in their attempts to escape from the system built by men.
In the poem, the wilderness also serves thereby as the internal landscape of the female speaker and the destination she chooses in her

effort to escape from the festival, a homosocial sphere, from which women and nature are excluded by heterosexual men.

The speaker assumes for herself not only the "female" role but also the "male" role that the culture has allotted only to men: leading. In the lines quoted here, it is the female speaker who takes the leading role and leads the horse out of the men's domain, the cannibalistic festival. We here witness an alternative vision of gender roles, in which the two roles replace each other's positions with the woman leading and piloting the horse. This sort of subversion is critical to queer ecofeminism as it aims to emancipate women and liberate them from the traditional, fixed roles assigned to them.

The text also strongly suggests that the relationship between the female agent and the horse is sexual.[7] Another formerly used name of the festival is "Boshita Matsuri," and there is another theory to it: that "Boshita" originates from "boboshita" in the Kumamoto dialect, meaning "to have sex." Indeed, Japanese festivals are sexually charged in various ways. At quite a few festivals, a *mikoshi*, an ornate palanquin-like portable shrine, stores a symbol of the penis. At the horse-chasing festival, the horse carries on its back an ornament called "hinokage," or yin/yang, symbolizing the male and female organs.

In the poem, it is not only that the female speaker is turned on and achieves orgasm by riding and jumping on horseback, but also that the speaker appears to be having sex, or queer, nonreproductive sex, with the horse: *bestiality*. It is of interest here that horses are in some cases associated with queers (Alaimo; Mortimer-Sandilands and Bruce Erickson, "Introduction").[8] Also, some parts of the world handle queer sexual acts and bestiality as equals, including Kenya, where they treat homosexuality and bestiality in the same way as sodomy; or Sweden, where they concurrently lifted bans on homosexuality and bestiality in 1944. In the lines just cited, the repeated plain phrase[9] "I don't need a person" inevitably invokes the image of bestiality, implying that the speaker does not need a man anymore because she is now with the horse. What we see here is something deconstructing the man-woman heterosexual relationship and beyond, questioning the "naturalness" of pervasive heterosexuality.

Queer sexual acts and bestiality have been consistent themes and long-standing concerns throughout Ito's poetry and poetics. One such example is "Chitô [Tito]," in which she problematizes the boundary between heterosexuality and homosexuality by implicitly questioning the naturalness of pervasive heterosexuality (see Morita, "Queer Ecopoet?" and "Ecopoeta Queer?"). Another example is

"Tanburuwído [Tumbleweed]," a prose poem, from *Koyóte Songu* [Coyote Song] published in 2007. It is worth citing a part of the poem here:

> The act of killing and
> the act of caring for you after too much of sex
> may be the same
> right, exactly, said the author in the book
> the coyote has the power to wield power over me
> to confirm it the coyote has sex, with me
> I have the power to wield power over the coyote
> to confirm it I have sex, with the coyote
> a tumbleweed tumbles in the plain
> do you know, the tumbleweed is a nonnative plant
> being misplaced in a sack of grain, it came from Ukraine
> it blooms, produces seeds, dries, and breaks away from the root
> it is blown by the wind and starts rolling. (140–41)

Reverting to "Matsuri," Ito's denaturalization of the modern heterosexual code does not stop there. It proceeds in the second stanza, again in the form of an erotic relationship between the woman and the nonhuman horse:

> The horse pees
> Its mane unhairs and falls, on me
> I get covered with the horsehairs all over my body
> The horsehead is even the armful size
> My breast, belly, everything to the face
> Without pushing them to it I can't caress it
> In fact in that way I caressed it
> Then to my mouth hot
> Snort it let out
> It falls for me I think. (79)

Here, the horse and the speaker that are excluded from the festival do not engage in the normative heterosexual intercourse; instead, they engage in intimacy without intercourse, a rather scandalous form of sexual practice in modern, masculine cultures. In so doing, they overcome the anthropological convention of kinship and scandalously break down the wall between humans and nonhumans. Then, why a horse? The article "Vegan Sexuality: Challenging Heteronormative Masculinity through Meat-Free Sex" by Annie Potts and Jovian Parry offers a clue. In a thorough survey of 141 vegetarians and vegans and 16 omnivores, they find that vegans tend to have sexual relations with other vegans more than with, say, carnivores. Based on the survey result, it is no wonder that a horse, which is a herbivore, and the speaker, who is a non-meat-eater, encounter each other in the poem. In the last line, "It falls for me I think," the poet eloquently hints at the romantic queer love relationship between the speaker and the horse. And, yet it does not appear as a violent, kinky, one-sided relationship and bestiality of "fucking" an animal, as lay people generally perceive; rather, the cited segment tacitly indicates that it is mutual affection with the horse covering the speaker with its hairs and with the speaker caressing the horse. It is an egalitarian relationship, in which the horse is the speaker's significant other of equals, thereby successfully escaping from anthropocentrism. This kind of relationship appears in folklore in Japan. There is a story derived from Iwate Prefecture, in which a young woman and a horse become a couple but the horse is killed and hung from a tree by the outraged woman's father. The daughter is clinging to the horse's head and accordingly the father chops it off and the daughter, riding on the horsehead, flies off into the sky. From that day on, they are known as the deity *oshira-sama*, the god of the horse (Yanagita). It is believed that when oshira-sama is at your house, you cannot eat meat and only women may touch oshira-sama. Here, we can link women and nonhuman-nature, or a horse in this example.

Queer communion is often only possible in the wilderness; this is probably because heterosexual men exclude wilderness as nature, an outsider like queers, from culture as defined by the men's heteronormative sphere and so wilderness (paradoxically) becomes a safe place for "outlaw," queer sex (see also Bell and Holliday, "Naked"; Mortimer-Sandilands and Erickson, "Introduction"), emerging as *queerscape*; as well as because as in the theory of vitalism, sexual energy is ubiquitous in nature. This reminds us of geographer Matthew Gandy, who researched queer ecology by using the example of Abney Park Cemetery in North London. He states that sex in parks is a means of escape from social mores and includes people who are excluded from the mainstream scene, raising issues of social inequality and cultural repression. This is undoubtedly embodied by the poem in that sex in wilderness is a means of escape from the social mores established by heterosexual men. In this sense, Ingram is correct in saying that "[t]he landscape is never just a backdrop" (123).

The horse per se, like the natural environment it signifies, is never a blank slate. Historically, the horse represents male virility, as indicated by the association of the word "stud." In fact, the horse in the dream in Freud's famous clinical case of the five-year-old Hans signifies a man, or more precisely the boy's father. And, if we go further, when we hear the word *horse* in this sexualized modern society, we automatically envision a male, not female, horse with a long penis. Therefore, it is not unnatural at all that the horse in the poem is a sexual agent.

Mizuta remarks that modern women writers have hardly written about men. In the case of Ito's poem, the man is not described as "he" but as a "horse"; moreover, when the horse represents a man, the poet depicts the man in a completely different way from traditional men as in the festival: the herbivorous boy, a sexually nonaggressive male, in contrast to the carnivorous girl, a sexually aggressive female, as coined by columnist Maki Fukasawa. The rest of the second stanza is reminiscent not only of the bestial interaction but also of a woman-man (read carnivorous girl-herbivorous boy) sexual intercommunication:

> The lip is red and soft
> I put it into my mouth
> And smash it so could I
> The smell of sex oozing from the hairline of the whiskers
> In my entire lungs I could smell it
> The horse's urine stinks
> The horse doesn't stop the urine that really stinks
> Doesn't stop the urine and perspiration that really stink
> Doesn't stop the secretion of saliva that really stinks
> Doesn't stop the secretion from every sexual gland that
>   really stinks. (80)

In this passage, which is overflowing with images of smell and water, the speaker kisses the horse and smells the sexual odor from the hairline of the whiskers; odor is important here as a queer reading of nature reveals a desire that extends beyond the human body to incorporate nonhuman-nature and smells. On the other hand, the horse is sexually excited and aroused and does not stop ejecting liquids like urine or golden shower, perspiration, and secretions from its sexual gland, constituting a queer bestial interaction between the two. In addition, on the assumption that the queer bestial interaction is woman-man intimacy, it informs a subversive gender relationship. This is because the woman herself takes the leading role of the carnivorous girl by progressively kissing and smelling the horse as a man, and the man as the herbivorous boy does not try to actively reach out to the woman and instead just becomes sexually excited and experiences incontinence. What we witness here (or rather what we have witnessed so far) is a heterotopia, not a utopia, marked by a mixed experience as philosopher Michel Foucault claims and an ecotopia of emancipation in the wilderness in terms of gender, nature, and queer sexuality. This is the very poetics which Gaard's original intention of queer ecofeminism does justice to and threatens the naturalness of heterosexuality in the androcentric sphere of culture, or the festival.

* * *

Queer ecology is not always feminist (Gaard, "Green" 125). However, the écriture féminine "Matsuri" is ecological, feminist, and queer and performatively presents our imaginary domain with another world where the three oppressed agencies in the modern, being derogated from the gender-asymmetric, andro-/anthro-pocentric, heteronormative domain, are liberated and emancipated. In the present poem, poet Hiromi Ito does not fall into positions of constructed heteronormative homosociality, questioning the naturalness of pervasive heterosexuality and problematizing the dichotomies of male/female, human/nonhuman-nature, and heterosexual/queer[10] and the unequal relationships of both sides. The result is, without doubt, to provide a powerful promise of confluent emancipations and again show us an alternative picture of emancipation of the long-oppressed three entities: women, nonhuman-nature, and queers.

NOTES

I am grateful to Associate Professor Simon Estok of Sungkyunkwan University, Associate Professor Daniela Kato of Zhongnan University of Economics and Law, and Brian Gueyser and Jessica Smarsh of Monterey Institute of International Studies for providing incisive comments. Please note that all the citations, including the poem itself, are translated from the original Japanese by the author and that in the case of books and papers, their English titles are shown in square brackets.

1. This volume includes works by queer ecopoet Caffyn Kelley whose two poems "Space" and "Water" have been translated into Japanese by the author and appear in volume 2 of *Journal of Queer Studies Japan*. (See also Morita, "Yakusha-Kaidai.")
2. In this regard, it is interesting that ecocritic Simon Estok's 2009 paper sees ecophobia and homophobia as being derived from a same root. One such example is the Shimkiba incident in 2000, in which a gay male was killed by several straight males at a publicly managed park in Tokyo after having picked up one of them during cruising. After the incident, the local government removed the trees in the park and turned them into

lawns in order, in part, to prevent such cruising. I am planning to analyze the tragedy from a queer ecological perspective in another paper.

3. I have positioned Ito as a queer ecopoet through an analysis of her poem "Chitô [Tito]," also from *Noro to Saniwa* ("Queer Ecopoet?" [English version], "Ecopoeta Queer?" [Portuguese version]).

4. The description of her biography here is based on my previous papers ("Queer Ecopoet?," "Ecopoeta Queer?," "Mother Leads Us"). Some of her works have been translated and published in English ("Killing Kanoko") and German (*Mutter Tötten, Das Anachische Aschenputtel*).

5. Hence, we can say that it is nothing but a myth that Japanese people coexist with and are in harmony with nonhuman-nature. In this regard, see Karen Laura Thornber's *Ecoambiguity: Environmental Crises and East Asian Literatures* (2012).

6. Bakhtin says that as carnival embraces all of the people and there is no other life outside it while it is going on, carnival is a participatory event (7). This might be misleading, for several reasons: (1) people in carnival do not necessarily stand on an equal footing as the marginalized agent of the poem, (2) carnival does not treat animals as equals, and (3) there is the life of nature outside carnival.

7. Catriona Mortimer-Sandilands and Bruce Erickson also pay attention to the correlation between sexuality and an animal (sheep, in their case).

8. For instance, recall a half-naked handsome and strong gay man riding on a horse; or the movie *Brokeback Mountain*, aka *Bareback Mountain* in the queer community.

9. Writer Tatsuhiko Ishii attributes the intensity of orality of Ito's poetry to her choice of plain words and tactical repetition.

10. Japanese literature scholar Nobuaki Tochigi discusses that one of the pivotal characteristics of Ito's works is what he calls *trans-ings*, or going beyond various things.

WORKS CITED

Adams, Carol J. *The Sexual Politics of Meat: A Feminist-Vegetarian Critical Theory.* New York: The Continuum, 1990.

Alaimo, Stacy. "Eluding Capture: The Science, Culture, and Pleasure of 'Queer' Animals." In Mortimer-Sandilands and Erickson, *Queer Ecologies.* 51–72.

Ayukawa, Nobuo, Makoto Oooka, and Toru Kitagawa. *Sengo-Daihyôshi-Sen: Tanikawa Shuntaro kara Ito Hiromi* [Selection of Post-War Representative Poems: From Shuntaro Tanikawa to Hiromi Ito]. Tokyo: Shichosha, 2006.

Bakhtin, Mikhail. *Rabelais and His World.* Trans. Hélène Iswolsky. Bloomington: Indiana UP, 1984.

Bell, David and Ruth Holliday. "Naked as Nature Intended." *Body & Society* 6.3–4 (2000): 127–40.

Berila, Beth. "Toxic Bodies? ACT UP's Disruption of the Heteronormative Landscape of the Nation." In Stein, *New Perspectives on Environmental Justice*. 234–56.

Estok, Simon. *Ecocriticism and Shakespeare: Reading Ecophobia*. New York: Palgrave Macmillan, 2011.

———. "Theorizing in a Space of Ambivalent Openness: Ecocriticism and Ecophobia." *Interdisciplinary Studies in Literature and Environment* 16.2 (2009): 1–23.

Foucault, Michel. "Of Other Spaces." Trans. Jay Miskowiec. 1984. *Michel Foucault, Info*. August 26, 2012. http://foucault.info/documents/heteroTopia/foucault.heteroTopia.en.html.

Freud, Sigmund. "Analysis of a Phobia in a Five-Year-Old Boy." In *The Complete Psychological Works of Sigmund Freud*. X Vol. The standard ed. Trans. James Strachey. London: The Hogarth Press, 1909. 5–149.

Fukasawa, Maki. *Sôshoku-Danshi Sedai—Heisei-Danshi Zukan* [The Generation of Herbivore Boys: A Picture Book of Heisei-Era Boys]. Tokyo: Kobunsha, 2009.

Gaard, Greta. "Green, Pink, and Lavender: Banishing Ecophobia through Queer Ecologies." *Ethics & the Environment* 16.2 (2011): 115–26.

———. "Toward a Queer Ecofeminism." *Hypatia* 12.1 (1997): 114–37.

Gandy, Matthew. "Queer Ecology: Nature, Sexuality, and Heterotopic Alliances." *Environment and Planning D: Society and Space*, 30 (2012): advance online publication, July 20, 2012. http://www.geog.ucl.ac.uk/about-the-department/people/academics/matthew-gandy/files/epd.pdf.

Ingram, Gordon Brent. "'Open' Space as Strategic Queer Sites." In *Queers in Space: Communities | Public Places | Sites of Resistance*. Seattle: Bay Press, 1997. 95–125.

Ishii, Tatsuhiko. "Ikiduku Nikutai toshite no Shi—Ito Hiromi no Ars Poetica" [Poetry as a Breathing Flesh: The Ars Poetica of Hiromi Ito]. In *Gendaishi toshite no Tanka* [Tanka as Contemporary Poetry]. Tokyo: Shoshi-Yamada, 1999. 221–32.

Ito, Hiromi. *Das Anachische Aschenputtel: Märchen als Medizin für den Hausgebrauch*. Trans. Richmod Bollinger and Yoriko Yamada-Bochynek. St. Pölten: Residenz Verlag GmbH, 1999.

———. *Kawara Arekusa* [Wildgrass Upon a Riverbank]. Tokyo: Sichosha, 2005.

———. *Killing Kanoko: Selected Poems of Hiromi Ito*. Trans. Jeffrey Angles. Notre Dame: Action Books, 2009.

———. *Koyôte Songu* [Coyote Song]. Tokyo: Switch Publishing, 2007.

———. "Matsuri" [Festival]. In Ito and Ueno, *Noro to Saniwa*. 76–80.

———. *Mutter Tötten*. Trans. Irmela Hijiya-Kirshnereit. St. Pölten: Residenz Verlag GmbH, 1997.

———. "Sen-Kyûhyaku-Nanajû-Nendai" [The 1970s]. In *Mahô no Kagami no Naka e—Rokku Orijinaru Yakushishû 2* [Going into Magic

72   KEITARO MORITA

Mirror: A Collection of Original Translations of Rock Music Pieces 2].
Tokyo: Shichosha, 1989. 26–30.
———. *Yoi Oppai Warui Oppai* [The Good Breasts and the Bad Breasts].
Tokyo: Tojusha, 1985.
Ito, Hiromi and Chizuko Ueno. *Noro to Saniwa* [Noro and Saniwa]. Tokyo:
Heibonsha, 1991.
Kawaguchi, Kazuya. *Kuia Sutadîzu* [Queer Studies]. Tokyo: Iwanami
Shoten, 2003.
Kelly, Caffyn. "Space." *QueerMap.com*, 2005. August 26, 2012. http://
www.queermap.com/orientation/Space-Intro.htm.
———. "Water." *QueerMap.com*, 2005. August 26, 2012. http://www.
queermap.com/orientation/Water-intro.htm.
Miura, Kokichiro. *Kankyô to Sabetsu no Kuritîku: Tojô/"Fuhô-Senkyo"/
Buraku-Sabetsu* [Critique of the Environment and Discrimination:
Slaughterhouse/"Illegal Occupation"/Discrimination against the Buraku
Untouchables]. Tokyo: Shin-yo-sha, 2009.
Mizuta, Noriko. *Monogatari to Han-Monogatari no Fûkei* [Landscape of
Story and Anti-Story]. Tokyo: Tabatashoten, 1993.
Morita, Keitaro. "Ecological Reflection Begets Ecological Identity Begets
Ecological Reflexivity." Diss. Rikkyo U, 2010.
———. "Ecopoeta Queer? Uma Análise de 'Chitô [Tito],' da Poeta Japonesa
Hiromi Ito." *Estudos Feministas, Florianópolis* 19.1 (2011): 265–82.
———. "'Mother Leads Us to the Wasteland Where We Settle Down': The
Natural Environment and Sexuality in Hiromi Ito's Deconstructive
Poetry." In *Proceedings of International Conference on Literature and
Environment*, Wuhan, 2008. Ed. Nie Zhenzhao and Chen Hong. Wuhan:
Huazhong Normal UP, 2011. 497–504.
———. "Queer Ecopoet?: An Analysis of 'Chitô [Tito]' by Japanese Poet
Hiromi Ito." The *Paulinian Compass* 1.4 (2010): 101–20.
———. "Yakusha-Kaidai" [Translator's Note]. *Journal of Queer Studies
Japan* 2 (2009): 138–40.
Mortimer-Sandilands, Catriona. "Unnatural Passions?: Notes toward a
Queer Ecology." *Invisible Culture* 9 (2005). August 26, 2012. http://
www.rochester.edu/in_visible_culture/Issue_9/issue9_sandilands.pdf.
Mortimer-Sandilands, Catriona and Bruce Erickson. "Introduction: A
Genealogy of Queer Ecologies." In Mortimer-Sandilands and Erickson,
Queer Ecologies. 1–47.
———, ed. *Queer Ecologies: Sex, Nature, Politics, Desire*. Bloomington:
Indiana UP, 2010.
Morton, Timothy. "Guest Column: Queer Ecology." *PMLA* 125.2 (2010):
273–82.
Plumwood, Val. *Feminism and the Mastery of Nature*. London: Routledge,
1997.
Potts, Annie and Jovian Parry. "Vegan Sexuality: Challenging
Heteronormative Masculinity through Meat-Free Sex." *Feminism &
Psychology* 20 (2010): 53–72.

Sandilands, Catriona. "Sexual Politics and Environmental Justice: Lesbian Separatists in Rural Oregon." In Stein, *New Perspectives on Environmental Justice*. 109–26.

Sasaki, Mikiro. "Hanmo Hanshoku—'Ito Hiromi' no Tadashii Yôhô ni tsuite" [Luxuriance and Fertility: The Right Way to Use "Hiromi Ito"]. In *Gendaishi Bunko 94 Ito Hiromi* [Library of Contemporary Poetry 94: Hiromi Ito]. Tokyo: Shichosha, 1988. 130–38.

Sedgwick, Eve Kosofsky. *Between Men: English Literature and Male Homosocial Desire*. New York: Columbia UP, 1985.

Stein, Rachel, ed. *New Perspectives on Environmental Justice: Gender, Sexuality, and Activism*. New Brunswick: Rutgers UP, 2004.

Thornber, Karen Laura. *Ecoambiguity: Environmental Crises and East Asian Literature*. Ann Arbor: The U of Michigan P, 2012.

Tochigi, Nobuaki. "Wild Grass upon a Riverbank: Transformational Narratives by 'the Poet Who Goes into a Trance.'" *Poetry International*. Trans. Yasuhiro Yotsumoto. 2006. August 26, 2012. http://www.poetryinternationalweb.net/pi/site/cou_article/item/7853/Wild-Grass-upon-a-Riverbank-Transformational-Narratives-by-the-Poet-who-goes-into-a-Trance/en.

Ueno, Chizuko. "Kannibarizumu" [Cannibalism]. In Ito and Ueno, *Noro to Saniwa*. 82–88.

———. "Matsuri to Kyôdôtai" [Festival and Community]. In *Chiiki-Bunka no Shakaigaku* [Sociology of Local Cultures]. Ed. Shun Inoue. Kyoto: Sekaishisosha, 1984. 45–78.

Yanagita, Kunio. *The Legends of Tono: 100th Anniversary Edition*. Trans. Ronald A. Morse. Lanham: Rowman & Littlefield, 2008.

Section II

KOREAN SECTION

5

MULTICULTURAL ECOCRITICISM AND KOREAN ECOLOGICAL LITERATURE

Won-Chung Kim

Under the banner of globalization the world today is becoming "Americanized," and while the spread of ecocriticism is by and large a good thing, there are nevertheless matters of globalization that strongly warrant our attention. One of the most widely discussed issues in the field of ecocriticism today is about how to get over the limitation of monocultural ecocriticism and make it a more viable muticultural and transnational discourse. Since its founding in 1992, the Association for the Study of Literature and Environment (ASLE) has aimed to launch a new ecological discourse applicable to every nation in this increasingly globalized world. More than ten ASLE branches have been established around the world to date, including ASLE-Korea (which was founded in 2001 following the inception of ASLE-UK and ASLE-Japan). But American-centered ecocriticism spread rapidly with the wave of globalization and through ASLE branches and has sometimes proved to be alien and inapplicable beyond the specific geographical conditions and sociocultural atmospheres of the United States. Diversity has been one of the key issues within ecocriticism from the very start. "Ecocriticism has been predominantly a white movement. It will become a multi-ethnic movement when stronger connections are made between the environment and issues of social justice, and when a diversity of voices are encouraged to contribute to the discussion," as Cheryll Glotfelty and Harold Fromm explain (xxv). Such an American-dominated ecocriticism and ecological literature has only reflected its own interests and points of view to the extent that ecocritical literature has become another literary theory divorced from the real world. The somewhat pastoral vision of American ecological literature that seeks to preserve the wilderness and harmony between humanity and nature is indifferent to the complex political, economic, and social problems of the other countries. The issues ecological literature and ecocriticism should address are not merely limited to the relationship between humankind and nature but must be mindful of socioeconomic problems holistically affecting humankind. In this respect, twenty-first-century ecocriticism should transcend national and geographical boundaries and be enlarged to a multicultural and transnational discourse, which considers not only Western viewpoints but also all the elements of politics, economies, societies, and cultures of the non-Western world. This chapter shows the need to expand the boundary of ecocriticism in this glocalized world and then examines Korean environmental literature to show the validity of the multicultural approach.

In *Farther Afield in the Study of Nature-Oriented Literature* (2000), Patrick D. Murphy points out that "if ecocriticism has been hindered by too narrow an attention to nonfiction prose and the fiction of nonfictionality, it also has been limited by a focus on American and British literatures" (58) and adds that "privileging of certain genres and certain national literatures" should be reconsidered to truly globalize the field of ecocriticism (58). In a similar vein, Ursula K. Heise argues, "[N]either environmentalism nor ecocriticism should be thought of as nouns in singular, and that the assumptions that frame environmentalist and ecocritical thought in the United States cannot simply be presumed to shape ecological orientations elsewhere" (9). Though the driving force of globalization was the economic interest of the First World, it has incidentally given people a more globalized sense of the world—that is, in this glocalized world, the local and the global are so inextricably intertwined that it is nearly impossible to talk about them separately. Our ecocritics' insistence that "the world is interconnected and environmental problems are not only local but also global at the same time" has never been more strongly felt. With all of this in mind, it is not surprising that ecocritics emphasize the need for ecocriticism to metamorphose into something more open and multicultural in order to encompass diverse cultures and literatures. Murphy advocates of transnational ecocriticism as "a theory that transcends and crosses the viewpoint or boundary of a specific nation and an attitude that compares, analyzes, and values the works of other culture and other nations (*Ecocritical* 63). In "Recent Critiques of Ecocriticism" Terry Gifford mentions Lawrence Buell as one of the first ecocritics to consider globalization and claims that "Buell suggests that the way forward might lie in exploring the dialectic of the local-global" (19). Buell's position goes hand in hand with Heise's comment that "it seems imperative to reorient current US environmental discourse, ecocriticism included, toward a more nuanced understanding of how both local cultural and ecological systems are imbricated in global ones" (59).

But present ecocriticism, even in Asia, has been mainly voicing Western views of literature and environment by limiting its scope mainly to American literature. As Simon Estok points out, more than half of the articles published in *Literature and Environment*, ASLE-Korea's house journal, are about American environmental literature (91). This fact is really striking, especially when we consider that more than half of ASLE-Korea members are Korean literature specialists and that the rest are English and American literature majors or other foreign literature specialists (of French, German, Russian, and other European literatures). As Graham Huggan notes, it seems as though a kind of cultural imperialism governs our academic field (702). Despite efforts to incorporate other cultures and languages from beyond the Anglophone region to ecocritical analysis, ecocritical research on non-Anglophone works is still scarce. Robert Hayashi, in his intuitive article "Beyond Walden Pond," convincingly demonstrates the seriousness of academia's failure to address the experiences of racial and ethnic minorities. Pointing out that the failure of white environmentalists lies in not being able to incorporate other voices (58), he argues that "the inclusion of multiethnic literature and the traditionally interdisciplinary discussion of its study can move ecological inquiry into more salient discussions of current environmental issues" (61). Though his research is mainly focused on Asian American literature, these remarks are applicable to Asian ecological literature as well. Though Hayashi laments "the absence of Asian American authors from the field of ecocriticism" (58), these authors are actually faring much better than the Asian writers writing in their own native tongues. In the ecocritical community, East Asian voices had a mere token presence. As Estok has observed in a variety of forums, whether because of language barriers (a topic that, in itself, is a complicated morass of colonial histories) or because of indifference, Asia cites America, but America doesn't cite us.

In order to truly globalize, it is necessary to broaden the academic sphere of ecocriticism to encompass literatures of non-English-speaking countries; and in this respect, the ecological writings of East Asian countries (including China, Japan, Taiwan, and Korea) deserve special attention, since their culture and environments are much different from those of Western countries. Because diverse ecologies produce diverse cultures and cultural practices, culturally monolithic ecocriticism that gives mere lip-service to diversity—a mere nod to the Asian voice and presence—will not be sufficient for ecocriticism that purports to be going further afield, extending boundaries, and glocalizing. Certainly, one way to understand each other and bridge the wide gap of cultural and ecological differences would be to study the literature that best represents the culture. But American indifference (and often simple inability) to read and study literary works written in languages other than English has been often proved to be a serious academic limitation.

In Korea, the flow is definitely one-way. Some works of major American nature writers have been translated into Korean, including Thoreau's *Walden* (a steady seller), John Muir's *My First Summer in the Sierra*, Aldo Leopold's *Sand County Almanac*, Edward Abbey's *Desert Solitaire*, and Annie Dillard's *Pilgrims at Tinker Creek*. Additionally, two books of poetry and two prose books (*Practice of the Wild* and *A Place in Space*) by Gary Snyder and four ecological essays (including *What're People For?* and *Home Economics*) by Wendell Berry have been translated into Korean. Gary Snyder is quite popular among Korean readers and scholars, and his name has almost become synonymous to ecoliterature.[1] Though American and Korean ecocritics share a similar agenda regarding environmentalism, the effort is heavily lopsided in favor of American scholarship.

The ecological literature of Korea deserves more attention because it can promote globalizing ecocriticism by introducing a new perspective. As a nation that has successfully moved from being one of the poorest countries in the world to a developed country through a relentless pursuit of industrialization in a very short period of time while simultaneously overcoming a military regime to establish democracy, Korea has suffered and still suffers many of the environmental problems of both the Third World *and* developed countries. Metaphorically speaking, Korea is comparable to a general hospital in which patients suffering from all kinds of environmental diseases are housed. But this fact, paradoxically, puts Korea's environmental literature in a unique position to contribute to the larger multicultural and transnational ecological discourse. Although not many of these

Korean works are recognized in the academic field of ecocriticism outside of Korea, they carry poignant insights to the dangers of rapid industrialization and a consumption-oriented society. They also consider the Buddhistic and Taoistic ideas of harmony between nature and humanity. Some of those major ecological writings have been translated into English, including *Cracking the Shell: Three Korean Ecopoets* (Chiha Kim, Hyonjong Chong, and Seungho Choi), Wonil Kim's "Meditation on a Snipe," and Se-hui Cho's *The Dwarf*. Korea has its own ecological ideas, and they are well documented in Hui-Byung Park's *Ecological Thinkers of Korea*, which analyses the ecological thoughts of five famous philosophers, including Kyubo Lee and Jiwon Park.

The most prominent characteristics of Korean environmental literature can be summarized in two parts. The first trait is its investigation of the close relationship between the division of the Korean peninsula and environmental degradation; both amount to the loss of the imagined original unity and harmony that once defined Korea. Korean people were obliged to suffer doubly, for the problems of division and environmental degradation have been occurring simultaneously. This idea is best explicated in Wonil Kim's "Meditation on a Snipe." The second feature is the close relationship between the democratic and environmental movements in Korea. Political persecution and environmental exploitation went hand in hand, and this is the reason why Korean ecowriters emphasize life, not only that of humans but also of nature. In a lot of Asian philosophy, humanity is not separate from nature but is a significant part of it: there exists a firm belief that nature and humanity are inextricably interconnected with each other. Not only were Korean people repressed and the environment exploited by colonialists, but also modern Korea has been marked by forced division of the country by political ideologies, the Korean War, and following military dictatorship, and blind pursuit of economic development. Two Korean ecowriters in particular, Wonil Kim and Chiha Kim, display these traits very conspicuously.

Wonil Kim's "Meditation on a Snipe,"[2] published in 1979, while Koreans still lived under a dictatorship and were enthusiastic for rapid industrialization, graphically shows links between development and environmental degradation. Rapid industrialization was accelerated by the geopolitical situation of the Korean peninsula; South and North Korea were competing with each other not only in an ideological but also in an economic war to prove each was better than the other. The environment has been destroyed due to the rapid economic development ruthlessly pushed by military regimes. Professor Paik's remarks in *The Swaying Division* aptly summarize this point:

> The anti-democratic reality which is antagonistic to all the NGO movements including the environmental movement controls the divided Korean peninsula—though the specific form and degree vary in South and North Korea. The environmentally devastating development has been practiced indiscriminately not only in the competition with other countries in the capitalistic world economy, but also in the competition of political system between the South and the North Korea. (44)

Kim's novel explores these relationships. Regarded not only as one of the pioneering works in ecological literature, but also as one of the best literary works to date in Korea, Kim's novel is set against the backdrop of the newly built industrial and chemical complex. It focuses on how the pristine land and rivers became a cursed dystopia, contaminated by toxic chemicals that were carelessly and sometimes intentionally discarded by factories. Byoung-kuk, one of the novel's protagonists, laments, "The Sokyo can no longer be called living water…It is already dead. Worse, a demon lives in it" (176). The demon here symbolizes the capitalist ideology that mercilessly exploits nature in its own interest. Rapid development not only altered the landscape of the region but also changed the relationship between humanity and nature. Losing the status of companion or cohabitant in the ecosystem, nature has been irrevocably isolated and regarded as an object for profit. The cost for development is not small; people worry about the possible mercury and chrome poisoning, and "the irreversible damage to [their] body" (176). This novel convincingly and graphically illustrates the rapid descent from ecotopia to dystopia, where the survival of humanity itself, as well as of other creatures, is put in danger. It is not mere reportage; it is, instead, a story that talks about the desolation of our life, a life that is intoxicated with the ideologies of progress and development.

Through the description of the physical and mental states of a father, the author vividly shows how the division of the Korean peninsula into two parts has destroyed people's lives as well. The novel portrays a family consisting of a father, a mother, and two sons, Byoung-kuk and Byoung-sik. The father, a North Korean refugee and injured veteran of the Korean War, is deeply scarred by the fact that he cannot go back to his hometown because of the separation of the peninsula, unlike the snipes, that can fly over the demarcation line. It affects his mind and body, which are externalized through his crippled leg and stuttering. His physical state serves as a metaphor for the division of the peninsula. The following two passages clearly exemplify how the division of the country has led him to lead a life of fear and despair:

> To put it mildly, he was the timid, cringing type, a man of few words and much fear. He attributed that to the war. He lamented that nothing short of unification would be able to fill the big hole that had opened up in him the time he lost his home. (156)
>
> [...]
>
> Dad is really a war victim. The country's division and the failure to reunite have drained him of hope. In a sense, his lifeline has been cut. (157)

The loss of his home is no less than the loss of place, "centers of felt values" according to Yi-Fu Tuan (4). Lawrence Buell argues that modern history has reversed the history of space becoming place (63–64). In this sense, the father's dislocation can be understood as the loss of place and as a forced move to a strange space where he can no longer maintain his own social and ecological identity. The division of the peninsula not only turns the land of pristine beauty into a land of fear but also completely deprives the Korean people of the possibility of leading a harmonious life in their own place.

The military government's antipathy toward the environmental movement that was burgeoning in the 1970s stems from their perception that nature can be exploited for humanity's profit. To the government, which had come to power through a coup d'état and was ruthlessly driving the whole nation toward economic development to justify itself, the environmentalists are "crazy" people who merely care for "useless bird and fish." The policy of "economy first" and "the supremacy of national security" were two most powerful weapons used to repress environmentalists. Two of Byoung-kuk's experiences illustrate the liaison between the military regime and the industries: one with his letter of petition to the government and the other with his trespassing of the military zone. In the first episode, unaware of the strong alliance between political and business circles, Byoung-kuk sends a petition letter to the city, but the city official forwards the letter to the same company that discharged huge amounts of toxic chemicals, including mercury and cadmium, into the river. The manager argues that the victims were only "useless birds and fish, you'll note, not people" (197). His companion adds, "[O]ur GNP is now one thousand dollars. Do you know sir, how modernization came about in our motherland?" (197). And another says, "[T]his is like catching a bedbug by setting the horse on fire!

We have to root out this type of crazy behavior" (197). According to their logic, environmentalists like Byoung-kuk are crazy people who do not understand the urgent need for modernization of the country. In the second episode, the fact that the ideology of the supremacy of national security goes hand in hand with the "economy first" policy is clearly shown. Byoung-kuk enters into the restricted military zone to find out the cause of the death of the birds and is arrested by soldiers. Major Youn severely criticizes Byoung-kuk's reckless behavior by summoning him and saying that "we are not in actual combat, but you must understand that we are still at war...In fact, the country's welfare and the development of all sorts of industries are due entirely to the maintenance of security" (204). These remarks clearly show how deeply the ideologies of modernization and industrialization have changed people's attitude toward nature. As Koreans are dislocated from their own homes, nature loses its status of ethical fellowship and is degraded to the status of mere resource.

On the opposite side of Byoung-kuk stands Byoung-sik, his mother, Byoung-sik's friend Wiesel, and Mr. Lee, the taxidermist. Their greed for money makes them indifferent to the misery of other people and the birds. The pollution of the land and water, the killing of birds for stuffing, and the sexual exploitation of female workers are also major problematic motifs within the novel. But the real misery is that people, blinded by this greed, do not recognize that this kind of life is suicidal. As Namho Lee indicates, "'Meditation on a Snipe' successfully overlaps the different stories; one, that the tragic history of Korea's division and corrupt political authority is the pollutant devastating people's lives, and the other, that the industrial complex is the pollutant turning a beautiful haven of migratory birds into a wasteland" (67). The inexorable drive for economic development by the Korean government and the industrial companies' blind pursuit of profit were too much for Byung-sik, a young man with intense moral passion, and thus the novel ends on a pessimistic note. Kim awakens us to the idea that we should be patient and dedicate ourselves to the recovery of the original ecosystem where we can live harmoniously with nature.

While Wonil Kim convincingly shows in "Meditation on a Snipe" how environmental problems are inextricably connected with the problem of political ideology and Korea's dividedness (Jeon 466), Chiha Kim's life and poetry offer us the best example of the close tie between the democratic movement and environmental movements. His life's journey from being the icon of Korea's democratic movement to an ecological poet and thinker witnesses the inextricable bond between these two movements, each a driving force of the Korean society in the last three decades of the twentieth century.[3] Born into a country under Japanese colonization in 1941, Kim experienced the Korean War at the age of nine and participated in the April 19 Revolution[4] as a college student. When he published "Five Thieves" (1970), a sarcastic and bitter parody of the military regime, high officials, and plutocrats, the government sentenced him to death on the absurd ground that he had violated the ban against anticommunist activity. But in the prison where he served for eight years, Kim paradoxically found a new meaning of life through which he drastically changed into an ecological poet. The episode of his awakening deserves a full quotation:

> Around that time I saw the dust filling the small gaps between the concrete wall and iron bars. The plant seeds, getting moisture from rain, were starting to sprout in those gaps. A wonder it was....How bitterly I wept in my cell that day! How powerful and fresh that one word—life. It held me! Before the one great life that fills the infinite universe and before the unending stream of life, there can be neither wall nor division, nor decay nor death. (*Heart's Agony* 28)

This experience of being awakened into the true meaning of cosmic life allows Kim to overcome the closed world of never-ending oppression and revolt and instead enter the sea of life where the whole creation cooperates to fulfill its cosmic life.

The change from the imagination of the sword to that of lotus, as it is expressed in a phrase in "A Wish 1" that "When I / Unsheathe my sword, / Oh, that it would change into / A lotus flower" (67), can be regarded as sudden and abrupt. But from the very beginning of his poetic career, Kim has aspired to live a "real" life in which human beings can be faithful to their own ideas and fulfill them freely. Therefore, both his fight for democracy and his agony for the ecological, cosmic self are two sides of the same coin: his unyielding yearning for a real life. Faced with suffocating oppression and merciless persecution, Kim, a man of courage and integrity, is determined to fight against the dark reality. Though he knows too well that the cost of his rebellion against the military regime will be the unbearable torture of his "fingernails plucked and flesh ripped apart" (50) and eventual death, he does not even wince. As the title of his poem, "With a Burning Thirst," indicates, he writes the name of democracy secretly in tears with a burning thirst. The act of writing the name of democracy is the only thing open to him at that time. It is a desperate effort to revive democracy in peoples' vocabulary, because that word, along with the word "freedom," was so rarely used that it almost became a distant memory. Though his own soul is "shriveled" by unending torture, he cannot help but write because:

> Somebody calls to me again and again
> Blood-stained, worn out underwear hanging from the windowsill.
> The crimson souls writhing so many nights in the cells
> And the cries of mangled bodies
> Call to me and my blood
> With their soft silence,
> With a shake of their heads. (45)

However, amid his fight against the dark power, Kim intuits that what should be broken down are not the outer worldly barriers such as political tyranny and persecution, but rather, the walls within oneself. The dark power that prevents him from enjoying real freedom also resides inside him. This recognition of dark powers in his own heart and of the powerful will of every living thing drives him to pursue another kind of revolution—that is, the revolution of the mind, rather than political revolution.

He diagnoses our current culture as the culture of killing and presents the culture of *salim* (which means both household and bringing things to life in Korean) as an alternative. By synthesizing and reinterpreting Korea's traditional folklore and Tonghak (東學),[5] he creates a new paradigm, which allows him to leap over the conflicting dualism of the world (Hong 190). Kim realizes that he himself could not help but live as the agent and as the victim of the culture of killing. What is needed most is to shed off his old self, which is accustomed to the imagination of the sword, and to put on the imagination of lotus. "Cracking the Shell" portrays this agony to be born again:

> I am burnt hollow
> And now a tree grows in me.
> Dead and transformed
> Into a crescent moon
> I rise over the trees.
> ......
> I'll break my shell
> Kick through
> To be born again
> As the Universe. (75)

As Chan J. Wu notes, the organic principle of the metamorphosis and circulation of the body tells us that life is imperishable and that this eternal life permeates our body. The new self the poet yearns for is the cosmic self who embodies the principle of interconnectedness and circulation of all things in this universe (31). This universe is based on the solidarity of all living things, in which the distinction between life and death is broken down and every creature helps the other realize life fully by supporting, embracing, and interpenetrating each other freely. As we can see in "Let's See Small Things" when Kim writes, "But nature is wise and merciful, / And with her symbiotic principle, / Harmonize all creations" (63), Kim turns his eyes toward the small things, and there he finds the harmony and symbiotic principle of nature. The cooperation and mutual living of the crocodiles and crocodile birds serve as an example of an ecological way of living in the biotic community. What governs this community of whole creation should be love, compassion, and respect, above all things, as we can infer from his words that, "Love is respect / That spins the world smoothly / By placing others on high" (84). To respect means first to acknowledge that an eternal cosmic life lives not only in our neighbors and others, but also in plants, animals, and even in inorganic things, such as earth and air. The core of Kim's life philosophy is to become one with the whole universe by respecting all things in it, and that is the reason why he prefers his philosophy to be called "life-philosophy," as he explains in "From the Burning Thirst to the Sea of Life."

In Chiha Kim's poetic career, the transition from political imagination to ecological imagination is prominent. While the former relies heavily on a worldview of binary opposition, the latter stems from a view of a cyclical and circular universe. His political imagination shows a strong pathos of confrontation, revolt, criticism, and satire, while his ecological imagination is one of compassion, interconnectedness, love, respect, and transformation. This shift is representative of the change in thinking within Korean society during the latter half of the twentieth century, and Chiha Kim's writings can be understood more clearly in this specific context. His poetry lends us a more comprehensive insight that ecological thought should not limit itself to merely seeking a harmonious relationship between humanity and nature but should expand to actively pursue a symbiotic living of every creature suffering in the social, political, and cultural realms. By reinterpreting traditional Korean thoughts and old cultural discourse of "Tonghak," he insists that not only all living things, but also all inorganic things should be respected and loved, thereby enlarging the boundary of nature in ecological discourse.

In "'Greening' Postcolonialism: Ecocritical Perspectives," Huggan insists that "political colonialism has ended, but a more benign form of colonialism has taken root" (702). Unfortunately, our ecocritical world has proved no exception, and this benign cultural colonialism has made its way into our interpretive strategies for environmentalist texts. Currently, a naively globalized ecocriticism that hears only voices that it understands, only voices that it wants to hear, and does not make a concerted effort to hear other voices has been dominant: this does not bode well for the future. As the aforementioned analysis of the peculiar characteristics of Korean environmental literature shows, the specific geopolitical and cultural situation of each country should be considered to ensure a better and meaningful understanding of each country's environmental problems. We must be careful not to impose one specific country's literary tradition or interpretation on the other countries, for every country has different customs and literary traditions. In this respect, Murphy's insistence is appropriate: "The internationalization of nature-oriented-literature studies should not lead toward globalization of generic or aesthetic criteria, nor should it lead to a hierarchical ranking of the best the world has to offer" (*Farther* 74). His words sound more powerful here in East Asia than anywhere else, because our cultures are much different from those of Western countries. Considering that the population of China, Japan, Korea, Taiwan, and India combined makes up a little less than half of the world's population, and given the great power these countries have on the global economy, the world *must* recognize the voices of these countries. Without addressing the environmental problems of this region, the ailing world will not be healed. Therefore, the first step would be to listen to other voices and concerns, because only that kind of open attitude will change the status quo of the unilateral dispersal of American ideas on literature and environment to the world, and open a new era of multilateral cross-fertilization, from which the real global discourse will bud.

NOTES

An earlier and substantially different version of my discussion on Wonil Kim's "Meditation on a Snipe" appeared as "Dystopia and Toxic Discourse in Wonil Kim's 'Meditation on a Snipe.'"

1. About the importance and reception of Gary Snyder in Korea, see Won-Chung Kim's "Gary Snyder Studies in Korea."
2. Because Brendan Machale's translation of the title of the novel, "Dreaming of the Snipe," is inaccurate and somewhat confusing, I use a new title, "Meditation on a Snipe," in this chapter.

3. Military dictatorship officially ended in June 1987 when the civilian government was launched by the election. Many of the democratic movement supporters have turned their eyes to environmental issues since then.

4. Civilian and student uprisings in April 1960 against the First Republic of South Korea led to the peaceful resignation of then president Syngman Rhee.

5. Tonghak (Eastern Learning) is a Korean religion founded in 1860 by Choe Je-u. As a syncretic religion based on Korea's traditional folk belief in Haneullim ("Lord of Heaven"), it incorporated some ideas of Buddhism, Confucianism, Taoism, shamanism, and Christianity, though it opposed Western culture and learning as the very name of the religion indicates. Its core tenet is called Innaecheon (人乃天), which states the identity of human beings with a higher being and the right of all people to equality on earth.

WORKS CITED

Buell, Lawrence. *The Future of Environmental Criticism: Environmental Crisis and Literary Imagination*. Oxford: Blackwell Publishing, 2005.

Estok, Simon. "Discourses of Nation, National Ecopoetics, and Ecocriticism in the face of US: Canada and Korea as Cases Studies." *Comparative American Studies* 7.2 (June 2009): 85–97.

Gifford, Terry. "Recent Critiques of Ecocriticism." *New Formations* 64 (Spring 2008): 15–24.

Glotfelty, Cheryll and Harold Fromm, eds. *Ecocriticism Reader: Landmarks in Literary Ecology*. Athens: The U of Georgia P, 1996.

Hayashi, Robert. "Beyond Walden Pond: Asian American Literature and the Limits of Ecocriticism." In *Coming into Contact: Explorations in Ecocritical Theory and Practice*. Athens: The U of Georgia P, 2007. 58–75.

Heise, Ursula K. *Sense of Place and Sense of Planet: The Environmental Imagination of the Global*. Oxford: Oxford UP, 2008.

Hong, Yonghee. "The Dream and Language of New Life." In *The Way for Green Life: A Critical View of Ecotopia*. Ed. Shin Deokryong. Gangju: Siwasaramsa, 1997. 189–210.

Huggan, Graham. "'Greening' Postcolonialism: Ecocritical Perspectives." *Modern Fiction Studies* 50.3 (Fall 2004): 701–33.

Jeon, Hongnam. "A Study of Environmental Crisis and the Counterforce of Novels." *Korean Language and Literature* 43 (1999): 453–69.

Kim, Chiha. *Heart's Agony: Selected Poems of Chiha Kim*. Trans. Won-Chung Kim and James Han. Fredonia, NY: White Pine P, 1998.

Kim, Won-Chung. "Dystopia and Toxic Discourse in Wonil Kim's 'Meditation on a Snipe.'" *Literature and Environment* 12 (December 2009): 53–58.

———. "Gary Snyder Studies in Korea." *Proceedings of the ASLE-Japan and ASLE-Korea First Joint Symposium on Literature and Environment*. Kanazawa (August 2007), 113–20.

Kim, Wonil. "Dreaming of a Snipe." Trans. Brendon MacHale. In *Anthology of Korean Literature* vol. 2 Ed. Seunggil Paik. Seoul: Dong-Suh-Munhak-Sa, 1988. 141–227.

Lee, Namho. *Literature for the Green.* Seoul: Minumsa, 1998.

Murphy, Patrick D. *Ecocritical Explorations in Literary and Cultural Studies: Fences, Boundaries, and Fields.* New York: Lexington Books, 2009.

———. *Farther Afield in the Study of Nature-Oriented Literature.* Charlottesville: U of Virginia P, 2000.

Paik, Nak-chung. *The Swaying Division.* Seoul: Changbi, 1998.

Tuan, Yi-Fu. *Space and Place: The Perspective of Experience.* Minneapolis: U of Minnesota P, 1977.

Wu, Chan J. "Cosmic Buds Burgeoning in Words: Chiha Kim's Poetics of Full-Emptiness." In *Heart's Agony.* 15–33.

6

THE CHEONGYECHEON AND SUSTAINABLE URBAN ECOLOGY

(RE)CONFIGURING KOREAN ENVIRONMENTAL DISCOURSE AND ECOCRITICISM

Dooho Shin

The Cheongyecheon is a stream that runs through the heart of Seoul. Its restoration was conducted between 2003 and 2005. Much controversy and debate went on before, during, and even after the project, and almost every field of Korean society jumped into the debates. Business circles and politicians embraced this project, while many civic and environment movement groups criticized it as representing one of the worst cases of government-driven ideology of development. This project and the controversy epitomize two contrasting but interrelated matters facing modern Korea: urbanization and the confrontation between preservationism and development.

Korea is one of the most heavily urbanized and densely populated countries. More than 80 percent of the whole population lives in urban areas, and nearly half of Koreans reside within Seoul and its satellite cities. Understanding urban environment and environmental issues such as the one concerning the Cheongyecheon requires attention from more than just a simple preservationism versus development confrontation because this confrontation is based on the assumption that nature and culture or nature and urban are two distinctive things. The urban environment cannot be understood within the framework of the nature-culture and preservationism-development distinction, because nature and culture in urban areas do not exist independently, nor are they easily distinguishable. Romanticism scholar and ecocritic Ashton Nicholas recently introduced the term "urbanature" to describe the idea that "nature and urban life are not distinct" and that "all human and nonhuman lives, as well as all animate and inanimate objects around those lives are linked in a complex web of interdependent interrelatedness" (xiii). Based upon this recognition, Nicholas calls for a "resituation" of humanity's awareness of nature: "The time has come to acknowledge humanity's position in a nature that is always urban and urbanity that is always natural" (188–89). I suggest here that Korean ecocritical discourse and environmental discourse in general, however, are yet trapped in a dualistic nature versus culture paradigm marked by conflicts between an ideology of nature preservationism and one of economic development, and that these conflicts originate from Korea's unique social circumstances. Consequently, ecocritical and environmental discourse has not appropriately represented the range of connections between environmental concerns and human social conditions.

Ecocritical and environmental discourse in Korea, therefore, should reflect characteristics of urbanized Korean social and environmental concerns—the crucial connection of environment with society and culture. This chapter focuses on the Cheongyecheon project and some novels that were inspired by this project and proposes three things: first, that the Cheongyecheon restoration is an example of a sustainable urban ecology whose understanding escapes the simple preservationism-development dichotomy; second, that there are four important perspectives involved in the Cheongyecheon discourse; and third, that the Cheongyecheon novels and the Korean ecocritical approach to them reveal how much ecocritical studies in Korea have been entrapped by a conceptual and preservationist ethos. At the same time, these novels well recognize characteristics of the sustainable development of urban ecology in this restoration project and embody them in narrative forms. Through this analysis and examination, this essay finally will suggest ways, through viable literary study, that Korean ecocriticism can come up with a transformative approach to the environmental issues of its society.

Before analyzing the Cheongyecheon project and its consequential environmental discourse, it will be helpful to give a brief examination of how Korean environmental and ecocritical discourse have been characterized by the conflicts between preservationism and development. Clashes between preservationism and development often occur in environmental discourse, but these conflicts are especially intense in Korea and the causes derive from the unique characteristics of its modern sociopolitical and economic circumstances, rather than from issues such as wilderness ethics that characterize much of Western and especially the American environmental discourse. Within the compressed time period of 40 years or so, Korea has achieved a rapid economic development, but with consequential environmental degradation. And when Korean society achieved democracy in the late 1980s, environmental awareness and discourses (which had been suppressed by the former dictatorial governments' push for national development through industrialization) suddenly erupted and became a symbolic means for obtaining citizens' rights. As a reaction to the government-led development ideology and its consequent environmental destruction, the preservationist causes aided by environmental civil groups and academic humanities pitted radical preservationism against government-led economic development and environmental policies. Accordingly, the conflicts between environmental causes and unrestrained development have intensified.

These conflicts have had some problematic consequences. For one thing, the conflicts have precluded efforts in environmental discourse toward developing the realistic and comprehensive approaches that are needed in order to understand environmental issues in modern urbanized Korean society. Moreover, the Korean humanities have opted for a preservationist stance derived from East Asian traditions and, more specifically, Korean thought, and they have given insufficient consideration to the real social circumstances of modern Korean society. Such a preservationist stance and retrospective attitude have characterized Korean ecocritical studies as well. In order to interrogate developmental policies and the industrial-capitalist system, Korean ecocriticism has conventionally resorted to a conceptual framework that creates boundaries between traditional preservationist perspectives and ones geared toward development. With regard to the causes of and the solutions for the environmental problems, Korean ecocriticism has not given much consideration to the specificity of real social and environmental circumstances; instead, it has relied on two types of environmental literary discourse. One is to attribute environmental destruction to the anthropocentrism of Western modernism and to look, instead, for solutions from East Asian or, more specifically, traditional Korean positions.[1] The other tendency finds the cause of environmental destruction in human greed and rapacity.[2] Both of these tendencies uncritically reify the conceptual framework of an East-West division, rooted in deep ecological and retrospective perspectives.

Korean ecocritic Yong-hee Hong analyzes the 1990s Korean eco-poetics and concludes that it is unanimously "inclined to deep ecology and attribute the destruction of the ecosystem to anthropocentrism and modern industrialism, putting an emphasis on reconstructing an escapist eco-cosmopolitan world." He adds that Korean ecopoetics "failed to analyze human-human and human-nature relations and nature of human existence, and, therefore, they failed to suggest specificity of life community" (48). The persistent reliance of Korean humanities including literary critics on a preservationist perspective may have contributed to raising environmental awareness, but this retrospective attitude is naïve and unrealistic for coping with modern Korean urbanized and modern society and its environmental issues.

The urban environment and human society have continually become the subjects of ecocritical attention in the West, under the recognition that "the country" and "the city" are not divisible. As Lawrence Buell puts it, the "brown" landscape and the "green" landscape need to be understood as being "in conversation" (7). With this recognition, Lance Newman early on called for an extended ecocritical practice: "In order for ecocriticism to earn its claims to relevance, its critical practice must be greatly extended... [and] the environmental crisis threatens all landscapes—wild, rural, suburban, and urban. South Boston is just as natural (and wild) as Walden Pond" (71; cited in Buell 7).

Korean ecocriticism, however, has stood firmly by the nature-versus-culture preservationist position and has ignored the specificity of environmental issues in urban areas. The Cheongyecheon and its project-inspired novels show good examples of why ecocriticism needs to correct its limited environmental thinking and approach.

Most of all, the Cheongyecheon restoration project needs to be understood as a sustainable project of urban ecology. The Seoul Metropolitan Government rolled out an ambitious plan for a large-scale restructuring of the stream, listing the main purposes as follows: (1) to pursue a sustainable urban development paradigm through a balance between economic development and environmental conservation; (2) to restore the ecosystem of the stream; (3) to uphold public health and safety through removal of urban hazards and nuisances of the rundown concrete roads and the elevated highway built over and along the stream; (4) to correct uneven social and environmental conditions of the two sectors located on each side of the stream; and (5) to restore the stream's historical and cultural assets ("History and Transformation"). The plan made it clear that environmental conservation would not sacrifice economic development and that cultural and historical restoration would be an integral part of such development.[3] These declared purposes illustrate the fact that the project was in principle an example of sustainable urban (re)development, which includes the dimensions of economic, sociopolitical development, environmental preservation, and cultural restoration. The confluence of these factors, such as economic and social development, and environmental and cultural preservation that the Cheongyecheon project declared as its main purpose have been recognized as representing the core principles of sustainable development. In 1996 the United Nations City Summit Habitat Agenda declared that "[t]here is a sense of great opportunity and hope that a new world can be built, in which economic development, social development and environmental protection as interdependent and mutually reinforcing components of sustainable development can be realized through solidarity and cooperation within and between countries and through effective partnership at all levels" (Chapter 1, June 1996, 1). The United Nations 2005 World Summit Outcome Document also refers to economic development, social development, and environmental protection as the "interdependent and mutually reinforcing pillars" of sustainable development ("2005 World Summit Outcome"). These three "pillars" are specifically recognized as constituent parts of a sustainable urban city as was manifested in the findings of the Conference on Strategies for Sustainable Cities: "Economy, ecology, social cohesion are the pillars of a sustainable city. These must be in balance and therefore require an integrated approach" ("Strategies for Sustainable Cities"). Otherwise, a community cannot be sustainable: "A major assumption of the sustainable community definition is that trying to address [economic, social, and environmental] issues in isolation eventually ends up hurting some other part of the community's health" (Lachman 19–20). Sustainable development is, then, an eclectic concept, comprising a wide array of views. With an increased awareness of the importance of cultural diversity, cultural factors have recently come to be taken into account by sustainability metrics, too. Some organizations and institutions define environment as a combination of nature and culture and argue that culture should be added as a key element of sustainable development in order to reflect the complexity of modern society. The United Cities and Local Governments (UCLG), which is an international organization that represents the interests of local governments throughout the world, proposed the "Agenda 21 for Culture" in 2004. This reference document aimed to draw up cultural policies for local governments that, at the time, employed only the three pillars of sustainable development in their local policies. Being aware of the importance of the role of culture in urban policies, Agenda 21 advocates the integration of cultural issues within sustainable development, along with environment, economics, and social inclusion. Prepared by the UCLG Executive Bureau, the policy statement document "Culture: the Fourth Pillar of Sustainable Development" was approved at the 2010 UCLG World Congress. Through the successive approval of the document by the UN General Assembly, cultural issues have become an integral part of sustainable development ("Cultural Policies and Sustainable Development").

The restoration project of the Cheongyecheon, completed in 2005, has produced heated debates and controversies, resulting in a wide range of urban environmental discourse. This discourse can be categorized according to the canonical triangle of sustainable development plus cultural factors. A confluence of these factors such that sustainable development would be deemed essential, however, was not feasible in the Cheongyecheon discourse. The issues of economic development, environmental preservation, social development, and cultural restoration were addressed in isolation or in contradictory terms.[4]

First, economic development through the restoration project was advocated by Seoul authorities, economists, and urban (environmental) architects. They focused on economic revitalization and urban environmental improvement for citizens through the restoration of the stream and renovation of its vicinities that had been economically inactive and environmentally degraded. The goal has been to renovate a polluted and repugnant urban space into an environmentally sound urban park. As landscape scholar Jeong-han Bae remarks, "An urban park is the most candid name for the Cheongyecheon and, at the same time, the stream's potential" (cited in Lee and Kim 108). Though preservation and economic growth have been historically at odds, they argue that such an environmentally renovated space would likely boost economic activities, because more people and businesses would be likely to pour in. Such economic development through environmental renovation of the stream was suspected by civic groups to be the real motivation behind the project.

Second, the stance of environmental preservation was taken by ecological scientists, who argued that the priority of the project should be restoration and preservation of ecology. In conflict with economic development, this stance considered the stream as an ecological space and approached the project primarily as a restoration of a degraded space into an ecologically sound space, with rehabilitation of aquatic plants and animals and the diversification of vegetation. Korean environmental scientists Baek-ho Kim and Myeong-soo Han consider the Cheongyecheon project as an instance of ecosystem restoration; meaning, "to restore the structural and functional elements of the stream so that the biota and food chain are maintained" (38). Scholars in the environmental humanities—including ecocritics—value the importance of nature preservation and cast strong doubt on the feasibility of such restoration to its original state.

Third, to some progressives and political NGOs, the restoration work was meant to be a form of social development, aiming to correct social and environmental injustice for the disadvantaged. This stance approached the restoration project from the perspective of social and environmental justice, which advocated that restoration should contribute to the benefit of the disadvantaged who have been exposed to all kinds of urban environmental harms and hazards. The middle and lower parts of the stream had been environmentally devastated and, accordingly, only the disadvantaged have resided there. Sociologist Seong-bok Yun interprets this project as an example of sustainable urban development and emphasizes the social aspects along with economic and ecological ones. He argues that "sustainable development with no consideration of social aspects will deepen the social inequality and worsen disproportion of urban spaces...The Cheongyecheon project should give the first priority to the disadvantaged in this area through benefits distribution; otherwise, this project can't be justified" (274).

Fourth, an advocacy of the stream's aesthetic and cultural restoration has been mainly maintained by artists and historians. They have stressed that the restoration project should include restoration and preservation of the cultural and historical heritage and assets of the stream, whose space, located in the urban center of the capital city, has been the site of political, economic, and cultural events for 600 years. Popular Korean philosopher Do-ol approaches this project not just as an example of physical beautification or betterment of the urban environment but as "a paradigm shift" in the nature of the city. He believes that this project will transform the industrial and capital city into a future model city of high culture and mind through the realization of Confucian moral and values. Considering the restoration of cultural and historical heritage, as well as the promotion of a citizen-friendly environment, both scientists and even some opponents of this project acknowledge that the stream will be reborn as the aesthetically and culturally restored space. Environmental scientists Baek-ho Kim and Myeong-soo Han point out that the Cheongyecheon project should not mean a physical restoration but a restoration of the stream where "our ancestors' joys and sorrows are stored" and go on to argue that "the eco-friendly city boasts its new face as a symbol of post-industrial Korean economic and cultural takeoff toward being a developed country" (38).

The opinions of these four approaches have produced diverse responses, and much controversy and debate have been carried out between two extreme poles; those of economic development and deep ecological preservationism. Additionally, social development groups have joined this debate, criticizing the two stances for their negligence of taking into consideration themes of social factors such as environmental injustice. The significance of this urban stream, however, cannot be understood fully from either perspective alone. As a work of sustainable development, the restoration of the stream requires attention to all these dimensions. Korean sociologist Seong-bok Yun remarks that "[b]uilding sustainable urban Seoul through the restoration and renovation of the Cheongyecheon requires us to take economic, ecological, and social stances into consideration. Emphasis on a certain stance alone will result in negligence of the other two stances. Then, building sustainable Seoul will be distorted" (247–48).

A brief survey of historical and current functions and circumstances of the stream will furthermore show that a confluence of these different stances is needed in understanding the project. First of all, as an urban stream, the Cheongyecheon had been under constant management. The Cheongyecheon had existed as a natural stream, with clean water flowing down from the neighboring mountains, and this stream eventually joined the Han River. As the capital's population increased, the Cheongyecheon shifted from being a natural stream to a site of drainage and sewage and then to being a hub of urban industry, eventually with the stream cemented over and an elevated expressway built over it. Second, as Seoul was a central stage for activities for 600 years as the capital city, the Cheongyecheon had become an important space for economic activities. Markets naturally began to spring up in this area where people most frequently passed through or gathered, and it had become a symbolic place for showing the industrialized urbanity of modern Korea. Big markets developed along the stream as the financial hub developed upstream. Third, throughout Korean history, the Cheongyecheon (an area where social injustices became prominent) played a pivotal role in dividing Seoul geographically, politically, and socially, thus producing social and environmental injustice. The stream functioned as a social and environmental borderline, with rich and aristocratic classes settled in the upper region of the stream, and middle and lower classes, respectively, living along its middle and lower courses.

With industrialization, small- and middle-scale factories sprang up and packed the regions along its middle and lower courses and, consequently, this area suffered from environmental problems of air pollution and traffic congestion. Fourth, historical and cultural assets have been an integral part of the stream. Over a 600-year span as a central space for political, social, economic, and cultural activities, the stream and its vicinity had left historic relics and artifacts such as stone bridges, stone walls, and paintings. This stream had become a site for cultural activities. Bookstores and print shops had been built in this area, and various cultural activities and celebrations had also been held. In sum, the Cheongyecheon had become a hybrid space where elements of the natural environment, economy, sociopolitics, and culture overlapped.

Considering the fact that the stream had traditionally functioned in supporting such diverse aspects of ecology, economic activities, sociopolitics, and historical-cultural activities, and that it had been environmentally desecrated, resulting in social stratification and injustice, all these aspects were taken into consideration in the discourse of the restoration project. That is, the nature of this restoration project demanded that people "think beyond" the nature-society dualism. The actor-network theory (ANT) provides a theoretical ground for such a corrective approach. ANT not only challenges the nature-society dualism but also conceptualizes relational socionatural imbrications, which include humans and nonhumans. Geographers Noel Castree and Tom MacMillan explain ANT by the process of its application to the restoration of the Cole River in England. According to them, the restoration process "was predominantly one of *hybridity* involving multiple, indissoluble links" among the actors involved such as nearby residents, government authorities, workers, machines, organisms, plants, animals (219). All these actors should be understood to form "socionatural networks" in which every actant is intimately interrelated. Therefore, they argue for "the necessity for a hybrid politics in which the fate of [such actants] are considered simultaneously" (220).

Based upon this recognition of complexities of environment-related matters, environmental communication scholars Tracy Based Marafiote and Emily Plec direct our attention to the "multivocality of discourse." Adapting Mikhail Bakhtin's conception of heteroglossia, they note that the way humans understand the natural world and environmental issues is full of "heteroglossic contradictions and complexities." They state that "[the Bakhtinian hybridity] acknowledges and searches for the multiplicity of discourses and sociological views within linguistic utterances about the environment...[It] acts as a centrifugal force in decentering and disrupting limited, monoglossic discourse or dualistic meanings, and helps us to locate occurrences of linguistic and ideological disjunctures" (61).

From such perspectives as ANT and hybrid discourse, the nature-society dualism that has characterized most of the Cheongyecheon discourse is too narrow and dichotomous. Responses to the Cheongyecheon project (especially from the humanities) can be characterized by "monoglossic discourse" of preservationism with "dualistic meanings" of the nature/culture division. The Korean humanities either have shown little interest in the debates or have criticized this project from conventional deep ecological perspectives. Out of a handful of humanities papers dedicated to this project, Korean philosopher Seok-young Cho, for example, weighs the meaning of the restoration work. The approach he makes to the restoration project is an ecocentric theory of restoration, and he brushes off any type of restoration of nature as "artifact." He states that justification for the Cheongyecheon project depends on whether the stream can be restored to its original state and argues that the project cannot be justified because the restoration of the stream to its original state is an impossible task. Therefore, he concludes, "the Cheongyecheon restoration is none other than one of the cases of human domination of nature" (224), and the new Cheongyecheon is nothing more than an "architectural structure of artificiality and industrial development" (236).[5]

Responses to the Cheongyecheon project from literary studies in Korea have also been characterized by willful negligence and harsh criticism from the perspective of preservationism. This attitude is well illustrated in the treatment accorded it in the Cheongyecheon novels, written by members of The Association for Korean Fiction Writers in commemoration of the Cheongyecheon restoration, and on commission by the Seoul Metropolitan Government. Eleven writers participated and, under the title of "The Selection of Clean Stream Novels,"[6] the same number of novels came out in time for the completion of the restoration project in 2005. Spanning 600 years of temporal settings, the novels deal with the history and stories related to the same number of bridges over the stream respectively through an amalgamation of historical records and storytelling imagination.

For the most part, literary circles have considered the participation of literary writers in the production of the "Clean Stream Novels" as conformist deportment. The majority of modern Korean writers traditionally have taken a nonconformist stance against dictatorial rulings of government-led policies and projects. Their nonconformist behavioral attributes have continued even after the democratization of Korean society in the late 1980s. Many Korean writers have shown concerns about environmental problems, and some of these writers have engaged in environmental activism. This activist-orientation has led the writers to stand in opposition to government-led environment policies. The nonconformist stance of the Korean literary circle has resulted in a general disregard for or indifference to the series of the Cheongyecheon novels produced by their colleagues, despite the fact that some leading fiction writers participated in this writing project, and despite the fact that some of the works turned out to be of high quality. Being commissioned products, these novels have been suspected of being political propaganda that Seoul city authorities promoted in order to justify this project that had already become a target of heated controversies even before it was launched.

In keeping with this nonconformist stance, Korean literary scholarship also shares the same critical attitude with the Korean writers toward the Cheongyecheon novels. In addition, Korean ecocritical studies have been critical of the novels. In "The Cheongyecheon Restoration and Storytelling Imagination" (2007), which is surprisingly the only full-scale ecocritical article on the project ever produced, Korean ecocritic Yoon-ho Oh questions the ontological validity of the restoration work from a deep ecological sense of restoration. He argues that this restoration, regardless of its success or failure as an ideal restoration of ecology and environment, is nothing more than an "artificial work," and adds that the project is "anti-ecological, anti-natural development politics of a modern nation." Therefore, to Oh the "restored" stream represents "a space represented by modern Korea's myth of industrialization and modernization and a contemporary myth of environment-friendly urban ecology" (35). To him the restored Cheongyecheon is like one of Jean Baudrillard's *simulacra*, a space that exists only in imagination, not in actualized reality.

Oh states that his "ecocritical evaluation" of the novels is a pioneering work in Korean ecocriticism, because these novels "do not foreground environmental or ecological problems and issues" (37). The novels, according to him, deal with the Cheongyecheon restoration and urban culture and, therefore, require an alternative ecocritical approach that points out antiecological characters of the modern novels as well as ecological ones. His intention of including antienvironmental or antiecological factors in ecocritical studies was timely and well directed, considering the fact that "the green rush" in Korean literary studies had just ended and Korean ecocritics

were seeking alternative approaches. His dealing with environmental restoration and urban culture as characteristics of "anti-ecological
literature," however, illustrates how much he is inclined to the preservationist ethos. His inclination to the preservationist perspective leads
him to conclude that the literary imagination of these novels "failed
to capture visions of eco-fiction and lacked critical mind because they
upheld the city government's ideology" (44). Oh suspects that the
writers were either inadvertently mobilized by or willingly complied
with Seoul city authorities in the act of creating such *simulacra*.

The Cheongyecheon novels, however, are worthy of ecocritical
attention in the sense that they describe the Cheongyecheon not
simply as a natural stream but as a space for various human activities
and they also deal with diverse environment-related aspects and issues
that Korean ecocritical discourses need to address. First of all, some
novels lead readers to question the meaning of the "restoration" of
the stream by showing that in the past the stream was under constant
management and that it ran with clean water because of management
efforts. Coexistence of humans and nonhuman nature in urban spaces
largely depended upon such management. *There Live Kingfishers in
Cheongyecheon Mojeon Bridge*, a "Clean Stream Novel" by Yong-woo
Kim, deserves ecocritical attention from this perspective.

Set at the turn of the twentieth century when Japan was beginning to colonize Korea, this novel describes how and why the stream
was left abandoned by the colonial government. Observing that the
running stream now turned into scattered puddles with foul smells
coming from them, the protagonist asks, "Isn't there any more
dredge work in this stream?" What he hears in answer to this question is, "Those damn Japanese! For this work to be done, thousands
of Korean workers need to be called in. That's what they are afraid
of! Kingfishers do not come any more and this stream is dead."
As the stream became worse, the kingfishers left, and so did the
residents near the stream. The message is clear. Fish, predator birds,
and residents in and near the stream are ecologically interdependent and their healthy existence depends on the management of the
stream, and when the management fails, they all disappear.

This novel infers that it is impossible to "restore" the Cheongyecheon
to its original state because it had remained as a natural stream only
before people had settled around it. The stream stopped being a
natural stream but has been under constant improvement and management since people started coming to this area. In its natural state,
water that ran down from its nearby hills was normally scarce, and
the stream remained almost dried up most of the time and flooded

during the rainy season. To keep it running with clean water, the stream used to be regularly dredged and carefully managed. Because of careful improvement and management efforts, fish and water plants and trees were able to survive in the stream.

From the perspective of environmental preservation, restoration of a damaged urban ecology, such as a "restored" stream, needs to be understood as a work of renovation and rehabilitation where the stream is ecologically revitalized with aquatic plants and animals.[7] This is what Yong-woo Kim deals with in his novel, and this is a point that ecocritics need to listen to from environmental scientists. Environmental scientists admit that "restoring" nature to its original state and condition is in itself an impossible task. Unlike ecological philosophers, who downplay the meaning of restoration as a degradation of original nature, scientists emphasize spontaneity and transformation of ecosystems over time; a process that includes complicated physical and biological activities. Environmental scientists Baek-ho Kim and Myeong-soo Han admit that the literal "restoration" of the stream cannot be realized, nor is such restoration important. However, they argue that the restoration should mean "a betterment of the deteriorated stream, a restoration of autogenesis of the stream with various creatures inhabiting it, or a realization effort of esthetic value through landscape renovation" (37–38). Korean ecocriticism also needs to pay attention to Paul Taylor who considers nature restoration as "the rule of restitutive justice" that "imposes the duty to restore the balance of justice between a moral agent and a moral subject when the subject has been wronged by the agent" (186). Taylor acknowledges that a perfect restoration of disturbed nature cannot be possible, but he still insists that humans "must further the good of the organisms in some other way, perhaps by making their physical environment more favorable to their continued well-being." He considers this compensation effort to be "a natural extension of respect from the individual to its genetic relatives and ecological associates" (188). As environmental scientists and Taylor suggest, the impossibility of original restoration should not mean that a disrupted and damaged ecology like the Cheongyecheon should be left as it is.

Second, the novels in the "Clean Stream Selection" are worthy of ecocritical attention because they deal with the interrelated theme of social inequality and environmental (in)justice. They touch on the subject of spatial injustice by showing the lives of the disadvantaged who have settled in the Cheongyecheon. A Female Barber by Sung-tae Jeon, for example, deals with the ordeal of a "Japanese wife" who was deserted by her Korean husband after the Japanese colonial period ended. Being a descendent of the oppressive colonizer, this woman faced continuous harassment and maltreatment by Koreans, and this forced her to keep wandering across the country. She eventually drifted into the Cheongyecheon area and opened a barber shop there, where at the time homeless people and poor migrant workers swarmed in and made makeshift dwellings. By depicting the miserable lives of such disadvantaged people, the author reminds modern readers of the fact that the Cheongyecheon used to be a dwelling place for these neglected people, and that even in modern days, just a few blocks away from the luxurious and jubilant downtown Seoul, environmentally and socially marginalized have resided along the stream mostly forgotten.

The Cheongye Stream Dandelion by Yong-un Kim also describes the lives of the poor people of the writer's childhood from the Cheongye stream area during and right after the Korean War. Kim graphically illustrates how people gathered and took shelter at the stream and how the steam consequently became polluted. Unlike Sung-tae Jeon, Kim describes these people and the place with warmth and even nostalgia, no matter how hard and dark their lives had been, but, at the same time, like Jeon, he asks readers not to forget that the Cheongye Stream has been a place for such disadvantaged people. Probably because the stream had supported the poor people and their environment and the living conditions had been miserable, Kim was pleased with the restored stream. In the "Author's Note," he recognizes that the restored Cheongyecheon and the bridges over it are not what they used to be. But he is much relieved by the fact that we are still able to "feel our history and the people who lived there" (5).

As Jeon and Kim narrate in their works, the Cheongyecheon has been a residential and working space for the disadvantaged. The improvement of its environment, therefore, should also mean an improvement of environmental conditions for these people.[8] Improving living conditions is an effort toward social equality for the disadvantaged as well as people in general, and, therefore, economic development and social development are interconnected. Seoul authorities have made it clear that the goal of the restoration project is to contribute to correcting social and environmental injustice for the disadvantaged living near the stream and to improve "uneven social and environmental conditions of the two sectors respectively located on each side of the stream" ("History and Transformation"). The environment's necessary interrelation with society has been recognized in ecocritical thinking from its initial stage by such ecocritics as Patrick Murphy and Andrea Parra, who have contended that ecocriticism needs to pay more attention to the social injustice that has been apparent in many urban communities.⁹ As Cheryll Glotfelty notes in her introduction to *The Ecocriticism Reader: Landmarks in Literary Ecology*, this interrelation will be the major theme of "The Future of Ecocriticism" (xxv), and ecocriticism has increasingly taken keen interest in social conditions and human environment.

In recent years, a new approach toward space or spatiality, called "a spatial turn," has emerged, and Edward Soja represents this spatial thinking from studies about the geography of social justice. In his *Seeking Spatial Justice*, Soja highlights sociospatial dialectics and adopts the view that "the spatiality of (in)justice…affects society and social life just as much as social processes shape the spatiality and specific geography of (in)justice" (5). He points out that social processes never take place uniformly over space and that geographically uneven development "is a contributing factor to the creation and maintenance of individual and social inequalities and hence to social and spatial injustices" (72). Even though Soja focuses on social and environmental injustice based on specifically racial divisions in Los Angeles, his theory of spatial justice still offers an insight toward understanding the correlations between social inequality and environmental injustice in other urban spaces (such as Seoul).

Third, the Cheongyecheon novels are worthy of ecocritical attention from the perspective of cultural restoration. All these novels deal with themes about the historical and cultural restoration of the Cheongyecheon space. The restoration project involves a realization of historical and cultural values, since the Cheongyecheon has staged important cultural activities and political events throughout Korean history, and the novels have contributed to restoring the history and culture of the Cheongyecheon.¹⁰ *The Bridge of Time* by Eun-joo Go is another work of the Clean Stream Selection that enriches our cultural and historical understandings of the stream. It does so by telling the story of King Seong-gye Lee, the founder of the Chosun Dynasty, and his beloved second wife Shindeok. These two historical figures are reincarnated as a middle-aged banker and a girl working in sales promotion, respectively, and the girl guides this banker (and the readers as well) through the historical events and places of some 600 years back, along the site of the stream being restored. She takes him to certain slabstones of elaborate decoration, which were unearthed during the restoration. Then she explains to him that these stones were originally used for the queen's tomb by King Lee's command but later, as a political retaliation by a later king, were removed to this stream and used as bridge building material. Such historical stories and relics, as this work describes, certainly helps enrich the environmentally restored urban stream as an imaginatively, historically, and aesthetically charged place. Go wrote the story through her research on historical documents and frequent field trips to the related places with the intention of integrating accurate historical fact with her imagination. In the preface of the novel, Go discloses how she made field investigations in order to write this story of the queen and the king and their time, remarking, "I often walked up and down the Cheongyecheon which was under construction, visited palace, shrines, and the queen's tomb, and climbed up and down a mountain tracing the old castle walls" (4).

Ecocritical practices of deep ecology ethos are challenged by Go's integration of history and culture into the discourse of this restoration and her resort to field exploration and historical materials. The "earth-centered approach" in ecocriticism tends to ignore not only the materiality but also the aesthetic values and specificity of culture and history, prioritizing spiritual values. Daniel Gustav Anderson points out a commonality between cultural studies and ecocriticism showing that both, in fact, "are species of materialism": both ecocriticism and cultural studies are "concerned with the material specificity of cultural production and practices," and this material specificity is formed both by nature and culture in a specific time of history. However, according to him, this materialism is often expressed in ecocriticism "in an obfuscated and contradictory way." Gustav's point is exactly applicable to Korean ecocriticism, and Go's work demonstrates the necessity of incorporating cultural and historical materialism into ecocritical analysis.

Government-initiated environmental projects normally tend to incline toward populist development, and such development is often motivated by political purposes and intentions. Seoul's developmental ideology and the mayor's political calculation cannot be totally denied as a motivation behind the Cheongyecheon project. Nor can antiecological aspects of the project be denied: the water is electrically pumped from the Han River, the stream was not restored to be a natural stream, the water flows in the opposite direction, and so on. Contrary to the charges made by many literary critics that the Cheongyecheon novels represent epistles to conformity, a majority of the Cheongyecheon novel series remain vigilant to the project's rhetoric and antiecological characters. *The Bridge of Time*, for example, finishes with an ecological and political suspicion that many have with this project: "In Cheongyecheon, an unidentified modern stream park is under development...It makes me feel bitter that developmental profits and political interest might be the real reason for the Cheongyecheon restoration" (182). In *A Female Barber*, Sung-tae Jeon also questions the status quo of the restored Cheongyecheon. The novel describes the Cheongyecheon as a place of contradictions in Korean history where, during the postcolonial period, a "Japanese wife" was in turn deserted by her Korean husband and led a miserable life among the hostile Korean people, and where, during the industrial period of the latter 1900s, most miserable lives had been led just a few blocks away from most affluent lives. This legacy as a contradicting space still lingers in the restored stream where development and preservationism coexist and collide; some people cheer when seeing this "clean" brook murmuring along whereas some others angrily avoid the "artificial" urban park.

Almost all of the Korean ecocritics have dismissed these novels with suspicion and prejudice, even before reading them. This is immature and narrow-minded. It is important and fundamental for Korean ecocriticism, first, to be vigilant and to critically examine its society's inclination toward the developmentalist ideology evident in government-led environment policies and, second, to recognize the value and importance of deep ecological environmental ethics. What is equally important for them is to rethink their habitual reliance on preservationist ethics and then to freshly look at environmental issues from the perspectives of environmentally sustainable urban development, which would be more congruous with the characteristics of modern Korean society.[11] When Korean ecocriticism addresses and envisions this transformative perspective, it will be able to overcome the academic isolation and stagnation that it has recently encountered and become sustainable in the constantly reshaping world of environmental discourse.

NOTES

1. See Hyo-gu Jeong's "Cosmic Community and Literature"; Shin 94–120. This tendency has not been a bit altered even in recent years. Sung-am Hong, in "A Study of Korean Ecological Literature" (2005) repeats this line of argument, stating, "Our ecological literature should be approached from the perspectives of how it respects and confirms Koreanness" (29).
2. See Suk-joo Jang's "For Ecological Imagination of Poems," 67–71.
3. Whether all these goals have actually been achieved is still debatable. This study does not deal with the evaluation of the project, but it focuses on the characteristic features of the environmental debates over the project.
4. Mi-Kyung Lee and Han-Bai Kim classify the topography of discourses of the restoration project into four tendencies according to ideological

inclinations: tendencies of practicality, radicalism, preservationism, and eclecticism.

5. His argument reflects the 1980s environmental ethics argument over nature restoration in the United States. The environmental philosopher Robert Elliot denounces any type of nature restoration based on value discrimination between the original and the replica. His reluctance to acknowledge nature restoration comes from the fact that he "value[s] the original as an aesthetic object, as an object with a specific genesis and history" (145). Even the perfectly restored environment, he argues, is "faked" nature and counts for less than real nature, using similar reasons as in arguing that "faked works of art count for less than the real thing" (149).

6. The literal meaning of the "Cheongyecheon" is "clean stream."

7. With regards to resultant ecological recovery of the stream, the theme of rehabilitation that this work tries to convey to modern readers has actually been verified by scientific data on the restored Cheongyecheon. Some research from environmental sciences has demonstrated that the stream has been in the process of ecological recovery with the BOD (biochemical oxygen demand) level having been reduced, aquatic plants and animals increased in population and species (see Hyea-Ju Kim), and introduced binary and perennial vegetation also increased (see Hyeong-Guk Kim and Bon-Hak Koo).

8. With the completion of the restoration work, the wind speed along the stream has been increased, which helps summer temperatures drop about three degrees Centigrade and improves air pollution problems with the decrease of PM10 (particulate matter) and NO2 (nitrogen dioxide) concentration (see Yong Kee Jang).

9. See Murphy (1098–99) and Parra (1099–100).

10. The majority of the Cheongyecheon novels are devoted to the events and the stories of the Chosun Dynasty (i.e., Eun-ju Go's *Bridge of Time*, Byul-a Kim's *Eternal Parting*, Sung-woo Lee's *Two-Parting Path*), followed by stories during the Japanese colonial period (Sang-woo Park's *The Sword*, Sung-tae Jeon's *A Female Barber*, Yong-woo Kim's *There Live Kingfishers in Mojeon Bridge*), during the Korean War (Yong-un Kim's *The Cheongye Stream Dandelion*), during the 1960s–1980s of industrialization and dictatorship (Su-kwang Lee's *Doomul Bridge*, Soon-won Lee's *A Song of Mirror*).

11. Greg Garrard sees a future model of ecocriticism in the Eden Project, the world's largest greenhouse experiment, whose prime mover Tim Smit summarizes it as "the sustainable development of human potential and the achievement of the optimum quality of life for all, across economic, social and cultural boundaries" (302). When sustainable development is a model for future ecocriticism, as Garrard notes, "It is a long way from the pastoral we started with, and it is a great-souled vision with its feet planted solidly on the ground" (182). Some Korean ecocritics like Yong-hee Hong are well aware of the fervency and inappropriateness of the preservationist inclination of Korean ecocriticism and they call

for a concrete and reality-based analysis and suggestion for ecological solutions of Korean society.

WORKS CITED

"2005 World Summit Outcome." *United Nations General Assembly.* 2005. World Health Organization. September 10, 2011.

Anderson, Daniel Gustav. "Activism, Aesthetics, and 'Spiritual Values': Contradictions in Ecocriticism." *Scribed.* August 4, 2012.

Buell, Lawrence. *Writing for an Endangered World: Literature, Culture, and Environment in the U.S. and Beyond.* Cambridge: Belknap Press of Harvard UP, 2001.

Castree, Noel and Tom MacMillian. "Dissolving Dualisms: Actor-network and the Reimagination of Nature." *Social Nature: Theory, Practice, and Politics.* Ed. Noel Castree and Bruce Braun. Oxford: Blackwell, 2001. 208–24.

Cho, Seok-young. "An Analysis of the Cheongyecheon Restoration from the Perspective of Environmental Ethics" (in Korean). *Ethics Studies* 65 (2007): 219–37.

"Cultural Policies and Sustainable Development." *Culture 21.* United Cities and Local Governments, n.d. June 25, 2012.

Do-ol. *Do-ol's Cheongyecheon Story: Seoul, a Future City of Confucian Refinement* (in Korean). Seoul: Tongnamu, 2003.

Elliot, Robert. "Faking Nature." *Inquiry* 25.1 (March 1982): 81–93; Rpt. *People, Penguins, and Plastic Trees: Basic Issues in Environmental Ethics.* Ed. Donald VanDeVeer and Christine Pierce. Belmont, CA: Wadsworth Publishing Co, 1984. 142–50.

Garrard, Greg. *Ecocriticism.* New York: Routledge, 2004.

Glotfelty, Cheryll and Harold Fromm, eds. *Ecocriticism Reader: Landmarks in Literary Ecology.* Athens, GA: U of Georgia P, 1996.

Go, Eun-joo. *Bridge of Time* (in Korean). Seoul: Changhae, 2005.

"History and Transformation." *The Cheonggyecheon.* Seoul Metropolitan Facilities and Management Corporation, n.d. Web. December 10, 2011.

Hong, Sung-am. "A Study of Korean Ecological Literature" (in Korean). *Hanminjok Cultural Studies* 17 (2005): 1–34.

Hong, Yong-hee. *Spirit and Sense of Modern Poems* (in Korean). Seoul: Millennium, 2010.

Jang, Suk-joo. "For Ecological Imagination of Poems" (in Korean). In Shin, *A Way of Green Life.* 67–71.

Jang, Young Kee. "Analysis of Air Quality Change of Cheongyecheon Area by Restoration Project" (in Korean). *Environmental Affect Analysis* 19.1 (2010): 99–106.

Jeon, Sung-tae. *A Female Barber* (in Korean). Seoul: Changhae, 2005.

Jeong, Hyo-gu. "Cosmic Community and Literature" (in Korean). In Shin, *A Way of Green Life.* 94–120.

Kim, Baek-ho and Myeong-soo Han. "Value of Restoration of the Cheongyecheon Ecological Function and Water and Ecosystem

Management through Periphyton" (in Korean). *EnvScience* 13 (December 2005): 37–42.

Kim, Hyea-Ju, et al. "Changes in Water Quality, Flora and Vegetation of Cheongye Stream Before, During and After its Restoration" (in Korean). *Korean Journal of Environment and Ecology* 20.2 (2006): 235–58.

Kim, Hyeong-Guk and Bon-Hak Koo. "Floral Changes during Three Years after Cheongyecheon Restoration" (in Korean). *Journal of Korean Environmental Restoration Technology* 13.6 (2010): 107–15.

Kim, Yong-un. *The Cheongye Stream Dandelion* (in Korean). Seoul: Changhae, 2005.

Kim, Yong-woo. *There Live Kingfishers in Cheongyecheon Mojeon Bridge* (in Korean). Seoul: Changhae, 2005.

Lachman, Beth. *Linking Sustainable Community Activities to Pollution Prevention: A Sourcebook*. Santa Monica: RAND, 1997.

Lee, Mi-kyung and Han-Bai Kim. "A Study on Environmental Cognition Patterns through Discourse Analysis Regarding the Cheonggyecheon Restoration" (in Korean). *Journal of the Korean Institute of Landscape Architecture* 131 (2009): 102–14.

Marafiote, Tracy and Emily Plec. "From Dualism to Dialogism: Hybridity in Discourse about the Natural World." In *Environmental Communication Yearbook*, vol. 3. Ed. Stephen P. Depoe. Mahwah, NJ: Psychology Press, 2006. 48–72.

Murphy, Patrick. "Forum on Literatures of the Environment." *PMLA* 114 (October 1999): 1098–99.

Nicholas, Ashton. *Beyond Romantic Ecocriticism: Toward Urbanatural Roosting*. New York: Palgrave Macmillan, 2001.

Oh, Yoon-ho. "The Cheongyecheon Restoration and Storytelling Imagination" (in Korean). *Literature and Environment* 7.1 (2008): 21–42.

Parra, Andrea. "Forum on Literatures of the Environment." *PMLA* 114 (October 1999): 1099–100.

Shin, Duk-ryong. *A Way of Green Life: Poetics for Ecotopia* (in Korean). Gwangju, Korea: SiwaSaramsa, 1997.

Smit, Tim. *Eden*. New York: Bantam, 2001.

Soja, Edward W. *Seeking Spatial Justice*. Minneapolis: U of Minnesota P, 2010.

"Strategies for Sustainable Cities." *Regional Conference Statements*. Euronet, University of the West of England, n.d. July 15, 2012.

Taylor, Paul. *Respect for Nature*. Princeton, NJ: Princeton UP, 1986.

Yun, Seong-bok. "Isolation: Cheongyecheon Restoration and Sustainable City Seoul" (in Korean). *Seogang Social Science Studies* 12.1 (2004): 240–76.

7

KOREA'S DIVIDED CIRCUMSTANCES AND THE IMAGINATION OF THE BORDER

Chan Je Wu

Boundaries define the world. The countless natural, artificial, and psychological boundaries that govern the world interact in complex ways with each other, simultaneously forming new boundaries and dissolving existing ones. The Demilitarized Zone (the DMZ) along the 38th parallel that has divided the Korean peninsula since 1953 is the most conspicuous sign of the two divided Koreas in political, social, and natural senses. Both countries have paid huge costs militarily, politically, economically, socially, and psychologically, costs that would not have been necessary without the line. Had it not been for this boundary, Koreans could have lived entirely different lives in completely different circumstances. The ecologies of Korea cannot be discussed without referring to this border; the boundary line explains why Korean literary works have produced diverse characters showing both a politically and ecologically unique consciousness and unconsciousness.

The ceasefire line, as an emblem for the loss of ecological identity, is a very significant and complex sign for the ecological circumstances of Korea. On the premise that the political condition of the Korean peninsula's division into South and North Koreas has had a significant impact on the ecological environment of Korea, this chapter investigates how this divided circumstance constitutes and affects Koreans by examining three representative novels of Korean literature: Choi In-hoon's *The Square* (1960), Park Sang-yeon's *DMZ* (1997), and Kang Hui-jin's *The Ghost* (2011). They evoke the ecological circumstances and the character of the division in the Cold War era, the post–Cold War era, and the digital era, respectively. This chapter also examines the ecological implications of the loss of home and the psychological consequences of being forced to live with borders.

The ecological consciousness about the DMZ is as complicated as the line itself. Because the demarcation line has posed a heavy burden of loss to Koreans, especially the loss of ecological identity, Korean writers have been investigating this issue very consistently. To fully understand the implications, it is important first to comprehend the notion of "ecological identity," a term used to denote one's total, harmonious life with environment. In discussing the characteristics of romance, literary critics usually mention the protagonist's drama of the loss and recovery of identity. In romance, the recovery of identity means the reconciliation of the self with the world without any conflict. But because of the division of self and the world in the modern age, recovering of the lost identity is no longer possible. Romances turn out to be based on a dualistic view of the world; the heavenly versus the terrestrial worlds, or paradise versus the terrestrial. Georg Lukács presents theory that goes beyond such a dualistic view of the world and emphasizes totality as a key for understanding the world more realistically (29). His main concern is socioeconomic life and the ideologies that govern people's mind and the world. But the concept of totality raised by Lukács has become an object of suspicion in the modern age, particularly in the postmodern era, for being too anthropocentric and rationalistic. Ecological identity is a more complex and broad concept than his totality because it takes two additional points into account: the natural element of the ecological environment and the psychological element of the ecological consciousness and unconsciousness.

All living things on earth are bound to be interconnected with other beings through very complex networks. Ecological identity can be preserved only when these beings can maintain or improve their own life in a given environment. But maintaining ecological identity in the modern era is not easy at all, because it is repressed in numerous ways. By insisting that "repression of the ecological unconscious is the deepest root of the collusive madness in industrial society" and that "open access to the ecological unconscious is the path to sanity" (320), Theodore Roszak emphasizes a return to ecological unconsciousness as a way to recover ecological identity. Ralph Metzner also acknowledges the importance of ecological unconsciousness, but in a slightly different context: he emphasizes ecological conscience or consciousness more in order to understand or embody the ecological unconscious (63). What is important here is the fact that both ecological unconsciousness and consciousness are important in keeping one's ecological identity whole. They are highly useful in the actual approach, since the world of ecological identity is a compound area of ecology and psychology. In literature, ecological unconsciousness can be read through the dream or hope for ecological identity, or the symptoms of the loss of ecological identity. Ecological consciousness, structured into texts through language and plot, can reveal a dynamic psychological spectrum between ecological unconsciousness and the actual ecological reality.

The Square, published in 1960, was written on the foundation of ideological reflections regarding the divided circumstances of Korea and the global situation during the Cold War era. As the title suggests, the imagination of space plays a very important role in the novel. The main story is about Lee Myong-jun, a Korean War veteran and prisoner, who chooses to go to an ideologically neutral third country, being disappointed at both the capitalist South and the communist North Korea. The author depicts capitalist life in the South through the metaphor of a secret room in which each individual's voice is respected but is not heard in the public square; he presents life in the North as being in a square in which only the public voice sounds loud. The square in the novel represents a collective and social life, while the secret room stands for an individual's private life. The novel's basic frame consists of Lee's search for a way to resolve the confrontational phases symbolized by the square and the secret room. Unable to find any solution, Lee eventually jumps from the ship bound for another country and drowns in the sea.

For the protagonist of the novel, ecological identity can only be realized in a world where squares and secret rooms coexist in harmony, but this desire is rarely fulfilled. Because reality is so far from the idealized world of ecological identity, Lee could not be satisfied with life in the secret room with squares removed. He was disgusted and hurt by life in the South, because the secret room itself fails to exist in its entirety. Realizing how far the distance is from the present world to the world of ecological identity that he hopes for, Lee attempts to move horizontally to the North, hoping to find there a utopian world of ecological identity. But to his dismay, he finds that life in the North is just as far removed from the world of ecological identity because the secret individual rooms are shut down, and only the collective squares are open. At last, he chooses to go to the third country. During the Cold War era, however, this third ideology, beyond the two major ideologies of capitalism and communism, is virtually impossible. Caught between these two ideologies, the protagonist ends up lodged on a reef of ideology.

The two ideologically contaminated Koreas have lost the status of "place" and degenerated into "space," to use Yi-Fu Tuan's terms. Presupposing that "space and place are basic components of the lived world," he says "place is security, space is freedom: we are attached to the one and long for the other" (3). The most important qualities of place are security and stability, the same qualities that define a home. The geographical division of the Korean peninsula was followed by an ideological division; the peninsula became the war zone of the Cold War. In this state, most Koreans, including Lee, became aliens to their own homeland; the old Korea, which was not divided and the very place of affection and allegiance for Koreas, existed no more. Therefore, in this dreadful situation, Lee resorts to love as the only way to achieve his ecological identity (Oh 291). He finds in his lover, Un-hye, a hopeful prospect of life, where the square/secret room conflict is finally resolved. The two make love at the cave on the front line of the Nakdong River, finally free from any political or social oppression. In this lovemaking, Lee glimpses a possibility for living the "whole" life for which he had hoped. But the war, fueled by the political ideology, mercilessly destroys even their earnest love.

In this deadlock, the gap posed by the conflicting ideologies is too wide to cross horizontally, and the protagonist seeks another way, a vertical leap into the mythic world. On the ship bound for the third country, Lee is influenced by two seagulls he sees flying above the sea:

> Myong-jun turned around and looked up at the mast again. They were not visible. He looked at the sea. The two birds were coming down towards the sea, as if sliding. A blue square.[1] For the first time, Myong-jun recognized the square in which these women were flying around to their heart's content. He had been walking backwards towards the pivot of the fan, and now he turned around. Back to a normal state of mind, there was a blue square reflected in his eye. (Choi 153)

Though at first he does not heed them, he eventually perceives that they are none other than Un-hye and their unborn baby. Though she has fallen in the real world for reasons of love and ideology, she rises vertically on wings as a seagull in the mythical world. When Lee looks up at the seagull in the sky, the sea below his eyes flashes upon him like a lost square. His jump into the dark blue sea symbolizes his inability to move horizontally in reality, or vertically in the mythical realm.

The blue square that Lee Myong-jun sees just before throwing himself into the sea is, above all, an ecotopia—a fictional response to the real division of Korea. Furthermore, it symbolizes the yearning for the circumstances of life in which ecological identity is not damaged and can be fully realized. The protagonist finds no place to call home and oscillates among the three borders: square/secret room, South Korea/North Korea, and the Korean peninsula/the third country. But Lee finally realizes that he cannot find his hoped-for space through such horizontal movements because the present world is irrevocably ruined. The protagonist gives up his horizontal search on the conscious level and investigates it at the unconscious level. It is at this very moment that Lee's vertical movement between "the sky/the sea" is introduced to the novel. He soon realizes that such a mystical union of the sky and the sea, or figuratively the union of ideology and love, seldom occurs in the real world. Having lived in a divided nation during the Cold War era, in which ideologies were firmly enforced, Choi could not help but lead his protagonist to death and mourn for him. Lee's death illustrates the futility of the yearning and pursuit of the hopeful blue square where the totality of love and ecological identity can be realized. The fact that even the third country is not the real destination for the protagonist, but a mere temporary escape, shows the dire situation of the ideologically torn country and its dwellers.

If *The Square* depicts how the political border corners a man into suicide, Park Sang-yeon's *DMZ*[2] portrays how geopolitical and mental borders construct and influence the ecological consciousness of the Korean people. Picking up where *The Square* left off, *DMZ* chronicles the journey of subsequent generations. In the novel, Lee Myong-jun is replaced with Lee Yeon-woo; both are almost identical people, except that the latter didn't commit suicide and instead led a life in a third country. Unlike Lee Myong-jun, who took the initiative in his actions, Lee Yeon-woo is reduced to the status of mere object and is viewed in retrospect by his son Versami. But to the son who lives in the post–Cold War era, his father, a victim of the Cold War era, is an obscure being totally beyond his understanding:

> Talking about the novel *The Square*, my father added that it is a story about the protagonist whose life is similar to his. The hero is said to have killed himself in the last scene. My father should have thrown himself into "the Indian Ocean darker than crayon" like the protagonist who first Lieutenant Gang talked about. It would have been better if the novel that is the life story of my father should have ended so fascinatingly. That was better for Cuby and me, and my father himself, as well. (Park 162)

To Versami, his father is nothing but a man who would have been better off if he had died earlier.

DMZ deals, as a sort of detective fiction, with the investigation of a shooting incident in which South Korean soldiers shot at North Korean soldiers in the northern area of Panmunjeom.[3] The narrator-protagonist and chief investigator in charge is half Korean and half Celtic, a Swiss national and a major of the Neutral Nations Supervisory Commission. During the investigation, he is able to see freshly his own family history in the context of the division of the Korean peninsula. His father was born in a region that is now the demilitarized zone and went to North Korea as a member of Workers' Party of South Korea during the Korean War. Fighting in the Korean War as a major of the North Korean People's Army, he is taken prisoner in the battle of the Nakdong River. Taking the lead of the violent communist POWs, Lee fortuitously kills his own brother. After that, he settles in Brazil, where he marries a Swiss journalist and gives birth to the protagonist. Such a father's last hope is to return to a *united* Korea: that is, neither South Korea nor North Korea. Though at first the son cannot comprehend such a father, he gradually comes to understand him and finds his own identity in the process of investigating the shooting incident. In the northern area of the truce line, the South and North Korean soldiers would secretly meet, but they opened fire on each other unawares. Feeling remorseful at their own incomprehensible actions, they commit suicide later.

Though his father had left for the third country in despair over the situation in the Korean peninsula, he became homesick and made sure that his son kept in mind his being Korean and encouraged him to learn Korean. Carrying his father's journal, written during the war, Versami came back to Korea in search of his father's and his own lost identity. There he read his father's journal and visited his father's hometown, all the while investigating Kim Soo-hyuk, the main suspect in the shooting spree that occurred in the northern area of the DMZ. Though he initially proceeded with the investigation from the perspective of an indifferent stranger, he ended up getting psychologically involved:

> I am neither in the South nor in the North any more. I wonder which country the small upper side of this brick with fifteen centimeter width belongs to. If people fall down from the brick to the left, they will find themselves in the Democratic People's Republic of Korea; to the right, in the Republic of Korea...I tried to walk on the narrow surface of the brick, keeping my balance. And I got down to the side of ROK.

If anyone could live on the surface of the brick, my father would not
have had to go as far as Brazil. He wanted such a place, didn't he?
Somewhere, which is neither north nor south. (148)

Newly recognizing the divided reality of the border, the son understands that, without the border line, the ecological identity of the
father would not have been damaged so terribly, and his father's life
would not have been so tough. Thus, on the very spot in which his
father's tragic life originated, the son undergoes a change of mind
about his father.

In "Varieties of Environmental Nostalgia," Scott Slovic sheds
light on understanding Lee Yeon-woo's life and reinterprets nostalgia
environmentally. Slovic defines nostalgia as "an excessive tendency to
look forward the past, to wish painfully for something or some place
or some relationship that no longer exists" (142) and argues that
nostalgia can be "one of the most powerful concepts and one that
can be harnessed both to explore the meaning of human relationships
to specific places and to the larger planet and to inspire effective environmental action" (142). Lee's long and painful journey of life can be
characterized as a severe case of nostalgia for his homeland. But the
problem is that the Korea he so earnestly longs for no longer exists,
as his son explains: "He wanted such a place, didn't he? Somewhere,
which is neither north nor south" (Park 148).

Because the Korean War has drastically changed the Korean peninsula, the place he imagines exists *only* in his own imagination.
In this sense, Lee's nostalgia is very similar to what Slovic defines
as "conditional nostalgia," which is "the fundamental human psychological impulses of desire and regret that the 'lifestyle traumas'
that might include geographical movement, fracturing of human
relationships, the devastations of war, and diminishment of nature
that occur through industrial and urban development" (142). The
trauma of war still governs the people who were involved in the war,
even long after the war ended and in the faraway places such as
Brazil.

DMZ reminds us of the tragedy of the Cold War period by reflecting
upon its historicity and its continuing presence. Both his father's
departure from the Korean peninsula and his birth as a half Korean
and half Swiss originated from the divided circumstances of the
Korean peninsula. The writer investigates these issues through
the sociobiological lens of operant conditioning.[4] The key incident in
the narrative of *DMZ* is the investigation process of the murder case
of North Korean soldiers by Kim Soo-hyuk.

Kim's job as a soldier is to train military dogs. Just as his predecessor did in the Pavlovian way of operant conditioning, Kim subjects the dog to abnormal treatment until it dies. He poses the following question: who pays the price for the dog's spirit, which is helplessly subjected to this operant conditioning? Park uses this episode to illustrate the inhumane way in which both the North and South Korean soldiers are ideologically brainwashed and manipulated to kill each other. Kim himself becomes subject to operant conditioning, killing his North Korean counterparts whom he had befriended just moments before. The soldiers' ability to make friends with each other without reserve implies the possibility of the harmonious living of the two Koreas in the post–Cold War era. But their conditioned-response firings show how the hostile ideologies of the Cold War era still define the mindset of the Koreans.

Brainwashed by anticommunist ideology and strongly affected by the environment of Korea's divided society, Kim succumbs to shooting North Korean soldiers. His criminal action exactly mirrors the incident of the protagonist's father, Lee Yeon-woo. Even though one generation has passed since the Korean War, the remnant of the political ideologies lingers powerfully in the memory of the survivors and controls people's behavior in Korea. The border between memory and reality is heavily lopsided toward memory. Not only the steel, barbed wire of the physical DMZ but also the DMZ of political ideologies still lurks in the common people's mind as the most powerful agent of action.

The Ghost, written by Kang Hui-jin in 2011, is a novel that expands the theme of border imagination into the digital era of the twenty-first century. The novel delves into not only the topic of the border between the North Korean defectors and South Koreans but also into the topic of the border between the real world and virtual reality. The protagonist of *The Ghost*, a defector from the North, belongs to the third generation of the Korean War. During the Korean War, the grandmother of the protagonist was pregnant with his father. His grandfather, who was a landlord, crossed the border into South Korea during the war, leaving his family behind. In North Korea, his father could not realize his dream of singing on stage as a professional but became a farmer, owing to the disgrace of being the son of a defector. Nevertheless, espousing North Korean communism, his father flatly refuses his son's suggestion to go to South Korea. The protagonist, though, resolutely gives up his life in North Korea (where people barely make a living) and escapes to South Korea.

But in the South, the protagonist cannot keep even his own identity. He uses "Harim," the name of a friend who starved to death in China, instead of Joocheol, his real name. Though in the South he can finally realize his dream of becoming an actor, he refrains from appearing on television, afraid that his remaining family members in the North might be persecuted if his identity is discovered. He cannot help but remain unemployed and live hand-to-mouth in shoddy places with other North Korean defectors (Ryu 461). In this situation, he plays the video game "Lineage," in which he is Lord Kusanagi, the leader of brave and strong allies. This game becomes his only solace. Though in reality he lives in abject poverty, in virtual reality, things are quite different. The wider the gap between reality and virtual reality becomes, the harder he struggles to erase the border. But the situation gets worse, and he finally shouts that "Kusanagi is not my avatar. It's me" (Kang 25). The protagonist's perception that Kusanagi is his real self shows how delusional he has become from his gaming addiction. While he is being treated for posttraumatic stress disorder symptoms, he goes as far as to tell the doctor, "Games are real. They are the reality of life" (51). To him, reality is the environment that makes him more insecure as an alien in South Korea, whereas virtual reality is a thriving, living space like a mother's comfortable womb.

But North Korean defectors find a "home" not in South Korea but in cyberspace. It is noticeable that a game space of virtual reality gave the protagonist and his fellow North Korean defectors such an impression:

> The defectors become not just "game maniacs," but, frankly speaking, the game-disabled. The internet or games were like the instruction of the great general giving orders to us, who were living very wretched lives. Though it was just a mid-summer night's dream…at least at those moments we felt happy. We could forget who the contemptible fools were, even though it was at the moment only. Our native country South Chosun, or South Korea, where we had arrived going through hardships, allowed us heaven on earth. At last we found Paradise. (285–86)

The fact that North Korean defectors feel the sense of being alive and are happy only in cyberspace is tragic indeed. Since they have left North Korea, they are no longer North Koreans. Nor did they settle wholly as South Koreans, who treat North Korean defectors poorly, showing no sympathy for them. If ecological identity is "the ways people construe themselves in relationship to the earth, as manifest in personality, values, and sense of themselves," as Mitchell Thomashow defines in *Ecological Identity* (3), their ecological identity cannot help but be severely endangered in the hostile circumstances of South Korea. Being neither North Korean nor South Korean, they are unable to keep their own stable identity and are driven into assuming a hybrid identity of an immigrant: they have strong bonds with two nations—the country in which they are living and the country of their or their parent's origin. Like immigrants, they have no sense of feeling at home in either of the two Koreas.

It seems almost inevitable that North Korean defectors, being bereft of the world of ecological identity, try to find a new and "possible world" in virtual space. As a result, young defectors end up being game-disabled or exhaust themselves by becoming drug-addicts. David Bolter notes, "[C]yber space is not, as some enthusiasts have argued, divorced from the natural and social world that we know; rather it is an expression and extension of both" (98, cited in Murphy 54). But that is possible only when one can move freely between the two worlds. To the North Korean defectors, South Korea is a society whose door is practically closed to them, while cyberspace welcomes them without any discrimination. In this sense, their indulgence in cyberspace should be regarded as a kind of escapism. The narrator of the novel comments on the posttraumatic stress disorder symptom with which he is afflicted as follows: "This is a disease through which the past torments the present and future, before one knows it. Some wounds gnaw at memory and heart fast, and some very slowly" (Kang 136). He suffers from schizophrenia and is in a state of identity confusion, unsure whether he is Harim or Joocheol. As we can see when he explains that "[t]his is neither a dream, nor a game," he is confused about whether he lives in the real world or in a world of virtual reality. The two worlds look like a Möbius strip, and reality becomes virtual reality, and vice versa. Between reality and virtual reality, he cannot be sure of anything. *The Ghost* shows the misery of the North Korean defectors who were transplanted to the South due to the divided circumstances of the Koreas. As the title of the novel suggests, the ghost of political ideologies dislocates people from their own place and drives them into a cyberspace of no hope.

It is not an exaggeration to say that the division of the Korean peninsula still haunts the minds of Koreans and forms the deepest ecological consciousness and ecological unconsciousness. Of course, not all of the ecological problems of Korea are related to the divided circumstances of the Korean peninsula, but we can safely say that such circumstances are the direct or indirect cause of many issues affecting Korean society. Problems arising from the division of the country are too numerous to mention, but they include damage to ecological identity, dispersed families, displaced families, an arms race between the two Koreas, regional conflicts, and local military confrontations such as the Battle of Yeonpyeong[5] or the Cheonan sinking.[6] Choi graphically portrays in *The Square* how the division of the nation takes away from Koreans the possibility of ecological identity by destroying the land where they can live harmoniously. The protagonist's suicide on his way to a politically neutral third county is due to his perception that the political ideology and the power games of the Cold War era have turned the world into a cold dystopia where no one can keep his or her ecological identity undamaged. Park's *DMZ* shows how division dislocates people from their homes and thereby makes them aliens and strangers wherever they might find their residence. The trauma haunts them, and their whole life is characterized as a life of nostalgia for a land that no longer exists. Finally, in the digital era that *The Ghost* depicts, a North Korean defector (who is unable to find the hoped-for place in the real world) falls into a digital game space. Driven to live in agony, he becomes deranged and schizophrenic, on the border of reality and virtual reality.

Though more than 60 years have passed since the division of the Korean peninsula and the Korean War, the tragic situation still governs both Koreas geopolitically. But the more serious problem is the fact the division has brought irrevocable destruction of the natural environment of Korea along with the loss of home. This sense of loss and displacement constitutes the basic ecological (un)consciousness for Koreans. The scar is not yet healed and keeps on appearing in a new shape. The road to recovering the ecological identity these writers dreamed of is dim yet present in the distance.

NOTES

1. The literal translation of the original text is "the sea."
2. This novel was made into a film in 2000 entitled *Joint Security Area*.
3. Panmunjeom is located in the demilitarized zone, 50 kilometers north from Seoul. When the ceasefire was signed in 1953, it was designated the Joint Security Area.
4. As one of the key concepts in behavior psychology, it is first used by B. F. Skinner to describe the effects of the consequences of a particular behavior on the future occurrence of that behavior.
5. The Battle of Yeonpyeong was a military confrontation between North and South Korean patrol boats near Yeonpyeong Island in the Yellow Sea on June 29, 2002.

6. On March 26, 2010, the South Korean navy ship "The Cheonan" sank near Baengroyng Island in the Yellow Sea. Forty six soldiers died in the incident. The South (and the international community) blamed North Korea for the sinking, but the North denied any involvement.

WORKS CITED

Bolter, Jay. *Writing Space: Computer, Hypertexts, and Remediation of Print*. Mahwah, NJ: Lawrence Erlbaum Associates, 2001.

Choi In-hoon. *The Square*. Trans. Kevin O'Rourke. Seoul: Spindlewood, 1985.

Kang, Hui-jin. *The Ghost*. Seoul: Ehnhaengnamoo, 2011.

Lukács, Georg. *The Theory of the Novel*. Cambridge: MIT P, 1974.

Metzner, Ralph. "The Psychopathology of the Human-Nature Relationship." In *Ecopsychology: Restoring the Earth Healing the Mind*. Ed. Theodore Roszak, Mary E. Gomes, and Allen D. Kanner. San Francisco: Sierra Club Books, 1995. 62–63.

Murphy, Patrick D. *Ecocritical Explorations in Literary and Cultural Studies: Fences, Boundaries, and Fields*. Lanham: Lexington Books, 2009.

Oh, Saengeun. "Beyond Window to the Life at Square." In *The Square: The 40th Year Special Edition*. Choi In-hoon. Seoul: Moonhakgwajiseongsa, 2001. 267–91.

Park, Sang-yeon. *DMZ*. Seoul: Minumsa, 1997.

Roszak, Theodore. *The Voice of the Earth*. New York: Simon & Schuster, 1992.

Ryu, Shin. "The Bridge of Poetic Imagination Connecting the Daedong River and the Han River." *Silcheon Moohhak* 83 (Autumn 2006): 459–83.

Slovic, Scott. "Varieties of Environmental Nostalgia." *Proceedings of Ecological Literature and Environmental Education: Asian Forum for Cross-Cultural Dialogue*, Beijing (August 2009): 142.

Thomashow, Mitchell. *Ecological Identity: Becoming a Reflective Environmentalist*. Cambridge: MIT P, 1996.

Tuan, Yi-Fu. *Space and Place: The Perspective of Experience*. Minneapolis: U of Minnesota P, 1977.

Section III

Taiwanese Section

8

CORPORATE GLOBALIZATION AND THE RESISTANCE TO IT IN LINDA HOGAN'S *PEOPLE OF THE WHALE* AND IN SHENG WU'S POETRY

Peter I-min Huang

Chickasaw writer Linda Hogan and Taiwanese writer Sheng Wu are from two very different places in the world. Hogan, born in the upper west region of the United States, has written many novels and poems about Native North American peoples—especially the Chickasaw, whose traditional homelands are in what is now Oklahoma state in the southern central area of the United States. Wu, born in the county of Changhua in the central part of Taiwan, a small island located just east of mainland China and south of Japan and the Korean peninsula, has written extensively on his people and their place in Taiwan. Despite the differences in history, geography, and environment that separate them, Hogan and Wu share closely related environmental justice, or ecojustice, concerns and interests. These inspire much of their activism, public appearances, participation in conferences, and also their poetry and prose. This chapter addresses these interests as they relate to *corporate globalization*, a phenomenon closely tied to many environmental problems in the world today. Drawing mainly on the work of the ecojustice and ecofeminist activist and scholar Vandana Shiva, including the book *Earth Democracy* (2005), in which appears an extended discussion of corporate globalization, this chapter analyzes Hogan's recent novel *People of the Whale* (2008) and five poems by Wu: "Loss," "Don't Sigh When You Go Out," "I Can Only Write A Poem For You," "My Dear Hometown," and "Black Soil." Toward its conclusion, it draws on arguments Stacy Alaimo advances in her book

Bodily Natures: Science, Environment, and the Material Self (2010).
Hogan's *People of the Whale* and Wu's poetry represent resistance to
corporate globalization in the writers' eastern and western, material
places in the world.

Broadly defined, corporate globalization refers to the major shift
of power from national governments to semiautonomous, multinational corporations in the period between the last two-thirds of
the twentieth century and the present twenty-first century. Born in
1944 and 1947, respectively, Wu and Hogan have seen and drawn
attention to the negative side of corporate globalization, including the destruction of local communities and the local environments upon which these communities depend. Wu does so in the
context of Taiwan, where corporate global interests have contributed significantly to the loss of Taiwan's natural environments and
Taiwan's agricultural base, as well to the industrial "trashing" of the
island (Clark 87). Hogan focuses on Native American peoples in the
United States, whom corporate globalization has negatively affected
socially and economically. Wu's and Hogan's efforts are supported
by many other ecojustice writers, activists, and scholars, including
the ecofeminist Vandana Shiva. In her book *Earth Democracy*, Shiva
defines corporate globalization specifically according to eight main
purposes and effects:

1. the enclosure or constriction of democratic interests and
   traditional "commons" (publically used lands) as opposed to the
   expansion of democratic interests and publically shared lands
   (2–3);
2. the accretion of wealth by a minority of the earth's population
   (2–3);
3. the control or privatization of "knowledge, culture, water, biodiversity, and public services such as health and education" by this
   same minority (3);
4. the devaluation of the intrinsic worth of "all species, all peoples,
   [and] all cultures" (6);
5. the destruction of beliefs that hold that "all things are connected" (7);
6. policies and practices by global corporations that they falsely claim
   will reduce the number of violent military-industrial conflicts
   around the world (30–32);
7. the deregulation of commerce by governments complicit with
   global corporations (73); and
8. the false marketing of corporate globalization policies and practices
   under the euphemism "economic reform" (74–75).

The characteristics of corporate globalization that Shiva identifies are either implicitly or explicitly targeted in Hogan's novel *The People of the Whale*. The main background event of the novel is a secret deal that several leaders of the Native American A'atsika have made with a small group of Japanese businessmen and small group of whale market operators in Norway. The handful of A'atsika leaders will be paid handsomely for telling their community that the resumption and legalization of whale hunting will restore the cultural identity of the A'atsika and bring their people economic prosperity. In exchange, the A'atsika leaders will negotiate with the US government to permit foreign commercial whale operators to access the traditional waters of the A'atsika, engage in whale hunting and whale slaughter, and commodify and export the meat from the whales that they slaughter to foreign markets.

As Hogan describes the first whale slaughter that ensues following the government's agreement to the corporate global deals, the key stakeholders fail to address questions of ethical responsibility, compassion for the whales, or the need for sophisticated understanding of both the whales that are hunted and the A'atsika who once worshipped the animals. The proposed resumption of whale killing would endanger the already threatened whale species, which survive in diminished numbers in the waters that used to be a "commons" shared with other Native American and First Nations peoples in the United States and Canada. In the past, the killing of whales had been a sustainable practice. The animals thrived along with the A'atsika. In their critical dependence on whales, the A'atsika recognized that their people's identity was bound up in the identity of the whales. These animals, the totem animal of the A'atsika, are the incarnation of the A'atsika's ancestral peoples: the loss of them would spell both the cultural and material demise of the A'atsika.

In the whale slaughter described by Hogan, the whales are objectified and commodified. The men who operate the buses, speedboats, and helicopters that bring sightseers, news reporters and other outsiders to observe the hunt do so mostly to make money. They and the other people who arrive on the scene by foot, car, or motorcycle, passively view the killing of whales. This killing functions as mere entertainment, as mere diversion for them. They have no other interest in either the A'atsika or the whales. As several men drag the carcass of a whale to shore and cut it open, they make offensive remarks about the whale's genitalia. In an deed typical of the men's many acts of "irreverence" and "stupidity" (95), one of the group that is drinking beer and smoking marijuana, pours beer into the whale's blowhole (95). He and the other men no longer "apologize to the spirit of the whale" (95) or sing or pray to the animal as they used to. "All the love for the animal" that used to characterize whale hunting for the A'atsika is "missing" from the whale hunt and slaughter (95). The A'atsika who participate in it and the other people present at the whale hunt—passers-by, onlookers, and news reporters—have "fill[ed] themselves up... but not with the heart, not [with] the soul" (90).

Hogan contrasts the ugly spectacle of a whale being killed and slaughtered with another scene in the novel where Ruth Small, one of the A'atsika tribe who is vehemently opposed to the whale hunt, remembers the traditional whale hunting of the A'atsika. In the past, when the A'atsika took their boats to the sea to hunt for whales, the whole town came to a sort of stop. Physically, materially, culturally, and ritually bearing some part of the whales' death, the people in a way *stopped living*: "No one laboured. No one bought or sold. No one laughed or kissed. It was the unspoken rule. All they did was to wait, the women singing, eerily, at ocean's edge. They were solemn and spoke softly" (20). The wife of Witka, one of the tribal elders and the grandfather of Ruth's estranged husband Thomas Just, digs a hole under the tree and stays there waiting for her husband to return. Throughout the duration of the whale hunt, the people endeavor to be "pure in heart and mind" (22). Witka and the men speak to the whales, entreating them to send one of their members to offer itself to the poor people on land. They also sing and pray to the whales. In one song, they chant:

> Oh brother, sister whale, grandmother whale, grandfather whale. If you come here to land we have beautiful leaves and trees. We have warm places. We have babies to feed and we'll let your eyes gaze upon them. We will let your soul become a child again. We will pray it back into a body. It will enter our bodies. You will be part human. We'll be part whale. (22–23)

In "Homeless in the 'Global Village,'" Shiva argues that the process of desacralization is a particularly unsalutary aspect of corporate globalization (103). She explains desacralization as the transformation by global corporate interests of "sacred spaces" revered and depended upon by people who have lived with and in these spaces for many generations, extending to preindustrial times (103). Such is the place of the A'atsika and the whales that coexist with the A'atsika. Under the global corporate negotiations, their and the whales' place is being transformed into a "location" in "Cartesian space" that has global market value only (103).

In his book *The Future of Environmental Criticism* (2005), ecocritic Lawrence Buell also addresses what Shiva calls "sacred spaces." Buell uses the term "space" to refer to "geometrical or topographical" abstracted places and the term "place" to mean geographical and concrete spaces that one can see, hear, smell, and feel as well as imagine, love, and revere, and also hate or fear (63). The latter kind of spaces specifically correspond to what Shiva calls "sacred spaces" and to what Hogan identifies in her novel as the traditional place or environment of the A'atsika people. The whale hunt staged by the corporate global businessmen, which occurs at the physical and geographical location where the traditional whale hunt of the A'atsika used to occur, materially, culturally, ethically, and environmentally desacralizes and disfigures the place that this location once was.

As Ursula Heise compellingly argues in *Sense of Place and Sense of Planet* (2008), defending place against space in absolute terms is not always salutary. She cautions ecocritics about the implications of defending places in unqualified terms by noting that this kind of argumentation in fact is used by many individuals and groups opposed to ethnic, racial, cultural, social, and ecological diversity in the world. In *The People of the Whale*, the rhetoric of place is thus used by the commercial whale operators and corporate global stakeholders. They use the rhetoric of place against the interests of preserving the "sacred spaces" of the A'atsika. They seek to revive a local traditional custom under a false, sentimentalized rhetoric of place. Only a very small group of men motivated by the prospect of earning money quickly and easily stand to benefit from the revival of the ancient custom. Among the few A'atsika aware of this initially is Witka's grandson (Ruth's husband), Thomas Just. Other A'atsika take advantage of the opportunity to profit from the proposed deal. These individuals include Dimitri and Dwight.

In an interview with Hogan, Summer Harrison asked Hogan to sum up the main difference between Ruth, who is against reviving whale hunting, and Dwight, who participates in the corporate global transaction between the A'atsika and Japanese and Norwegian businessmen. Hogan calls Ruth an "authentic" character in contrast to the character of Dwight (qtd in Harrison 170). Hogan's use here of the word "authentic" brings to mind the postmodernist thinker Jean Baudrillard's critique of the notion that a copy of anything is based on or can be traced to an originary source or "real" object, subject, or identity. For Baudrillard, there is no original: every object, subject, or identity, and even any representation or purported "authentic" statement or sign, is a copy of a copy. All "artifice lies at the heart of reality" (75). In the countersense that Hogan uses the word "authentic" when she contrasts Ruth to Dwight, it refers to a person who is interconnected and integrated with his or her local community and who desires to be part of this community. Hogan does not claim Ruth is an "authentic" Native American, but her characterization of Ruth, a figure who is keenly sensitive and receptive to her community's interests, suggests that Ruth indeed is authentic in comparison to individuals such as Dwight, who trades his authentic identity as an A'atsika for an inauthentic identity as a member of a corporate global business deal.

Baudrillard's postmodern critique of the notion and concept of authenticity has clashed with much ecofeminist, postcolonial, and ecojustice scholarship and with the work of such writers as Hogan (and Wu), the literary output of whom constitutes a passionate defense of authentic identities and places. However, his concept of authenticity, as well as his concept of *simulacrum*, is useful for reading their work. For *The People of the Whale*, it highlights the reducing to an empty image or symbol by corporate global interests of traditions that once had real material and symbolic value. Baudrillard identifies three kinds of copies or "simulacra." The first he calls *"counterfeit"* (50). This is "the dominant schema in the 'classical' period, from the Renaissance to the Industrial Revolution" (50). The second he calls *"production."* This is "the dominant schema in the industrial era" (50). The third, *"simulation,"* defines the current (post)modern era (50). It refers to the ways in which we are seduced, and controlled, by goods and services divested of real meaning, either real material or real symbolic meaning. That is to say, we are given products that do not fulfil us in ways that are culturally, politically, or environmentally durable or sustainable. The products, goods, and services are not very lasting, but, paradoxically, they consume us. *The People of the Whale* targets the spectacle of the whale hunt staged by the corporate global interests. Only a small number of A'atsika are aware it is a false front for selling whale meat in overseas foreign markets. One of these individuals, Ruth, challenges the members of the deal at a meeting organized to cast votes for the restoration of whale hunting. She questions the reputed authenticity of the whale hunt and implies that it is an empty sign, symbol, or simulacrum:

[W]ho here has the kind of relationship to the whales that our ancestors had? Who among us knows the songs and the correct way to bring in the whale? Who will prepare by fasting? Who will sew its mouth shut so it doesn't sink to the bottom of the ocean? Which of you knows what our grandparents knew? We can't jump into this because someone has made an under-the-table offer of money. (82)

Earlier she addresses the entire A'atsika community about this same issue. The global corporate interests are, she says, "not even near the original meaning of a whale hunt" (69). They are "not the voice of our community" (69).

The issues of authenticity and simulacrum also are addressed by Wu, a writer who in many ways is very different from Hogan, but whose passionate commitment to environmental and social justice in Taiwan and skepticism of corporate globalization bring him ideologically close to Hogan. Wu has written extensively on the loss of agriculture in Taiwan that have resulted from corporate global interests and aggressive industrialization since the 1980s. Born in 1941 in the central part of Taiwan in the agricultural county of Changhua, Wu graduated from Pingtung Agricultural College in 1971 and taught biology at a junior high school in his hometown. He also was a farmer and a writer. Since retiring in 2000 he has continued to practice farming and to write poetry. In 1980, in recognition of the latter, he was invited to the Iowa International Writers Program as a visiting poet. Wu has several published collections of poetry, including *Poetry Anthology* (2000), from which some of the poems cited here are taken, and he has received a number of prestigious literary awards. He is most famous for capturing images of rural life in Taiwan and is one of the country's most recognized pastoral poets. His poetry is deceptively simple and follows the rhythms and patterns of everyday speech. His humility is also much remarked on by critics.

In the poem "Don't Sigh When You Go Out," Wu adopts wry tones to criticize the corporate global impact on Taiwan's local domestic economies and the disingenuous use of authentic language by corporate global companies to market goods to Taiwanese people: he narrates an experience of taking his son for an outing on a holiday. When he is worried that he doesn't have time to prepare breakfast, his son comforts him offhandedly: "Don't worry; we can use milk powder." Wu notes that the trademark says it is an "authentic import from Europe." They go past a large area where there used to be vast rice paddies. The area is now a construction site. Between the newly erected skyscrapers are squeezed what is left of the rice paddies and their "few rice stalks about to die." Wu's son again tries to comfort his father, saying: "Don't worry. It is convenient to buy hamburgers

at McDonald's." Wu observes that the trademark says the meat is an
"authentic import from America." When Wu brings his son to a river
that he remembers from the past, he finds that the river has dried up
and its riverbed is filled with "randomly dumped" garbage. He has
hoped to be able to drink from the river as he did in the past. His
son, again trying to comfort his father, responds that it is more convenient to drink from a "bottle of mineral water." The label on the
bottle states that the water has been "imported authentically from
Australia." Hoping to find a place that "still retains the pristine natural
beauty" of the past, Wu brings his son to a mountain that he also
remembers. Where there was once forest there is now only "helplessly
exposed" yellow earth. All of the "trees and grasses" on it have been
destroyed. As Wu and his son leave the mountain, they are caught in a
thunder storm. They see that part of the mountain cliff has collapsed,
and the bridge across the mountain has broken. They get stuck in
one of the mudslides on the mountain. It has become "like an island
ravaged by high waves." Wu's son, holding some empty cans to his
chest, worriedly asks his father, "What shall we do now?" Corporate
notions of "authenticity" are just rhetoric to engage in "green wash-
ing" their businesses.

The poem points to Shiva's arguments in *Earth Democracy* of the
strategy powerful global corporations use to force local and federal
governments to deregulate their economies, waive or reduce taxes
on big corporations, and reduce or eliminate import and export
taxes. These powerful corporations use phrases such as "sustainable
development" and "economic globalization" simply as shortcuts to
purchasing cheaper resources and using cheaper labor in one part
of the world and to sell those products cheaply in markets in other
parts of the world (*Earth Democracy* 73). Rather than encouraging
competition, this can reduce competition. Rather than expanding
the range of goods available to a local community in many cases,
this can narrow the range and make communities and consumers
more dependent upon products that they would not choose to buy
if corporate globalization had not made it expensive to produce
goods locally. Further, corporate globalization practices that result
in the replacement of local market models by neoliberal market
models often are no more environmentally sustainable or politically
equitable than the practices they rendered obsolete. In place of traditional power structures (national-based governments or older kinds
of power structures such as monarchies and the church) that highly
visible individuals depended on (people who desired to be visible) to
wield power, the individuals who make up the major stakeholders of

corporate globalization today hide (and desire to hide) behind the "anonymous face" of their companies. This gives them extraordinary license in their practices, practices they might not engage in if they were held accountable for them. Heather Eaton in her essay "Can Ecofeminism Withstand Corporate Globalization?" characterizes such individuals as having "no accountability to anything" but their own "hegemonic economic agenda" (25).

"Don't Sigh When You Go Out" draws attention to the increasing dependence of Taiwanese people on products imported from overseas that could be produced locally and more sustainably. In addition, it alludes to the problem of the replacement of diverse crops cultivated on relatively small areas of land by monoculture or cash crops culti-vated on much larger areas and in places where once there was for-est and the soil was held in place by the forests. Deforestation and cash crops have contributed significantly to mudslides, flooding, and soil loss and erosion in Taiwan. When Wu tells us that "[t]he cliff is collapsed, the bridge broken, and mud obstructs the mountain roads," he is not exaggerating the seriousness of this environmental problem.

In their book *Postcolonial Ecocriticism* (2010), Graham Huggan and Helen Tiffin discuss how in the period between the late eighteenth century and first half of the twentieth century, before the era of cor-porate globalization, Western European imperialist powers not only subjected human populations in many places in the world—Africa, Asia, and the Middle East—but also took control over and destroyed the older natural environments that these populations depended on and closely identified with *as* peoples. Corporate globalization is the postcolonial extension of older colonial imperialist, racist, and eth-nocentric practices. In many instances, as Shiva argues, corporate globalization has been more destructive than colonization processes despite its claim of reducing violent military-industrial conflicts in the world (*Earth Democracy* 30). It incites conflict where formerly there was no conflict or intensifies an existing conflict in a political region or territory and destroys the identity of the community caught up in the conflict (30–32). Hogan refers to this colonial history in her fictional portrayal of the North American A'atsika.

As Harrison notes, Hogan refers also to a more recent (post)colonial history in her novel: the US government's military intervention in the civil war in North Vietnam (169). Thomas, a Vietnam War veteran, was conscripted with many other A'atsika men to serve in the US government's aggressive military venture. Many still suffer deeply from the horrors that they participated in or witnessed. They bear emotional and physical scars. They externalize this experience as well as internalize it. This has deeply marked their place at home, which has become a place where "kids [shoot] guns, kill dogs and die of alcohol poisoning" (Hogan 95).

Thomas regards himself as a person without an identity, "a stolen person," a mere "body walking" (46). He feels his body is steeped in "dishonesty" because of the killing he witnessed and participated in as a US government soldier (46). When he makes a pilgrimage with his friend Dimitri to The Wall, the Vietnam Veterans Memorial site in Washington, D.C., he finds his name "listed as one of the dead" (248). "Geez," Dimitri says to him teasingly, "you're not only a hero. You're a dead one!" (248). This comment epitomizes Thomas's loss of identity as an individual and as an A'atsika. When he reads the many names listed on The Wall at the Vietnam Veterans Memorial, he wishes he could have known some of the men identified by these names. He wishes he could have "touched their skin" and "held their sweaty bodies" to him (248). When a man comes by and touches Thomas's body, saying to him in greeting, "Hello, brother," Thomas is overwhelmed with emotion and begins to cry (248). It is one of the rare moments when Thomas gives in to his feelings. Previously, at the time when he participates in the whale hunt and his young son Marco asks him if he can hear and feel the voices of their ancestors, we learn that he has lost the ability to hear and feel the suffering of either himself or others (99). Also, his distrust of words is deepened when he sees his name listed among the names of deceased Vietnam veterans. He characterizes the writing on The Wall as writing that both "[proves] history" and "[proves] lies" (252). Yet, the stone wall also inspires Thomas. It gives him some hope that the memory of his own people will not be lost and his people will survive the attempt by corporate global interests to reduce his and the A'atsika's identity. In one of the stories of the A'atsika, stones speak. For Hogan, history epitomized in the Wall can be fabricated and engraved. But the material stone will not lie. The stone tells a lost boy how to find his way home (245). Thomas recalls these stones when he sees The Wall and so he sees in it, in "this stone," "a direction home, speaking to him" (245). Hogan uses the example of the stone to suggest a paradigm shift from the discursive to the material.

Hogan is not blind to the difficulty that local communities face when they have to determine how much they should preserve of older traditions and how much they should change in order to be able to continue as a community and maintain their identity. Her novel shows us this in particular through the character of Thomas. He comes to understand the implications of the corporate global deal that

will putatively restore to his people one of their most venerable
traditions. Another character, Dwight, does not or is unwilling to
try to understand the murky negotiations: "It was an intrigue too
large...for [him] to figure out, too complex. All he saw was the
money on the table for meat in another country" (69). Yet another
character, Dimitri, is similar to Thomas in that he is fully aware of
the consequences of the deal. However, unlike Thomas, Dimitri sacrifices the long-term interests of his A'atsika people to short-lasting,
temporary gains. Standing with "his shirttail out," in a posture
meant to show superior knowledge, and speaking in bragging tones,
he boasts: "Whale-hunting...will bring us back to ourselves" (69).
Thomas, wanting to restore his people's confidence but dubious of
the corporate global deal, is more reluctant to vote in favor of the
deal. Through his character, Hogan represents the dilemma that
many people today confront when their communities are offered an
enticing, lucrative business proposal that promises to preserve and
sustain their communities' way of life. She writes:

> It was so difficult to have to go against your own people who had
> already been wounded and persecuted and to want to see them thrive,
> to really *be*, like they once were, and to see how compassion had been
> taken away from their lives by their experience in the new and other
> world as if they'd been transformed away from themselves. (90)

Thomas does not succumb to what seems to be a solution to the
crisis of identity and economic difficulties of the A'atsika. Dwight
capitulates and in doing so loses his identity anyway. Desperate to
restore the so-called tradition of whale hunting, to "retain the old
way of being in the world" (69), he becomes "a man without a heart"
and "a liar about the whales" (253).

The problem Hogan implicitly confronts in *The People of the Whale*
of continuing traditions divested of the ethnocentric practices that
are seen by many to be central to those traditions has been addressed
by many scholars, including the German sociologist Ulrich Beck.
Beck has written on globalization as well as on the related issues of
management of risk associated with corporate globalization practices
and environmental politics. Similar to Ursula Heise, who cautions
ecocritics against an unreflected defense of local places and unqualified excoriation of globalized spaces, Beck addresses the problem of
continuing ethnocentric practices that were never or are no longer
in the interest of some of the members of the community that traditionally engaged in those practices. Thus, he suggests not to accept

tout court arguments in defense of "tradition." "[L]ocal cultures," he states, "can no longer be justified, shaped and renewed in seclusion from the rest of the world" (47). In support of his argument, he points to the "fundamentalism"—religious, ethnic, and so on— behind the "knee-jerk defenses of tradition" that are "by traditional means" (46–47). However, as he might recognize, and as Hogan recognizes in her writings, one need not throw out an entire tradition or culture on the basis of some of its practices, for example, practices associated with the oppression of women, animals, or outsiders to the community. Such practices can be discontinued without destroying the entire tradition or culture. Nonetheless, Beck seems to support the idea of simply relocating "detraditionalized traditions *within a global context* of exchange, dialogue and conflict" (47; emphasis in original). Hogan, however, would respond that before a tradition can be reformed or detraditionalized, one must try to fully understand and respect it.

Harrison asks Hogan the question that Beck addresses in *What is Globalization?* (2000) and that Thomas confronts in *The People of the Whale*: "[H]ow to practice tradition in the contemporary world without trying to replicate the past" (169). Hogan's response, a qualified defense of tradition, is as controversial as Beck's contextualized denouncements of tradition. Her target is not "fundamentalism," or the minority fundamentalist communities that Beck attacks (which Hogan probably would regard as already taking a battering from corporate global interests), but rather an entire Western European history of oppression and domination. She responds: "[T]he Western mindset is so pervasive that you have to decolonize your own mind and heart and soul, and then reeducate yourself into understanding what tradition is" (168). Her words echo the famous writing by postcolonial scholar Ngũgĩ wa Thiong'o entitled "Decolonizing the Mind." She urges her people to "re-indigenize" themselves and "understand and love the earth" that is closest to them and from which they come (qtd in Harrison 168). Toward this goal, she warns us against the ways in which corporate globalization interests use "tradition" to destroy the very traditions they claim they are promoting.

Similar to Hogan, Wu in his poetry and other writings has argued for the preservation of politically, socially, economically, and ecologically sustainable traditions. Many of his poems speak to the immense effort in Taiwan of local farmers who are resisting corporate globalization. Often it seems Wu is pessimistic that the latter will defeat the former, as the poem "Loss" represents in its description of local fishing traditions that barely survive. In this poem, Wu visits an old fishing village and is saddened by what he sees. A vast stretch of oyster fields along the western coast of Taiwan has been almost totally devastated by the pollution of the petrochemical plants. He laments the loss of local food of oyster cake and oyster soup due to the inroads of this industry, which is heavily backed by corporate global interests. Banners raised by protesters against the industrial development of the fishing village are faded and listless. The heritage and tradition of this "little town on the seashore" are broken up by "new signs," "new development," and "pollution." They survive only in pockets or otherwise remain as a record, "[e]tched" on the faces of people that have lived in the village for most of their lives. Wu asks, "[Does] the heritage of the town remain?"

Wu's poem "Loss" is based on his intimate knowledge of environmental protest movements in Taiwan and the formidable opposition they face. This may be illustrated by some very recent events. In April 2010, farmers from the counties of Miaoli, Hsinchu, Hualien, and Changhua gathered to protest a draft act by the government to expropriate farmlands in their counties for industrial development. Under the proposed act, farmlands that previously were protected from other kinds of development now were at risk. Despite opposition to the act, it was passed. As a result, 362 hectares of farmland in Miaoli County were scheduled to be turned into an "industrial science park." The term "industrial science park" typically designates a petrochemical or plastics manufacture plant. Heavily backed by corporate global interests, the petrochemical and plastics industry in Taiwan has greatly boosted the economy. However, many Taiwanese, including Shih-jung Hsu, chair of the Department of Land Economics at National Chengchi University, are critical of the aggressiveness of the industry, and Taiwan's land expropriation system, which favors the industry. As they argue, the locations chosen by the industry's stakeholders often are coastal areas and wetlands that are ecologically diverse or lands that support agricultural communities or aboriginal communities (Loa, "Group calls for purchases to scupper refineries plan"). Industrial developers target these areas because of their vulnerability, or "minimum resistance" (Loa, "Group Calls for Purchases"). This practice is seen in many other parts of the world, as ecofeminist and ecojustice scholar and activist Greta Gaard has written extensively on. Minority, underprivileged, marginalized communities mostly bear the negative costs of globalized spaces. They are "pillaged, resourced and outsourced, as well as polluted and degraded in the process of globalization" (654).

In June 2010, more than two hundred police officers surrounded the Jhunan township of Hsinchu County to prevent protestors from accessing agricultural land designated for an industrial park. Twenty excavators were brought in and used to dig up the rice paddies little more than a month away from harvest (Loa, "Miaoli Destroys Farmland"). Later in the same month, approximately one hundred police officers blocked off roads to the township of Dapu in Miaoli County, where another science park was planned, and excavators were brought in to dig up the land. In response to increasing public protest, the government wooed voters with its controversial Farm Villages Revival Act. This act was passed (in July 2010) despite the attempts that were made to boycott it. Under this act, the government announced it would spend 150 billion Taiwan dollars (5 billion US dollars) on "farm village revival projects" over the next ten years. The government promised these projects will "stimulate" agriculture, "protect" farm village culture, and "improve" farm villages, village commons areas, and farm houses (Wang and Loa).

Wu and many other environmental activists in Taiwan are deeply critical of the Farm Villages Revival Act. Pei-hui Tsai, speaking for The Taiwan Rural Front, argues it will do nothing to improve the interests of local farmers. She compares it to "spending money to repaint the outside of a house when the roof is leaking" (qtd in Wang and Loa). Sulak Sivaraska, author of *The Wisdom of Sustainability* (2009), discusses acts such as these by pointing out they are created under agreements between governments and multinational corporations and impose "structural violence" on local communities and places because they pervade—socially, culturally, economically, and ecologically—every aspect of these communities and places (29).

The efforts of many people around the world to retain control of their local identities and places is not, however, a doomed enterprise. In Taiwan in Changhua County, Wu's home county, Wu and others successfully opposed the building of a petrochemical plant. Beginning in July 2010, Wu and other environmentalists (including over a thousand Taiwanese scholars) signed a petition against the planned oil refineries (Loa, "Activists Apply for Wetlands"). The existing oil refineries have been disastrous for the diverse wetland ecology of the region—the Jhoushuei River, the coastal wetlands, which are fed by the river, and coastal waters. More oil refineries would further endanger the already threatened species of pink dolphin (also known as white or humpbacked dolphin) that makes its home in the coastal waters of western Taiwan. These dolphins survive only here and in the coastal waters on the east coast of mainland China near Xiamen. Environmentalist groups also launched a campaign asking the public to buy two hundred hectares of the most sensitive coastal wetland areas in this area. Thirty-one thousand people signed up to purchase 1.5 million shares, or enough shares to purchase 150 hectares of wetland (Loa, "Activists Apply for Wetlands"). On May 8, 2011, a group of local artists and activists headed by Wu gathered in Taiwan's northern capital, Taipei, at the entrance of the Museum of Contemporary Art, to call for more public support for designating Dacheng wetlands, the site of the proposed Kuokuang petrochemical factories, a permanent natural reserve (Lee). In June 2011, they established an environmental trust fund for donations from the public. This fund is the first of its kind in Taiwan (Lee). Eighteen research fellows from one of Taiwan's most prestigious institutes, Academia Sinica, including Dr. Chou Chang-hung, who heads the institute's Life Sciences Division, were involved in the effort.

In a recent article published in the *China Times*, Wu asked, "Do we want to pay the price of an enormous environmental catastrophe for an increase of 4% GDP promised by big corporations and government?" ("Strive for Whose Economics?"). In his poem "I Can Only Write a Poem for You" (printed in the Chinese edition of *Business Weekly*), Wu criticized big corporation and government interests in the specific context of one of Taiwan's petrochemical industry giants, the Kuokuang Petrochemical Technology Company (KPTC). The poem is one of Wu's most explicit statements against the continuing industrialization of Taiwan by powerful corporate global interests. He points out that it is a minority, "a few people," who are responsible for the decrease in water supplies, the increase in "drought and famine," and the loss of Taiwan's ecologically diverse environments. He also condemns the "silent majority" of people in Taiwan who seem not to care. He asks: will Taiwanese people continue to allow big industrial interests to "block off the sea," "give us pollution," "give us smoggy sky," and let "fish, crabs, cranes, and dolphins" be wiped out "in the name of prosperity?" Although in the poem Wu expresses a sense of futility in response to the escalation of big industry, when his poem appeared in print in several major newspapers in Taiwan, the public responded with an enormous outpouring of support. In response to his poem and the public protests it inspired, the government suspended one of the construction projects that Wu spoke out against in the poem.

In another poem, "My Dear Hometown," Wu targets the language of "risk assessment" used by corporate global companies in their efforts to tightly control people and places and rationalize "acceptable levels" of environmental and social risk. He questions the way in which enormous environmental and social costs are reduced under risk assessments to amoral abstractions, words, and figures. He writes that when he leafs through voluminous stacks of environmental risk assessments and long lines of statistics, he cannot repress his strong sense of anger and frustration because such risk assessments and statistics "create shadows of phantoms and ghosts" to haunt the future of his dear hometown. The statistics announce that this "remote" and "barren" place has no future but that of being turned into "chimneys and sewage sites to accept their baptism of pollution day and night" in exchange for "progress" and "development." Wu then asks, "Who has the right to decide/to abandon the sustainable blessings" of his "hometown?" He charges that corporate global companies "fabricate the graphs and numbers/to evaluate how much abuse of pollution/ such a small island can endure." In referring to "[e]nvironmental risk assessments," which corporations routinely use to rationalize the construction of industrial plants and the "baptism of pollution by day and night" that these plants emit, Wu offers his critique to insist on his lifelong faith in environmental justice of the land.

In *Bodily Natures*, ecofeminist Stacy Alaimo discusses Beck's risk theory and his claim that the practice of determination of risk itself is a form of ethics (Beck 28). Alaimo both puts pressure on and extends Beck's argument by critiquing corporate global economic and political practices that do not adequately or at all reflect the understanding that the material world is a "trans-corporeal" body and a body that possesses *agency* (21). As Alaimo argues, the material world is not static or fixed, or an "object." Risk assessment models that in effect treat it as such are bound to be unreliable. For ecofeminists such as Alaimo, the body of the material world is intimately, deeply connected to the body of the human, and it also possesses its own kind of agency: "Understanding the material world as agential" means understanding it as more than a passive and "pliable" resource for industrial production and social construction (Alaimo 21). As Alaimo asserts in the introduction coauthored with Susan Hekman to *Material Feminisms*, our use of the material world has consequences for us as well as for the nonhuman world (4–5).

Yet, in standard, common risk assessments by corporate global companies, the material environment is not considered from any moral or ethical perspective. As Alaimo argues, this is an enormous oversight, and, as Shiva shows, it is a gross environmental injustice. Alaimo urges that since "material agencies can be neither adequately predicted nor safely mastered," a "precautionary principle" should be adopted minimally, at least when relying on risk assessment findings for analysis of any threat of harm to humans and the material environments that support them (21–22). She draws on Sandra Steingraber's book *Living Downstream: A Scientist's Personal Investigation of Cancer and the Environment* (1998), in which Steingraber also urges that while the "precautionary principle" should not be extended to all ecological and technological risks assessments, the principle should be used in scenarios where a risk assessment is used by an industry to obscure human and environmental health dangers (284).

Vandana Shiva in *Earth Democracy* argues that globalization is, in fact, "the ultimate enclosure—of our minds, our hearts, our imaginations, and our resources" (30). Patrick Murphy calls it part of "an instrumentalist mind-set" that is "willing to commodify everything and everyone" (127). One of the ways it is promoted in Taiwan is through the kinds of duplicitous marketing that Linda Hogan addresses in *People of the Whale* and Wu addresses in such poems as "Don't Sigh When You Go Out." In Hogan's novel, whale hunting is promoted on the grounds that it restores a traditional Native American practice. In "Don't Sigh When You Go Out," Wu focuses on the language of "authenticity" that corporate global companies use to destroy local domestic markets. In "I Can Only Write A Poem For You," Wu focuses on the rhetoric of progress and development used by multinational industrial corporations in order to transform farmlands, wetlands, and coastal areas into petrochemical plants. His and Hogan's writings belong to the growing body of ecojustice protest literature. Huggan and Tiffin characterize such writings as vitally contributing to "consciousness-raising" in the context of "the twin demands of social and environmental justice," and they "conspicuously display" those demands (33). As Alaimo urges us to do, they cultivate "a tangible sense of connection to the material world" (16). Perhaps this is nowhere better expressed than in Wu poem titled "Black Soil."

An especially strong piece of ecojustice writing, "Black Soil" works against much of contemporary cultural theory's promotion of the "disdain of nature" and against the complicity between social constructionism and commercialism, which replaces "the natural" with "the artifactual" (Alaimo 4, 8). It articulates Alaimo's argument that there is an urgent need to critique the postmodern humanism that seeks to transcend material worlds and an equally pressing need to shift our focus from linguistic and discursive concerns to material concerns. "Black Soil" also laments what Alaimo critiques as the denial of the agency of the material world by corporate global interests and what Shiva characterizes as the desacralization of soil. It works against the disconnection between humans and their environments, which are being increasingly transformed into "universally globalized, undifferentiated or abstract, replicable spaces" (16). Wu writes that when he used to work on the paddy fields along the Jhoushuei River, a main river in central Taiwan, the sweat of his body dropped on the soil and sprouted the seeds in the ground into leaves and flowers, solidifying his covenant of love to the land. He vividly describes the physical touch with the black soil in celebration of human embodiment. He writes of his memories of "tilling and farming in tranquillity one season after another, in the thick black soil along the Jhoushuei River," and "planting seedlings that would shoot into lush greenness." The pact between himself and the black soil created hope and enriched his youth and adulthood. Celebrating humans' agricultural bonds with the earth, Wu affirms an ancient covenant between the human body and the earth's body. He confronts the global corporate entities that seem intent on transforming the earth's entire surface into an industrial vat. He argues that our future depends on continuing older, bodily, relations with the earth and engaging in sustainable agricultural practices. "Black Soil" represents his resistance to the postmodern fantasies of disembodiment and modern myths of creativity. These often are enlisted by corporate global interests in their rationalizations of the destruction of natural environments and local communities. Many of these have been or are being reduced to mere commodities or even mere symbols; many others have been or are being eradicated altogether. Both Wu and Hogan have tirelessly fought to encourage local communities to be aware of and active in sustainable economic practices. Their writings foster understanding of, commitment to, and respect for the natural world. They celebrate the belief that the soul of our societies is the body of this world.

WORKS CITED

Alaimo, Stacy. *Bodily Natures: Science, Environment, and the Material Self.* Indianapolis: Indiana UP, 2010.

Alaimo, Stacy and Susan Hekman. "Introduction: Emerging Models of Materiality in Feminist Theory." In *Material Feminisms.* Ed. Stacy Alaimo and Susan Hekman. Indianapolis: Indiana UP, 2008. 1–22.

Baudrillard, Jean. *Symbolic Exchange and Death.* Trans. Iain Hamilton Grant. London: Sage Publications, 1993.

Beck, Ulrich. *What Is Globalization?* Trans. Patrick Camiller. Cambridge: Polity P, 2000.

Buell, Lawrence. *The Future of Environmental Criticism.* Oxford: Blackwell, 2005.

Clark, Timothy. *The Cambridge Introduction to Literature and the Environment.* New York: Cambridge UP, 2011.

Eaton, Heather. "Can Ecofeminism Withstand Corporate Globalization?" In *Ecofeminism & Globalization.* Ed. Heather Eaton and Lois Ann Lorentzen. Oxford: Rowman & Littlefield, 2003. 23–37.

Gaard, Greta. "New Directions for Ecofeminism." *ISLE* 17.4 (Autumn 2010): 643–45.

Harrison, Summer. "Sea Level: An Interview with Linda Hogan." *ISLE* 18.1 (Winter 2011): 161–77.

Heise, Ursula. *Sense of Place and Sense of Planet.* Oxford: Oxford UP, 2008.

Hogan, Linda. *People of the Whale.* New York: Norton, 2008.

Huggan, Graham and Helen Tiffin. *Postcolonial Ecocriticism: Literature, Animals, Environment.* London: Routledge, 2010.

Lee, I-chia. "Environmental trust fund launched." *Taipei Times.* June 1, 2011: 4.

Loa, Iok-sin. "Activists apply for wetlands purchase." *Taipei Times.* July 8, 2010: 1.

———. "Group calls for purchases to scupper refineries plan." *Taipei Times.* June 25, 2010: 2.

———. "Miaoli destroys farmland for science park." *Taipei Times.* June 29, 2010: 3.

Murphy, Patrick. *Ecocritical Explorations in Literary and Cultural Studies.* Plymouth: Lexington, 2010.

Shiva, Vandana. *Earth Democracy. Justice, Sustainability, and Peace.* Cambridge, MA: South End P, 2005.

———. "Homeless in the 'Global Village.'" Shiva and Mies. 98–107.

Shiva, Vandana and Maria Mies. *Ecofeminism.* London: Zed Books, 1993.

Sivaraksa, Sulak. *The Wisdom of Sustainability: Buddhist Economics for the 21st Century.* Kihei, Hawaii: Koa Books, 2009.

Steingraber, Sandra. *Living Downstream: A Scientist's Personal Investigation of Cancer and the Environment.* New York: Vintage, 1998.

Wang, Flora and Iok-sin Loa. "Legislature passes farm villages act." *Taipei Times.* July 15, 2010: 1.

Wu, Sheng. "Black Soil." In *Poetry Anthology.* Taipei: Hong Fang Books, 2000. 222–24.

———. "Don't Sigh When You Go Out." In *Poetry Anthology.* 244–47.

———. "I can only write a poem for you." *Business Weekly.* June 28, 2010: 116–17.

———. "Loss." In *Poetry Anthology.* 285–87.

———. "My dear hometown." *Liberty Times.* July 18, 2011: D11.

———. "Strive for whose economics? Satisfy whose belly?" *China Times.* September 20, 2010: A14.

9

Sense of Wilderness, Sense of Time

Mingyi Wu's Nature Writing and the Aesthetics of Change

Shiuhhuah Serena Chou

Taiwanese writer Mingyi Wu (吳明益, b. 1974) has garnered widespread scholarly attention for his perfection of Taiwanese nature writing. His nature writing *The Book of Lost Butterflies* (迷蝶誌—*Midiezhi*, 2001), *The Dao of Butterflies* (蝶9053—Diedao, 2003), and *So Much Water So Close to Home* (家離水邊那麼近—*Jiali shuibian name-jin*, 2007) enjoyed wide circulation and received numerous literary awards.[1] Celebrating "the experience of 'wilderness,' if not 'wildness'" (著眼在野性—wildness, 而僅止於荒野—wilderness),[2] Wu attempts to localize the nature writing form and turn this Western literary genre introduced to Taiwan in the early 1980s into a culturally nativized environmental criticism ("Forward" 12). He supplemented "*huangye*" (荒野) with its English equivalent, "wilderness," when delineating a "modern Taiwanese nature writing" (現代台灣自然書寫—*xiandaiziranshusie*), relating, referencing, and reinforcing its English/American origin and value. Huangye or wilderness appears frequently as a readily available ecocritical nomenclature for the whole complex of fantasies surrounding and constituting nature—that is, as an evocative name for the ideal nature of Taiwanese ecocritical imagination. In Wu's nature writing, interestingly, wilderness, as a translated Euro-American concept, has also taken on Taoist and local meanings to suggest an enduring record of and testimony to nature's process of evolution and regeneration. Wu's wilderness, characterized by transience and temporality, symbolizes an aesthetics of change where nature's autonomy constantly resists the reduction of nature to resources. Wilderness not only helps Wu define "modern Taiwanese nature writing," but also offers another dimension to ecocriticism by urging a perception of nature beyond a scale of direct human experience.

Henry David Thoreau's 1862 remark that "in wildness is the preservation of the world" has long inspired writers and activists, cultivating environmental preservation movements worldwide (644). The notion finds favor in Taiwan and in some ways epitomizes Wu's position. Like his American counterparts, Wu foregrounds the notion of "wild reserve" as the type of nature that is most worthy of safeguarding.

Euro-American environmental writers and critics, however, are prompted to reexamine their reading of pristine wilderness when environmental historian William Cronon declared in 1995 that "[t]he time has come to rethink wilderness" (69). In this movement where scholars dedicate themselves to complicating the notion of wilderness, postcolonial ecocritics are most notable for their trenchant critique of ecocriticism's Anglo-American centricity and its appreciation for wilderness without historical differentiation and cultural specificity. As Graham Huggan and Helen Tiffin note in *Postcolonial Ecocriticism: Literature, Animals, Environment* (2010), mainstream environmental studies often "privileges a white male western subject" and "fails to factor cultural difference into supposedly universal environmental and bioethical debates" (3). In a similar vein, Bonnie Roos and Alex Hunt demand the recognition of both the globality of current environmental crises and the transnational economic realities that have created such natural catastrophe (2–3). Documenting a wilderness history of race, class, and gender conflicts, these critics unravel how the configuration of wilderness as moral, ecological sanctuary deprived of change is, in fact, a cultural product of nineteenth-century American nature appreciation and of the subsequent preservation movement. Their investigation of wilderness invites further study of this American idea that has not only defined US environmentalism before the 1960s but has arguably become the most celebrated type of natural landscape among Wu and Taiwanese environmental writers and critics alike.

In their introduction to *Postcolonial Green*, Roos and Hunt most famously declare that "scholars certainly must account for the fact that what it means to be 'postcolonial' or 'green' varies radically in different geographies" (7). One then might ask: what is this wilderness, or *huangye* (荒野), popularized by Taiwanese environmental writers and critics such as Wu in the 1980s and 1990s that has become an integral part of the vocabulary of the so-called *huanjing baohu yundong* (環境保護運動—environmental protection movement)?[3] If the appreciation for the wild and the pristine come to suggest for Wu an objective nature abstracted from human value, how has this American wilderness aesthetics helped shape Taiwanese environmental literature or, more specifically, nature writing? Postcolonial ecocritics Elizabeth DeLoughrey and George B. Handley accentuate the importance of historicization to "our understanding of land and, by extension, the earth" (4). How does this cross-fertilization help Wu address postcolonial economic and cultural imperialism and envision an environmental literature/criticism that foregrounds nature's historical processes?

A highly developed island with the world's sixteenth highest population density (1,730 per square miles) in 2011, Taiwan has designated 8.64 percent of its 13,902 square miles of land for national parks since 1982. The Ministry of Interior has enclosed these natural landscapes and wildlife areas as nature reserves, and yet these national parks seldom register the image of "wilderness" as sacred land in Taiwan as they commonly would in the United States. Although *huangye* first came to the Chinese language sometime between the ninth and sixth centuries BCE in *Shujing* (書經—*Classic of History*), it has not moved beyond the meaning of "desolate fields" until very recently.[4] In the language of everyday conversation, "*daziran*" (大自然—Nature) or "*ziran*" (自然—nature) are terms that describe the non-human: "wilderness" seldom appears in everyday conversation, not so much because of the shortage of primeval forests, but because of the lack of cultural equivalence in Taiwanese/Chinese language and epistemology until its import in the early 1980s. Even now, one most often detects traces of "wilderness" in American-influenced nature writings such as Jiaxiang Wang's *Civilization, Wilderness* (王家祥, 文明荒野— *Wenming Huangye*, 1980), Ka-Shiang Liu's *The Heart of Wilderness* (劉克襄, 荒野之心—*Huangye zhi Xin*, 1986), Ling Fu's *Encountering Wilderness* (凌拂, 與荒野相遇—*Yuhuangye siangyu*, 1999), and Renxiu Xu's *Song of Wilderness* (徐仁修, 荒野有歌—*Huangye you Ge*, 2002), and they are the chief concerns of major environmental conservation and the education nonprofit organization founded by Xu and Weiwen Li (李偉文), The Society of Wilderness (荒野保護協會—*Huangye Baohu Xiehui*, 1995–). "Wilderness" has taken the place of "*daziran*" or "*ziran*" as the ultimate modern symbol of ideal nature in Taiwanese ecocriticism.

The very appearance of Wu's nature essays is something of a curiosity and wonder to Taiwanese readers and writers alike. As Wu himself notes, libraries and bookstores that are unfamiliar with "nature writing" continue to place his "field notes that recount butterflies through words, photographs, and sketches as a mode of life" in the insect or natural science sections (Huang 253).[5] For those Taiwanese writers and critics constantly haunted by the need to explore a new literary form for voicing their environmental concerns under a global capitalist economy, the American imported nature writing that Wu adopted has been the most suitable genre for the development of ecocritical modes of expression. Wu, however, was not the first to adopt and translate this product from abroad into the terms of Taiwanese culture. Capturing communication patterns and behavioral processes of over 30 tropical butterflies of northeastern coastal regions of Taiwan in first-person, nonfiction narratives, Wu followed Liu, Wang, and other nature writers of the 1980s. He carefully documented flora and fauna of Taiwan in nonfiction prose writing often referred to as "*ziran shuxie*" (自然書寫—nature writing). Before Wu's book-length study of nature writing and its move toward localization, Liu traveled, observed, and recorded extensively data on migrant birds, river paths, and vegetation and wildlife of the Taipei basin in personal reflections. His scientific investigations of wilderness in the cosmopolitan Taipei neighborhood where he dwells has customarily won him the title "father of Taiwanese nature writing." In 1996, Liu contends that "Taiwan's nature writing" (*taiwandeziranxiezuo*), in comparison to the tradition of "environmental protection literature" (環保文學—*huanbaowenxue*) and "pastoral literature" (田園文學—*tianyuanwenxue*), is characterized by scienticism.[6] He writes, "[T]he language [of nature writing] is filled with elements from natural science and is more informative. It emphasizes field observation as well as the direct experience and the particular moment of observation" ("Introduction" 34). But even for Liu, Wu's narratives appear to be a "new species" ("New Face" 29).

As Liu remarks, Wu's nature writing is a "new prototype" that finally breaks free from the shackles of the narrowly defined Western nature writing structure. For Liu, Wu has surpassed himself and other Taiwanese writers of the 1980s by integrating "local perspectives" (本土思維—*bentusiwei*) into the naturalist's encounter with the primitive land (野外—*yewai*) ("Encountering" 25). Undertaking the task of unraveling Wu's breakthrough as a "modern Taiwanese nature writer," Liu, like most Taiwanese ecocritics, is dedicated to exploring what nature writing is.[7] His determination to examine local/Taiwanese formulations of nature is nonetheless undermined by his lasting interrogations of the epistemological origins of nature writing,

or the formation of Taiwanese nature *writing*. As DeLoughrey and
Handley comment, "[T]he discourse of nature is a universalizing
one, and thus ecocriticism is particularly vulnerable to naturalizing
dominant forms of environmental discourse, particularly those that
do not fundamentally engage with questions of difference, power,
and privilege" (14). Liu's attention to the representation of wilderness
indeed anticipates Wu's preoccupation with the nature writing genre.
As he continues to promulgate first-person, nonfiction accounts of
first-hand field observations, however, he in fact participates in what
DeLoughrey and Handley point out as "an increasing tendency to
naturalize a dominant American origin for ecological thought, and
by extension a displacement of postcolonial, feminist, ecosocialist, and
environmental justice concerns" (14). When pondering the "mod-
ernness" (現代性—*xiandaixing*) of Taiwanese nature writing in "An
Epistemological Reflection on the Definition and the Discourse of
Contemporary Taiwanese 'Nature Writing'" (一個知識語述的省察：
對台灣當代 "自然寫作" 定義與語述的反思), professor of Chinese literature Yiling Xiao (蕭義玲) confronts the oversimplification of *nature*
writing by Taiwanese ecocritics. She asks, "Does 'nature' refer to the
Western naturalist tradition, or does it implicate a nature-oriented
literature? Does 'nature' buttress a wilderness aesthetics that insists
on a natural landscape that is neither the city nor the country and
neither the land nor the nature that humans depend on for survival?"
(493–94). While this set of questions puts forward a powerful
critique of the belief in the authenticity of nature representation, it
also suggests a possibility for "modern" Taiwanese nature writing.
Yet, question remains for ecocritics: in what ways is Wu's faith in a
naturalist engagement with wilderness "modern"?

The 1980s and 1990s were crucial to the development of
"modern" Taiwanese nature writing and the formulation of Wu's
American-influenced wilderness aesthetics. This was a time when
Taiwan first tasted the fruit of modernization and what seems to
be the success of industrial capitalism.[8] With a population that has
more than doubled since 1945 to close to 15 million, Taiwan in the
1980s witnessed a rapid social and economic change that involved the
structural transition from an agricultural and labor-intensive economy to an export-oriented, capital-intensive system of production.
For American economist Manuel Castells, Taiwan, along with Hong
Kong, Singapore, and South Korea, has become one of the "Four
Asian Tigers" or "Four Asian Dragons" whose exceptional economic
growth in the 1980s impressed the world. For Liu and Wu, the culmi-
nation of economic expansion efforts in the 1980s and 1990s implies

environmental exploitation projects implemented under the banner of developmentalism first by Japanese colonial powers (1895–1945) and later, by the pull of global economic tides.

In the imperial/capitalist thirst for mastery and conquest of land, more importantly, Liu and Wu recognize the root of modern Taiwanese nature writing. Liu, for instance, compiles a series of nineteenth-century European and Japanese travel writings on Taiwan during the late 1980s and takes them as the primary source of inspiration for his nature writing.[9] In *Great Travels in Formosa* (福爾摩沙大旅行—*Fuermosha Daluxing*, 1999), Liu notes, "[T]o recover what the explorers had felt one hundred years ago, I (re)visited almost every spot and took photos of related landmarks. I reconstructed the environment back then so one could learn more about the historical events and feel present in history" (7). Wu, similarly, traces modern Taiwanese nature writing to eighteenth-century Qing Dynasty imperial chronicles and nineteenth-century Euro-Japanese travel narratives in his *Liberating Nature by Writing: Exploration in Modern Nature Writing of Taiwan* published in 2004 (以書寫解放自然: 台灣現代自然書寫的探索). In light of colonial geographical/ecological exploitation, he examines the deteriorating environmental condition of Taiwan in the 1980s and 1990s. For Wu, these accounts are rich in "naturalist information" (自然史材料—*ziranshi cailiao*, 113), show great attention to indigenous tribes (132–33), but offer an "Other" perspective of Taiwan (134–35). He writes, "[W]hat modern Taiwanese nature writers of the 1980s confront is a Formosa that has been drastically altered by various colonial powers" (161). He also introduces questions about the impact of colonialism on the environment through American historian Alfred Crosby's notion of ecological imperialism (154–56) and Lester Milbrath's theory of "dominator society" (167–68). Documenting the postwar capitalist mentality in Taiwan (169–73), questions of social justice, however, remain in the periphery as historical backgrounds to the rise of modern Taiwanese nature writing. Along with Liu and mainstream American ecocritics, Wu's struggles to contextualize nature within the complex global capitalist network, unfortunately, fails to reach beyond the nonhuman and is absent in his creative works.

In both his critical and creative works, Wu is sympathetic toward the colonial legacy and uneven capitalist development. For him, Taiwan in the 1980s and 1990s was desperately in need of a new, authentic type of nature representation—a "modern" Taiwanese environmental literature that operates on an epistemology distinct from traditional Chinese/Taiwanese literature, whose anthropocentrism shares interests with industrialists. The systematic introduction and translation of American nature writing classics such as Thoreau's *Walden* (trans. 1990), *The Maine Woods* (trans. 1999), *A Week on the Concord* (trans. 1999), John Muir's *My First Summer in the Sierra* (trans. 1998), Aldo Leopold's *A Sand County Almanac and Sketches Here and There* (trans. 1987), Rachel Carson's *The Silent Spring* (trans. 1997), Annie Dillard's *Pilgrim at Tinker Creek* (trans. 2000), and Edward Abbey's *The Journey Home* (trans. 2000) in the 1990s served the Taiwanese appetite for nature retreat and the need for environmental solutions. Recognizing the limits of traditional literary genres and the lack of ecocritical vocabulary in Taiwanese/Mandarin/Chinese dialect for delineating contemporary environmental crises, writers and ecocritics experimented with eastern nature writing as a "modern" mode of representation; for them, nature writing's insistence on ecological sciences and wilderness aesthetics engenders a position beyond anthropocentrism. An attentive reader may easily discover that Wu very often begins each of his chapters on Taiwanese ecocriticism with an epigraph, a translated passage, of an American environmental classic, and that quotations from Euro-American sources also punctuate each page of his creative writing.[10] These limited and selected translations offered Wu and writers and critics who attempt to modernize and bring up to date Taiwanese environmental discourse fresh insights and accessible methods. Although these Western texts commonly served to inspire Taiwanese environmental literature and ecocriticism and functioned commonly as places of departure, they have helped construct a "modern Taiwanese nature writing" based on a wilderness aesthetics.

In the steps of his predecessors, Wu first developed from an American-imported nature writing form and wilderness aesthetics a "modern nature writing." In the introduction to the 2003 *An Anthology of Taiwanese Nature Writing* (台灣自然寫作選), the first Taiwanese environmental anthology, Wu declares that this modern Taiwanese nature writing, grounded in the experience of wilderness, is a first-person, nonfiction narrative that seeks to explore the nonhuman nature in objective scientific analyses (12–13). The 23 pieces of "modern Taiwanese nature writing" in this literary collection all consist of the following elements:

> First, nature no long plays supporting roles or serves as settings; it has become a leading figure. Second, a nature writer must immerse himself/herself in nature. The experience of focusing, observing, recording, exploring, and discovering are "nonfictional," and are essential to

his/her creative process. I should also emphasize one's experience of nature is grounded in "wilderness," if not, "wildness." Third, modern nature writing depends on the exercising of scientific knowledge such as biology, natural science, natural history, modern ecology, environmental ethics. Fourth, a nature writer should avoid a human-centered ethical and aesthetical position and moved beyond "anthropocentrism." Lastly, nature writing is a personal narrative. (12–13)

Here Wu argues that modern nature writing should first come under scrutiny through the lenses of naturalists: while first-hand observational research ensures the accountability and authority of representations, the expressive purity of such scientific knowledge complements the naturalness of wilderness. The "modern Taiwanese nature writing" that he sketched is not just any environment narrative: it is one that builds narrowly upon the supposed authenticity of the naturalist tradition and the American nature writing form. The scientific objectivism that modern life sciences conveys, in other words, connotes a sense of authenticity and transparency that functions as binary opposites to the anthropocentrism of both traditional Taiwanese and Chinese environmental writings and the economy-driven commercial society of the 1980s in Taiwan. As Wu explains a year later in his dissertation-turned-book *Liberating Nature by Writing*, "the '*zhenshixing*' (factualness), or the '*feixugou*' (nonfiction) character" ("真實性" (factualness), 或說 "非虛構性" (nonfiction)) of the Western field observations make modern nature writing possible (20).[11] All other Taiwanese/Chinese environmental writings belong to the category of "nature-related writing" (自然相關書寫—*ziranxiangguanshuxie*, 84).

Wu's insistence on the natural sciences and subsequent wilderness experience as constitutive of "modern Taiwanese nature writing" also evinces a faith in the moral superiority of "wilderness." As a timeless and unchangeable vacuum outside of human value systems, wilderness, for Wu, distinguishes "modern Taiwanese nature writing" from traditional Chinese travel writing and classic *tianyuan* (田園詩—field and garden) and *shanshui* (山水詩—mountain and stream) poetry where nature functions as the backdrop to human drama and adventures ("Forward" 84). As an embodiment of a universal order of things, Wu's wilderness encodes time. Even though Wu adds that one must not dwell on the essay form of nature representation, his commitment to "animal novels" (動物小說—*dongwu xiaoshuo*) and "science novels" (科學小說—*kexue xiaoshuo*) persists in the celebration of the nonhuman and hence a seemingly pristine notion of nature and an authentic form nature representation. As writer Jiaxiang Wang commented in 1992, "*ziran wenxue* (natural writing) is also called *huangyewenxue* (wilderness)" (19A).[12] Though Wang mistranslated "nature writing," his remark nonetheless reveals the obsession of a Taiwanese nature writer/ecocritic such as Wu with the "naturalness" of wilderness environments and nature representation.

In *The Truth of Ecology* (2003), ecocritic Dana Phillips ardently calls environmental criticism of the 1960s a "utopian discourse" that romanticizes ecological values and ecological forms of representation (42). He writes, "ecology has come to be identified in the popular mind with such values as balance, harmony, unity, purity, health, and economy. It's fair to say that many people regard these values, however utopian they may be, as all buy indisputable and as all buy synonymous with the very word 'ecology'" (42). In the search for "modern Taiwanese nature writing," Wu more than once proclaims the role an ecologically grounded "wilderness" plays in substantiating allegations against the shallow anthropocentric systems of domination, including environmental protectionist enterprises in Taiwan that continue believing in the omniscient power of the technological control of nature. Like early American ecocritics, Wu believes a wilderness of harmony and order challenges the disorder brought forth by industrialization. That is not to say, however, that Wu is committed to the notion of wilderness in the American sense of pristine areas untouched by humans and absent from history. Neither does he turn to what postcolonial ecocritics Elizabeth DeLoughrey and George B. Handley note as a postcolonial position that participates in the depiction of nature in "historical process" (4). Wu, in fact, forges for modern Taiwanese nature writing a localized concept of wilderness that fully engages in the larger cosmic process of time, in what seems nature's own process of regeneration and change.

Much of his first book on nature writing, *The Book of Lost Butterflies*, points to the ideological hypocrisy of Taipei butterfly conservation and with the exportation of the Magellan Birdwing butterfly (*Troides magellanus*) specimens during the Japanese rule (1895–1945; 56–57). The colonial butterfly collectors claimed their scientific uses were no different from Taipei butterfly conservatories who "mail-ordered and shipped butterflies from southern Taiwan in the name of nature preservation" (38–39). Butterflies are objects of display and victims of human valuation. Like "facsimiles of Cezanne" (45), engineered botanical gardens that "harvest [nature] as games" only further reinforce the impossibility of replicating primeval forests as habitats for butterflies (45). "Man-made nature" could not "create" nature in its original state, though humans also form important parts of nature (*Dao* 49). The Chinese title of *The Book of Lost Butterflies* (*Midiezhi*) slips from pun to pun with the first word "*mi*" (迷) suggesting the obsession with (迷戀—*mi-lian*) butterflies, the mysterious (迷樣—*mi-yang*) butterflies, and the lost (迷蝶—*mi-die*) butterflies who cross borders (*Lost* 171–73). Eager and desperate, Taiwanese nature enthusiasts often overlook how they are in reality the ones who trespass boundaries when admiring the evanescent butterflies.

For Wu, wilderness is nature's purest force; it is Tao—nature's original passage. "The artistic patterns tattooed on the wings of butterflies are the true touches of the wild, and the freehand *pomo* brushwork of life," Wu once wrote (139). For Wu, butterflies and rivers are not only embodiments of the material wilderness but manifestations of its wild essence. Nature's wildness redeems Wu's longing for the ever receding horizon of wilderness in Taiwan. Omnipresent, wildness crosses boundaries and the limits of material. Wu finds wildness in butterflies who await their metamorphoses to realize the different stages of life and to reproduce and multiply even in urban terrains (154, 70), in "deserted land" (荒地—*huangdi*) on campuses where yellow butterfly-like flowers blossom, and in the "lonely, horrifying, untamable, beast-like" and "unconscious-like" ocean (*Water* 205, 127).

Wu's second book on nature writing (*The Dao of Butterflies*, published in 2003) again takes on wildness as nature's untamed energy, but with a twist. Here in his struggle to construct a "private wildness reserve" (90), Wu moves beyond his preoccupation with details of his search for "routes" and "pathways" of butterflies (道路—*daolu*; 276) to investigate "the principles and philosophies" (道理—*daoli*; 278) of nature. "Tao," the fundamental nature of the universe, alludes to the ancient Chinese philosopher Lao Tzu's *Tao Te Ching* and suggests a larger cosmic order, constantly changing and yet ineffable to humans. As the passageway to existence, Wu's butterflies constitute a wildness, a unified organic structure of natural, unadulterated law, very much like the traditional Chinese notion of *ziran*.[13]

In *So Much Water So Close to Home*, Wu's third attempt to represent wilderness, the bodies of water represent nature's agency and its "divine savageness" (神聖蠻荒—*shensengmanhuang*; 262). When critiquing the desire of many to "control" the Meilun River by establishing dikes and channels, Wu warns of how this stream of water in its original state is the source of both nature's creative and destructive powers. Rivers, oceans, and lakes nourish "economy, culture, art, and memory" (21); and yet, for him, "the Meilun River, like all rivers and creeks, is not always gentle; she gets hot-tempered and angry and becomes hard to understand and please, too. From a topographic or climatic perspective, flooding and diverting waters are the norm" (33). Here Wu anthropomorphizes the Meilun River, unaware of his sexist language when referring to nature as "her" (*ta*) and attributes feelings to nature. "Nothing could stop the will of the flood from the mountain, which washes away ditches, power poles, and walls," Wu argues (90). Nature's spontaneity and wildness maintain a sense of wildness that reveals a nature devoid of conscious premeditation and intervention. Waters in their wild condition, uncontaminated and uncorrupted, evoke the Taoist notion of *wu-wei*—"not" or "non-" "'action,' 'making,' 'doing,' 'striving,' or 'straining,' or 'busyness'" (Watts 19). Wu's waters, as a state of wholeness that renounces the dichotomization of self and other, human and nonhuman, correspond to Lao Tzu's *Tao Te Ching*:

> The supreme good is like water,
> which nourishes all things without trying to.
> It is content with the low places that people disdain.
> Thus it is like that Tao [Dao]
> ...
> In thinking, keep to the simple.
> In conflict, be fair and generous.
> It governing, don't try to control.
> ...
> When you are content to be simply yourself
> and don't compare or compete,
> everybody will respect you. (8)[14]

Waters attest to binarizations and control, blurring ethnic differences. Wu notes, "I cannot not tell which of the children playing in the rivers are Han Chinese and which are indigenous Amis. Rivers blur the borders and boundaries between races and between the rich and the poor" (*Water* 38). In Wu's nature writings, one sees butterflies and various streams of water in detailed descriptions, sketches, photographs, and indexes of professional and amateur field study. The Latin scientific names, identification keys, and field notes present a foreign look, but these wild butterflies and waters convey a sense of nature and a wilderness aesthetics that is particularly "Taiwan."[15]

As symbols of the courses of change and in the contingencies of time and space, Wu's wilderness constitutes an important part of the local struggle for cultural and political recognition. Wu, in fact, began his career as a Nativist short story writer determined to define Taiwan against the authoritarian hegemony of the Kuomingtang (KMT) regime and the Kuomingtang's mainland Chinese cultural influence in Taiwan. In the foreword to *An Anthology of Taiwanese Nature Writing*, Wu indicates that a nature writer's ecological concerns share interests with Taiwanese nativist writers who switch to their native language to retell local stories of rooted communities in the late 1970s. The environmental movement of the 1980s was an extension of the earlier *Xiangtu wenxue yundong* (鄉土文學運動—Nativist literary movement) dedicated to the exploration of histories of *xiang* (鄉—home), memories of *tu* (土—land), and the "place we inhabited" ("Forward" 15). Ecological exploitations of nature parallel the history of colonization and development. The subordination of the earth was part and parcel of the oppression of the cultural and political structures of colonized societies: while Nativists view "Taiwan" in terms of the human subject under postcolonial conditions, nature writers examine the nonhuman in the context of developmentalism. Both Taiwanese Nativists and nature writers were concerned with the survival of the local and the indigenous through an understanding of the historical contingencies that continue to shape their experience of the world. As Wu demonstrates, the endeavors of Taiwanese ecocritics are derived from a "geographical and historical identification with Taiwan" (15). Calling attention to the violence of ecological colonialism, Wu attempts to connect ecocritical and postcolonial critique.

In Wu's nature writing trilogy, one can easily discern a heightened interest in the historicity and temporality of nature. The notion of wilderness as spontaneously self-generating life processes evokes images of natural forces that drive the course of time, be it historic, mythic, or evolutionary. Repeatedly, Wu prompts an understanding of nature in terms of history, and notably through the rewriting of the particular and the local within the "grand narratives" of colonization and environmental expropriations. Wu, for instance, first depicts the Jungle Queen butterfly (*Stichophthalma howqua formosana*) as a displayed specimen and contextualizes it as a victim of a history of expedition and discovery that reaches back into early-twentieth-century Taiwan (*Lost* 158–62). Finding the emigration history of these butterflies in Taiwan longer than the history of humans, Wu raises questions regarding land, ownership, and access (*Dao* 198). He tells of the loss and survival stories of various members of nature under human domination in an attempt to critique a master discourse of development. Nature also charts time periods and documents a history of environmental colonization. While Jungle Queens mark our age of extinction as "an era where Jungle Queens no longer blossom like chrysanthemums" (*Lost* 162), the Dwarf Crows butterfly species (*Euploea tulliolux koxinga*) characterize the current generation as one where humans no longer possess any memories of home (118). As Elizabeth DeLoughrey and George B. Handley suggests, "Place encodes time, suggesting that histories embedded in the land and sea have always provided vital and dynamic methodologies for understanding the transformative impact of empire and the anti-colonial epistemologies it tries to suppress" (4). Wu's butterflies may not be a place, but they are certainly sites of colonial cultural and material consumption.

In wilderness's purity and autonomous forces, Wu recognizes not only the nonhuman and hence the natural, but also the time and rhythm of the universe. Wu, however, is one of the few nature writers in Taiwan who delves into the concept of a nature embedded in time and history. In his nature writing, Wu prioritizes the position of butterflies and rivers within an historical timeframe. He also prioritizes (within this same time frame) their relations to other species, communities, and systems. Organisms and natural objects are part of the larger span of history across generations, whether on a mythic or evolutionary level. They are not only active agents of a larger historic passage, but they embody the temporal order of the universe. Celebrating Common Rose caterpillars (*Pachliopta aristolochiae interpositus*) waiting with patience for the right time to metamorphose, Wu depicts a sense of wilderness that trespasses human-induced meanings and values (152–53). Wu's portrayal of Taiwan reveals wilderness in a constant state of becoming on a time scale of creation and extinction: "Taiwan is a compound for all the living and nonliving on the island, a noun for endless movements. Every day, a part dies and another is reborn, becoming more 'Taiwan'" (*Dao* 239). For Wu, Bamboo Treebrown butterfly species (*Lethe europa pavida*) and wilderness provides the secret gateway to the mythic and poetic, reminding him of "Tiziano Vecellio, the golden Europa, and the cunning eyes of Zeus" (*Lost* 84). One should contemplate nature and its characteristics, behavior patterns, and evolutions in relation to the larger mythic and cultural sense of time: "[W]hat karma has made the Bamboo Treebrown inherit the name 'Europa?' Is it because of those eye-like spots on their wings that stare at you from all directions? Or is it because of the half moon-shape patterns on its forewings" (86-87)?

In "The Ambivalence toward the Mythic and the Modern: Wu Mingyi's Short Stories," Liangya Liou (劉亮雅) reveals a merging of the modern and the mythic in Wu's nativist short stories (119). Professor of English and Taiwanese literature, Liou is one of the first critics in Taiwan to make the connections between Wu's nativist and environmental roots. As she points out, one first uncovers mysteries of nature in modern times through scientific knowledge, though he/she eventually notices the inadequacy of such a learning process and hence again returns to rituals, dances, music, and other magical methods of imagining the environment (100). The juxtaposition of the mythic and the scientific in Wu's nature writing exemplifies what Liou notes as an ambivalence toward the mythic and the modern. Butterflies and rivers, as embodiments of nature's wildness and primordiality, enchant a Taiwanese generation devastated by the homogenizing forces of global capitalist economy; they invite dislocated Taiwanese urban dwellers to know nature intimately and imaginatively through the senses. Butterflies and the various bodies of water, in the eyes of modern ecology, also appeal to a Taiwanese society that strives to move beyond anthropocentrism as a method of perceiving nature that is authentic, objective, and universal. In Wu's nature writing, while the primitive wilderness commands a sense of wonderment, modern science, as a body of knowledge of inquiry and objectivity, suggests a universal truth that locates time and space in a global dimension. His characterization of nature as an autonomous entity grounded in time demonstrates for ecocritics an aesthetics of change that challenges the representation of nature in developmentalist history as merely inert object for manipulations and instrumental use. But here this scientific nature, like that of the mythic nature, also projects nature at a universal scale of time and history.

Wu's wilderness as a temporal entity highlights a relation with nature defined by spatiality—by one's understanding of nature's rootedness in communities; the temporality of wilderness also raises pertinent questions over the scale of time and space when foregrounding nature as participants in historical process. Inspecting the coastlines of Hualien, Wu identifies spatiotemporal scale as crucial to determining the scope, intensity, and changes in natural systems. The apparent regularity or randomness, balance or imbalance, and order and chaos of nature are relative to a particular scale or viewpoint.

In Wu's butterflies and water, one detects wilderness intimately entrenched in time; butterflies and water, in fact, call attention to what Professor of Environmental Studies Mitchell Thomashow indicates as "the scope of observation." In *Bringing the Biosphere Home: Learning to Perceive Global Environmental Change* (2002), Thomashow provides a series of observational approaches to explore scale and perception for members of fleeting communities in a biosphere of "ecological transience" that shed light on the global, cosmic scope that Wu situates his butterflies and various bodies of water in (170). In his discussion of naturalists Tom Wessels and John Hanson Mitchell, Thomashow writes,

> Of great interest is how they experiment with scale as a means to expand perceptual awareness. Stepping between landscapes and time frames provides a means of comparison and perspective...Scale is a conceptual language that allows for the amplification of perception. It's a tool for detecting patterns of connection across the boundaries of ecology, geography, history and psyche. (93)

As with Thomashow, scale for Wu provides an angle into processes where nature's parts integrate into a whole and the whole become parts again (*Dao* 240), into a cosmos that lives through its own "rule of wildness" (240–41). Nature as a self-regulating wild agent raises questions regarding the scale of time in environmental preservation and restoration for Taiwanese ecocriticism: what was the state of nature before it was degraded? What can be learned from past failures and successes of restoring nature? How has the endeavor of environmental protection changed over the years?

Wu's butterflies and waters reveal the complex and discursive literary traditions through which Wu formulates his conceptions of wilderness. Alluding to both Euro-American and Taiwanese perspectives of nature, butterflies and waters are products of miscegenation—a mixed race of, on the one hand, the naturalist and the wilderness aesthetics of the West, and Taoist and the local Taiwanese culture expressions, on the other. The layering of multiple images, languages, and voices creates a uniquely Taiwanese ecocriticism based on wilderness: butterflies and waters are uneven but potentially creative hybrids whose sense of time constantly challenges ecological notions of nature as a balanced, harmonious order. Through images of nature as change, Wu's wilderness confronts popular belief in an orderly nature of balance as seen in both Taiwan and the United States. "Change" not only demands a more critical understanding of the process of nature but also urges a more complex reading of nature in a cosmic scale of time.

NOTES

1. English titles of all three nature writings are Wu's. In the foreword to the book *So Much Water So Close to Home*, Wu indicates that he borrowed the title from Raymond Carver's short story of the same name, inspired by the image this simple line provides (5). *The Book of Lost Butterflies* is a winner of Taipei Literary Award (台北文學獎) in the year 2000 and

was voted one of the 60 Best Books of the New Century by *Wenshun* (文訊—2004). *The Dao of Butterflies* is a winner of *China Times Open Book Award for Best Chinese Writing* (中國時報開卷中文創作類, 2003). *So Much Water So Close to Home* had undergone three editions since 2007. It received numerous awards, including *China Times* Open Book Award for Best Chinese Writing (2007) and the Golden Ding Award of the Government Information Office of the Executive Yuan (2008).

2. The translations bracketed are original. In defining the nature writing genre, he provided the English words for *yexing* (wildness) and *huangye* (wilderness) in his texts, alluding directly to its Euro-American origin.

3. Translations of Mandarin sources are mine unless otherwise indicated.

4. See "The Charge to Yue" (說命下) of the chapter "Document of Shang [Dynasty]" (商書), *Shuing*: "I used to learn from Gan Pan, but then escaped to find shelter in *huangye*" (台小子舊學于甘盤, 既乃遯于荒野, 入宅于河).

5. "Field notes that capture butterflies through words, photographs, and sketches as a mode of life" is subtitle to *The Book of Lost Butterflies*.

6. *Tianyuanwenxuie* is a traditional Chinese poetic genre/mode that depicts the simplicity of country living like that of pastoral literature of the West.

7. Studies that attempt to reconstruct the genre around the 1980s and 1990s are extensive. Although most of these are graduate theses that remain unpublished, they are frequently referenced by students and ecocritics because of the lack of ecocritical research in Taiwan. Notable pioneering studies that sought new possibilities during this period include Jiaxiang Wang's "The Nature Writing and Taiwanese Land that I know" (我所知道的自然寫作與台灣土地, 1992), Jianyi Chen's "Discovering a New Literary Tradition—Nature Writing" (陳健一, 發現一個新的文學傳統), Ka-Shiang Liu's "An Introduction to Taiwanese Nature Writing" (台灣的自然寫作初語, 1996), Yiming Jian's MA thesis *A Study of Taiwanese "Nature Writing" from 1981–1997* (簡義明, 台灣 "自然寫作" 研究:以1981–1997為範圍, 1997), and Youmei Xu's dissertation *A Study of Contemporary Taiwanese Nature Writing* (許尤美, 台灣當代自然寫作研究, 1998).

8. For an average of 9 percent GNP rate advancement between 1952 and 1980, however, Taiwan had paid a high environmental price, including pollution and biodiversity loss. In particular, in the 1960s and early 1970s, Taiwan produced an average of 5,300 cubic feet of lumber, but suffered from the massive loss of forest land. The scarcity of natural resources in Taiwan also led to its dependence on nuclear energy. Currently, three active nuclear plants and six reactors supply 8.1 percent of national energy, while oil and coal produce another 81.1 percent. Renewable sources account for merely 0.5 percent of the total energy consumption in Taiwan—the fifteenth largest consumer of nuclear power in the world.

9. Selections of travel writings include *Across Formosa: Foreign Travels in Taiwan* (橫越福爾摩沙: 外國人在台灣的旅行—*Hengyue Fuermosha: Waiguoren zai Taiwan de Luxing*, 1989) and *Exploring the Back Mountain: Nineteenth-Century Foreigner Travels in the East Coast, Taiwan* (後山探險: 十九世紀外國人在台灣東海岸的旅行—*Houshantanxian: Shijiushiji Waiguoren zai Taiwandonghaian de Luxing*, 1992).

10. In *Liberating Nature by Writing*, for instance, Wu introduces his chapters with American ecocritical statements from Frank Stewart's *A Natural History of Nature Writing* (Chapter 1: "Defining Modern Taiwanese Nature Writing"), Abbey's *The Journey Home* (Chapter 2: "Characteristics of Modern Nature Writing"), Thoreau's "Walking" (Chapter 3: "Western Nature Writing"), Dillard's *Pilgrim at Tinker Creek* (Chapter 7: "Photographic Images in Modern Nature Writing"), and Aldo Leopold's *A Sand County Almanac* (Chapter 9: "Land Ethics in Nature Writing"). Another example would be that Wu borrowed the title "So Much Water So Close to Home" from Raymond Carver's short story of the same name. Wu himself notes his interest in the images Carver's title provides and is well aware that his book has nothing to do with Carver's short story (*Water* 5).

11. The translation of the title is Wu's. The English translations bracketed in the quotation are also original.

12. Ibid.

13. *Ziran* is the Chinese equivalent of "nature," but *ziran* implies the self-generating life process of nature. For an in-depth discussion of Chinese notion of "nature," see, for instance, Weiming Tu's "The Continuity of Being: Chinese Visions of Nature" collected in K. Baird Callicott and Roger T. Ames's *Nature in Asian Traditions of Through: Essays in Environmental Philosophy* (2001). Albany: SUNY P, 2001.

14. Translations of *Tao Te Ching* are by Stephen Mitchell.

15. As early the late nineteenth century, Taiwan has enjoyed its fame as the Kingdom of Butterflies. Naturalists East and West have identified over 380 butterfly species throughout history. Colonial travel narratives such as British biologist Alfred Russel Wallace and Frederic Moore's *Life of Lepidoterous Insects Collected at Takow, Formosa, by Mr. Robert Swinhoe* (1866), Canadian Presbyterian missionary George Leslie Mackey's *From Far Formosa: The Island, its People and Missions* (1896), and Japanese naturalist Kano Tado's *High Altitude Butterflies in Taiwan* (1930) first forged the indissoluble link between butterflies and Taiwan. Taiwan, with its coastline stretching 1,566 kilometers and rivers flowing over 68.4 percent of the terrain, is also a place, in Wu's words, "so much water, so close to home."

WORKS CITED

Cronon, William. "The Trouble with Wilderness; or Getting Back to the Wrong Nature." In *Uncommon Ground: Rethinking the Human Place in*

Nature. Ed. William Cronon. New York: W. W. Norton & Company, 1996.

DeLoughrey, Elizabeth and George B. Handley. "Introduction: Toward an Aesthetics of the Earth." In *Postcolonial Ecologies: Literatures of the Environment*. Ed. Elizabeth DeLoughrey and George B. Handley. Oxford: Oxford UP, 2011.

Huang, Tsungchieh. "Through the Passage of Butterflies: An Interview of Wu Mingyi". *Sixiang* 11 (2009): 251–62.

Huggan, Graham and Helen Tiffin. *Postcolonial Ecocriticism: Literature, Animals, Environment*. New York: Routledge, 2010.

Lao Tzu. *Tao Te Ching: A New English Version*. Trans. Stephen Mitchell. New York: HarperCollins, 2006.

Liou, Liangya. "The Ambivalence toward the Mythic and the Modern: Wu Mingyi's Short Stories." *Tamkang Review* 39.1 (December 2008): 97–124.

Liu, Ka-Shiang. "Encountering Aurora Swallowtail". In *The Dao of Butterflies*. Taipei: Fish & Fish, 2003.

———. *Great Travels in Formosa*. Taipei: Yushan Publishing, 1999.

———. "An introduction to Taiwan's nature writing". *United Daily News* January 4–5, 1996: 34.

———. "A New Face of Nature Writing". In *The Book of Lost Butterflies*. Taipei: Rey Field, 2000.

Phillips, Dana. *The Truth of Ecology: Nature, Culture, and Literature in America*. Oxford: Oxford UP, 2003.

Roos, Bonnie and Alex Hunt. "Introduction: Narratives of Survival, Sustainability, and Justice." In *Postcolonial Green: Environmental Politics and World Narratives*. Ed. Bonnie Roos and Alex Hunt. Charlottesville: U of Virginia P, 2010.

Thomshaow, Mitchell. *Bringing the Biosphere Home: Learning to Perceive Global Environmental Change*. Cambridge, MA: MIT P, 2002.

Thoreau, Henry David. "Walking." In *Henry David Thoreau: Walden and Other Writings*. Ed. Brooks Atkinson. 1962. New York: Modern Library, 1992.

Wang, Jiaxiang. "The nature writing and Taiwanese land that I know." *Zili Evening News* August 28, 1992: 19A.

Watts, Alan. *The Way of Zen*. New York: Vintage, 1985.

Wu, Mingyi. *The Book of Lost Butterflies*. Taipei: Rey Field, 2000.

———. *The Dao of Butterflies*. Taipei: Fish & Fish, 2003.

———. "Forward." *An Introduction to Taiwanese Nature Writing*. Taipei: Fish & Fish, 2003.

———. "Introduction: Thoughts on the Intricacies of Nature Writing." In *An Anthology* of *Taiwanese Nature Writing*. Ed. Wu Mingyi. Taipei: Fish & Fish, 2003.

———. *Liberating Nature by Writing: Exploration in Modern Nature Writing of Taiwan*. Taipei: Da-An, 2004.

———. "The Processes of Dialogue: Taiwanese Nonfictional Nature-Oriented Literature". In *Issues on Twentieth-Century Taiwanese Literature II: Creative Genre and Subjects*. Ed. Dawei Chen and Yiwen Zhong. Taipei: Wanhuanlou, 2006.

———. *So Much Water So Close to Home*. Taipei: Fish & Fish, 2007.

Xiao, Yling. "An Epistemological Reflection the Definition and the Discourse of Contemporary Taiwanese 'Nature Writing.'" *Qinghuaxuebao* 37.2 (2007): 491–533.

10

ANG LI'S *THE BUTCHER'S WIFE (SHAFU)* AND TAIWANESE ECOCRITICISM

Kathryn Yalan Chang

As a bridge between the physical environment and literary texts, ecocriticism—a term coined by William Rueckert in 1978—is composed of two parts: "*Eco* is derived from the Greek *oikos* (home, nature) and *criticism* comes from *kritikos* (to judge)" (Tsai, "Ecocriticism" 347). Examining the meanings of "home" and "place" is particularly important for Taiwanese ecocriticism at this stage in its development. In his 2011 summer course on "Current Trends in International Ecocriticism and Environmental Literature" in Taiwan, Scott Slovic argued that "place" as well as "animal" (animality) are two essential and dominant paradigms within environmental literature, ecocritical thinking, and more broadly, the environmental humanities. As ecocriticism has internationalized, two competing views on place have emerged, defining a controversy between bioregionalism and the local versus ecocosmopolitanism and the global. On the one hand, Tom Lynch advocates for a bioregionalist perspective, seeking to "develop and maintain diverse vernacular cultures—their music, food, rituals, and other traditions—against the spread of global monoculture" (19). Instead of subscribing to parochialism, Lynch promotes a new sense of bioregionalism, conscious of the interconnectedness of all places. On the other hand, Ursula K. Heise argues for ecocosmopolitanism, explaining that "the point of an eco-cosmopolitan critical project...would be to go beyond the aforementioned 'ethics of proximity'" (62). Lawrence Buell agrees, explaining that "fewer and fewer of the world's population live out their lives in locations that are not shaped to a great extent by translocal—ultimately global—forces"

(63). Attempting to bridge the local and the global, Buell proposes a "postmodern, place-based identity" or a "multivocal" and "multilocal" identity (92) as most descriptive for discussions of place and belonging in an age of globalization.

But feminist ecocritics aren't so sure; they point out significant exclusions and omissions from both bioregionalism and ecocosmopolitanism. As Greta Gaard asks, "[W]here are the analytical frameworks for gender, species, and sexuality?" ("New" 2). Gaard draws on feminist bioregionalists Michelle Summer Fike and Sarah Kerr, who acknowledge that the intensified focus on reconnecting and grounding oneself in a place enables bioregionalists to celebrate "the physicality of human beings as creatures of the earth" (24), but urge bioregionalists to redefine the notion of "home" in consideration of women's experiences. Fike and Kerr also warn that "if bioregionalism does not incorporate ecofeminist concerns, there is a danger of revaluing a home that is no different from the one that restricts so many women's lives today" (26). From an ecofeminist standpoint, globalization (and by association, "eco-cosmopolitanism") offers little hope of ecological, economic, or political justice, since its menu of "technology, capitalism, militarism, racism, and imperialism—[simply lists] the products of a globalizing patriarchy that exploits and subordinates women as it destroys the environment" (Robertson and Scholte 349). Only by taking gender and nature into account can we find sustainable solutions to the environmental crisis caused by global patriarchy. Bridging the new bioregionalism with a feminist ecocritical awareness of ecoglobalism, this essay offers a reading of Taiwanese writer Ang Li's *The Butcher's Wife* (*Shafu*) (1983),[1] revealing the entangled connections between gender politics and the fear of the natural environment (ecophobia) through the examination of gender, food animals, and dreams.

THE REIFICATION OF TAIWANESE ECOCRITICISM

Like American ecocriticism in its early stages, Taiwanese ecocriticism maintains a high level of interest in nature writing that celebrates the natural beauty of Taiwan, and reportage, a hybrid of journalism and literature. Unlike American ecocriticism, however, Taiwanese ecocriticism has not yet been developed, despite its manifestations in "Taiwan's ecoliterature" (Cheng), and "Taiwan's nature-oriented literature" (Yang; Wu). As Greg Garrard has observed, "Japanese, Korean and Taiwanese ecocritics have tended to align with developments in America" (32). But Patrick Murphy argues, "In order

to widen the understanding of readers and critics, it is necessary to
reconsider the privileging of certain genres and also the privileging of
certain national literatures and certain ethnicities within those national
literatures" (58). International ecocriticism and Taiwanese ecocriticism alike are moving toward a cross-cultural comparative framework
that goes beyond one specific genre or nation.

Taiwanese ecocriticism is rooted in Taiwan's ecoliterature and
ecocritical scholarship and thus theorizing Taiwanese ecocriticism
requires discussing its history as ecoliterature. In the long history of
Taiwan under colonialism, Hsien-yu Cheng discusses the relationships
between colonialism and Taiwanese ecoliterature. In his definition
and explication of Taiwan's ecoliterature, he criticizes some writers
for lacking a wide range of historical perspectives although their texts
may "each hold a different discourse towards nature and ecology"
(Cheng 4). He then gives credit to one indigenous writer, Syapen
Jipeaya, because his text "construct[s] eco-literature with a historical
axis based on local Taiwan geography (through the knowledge and
experience of ancestors)" (4). The definition of Taiwan's ecoliterature
that Cheng offers in this article shows part of the scope of ecoliterature
in Taiwan: nature writing/literature and indigenous knowledge(s) of
this island's geography.[2]

Since 2000, ecocriticism in Taiwan has been gaining the recognition of Taiwan's academic circles through several national and international ecological conferences and ecocritical publications.[3] One of
the distinctive trends in Taiwanese ecocriticism since the 1980s is the
popularization of the genre of nature writing. Prominent among the
early research, Ming-tu Yang's dissertation in English, entitled "From
Love of Nature to Frugal Lifestyles: Nature-Oriented Literature of
Taiwan Since 1981," hoped to draw the attention of Taiwanese literary critics to Taiwan's nature-oriented literature, inspired by Patrick
Murphy's *Farther Afield in the Study of Nature-Oriented Literature*
and his taxonomy[4] expanding the category of nature-oriented literature to include poems, stories, and environmental essays about
Taiwan. Ming-yi Wu's dissertation on "Modern Nature Writing of
Taiwan," aimed at discovering seven prominent Taiwanese nature
writers, including two female writers (Suli Hong and Fu Ling) and the
other five male writers (Ke-hsiang Liu, Jen-hsio Hsu, Yueh-fong Chen,
Jia-xiang Wang, and Hung-chi Lia) in light of the writing skills each
writer applied and how their writings traced the history of Taiwan's
landscapes and the mutually influencing affects between its residents and
lands. This trend parallels the development of US ecocriticism, where
"ecocritics initially focused on American nature writing, the British

Romantics, and environmentally oriented non-fiction" (Bracke and Corporaal 709). Taiwan's ecoliterary works have exhibited people's love and concern for the land of Taiwan, celebrated the beauty of Taiwan's landscape, given voice to species endemic to the island, and only recently have revealed the contemporary environmental problems in relation to the people in Taiwan and across the planet. For example, Han Han and Yi-kung Ma's *We Have Only One Earth* (1983) cannot be overlooked: their book is the first to address the environmental problems of excessive deforestation and hunting in Taiwan.

Yet, at this historical moment, merely praising the beautiful landscapes of Taiwan as shown in early nature writing and in ecological documentaries alike seems insufficient for ecofeminists, animal advocates, and ecocritics alike. While it is developing in scope, to maintain its immediacy and relevance, Taiwanese ecocriticism should not stop at the appreciation of local places, feminist ecocritics argues, but must develop by examining the association of sexism, speciesism, colonialism and ecophobia.

Following Ming-yi Wu's suggestions in "Engaging by Heart? Or Resigning to Fate?"[5] this essay argues that some undeveloped areas and directions could be put into consideration as well: the first is to explore associations among sexism, speciesism, and ecophobia in the literary/cultural texts of Taiwan because violence seldom occurs on one level alone. Second, Taiwan's nature-oriented writings should be more than a "praise-song school" in Michael Cohen's terms (21), and should emphasize both justice and the conceptual connections between various forms of discrimination in cultural narratives (literature or film). Accordingly, this essay brings Taiwan's ecoliterature into dialogue with Euro-American ecocriticism by exploring Ang Li's *Shafu* as a Taiwanese ecocritical text, taking eco/feminist ecocriticism as its referent point, and broadening the development of Taiwanese ecocriticism by reconstructing the relationships among humans and nonhuman species, nature, and culture.

Li's *Shafu* is not in the nature writing tradition that one sees in others' texts[6]; nor does it fit the "praise-song school" of nature writing. Its plot is profoundly disturbing even 30 years after publication, but Li's ideas in relation to sexism and speciesism remain relevant, illuminating associations among ecomasculinism, animality, and species. As a fascinating but a brutal story, *Shafu* portrays the baser animality of humans, gender politics, and animal exploitation. Although characters in *Shafu* do not endorse a "postmodern, place-based identity" or a "multivocal" and "multilocal" identity but rather "a closed community of traditional regionalist imagination" (Buell 92), the narrative still touches on the problems of others (other sexes, other species, other places, other nations) without ignoring the fact of every entity's quintessentially material environment.

As a prolific Taiwanese writer with more than 30 novels to her credit, Li often raises provocative issues and depicts both sexual experiences and sexual taboos in her writings. After *Shafu* was published in Chinese in 1983, it won the first prize in Taiwan's *United Daily News* but simultaneously got mixed reviews because it shocked both the academic circles and the general readers in Taiwan. *Shafu* is a story of a girl in poverty, Shi Lin, who is first exchanged by her uncle to a butcher named Jiangshui Chen for some pork, and then abused and tortured physically and mentally by Chen daily after he butchers hogs in the slaughterhouse. Despondent after Chen relentlessly slays the ducklings that Shi Lin raised in hopes of gaining economic independence, Lin murders her husband in the same way that she has seen him slaughtering hogs and is sentenced to death after the killing.

Depicting the traumatic experiences of women who are abused by husbands without any possibility of survival, Ang Li's novel can be hard to digest. In the "Author's Preface," Li explains that the story of the novel was adapted from a social news report that said a man was murdered by his wife in Shanghai in the 1930s. Grounded in this historical fact, Li exposes the implicit gender inequalities manifesting as economic and domestic violence in traditional—patriarchal, classist, and sexist—Taiwanese society and culture. As Gwen Hunnicutt comments, "patriarchy is a 'system,' and really needs to be tested at the cross-national level." By sketching out how patriarchy works, Li is able to explore how women and animals cross-culturally become oppressed minorities in the context of Chinese culture.

Many of Ang Li's novels expose the sexual and political violence that is imposed upon subaltern bodies of Taiwanese women, but *Shafu* in particular can be viewed as a text within Taiwanese ecocriticism, because the associations between gender, species, and nature are interrelated. There has been a lot of research on the novel, including both feminist criticism of the female image as a battered woman and investigations into the reasons for Lin's tragedy. Themes such as feminist emancipation and the female Gothic have become a focus, and both a psychoanalytic and a Nativist literary approach have proven useful in shedding further light on the many issues in this book (Chen, Hsu, Jing-mo Lin, Xiouling Lin, Kang). *Shafu* has been translated into "more than ten different languages, including English,

French, German, Italian, Japanese, Dutch, Swedish, Korean" (Liang).
Yi-ping Wu, for example, researched *Shafu*'s sexual descriptions and
obscene language by examining Howard Goldblatt and Ellen Yeung's
English translation to highlight "the ideological focalization of sexual
oppression and violence encoded in *Shafu*" (1). Doing a comparative
study of *Shafu* (Taiwan) and *So Long a Letter* (Senegal), Kai-ling Liu
compared and contrasted these two novels from the standpoint of
feminist theories in discussions of "polygamy, the sexual objectification of women, women's socialization into patriarchy and their search
for self" (25). Nevertheless, the ecological significance of *Shafu* has
seldom been acknowledged apart from Chia-ju Chang's "Putting
Back the Animals" (2009), which discusses "woman-animal meme"
in *Shafu* at length from a vegetarian ecofeminism perspective and
emphasizes that the animal suffering itself is worth noting.

LI ANG'S *SHAFU* AS A CASE IN POINT

Since the female protagonist Shi Lin's objectification and marginalization has been much discussed and examined, both from a feminist and
a vegetarian ecofeminist perspective, it is important to bring additional
critical aspects into focus, including nature in relation to ecophobia,
associations between sexism and speciesism, and Lin's dreams with
regard to environmental ethics. Offering such perspectives promotes
the development of a discourse of Taiwanese ecocriticism.

The place of the local in *Shafu* leaves readers a messy and unpleasant impression and is definitely a living hell for its female protagonist
Shi Lin. Home is not a place in which she can rest, and the local
patriarchal culture is the source of her oppression. Gendered space
and the natural environment in *Shafu* are significant elements in the
narrative, revealing the moral values and offering multiple perspectives
to approach the novel. Whether in *Shafu* or in a series of "Lucheng
Stories," Ang Li's creative writing has abundantly introduced Lugang
in terms of its landforms, natural conditions, and social customs. In
Li's description, Lucheng (the fictionalized town of Lugang) "had
a long and involved series of rites for the dead" with "each district
taking a turn in offering sacrifices" (45). In *Shafu*, the feudalistic
Chinese patriarchy has epitomized Lugang as the small seacoast town
of Lucheng, in which conservative, outdated, and outworn ideas of
chauvinism choke economically marginalized women such as Shi Lin.
Some specific places—her husband's home with his presence, the
well where the townswomen gossip, the temples grouped by family
clans, and the slaughterhouse where pig screams have been heard—all

become spaces of oppression, suffocating the female protagonist and demonstrating how a traditional Taiwanese woman's body negotiates her everyday environment by focusing on space and the bodily movement. As Fike and Kerr point out, "To expand the scope of what we understand to be 'home' without addressing issues of gender privilege and power differentials does not solve the problem" (26).

For Shi Lin, "home" does not possess any romantic interpretations; rather, it is a legal space where a married woman must submissively accept mental and physical exploitation from her husband and from society's value judgments. Neighbors' gossips and rumors, public apathy toward spousal abuse, and self-righteous morality from people oppress Lin in *Shafu*, burning every corner of her mind. As Chia-ju Chang's analysis of François Lyotard's etymological interpretation of the word "ecology" for reading *Shafu* indicates, home "is the shadowy space of all that escapes the light of public speech, and it is precisely in this darkness that tragedy occurs" (Lyotard 135). Tim Cresswell also indicates that "home can be an oppressive, confining and even terrifying place for many people—especially for abused women and children" (109).

Tragedy occurs both before and after Lin's marriage. The reproduction of power relationships is inherent in the patriarchy. After her father's death, Lin and her mother are driven out of her paternal house (the Lin Clan Ancestral Hall), since there are no brothers to maintain the legacy. Chinese people believe that "to be an ancestor one must have male progeny" (Tuan 119), so a woman in Chinese society is subordinated to her father/husband/son if widowed. After losing her mother as well, Lin is first reduced to a free-of-charge female slave whose obligation is to take care of her sick paternal aunt, and later bartered by her paternal uncle to the butcher Jiangshui Chen in exchange for pork. In the context of this arranged marriage, Lin is unable to establish a gender-equal relationship within Chen's home, or to create a space where she can feel "at home" as a woman. The small town of Lucheng and the ancestral house of the Chen family, Chencuo, are not a harbor of refuge but a space in which domestic violence and sexual abuse have always been committed.

From an ecocritical point of view, nature no longer serves as a backdrop or a setting subordinate to characters, but rather plays an important role in human drama. Geographically speaking, Lugang, famous for its "September Winds," usually is hit by sand and strong gales because of its proximity to the ocean. In Ang Li's narrative, nature as a character magnified the residents' physical or psychological pain and distress. Shi Lin's fear of patriarchal domination in both the public and private spheres is associated with her fear of nature. This patriarchally induced horror of the natural world is a result of ecophobia, which, as Simon C. Estok explains, is not simply an irrational fear of the natural environment ("Narrativizing" 144). Ecophobia expands clinical psychology's definition of this term—"an irrational fear of home"—to encompass the "fear of the agency of Nature" (Estok, "Introduction" 112). The "whistling sea breezes" endemic to the sea port of Lugang become "more clamorous" and "swirl in from all directions" (Ang Li 56), and the chilling and hostile atmosphere magnify Lin's phobia caused by an environmental threat. The howling sea gales and the barren landscape around her husband's house not only give a "dreary and bleak" vision (6) foreshadowing Lin's marital life, but also reinforce the image of Lugang as a ghost town in which spirits of women and animals who have died unjustly linger in the neighborhood.

The more violently Chen behaves toward Lin and the animals he slaughters, the more fiercely the weather outside the house is portrayed. When winter comes, "The weather really began to turn cold. Even in the daytime, the chilly, gusty wind blowing in from the distant horizon turned dry and blustery, churning and sweeping up the yellow sand from the beach" (125). Ang Li gives readers a sense that the representation of dark/Gothic nature symbolizes the patriarchal cultural environment that is imposed upon women and animals.

In Chinese culture, people pay a tribute to heaven and earth, and nature is widely praised, but as Huey-li Li indicates, "[T]here are no parallels between Chinese people's respectful attitude toward nature and the inferior social position of women" (276).[7] In Chinese domestic religions—Taoism, Buddhism, and Confucianism—the doctrines ask people to show filial respect to nature and one's ancestors. Nevertheless, this respect has nothing to do with women, who are valued only for their sexual, reproductive, and household services to men. For example, Golden Flower, Jiangshui Chen's favorite prostitute, is not only able to soothe Chen's savage violence with her "full, pendulous breasts" (81) but also shares her repetitive dreams in which a litter of twenty-five little pigs run up to her for milk. Golden Flower's exploited mothering body is compared to agricultural fields (i.e., nature), thereby reinforcing her subordination: "[H]er body resembled nothing so much as a water-soaked field after autumn harvest" (82). Devotion and self-sacrifice characterize Golden Flower as an image of "Mother Earth," and a prostituted Mother Nature, expected to be "selfless, generous, and nurturing" (Gaard, "Ecofeminism and Native" 302). As Western ecofeminists have observed, the metaphor of Mother Earth "grows out of a constellation of values" (301) and "authorize[s] humanity's limitless consumption of nature" and women (Gaard, "Vegetarian" 127). The naturalization of women reduces both Golden Flower and Shi Lin to a status of servitude and exploitation.

The association of women and animals does the same. Lin's neighbors and her husband see her equation with pigs as normal, mundane, and even a compliment to her value. The term "the mundanacity of violence," coined by Grant Farred, refers to "the quotidian everywhere-ness of violence" (354). Mundanacity is patriarchal violence normalized "as an everyday, routine possibility because it takes place with such great frequency and speed" (354). Chen's marital rapes occur whenever the opportunity presents itself. The fact that Lin's body is bartered for pigs' bodies enslaves Lin as an "actual" prostitute in Chen's eyes. Her scream in the spousal rape is equated with the hogs' squeals in the slaughterhouse: on the day after Chen's wedding, the slaughterhouse workers tease him when they hear the slaughtered hogs' squeals, asking "Is this how your woman squealed last night?" (Ang Li 18). The analogy between victimized women and slaughtered animals[8] reinforces the notion of a "conspiracy of silence" (Daly 158) as both woman and animal are sacrificed in this sadistic joke. Comparing Lin's scream to the pig's belittles her as a less-than-human woman. Chen brandishes the butcher knife in his temptation to make Lin into a dead object: "If you don't scream and yell this time, I'll fix you good with this knife" (Ang Li 137). In this speech act, he confirms that Lin has never been fully human to him, but rather has always been viewed as an animal-object to be manipulated for his pleasure. Her traumatized body is compared to an injured animal: "Shi Lin curled up into a ball, hugging herself tightly and whimpering like a wounded animal" (106). Using animal metaphors, Ang Li is able to portray Lin's timidity, submissiveness, and endurance: "[S]he began hunching over in an attempt to make herself as small as possible...she had the shriveled appearance of a wind-dried shrimp" (114). Both women and animals are silent: "[Lin] just gritted her teeth and bore it all in silence—except for the panting hisses that escaped from between her teeth, like the gasps of a tiny animal in the throes of death" (109). From the domestic violence and forced "exiles" around the neighborhood, Lin continues to suffer from psychological wounds, etched by patriarchy.

While animals are used as metaphor, the actual lives of economic animals present an involuntary servitude for human beings' consumption. As Chia-ju Chang indicates, "[D]etailed depictions of animal killing [in *Shafu*] are direct accusations of violation against animals, rather than just a trope to dramatize the psychological or emotional state such as the butcher's repressed anger and his wife's fear and wretchedness" ("Putting" 256). Ang Li's feminist text parallels the violence against women with the violence against nonhuman animals. A slaughterhouse is a living hell for all animals. Compared with the abattoir in Upton Sinclair's *The Jungle*, which revealed the slaughtering process in 1905 to expose the awful inhuman working conditions in Chicago's meat-packing industry, Ang Li's slaughterhouse in *Shafu* depicts "exactly how an animal dies, kicking, screaming, and is fragmented," but resists turning "the operations of the slaughterhouse [into] a metaphor for the fate of the worker in the capitalism" (Adams 51–52). Instead, Ang Li demonstrates the unbearable psychological impact of the slaughterhouse on the consuming public when its invisible and inaccessible slaughtering process comes into view.

Working daily in the slaughterhouse, Chen and the other butchers have become complacent and insensitive to what is overly familiar. Their economic needs make them numb to "the mundanacity of violence" against animals and deaf to the squeals of ready-to-slaughter hogs. The relationships people establish with animals in traditional Taiwanese society, imaginatively and materially, manifest the failed understanding of animal agency. Intensified and intricate focus on the food animal, hogs in this case, enables Li to write in a zone of intersection between feminist and ecological concerns, to elaborate an ecofeminist-oriented ethics that sharpens the critique of traditional patriarchal regimes that dominate and exploit fellow beings both human and nonhuman.[9]

Violence never stands alone. Resistance against emotional attachment with food animals extends to domestic violence and abuse, since "animal abuse and interpersonal violence do often go together" (Flynn 461). Several articles, sociology dissertations, and books document research from diverse disciplines, showing the interconnections among slaughterhouse violence, psychological diseases, and domestic abuse.[10] Being a "professional" butcher since his youth, Chen has mastered the "craft" of dismembering the hogs without getting a drop of blood on his clothes. In his "slaughterhouse rage" at home, Chen dismembers his wife's ducklings, her only companions and economic resources— her only hope for solace and for escape—relentlessly chopping them into pieces and fragments with his butcher knife and forcing her to witness the slaughter: "[T]his drive to kill, which was so necessary in his profession, had merged into his life and had become an integral part of it. Now, even when he wasn't on the job, it could be summoned with a mere thought, producing actions and consequences over which he had absolutely no control" (Li 123).

This persistent violence, which Li's narrative foreshadows as mounting and leading to gruesome consequences, turns Chen into a demon. Ecologically speaking, all of Chen's killing—especially the killing of a pregnant sow, whose "extraordinarily sad look" (121) conveys a mother's humble supplication for her eight piglets—symbolizes "the destruction of the womb, the source of all life" (121). Chen physically severs any mutuality between human and nature, human and animal, by reinforcing the exploitation of females, animals, and nature. Here, *Shafu* challenges what is to seen as the dividing line between "human" and "animal" suggesting that this failed attempt to eliminate and transcend animality is what makes patriarchy a life-denying system.

The slaughterhouse is a local place that exposes the violence of turning animals into carcasses, a place where Lin connects all the wretched souls in her life, realizing how and where relations of violent domination and exploitation are reproduced. The slaughterhouse scene produces a notable shift in the story. It elicits Lin's initial terror of the vengeful souls of pigs, for Lin's neighbor has warned her that in Chinese belief a butcher's wife must share a common karma (punishment) in hell if her husband slaughters hogs for a living. The unsavory spectacle of their deaths—the disgusting smell, the bloody images, and the terrible screams—forces her to connect the torment and the anguish of both women and animals. As Paul Rozin explains, "Disgust is triggered not primarily by the sensory properties of an object, but by ideational concerns about *what it is*, or *where it has been*" (108; original emphasis). Being aware of "what it is" and "where it has been" is like "the shock of the real" in a Lacanian psychoanalytic sense because "the real emerges as that which is outside language" (Evans 162); the glimpses of the brutality and violence underlying the processing procedure drive Lin over the edge.

When Lin finally takes her husband's slaughtering knife in hand to dissect and dismember him in the same manner in which she saw him butchering pigs, the narrative build-up has constructed her actions as a logical end to the oppression of both woman and animal. As Jovian Parry indicates, "[T]he preoccupation with performing hegemonic masculinity through violence towards animals extends through to the dismemberment of the corpse" (387). This decisive turning point in Lin's life occurs when she loses the ability to distinguish reality from hallucination, and thus inverts the relationship between Chen's domination of his wife and of the hogs he slaughters. Lin's increasing affinity with the bodies of the pigs on the block makes her associate traumatic memories of violence imposed upon her body and haunted by dreams of her mother's wretched death, her neighbor's mimicry of patriarchal violence through threatening gossip, her husband's foul language, and his sadistic acts of rape with the dismembered bodies of ducklings and pigs. The slaughterhouse triggers a return of the repressed elements, preserved in the unconscious and in her dreams, and they reappear in her consciousness and behavior. During her husband's final act of rape after the slaughterhouse scene, Lin "didn't struggle; she just whimpered softly like a small animal" (Ang Li 137). Silence articulates her acute pain and determination. The devastated bodies of women and animals, though lacking verbal expression, are encoded in Lin's dreams and subconscious to find a way through the butchering of Chen.

The scars inflicted by patriarchy manifest in Lin's dreams and ravings, in a space where hierarchically dualistic thinking cannot enter, allowing Lin to imagine a new territory and new possibilities. Interpreting the meanings of dreams, Kelly Bulkeley says, "Many dreams present us with challenges to our waking consciousness of what we can and can't do in life" (157). Li goes to great lengths describing Lin's dreams and nightmares in relation to the wretched souls of women and animals, exposing "flesh-eating as a form of patriarchal domination" (Gaard, "Vegetarian" 127), and the violence that is hidden in private and public spheres. These repeatedly haunting nightmares, including one of her mother as a hungry ghost and one of salty-as-blood pork and meaty pig's feet noodles, lead Lin to nausea, confirming that the "exploitation has gone too far" (Bulkeley 156). Dreams in this definition are not a fantasy or "'airy nothings' devoid of meaning and reality" but must be understood in the words of Stephen LaBerge: "[W]hat we do in dreams (or leave undone) can at times affect us as profoundly as what we do (or do not do) in our waking lives" (98).

In terms of the relationship between the natural environment and dreams, Bulkeley asserts, "the natural environment is the physical manifestation of what lies 'outside' our bodies, and dreams are the psychological expressions of what lies 'outside' our ego consciousness" (156). In *Shafu*, the natural environment in Lugang consists of its fierce sea winds, barren landscape, the insidious patriarchal ideologies, the ghost-like village, and the hell-like slaughterhouse and manifests itself "outside" Lin's body; however, her dreams represent the "psychological expressions of what lies 'outside' [her] ego consciousness." Dreams as well as sleep in this novel are "a go-between, a mediator of the very categories of 'the human' and all that lies beyond" the human world of culture and civilization and the natural world of animals, death, and noncivilization (Estok, "Unconscious" 111).

This go-betweenness, this neither-nor space of neither culture nor nature, respectively, is what Bulkeley called a "liminal moment," displaying nonduality and "the point which ritually symbolizes the transition from one state to another" (161). It is in this liminality that Lin flees from patriarchal dualism and experiences the realm of transhuman power, undergoing a transformation in relation to the unconscious, the invisible, and the unbearable, and allowing her energy and her courage to rise. Dreams "direct us beyond the limits of our ordinary categories of life" and expand "in many different directions—into the unconscious, into the natural world, and perhaps even into the collective psychic experiences of humankind and the realm of trans-human powers" (160).With this transhuman power, Lin finally slaughters the Chinese patriarchal "pig."[11]

CONCLUSION

Ang Li's *Shafu* articulates the ecofeminist associations among sexism, speciesism, and ecophobia. Instead of regarding ecofeminism as a one-sided grand narrative, Greta Gaard suggests, "Given the Taiwanese cultural contexts of Buddhism, Taoism, and Confucianism rather than Christianity, a philosophical reframing would be more strategically helpful in exploring connections of gender and species in Asian cultures" ("New" 652). Li's Lugang is certainly not a utopia-like place because it has been contaminated by patriarchal force and capitalist industry, but demonizing place is not my purpose. Nor was it Li's. Rather, this essay argues that the novel represents a traditional patriarchal society and the ways that society disregards the living rights of women and animals.

This essay has not only shown the interpretive power of Taiwanese ecocriticism, but also the reason *Shafu* is a Taiwanese ecocritical text. Feminist ecocritics recognize species oppression as a form of ecophobia, equally significant to other forms of oppression, and advocate the need to transform hierarchy and domination through "the liberation of all subordinated Others" (Gaard, "Wilderness" 5). A feminist ecocritical reading of *Shafu* shows that Taiwan's ecoliterature is capable of bridging the bioregionalism/ecocosmopolitan debate by showing that the local is also global. Li's *Shafu* encompasses the local scenario but never loses sight of the broader impact of the patriarchy system.

In Taiwan today, more and more writers are devoting themselves to animal advocacy—notably, the Huang sisters (Tsung-huei Huang, Tsung-chieh Huang), the Chu sisters (Tien-wen Chu, Tien-hsin Chu, Tien-I Chu),[12] and Chia-ju Chang's article "Trans-species

Care: Taiwan's Feral Dogs and Dog Mother Activism," concerning the problems of stray dogs and the identity of dog mothers in Taiwan. Some seem to approach the question of the animal in Taiwanese nature writing from the viewpoint of animal/animality studies. For instance, Sun-chieh Liang shows his interest in Ka-Shiang Liu's (pinyin: Kexiang Liu) animal fiction *He-lien-mo-mo the Humpack Whale* and explores "how the novel raises questions about both anthropomorphism and speciesism…" (Lunblad 10).

Although the clash of generations and genders may be sharper in traditional Taiwanese society than in other places, Ang Li's locally placed themes have cross-cultural and ecoglobal resonance. Li presents her story in a way that shows how the issues of patriarchal violence and the traumatized bodies of human and nonhuman are intertwined. Her writing offers a good foundation for developing a Taiwanese feminist ecocriticism.

NOTES

This essay was supported by the National Science Council of the Republic of China (under the grant number NSC 100-2410-H-211 -007 -MY2). I am grateful to Professors Greta Gaard and Simon C. Estok for their insightful comments on various versions of this essay.

1. The original title in Chinese is "Furenshafu," meaning "a woman killing her husband." The English translation of the title "The Butcher's Wife" focuses on the female subjectivity, whereas the Chinese title is more aggressive and provocative. As Chang Chia-ju points out, "The word 'Shafu' is polysemic: it not only denotes 'killing the husband' but also refers to someone whose career is related to killing, as in '*tufu*' (屠夫)" ("Putting" 262). Therefore, I prefer using the title "*Shafu*" in this essay.

2. Although many environmental (justice) movements are well-known to the public in Taiwan, most Taiwanese ecotexts are within the genre of nature writing or environmental writing; novels concerned with environmental justice movements not only need to be further researched but also to be translated into other languages. Few Taiwanese literary texts regarding ecological consciousness have English translations. See Ming-tu Yang's dissertation and, Tsai, Hsai-chu (蔡秀菊), *The Dancer in the Light: The Collection of Taiwan Ecological Novels* (夜舞者--台灣生態小說集) (Taipei: Taiwan Academy of Ecology, 2006).

3. The first ecological conference was held at Tamkang University, Taiwan, in 2000. Ecocriticism in Taiwan has been highly influenced by ecocriticism in the United States. ASLE-Taiwan was not founded until 2009 at Tamkang University. TKU has taken the lead in offering ecological courses and curricula in its English Department MA and PhD programs since 1998 and has consistently held the international ecological conferences

since 2000, the fifth in 2010. The first president of ASLE-Taiwan, Yaofu Lin, has published the ecojournal *Ecohumanism* since 2002; other journals related to Taiwanese ecological studies include *Taiwan Academy of Ecology* (生態台灣) and *Studies On Humanity And Ecology In Taiwan* (台灣人 文生態研究).

4. According to Patrick Murphy's taxonomy, nature-oriented literature can be divided into four categories: "[N]ature writing, nature literature, environmental writing, and environmental literature without any kind of value hierarchy imposed on these subcategories in terms of their thematic or informational value" (10).

5. Ming-yi Wu (吳明益) has suggested the following directions:
In the study of nature-oriented literature in Taiwan, I have always believed for the past several years that there are some [tasks] waiting to be developed: first is to clarify the definition of nature-oriented writings, nature writing, and environmental writing. The second is to use Taiwanese postwar novel and poetry as research subjects and continue to explore [the] hidden 'nature consciousness' in text. [Third] is to investigate writing meanings in specific environment and landscapes, [and] fourth is to discuss nature consciousness in Native Taiwanese Han language literature Han language writings. ("Engaging" 201).

6. Gender has produced very little difference when one examines Taiwanese nature writing. For instance, Hui-ling Wang's ecofeminist reading of female nature writer Yue-hsia Chen's "Love for the Mother Earth" celebrates positive images of mother and earth, just as many of Taiwan's male nature writers would do in their writings.

7. Even though Chinese philosophy, such as Taoism or Confucianism, to some extent suggests an ideal state of harmony between the heavenly world and secular life, nevertheless, the historical records of Chinese people's attitudes toward the natural environment reveal a great divide between the ideal state of philosophical teachings in terms of environmental protection and the consequences of the environmental pollution and ecological destruction in China. Karen L. Thornber's book *Ecoambiguity: Environmental Crises and East Asian Literatures* (2012) is worth noting for the way she highlights the ambiguous position between the philosophical thinking that celebrates the harmony of humanity with nature and the beauty of natural landscape, and the environmental problems that people have found in East Asian countries.

8. Carol Adams explains women are the absent referent in "the rape of animals," whereas animals are the absent referent of "the butchering of women" (Adams 43).

9. According to Greta Gaard, ecofeminism is insufficient if animal issues have been ignored or disregarded (*Ecofeminism* 6). Investigating ecofeminist anthologies, Gaard in *Ecofeminism: Women, Animals, Nature* had long ago pointed out that "animal" as a topic should not be overlooked within the discipline of ecocriticism and ecofeminism or be assumed to be implicit under the umbrella term of "nature." In her "New Directions

for Ecofeminism: Toward a More Feminist Ecocriticism," Gaard analyzes
how ecofeminism has been stigmatized as an "essentialist standpoint"
and advocates for a reinvigorated feminist ecocriticism capable of giving
voice to species (n1). Her research of feminist critics' works on "the sex-
ism/speciesism nexus since the 1980s" (2–3) shows that "species" has
not been a component of every ecofeminist standpoint but it is becoming
a research interest in cultural studies under the name of "animal studies"
or "animality studies." I will chiefly focus on feminist ecocritical viewpoints of "animal" here, because the debate between "animal studies,"
"animality studies," and feminist ecocriticism is the subject of another
forthcoming essay.

10. Consider Amy J. Fitzgerald, Linda Kalof, and Thomas Dietz's article in
sociology, "Slaughterhouses and Increased Crime Rates: An Empirical
Analysis of the Spill over From *The Jungle* Into the Surrounding
Community" or Gail Eisnitz's book *Slaughterhouse: The Shocking Story of
Greed, Neglect, and Inhumane Treatment Inside the U.S. Meat Industry.*
Jennifer Dillard from Georgetown University Law Center also has
one article called "A Slaughterhouse Nightmare: Psychological Harm
Suffered by Slaughterhouse Employees and the Possibility of Redress
through Legal Reform." Each of these shows both how monstrous the
slaughterhouse industry is and its relation to crimes and diseases.

11. As many cultural critics have already pointed out, there are numerous
associations between masculinity or "machismo" (Parry 385) and the act
of animal slaughtering in Western societies (Adams; Fiddes; Kheel; Luke).
Chauvinism in Mandarin Chinese literally means a "killing-pig culture,"
and in Chinese syntax, pigs are regarded as a symbol of macho men. In
this sense, Lin's killing of her husband stands for challenging a culture that
implies an unbalanced sexual status and taking revenge for the death of the
numerous slaughtered animals and the female orphaned ghosts.

12. These writers, having long been part of prominent Taiwanese writers,
now are shifting their concern to either environmental movement/eth-
ics or animal protection and animal advocacy on this Island. Take their
recent publications as examples. Tsung-chieh Huang from Chinese department of Donghua University largely focuses on animal literature and
protection in Taiwan. She had one book published in Chinese in 2011,
entitled *The Construction of Bioethics: Contemporary Taiwanese Literature
as an Example* (生命倫理的建構: 以台灣當代文學為例), in which she
discusses bioethics in animal writing, food writing, and ocean writing.
Tien-I Chu in her recent book *My Animal Companions in the Mountains
of My Life* (我的山居動物同伴們, 2012) shared her experiences of being
an animal advocacy social worker and her life living in the mountains with
animals. Both Tsung-huei Huang and Tsung-chieh Huang had academic
articles on Taiwanese nature writer Ka-Shiang Liu; however, the former
(Tsung-huei Huang) drew on Derrida's theory of the question of animal
as well as discussions of human-animal coexistence problems in terms of
theory of Martha C. Nussbaum and others to examine Ka-Shiang Liu's

animal fictions, in particular, "Animal Advocacy in Ka-Shiang Liu's *Hill of Stray Dogs*: Jacques Derrida's Animal Concern as a Point of Departure" (劉克襄《野狗之丘》的動保意義初探：以德希達之動物觀為參照起點).

WORKS CITED

Adams, Carol J. *The Sexual Politics of Meat: A Feminist-Vegetarian Critical Theory*. New York: Continuum, 1990.

Bracke, Astrid and Marguerite Corporaal. "Ecocriticism and English Studies: An Introduction." *English Studies* 91.7 (November 2010): 709–12.

Buell, Lawrence. *The Future of Environmental Criticism*. Malden, MA: Blackwell, 2005.

Bulkeley, Kelly. "Dreams and Environmental Ethics." In *Visions of the Night: Dreams, Religion, and Psychology*. Albany: State U of New York, 1999. 39–46.

Chang, Chia-ju. "Putting Back the Animals: Ecological-feminist Discourse and Woman-Animal Meme in Contemporary Chinese and Taiwanese Cultural Imagination." In *Chinese Ecocinema: In the Age of Environmental Challenge*. Ed. Sheldon H. Lu and Jiayan Mi. Hong Kong: Hong Kong UP, 2009. 255–70.

———. "Trans-species Care: Taiwan's Feral Dogs and Dog Mother Activism." *International Journal of Humanities and Social Science* 2.3 (February 2012): 287–94.

Chen, Shu-chun (陳淑純). "Discourse of Female Body in The Butcher's Wife, Dark Night, and The Garden of Mystery" (《殺夫》、《暗夜》、與《迷園》中的女性身體語述). *Literary Taiwan* (文學台灣) 19 (1996): 128–45.

Cheng, Hsien-yu. "Under Colonialism: Eco-literature on the Fault Lines." *Stepping Out of the Shadow of Colonialism*, Anthology, Proceedings of Pan-Asian Literature Symposium, 2004. 121–31.

Chu, Tien-I. *My Animal Companions in the Mountains of My Life* (我的山居動物同伴們). Taipei: Rye Field Publishing Co. (麥田), 2012.

Cohen, Michael P. "Blues in the Green: Ecocriticism Under Critique." *Environmental History* 9.1 (January 2004): 9-36.

Cresswell, Tim. *Place: A Short Introduction*. London: Blackwell Publishing, 2004.

Daly, Mary. *Gyn/Ecology: The Metaethics of Radical Feminism*. Boston: Beacon, 1990.

Dillard, Jennifer. "A Slaughterhouse Nightmare: Psychological Harm Suffered by Slaughterhouse Employees and the Possibility of Redress through Legal Reform." *Georgetown Journal on Poverty Law and Policy* 15.2 (2008): 391–409.

Eisnitz, Gail. *Slaughterhouse: The Shocking Story of Greed, Neglect, and Inhumane Treatment Inside the U.S. Meat Industry*. Amherst: Prometheus Books, 1997.

Estok, Simon C. "The Ecocritical Unconscious: Early Modern Sleep as 'Go-Between.'" In *Ecocriticism and Shakespeare: Reading Ecophobia.* New York: Palgrave Macmillan, 2011. 111–22.

———. "An Introduction to Shakespeare and Ecocriticism: The Special Cluster." *ISLE* (*Interdisciplinary Studies in Literature and Environment*) 12.2 (2005): 109–17.

———. "Narrativizing Science: The Ecocritical Imagination and Ecophobia." *Configurations* 18 (2010): 141–59.

Evans, Dylan. *An Introductory Dictionary of Lacanian Psychoanalysis.* New York: Routledge, 1996.

Farred, Grant. "The Mundanacity of Violence: Living in a State of Disgrace." *Interventions* 4.3 (2002): 352–62.

Fiddes, Nick. *Meat: A Natural Symbol.* London: Routledge, 1991.

Fike, Michelle Summer, and Sarah Kerr. "Making the Links: Why Bioregionalism Needs Feminism." *Alternatives* 21.2 (April–May 1995): 22–27.

Fitzgerald, Amy J., Linda Kalof and Thomas Dietz. "Slaughterhouses and Increased Crime Rates: An Empirical Analysis of the Spillover From *The Jungle* Into the Surrounding Community." *Organization Environment Online First.* June 2, 2009.

Flynn, Clifton P. "Examining the Links between Animal Abuse and Human Violence." *Crime, Law and Social Change* 55 (2011): 453–68.

Gaard, Greta. "Ecofeminism and Native American Cultures: Pushing the Limits of Cultural Imperialism?" In *Ecofeminism: Women, Animals, Nature.* Ed. Greta Gaard. Philadelphia: Temple UP, 1993. 295–314.

———. "Ecofeminism and Wilderness." *Environmental Ethics* 19.1 (1997): 5–24.

———. "New Directions for Ecofeminism: Toward a More Feminist Eco-criticism." *ISLE: Interdisciplinary Studies in Literature and Environment* 17.4 (2010): 1–23.

———. "Vegetarian Ecofeminism: A Review Essay." *Frontiers* 23.3 (2002): 117–46.

Garrard, Gregory. "Ecocriticism." *The Year's Work in Critical and Cultural Theory* 18 (2010): 1–35.

Han Han and Yi-kung Ma (韓韓、馬以工). *We Have Only One Globe* (《我們只有一個地球》). Taipei: Chiu Ko Publishing Co., Ltd. (九歌出版社有限公司), 1983.

Heise, Ursula K. "Deterritorialization and Eco-Cosmopolitanism." In *Sense of Place and Sense of Planet.* New York: Oxford UP, 2008. 50–62.

Hsu, Sophia Hwei-hsin (許蕙薪). "Nightmare Comes True—Social Confinement in Female Gothic Works: *The Italian* by Ann Radcliffe and *The Butcher's Wife* by Ang Li" (惡夢成真－女性哥德小說中的社會幽禁：以安．瑞克莉芙的《義大利人》和李昂的《殺夫》為例). Thesis, Fu Jen Catholic University, 2004.

Huang, Tsung-chieh. *The Construction of Bioethics: Contemporary Taiwanese Literature as an Example* (生命倫理的建構：以台灣當代文學為例). Wen Chin Publishing Co., Ltd (文津出版社有限公司), 2011.

Huang, Tsung-huei. "Animal Advocacy in Ka-Shiang Liu's *Hill of Stray Dogs*:
Jacques Derrida's Animal Concern as a Point of Departure" (劉克襄《野
狗之丘》的動保意義初探：以德希達之動物觀為參照起點). *Chung-Wai
Literary Monthly* 37.1 (2008): 81–115.

Hunnicutt, Gwen. "Patriarchy and the Victimization of Women:
A Cross-National Exploration of the 'Degrees of Patriarchy' and the
Violent Victimization of Females." Paper presented at the annual meeting
of the American Society of Criminology (ASC), Los Angeles Convention
Center, Los Angeles, CA, November 1, 2006. http://www.allacademic.
com/meta/p127299_index.html.

Kang, Jing-wen (康瀞文). "A Battle Won by Feminism? Starting from Li
Ang's *The Butcher's Wife*" (女性主義打勝的一場仗？由李昂的《殺夫》
談起). *Art Forum* (藝術語衡) 6 (2000): 99–110.

Kheel, Marti. "License to Kill: An Ecofeminist Critique of Hunting."
In *Animals and Women: Feminist Theoretical Explorations*. Ed. Carol
Adams and Josephine Donovan. Durham, NC: Duke UP, 1995.
85–126.

LaBerge, Stephen. *Lucid Dreaming: The Power of Being Awake and Aware in
Your Dreams*. Los Angeles: Jeremy Tarcher, 1985.

Li, Ang. *The Butcher's Wife* (*Shafu*). Trans. Howard Goldbratt and Ellen
Yeung. London: Peter Owens, 1986 (1983).

Li, Huey-li. "A Cross-Cultural Critique of Ecofeminism." In Gaard,
Ecofeminism. 272–94.

Liang, Min-min. "The Contemporary Chinese Writers Website Project: Li
Ang." http://web.mit.edu/ccw/about.shtml (retrieved on March 4,
2011).

Lin, Jing-mo (林靜茉). "Did the Woman Actually Kill Her Husband?—
Deconstruct the Feminism in Li Ang's *The Butcher's Wife*" (婦人真的殺
夫了嗎?--解構李昂「殺夫」中的女性主義). *Literary Taiwan* (文學台灣)
15(1995): 272–83.

Lin, Xiouling (林秀玲). "The Mutual Relations of Gendered Characters and
the Presentation of Individuals in Li Ang's *The Butcher''s Wife*" (李昂「殺
夫」中性別角色的相互關係和人格呈現). *Dong Hai Xue Bao* (東海學報)
37.1 (1996): 53–66.

Liu, Kai-ling. "To Whom Is the Letter Sent?: A Subversive Chinese Love
Letter." *Journal of National Cheng-Kung University* (Humanity and Social
Science Section) 26 (1991): 25–36.

Luke, Brian. *Brutal: Manhood and the Exploitation of Animals*. Champaign:
U of Illinois P, 2007.

Lunblad, Michael. "Introduction: Cetacean Nations." *Tamkang Review* 42.2
(June 2012): 3–12.

Lynch, Tom. *Xerophilia: Ecocritical Explorations in Southwestern Literature*.
Lubbock: Texas Tech UP, 2008.

Lyotard, Jean-François. "Ecology as Discourse of the Secluded." In *Green
Studies Reader: From Romanticism to Ecocriticism*. Ed. Laurence Coupe.
London: Routledge, 2000. 135–38.

Merchant, Carolyn. *The Death of Nature: Women, Ecology, and the Scientific Revolution*. New York: HarperCollins, 1980.

Murphy, Patrick D. "Refining through Redefining Our Sensibilities: Nature-Oriented Literature as an International and Multicultural Movement." In *Farther Afield in the Study of Nature-Oriented Literature*. London: U of Virginia P, 2000. 58–74.

Parry, Jovian. "Gender and Slaughter in Popular Gastronomy." *Feminism & Psychology* 20.3 (2010): 381–96.

Robertson, Roland and Jan Aart Scholte, eds. *Encyclopedia of Globalization*, II. New York: MTM and Routledge, 2006.

Rozin, Paul, et al. "Body, Psyche, and Culture: The relationship Between Disgust and Morality." *Psychology and Developing Societies* 9 (1997): 107–31.

Sinclair, Upton. *The Jungle*. Urbana: U of Illinois P, 1988.

Thornber, Karen L. *Ecoambiguity: Environmental Crises and East Asian Literatures*. Ann Arbor: University of Michigan P, 2012.

Tsai, Robin Chen-hsing. "Ecocriticism." In *Encyclopedia of Globalization: Volume One, A to E*. Ed. Roland Robertson and Jan Aart Scholte. New York: Routledge, 2007.

Tuan, Yi-fu. *Landscapes of Fear*. Oxford: Basil Blackwell, 1979.

Wang, Hui-ling (王惠玲). "An Ecofeminist Praxis in Yue-hsia Chen's 'Love for the Mother Earth: Plants of Four Seasons in Taiwan'" (陳月霞《大地有情》生態女性主義的實踐). In *Collection of Essays in Taiwan Nature Ecological Literature* (東海大學中國文學系(編)：臺灣自然生態文學語文集). Wen Chin Publishing Co., Ltd (文津出版社有限公司), 2002. 330–48.

Wu, Ming-yi (吳明益). "Engaging by Heart? Or Resigning to Fate?: Discussion on the Writing Features and Horticultural Concept in Liu, Da-Ren's Yuan Lin Nei Wai." *Journal of Taiwan Literary Studies* 15 (2009): 199–232.

———. "Modern Nature Writing of Taiwan." Diss., National Central University, 2003.

Wu, Yi-ping. "A Study on the English Translation of Eroticism: The Case of Li Ang's Sha Fu." 5th Global Conference—The Erotic, Salzburg, Austria. November 6–8, 2009 (unpublished).

Yang, Ming-tu. "From Love of Nature to Frugal Lifestyles: Nature-Oriented Literature of Taiwan since 1981." Diss., Tamkang University, 2001.

Section IV

CHINESE SECTION

11

ENVIRONMENTAL DIMENSIONS IN CONTEMPORARY CHINESE LITERATURE AND CRITICISM

Jincai Yang

Recently, there has been a boom of nature writing in China, displaying a multitude of genres that include not only fiction, poetry, and drama, but also essays, notes, and eco-concerned warning signs. Various forms of nature writing have enhanced Chinese critics' eco-concerned aesthetic awareness. Such writing embraces a unity of nature, human love, and beauty that urge a reevaluation of the relationship between nature and art, for contemporary Chinese environmental writing offers a unique aesthetic perspective toward the natural world. Such a perspective is mainly ecological and allows human subjects to take a benign and nonutilitarian attitude toward nature. In line with this attitude, one may easily agree that humanity and nature should coexist so as to set a harmony between each other. Human beings can only try to adapt to their environment without making an enemy of it. Contemporary Chinese literature seems to address such issues, providing a notion of literary ecology that is based on an ecological-systemic holism from which all human behaviors should be closely examined. Studying contemporary Chinese literature should thus transcend the scope of dominant anthropocentricism. Michel Foucault is instructive when he speaks about anthropocentricism, maintaining that humanity does not rule alone as the center of the world nowadays.[1] Having to live with others, humanity feels compelled to respect and honor nature and its species. All living entities on earth, human and nonhuman, have their own "niche," hence their own inherent worth. According to this ecological notion, all species should enter the horizon of ethical concern. In this sense, the Chinese expression of ecological aesthetics displays a significant understanding of the ecological-systemic holism.

From the 1980s to the 1990s, with a few exceptions, the most visible writers considering ecocriticism in China preferred to be social critics rather than academic literary scholars: they began to publish on ecocritical matters in literary studies; their articles appeared in general interest magazines, such as *Dushu* (Reading), *Shanghai wenxue* (Shanghai Literature), *Yishu guangjiao* (Art Panorama), and *Benliu* (Torrent). A book-length study of ecocritical subjects in literature did not appear until a decade later. Articles about ecocriticism also appeared in scholarly journals, such as *Wenxue pinglunjia* (Literary Reviewers), and especially toward the end of this period, Jincai Yang argues, "more and more Chinese intellectuals found themselves confounded in an impasse of environmental deterioration" (Yang 364). China's preoccupation with economic and material pursuits led to the Chinese negligence of environmental protection. According to a recent analysis by environmental experts both at home and abroad, there are several major factors that threaten China's environment— namely, a large growing population, rapid urbanization, fast economic growth, and industrial pollution.[2]

The emergence of ecocriticism has offered a favorable opportunity for Chinese scholars to take part in the critical trend and communicate with academic circles around the world. Many intellectuals took immediate action to handle the rising ecological issues in China's environmental deterioration. More and more began reflecting upon rapid economic development in China and its consequences. The most obvious achievement they made was to shift the focus of ecology to show ecological impacts on humanity. They addressed a variety of topics from an ecological perspective, giving rise to a cluster of ecoterms such as ecological philosophy, ecological aesthetics, ecological ethics, and ecological anthropology. Alongside the growing ecocritical turn in Chinese literary studies, Chinese ecological literature came into being, though at a slow pace. In October 1995, Meng Wang, a noted writer, cochaired the international conference on "Humanity and Nature" in the coastal city Weihai, China. At the conference, several scholars introduced nature writing and the paper "Awareness of Environment in Taiwanese Literature" caused great discussion among participants. Many writers in mainland China were then still unaware of ecological crises, though they could see water pollution and take in air pollution every day. The conference opened a new frontier for Chinese writers. Four years later, another international conference on "Ecology and Literature" took place in

Haikou, capital city in Hainan Province. Writer Shaogong Han came for the meeting and chaired the whole session. Professor Arif Dirlik from Duke University attended the conference. Chinese writers such as Tuo Li, Ping Huang, and Jinhua Dai all delivered their papers. In the following year Shuyuan Lu at Soochow University organized a seminar on spiritual ecology and scholars such as Zhiyang Zhang, Jiaqi Chen, and Zhanchun Geng addressed affirmatively that ecological discussions should also take into account spiritual matters. In his subsequent work, Lu devoted himself to the study of ecology in an attempt to unveil the subtlety of traditional Chinese understandings of nature and ecology. His exploration of the Chinese character "feng" (wind) from an ecocritical perspective is exemplary and fascinating, rendering an aspect of Chinese ecological thinking. His book *Shengtai piping de kongjian* (Space for Ecocriticism), having explored the source of Chinese ecology and attempted to examine the relationship between literary art and human souls, is a fundamental contribution to Chinese scholarship on ecocriticism, helping us to know about "a variety of exciting local particularities, such as the power of Taoist thought in Chinese culture" (Lu 114). Its critique of contemporary Chinese urbanization commands our attention.

From the 1990s onward, Chinese intellectuals began to turn to the Chinese traditional thought that highly appraises the idea of coexistence between humanity and nature. Professor Xianlin Ji at Peking University took the lead, maintaining that "human beings are destined to suffer from mountainous problems and even cannot survive on earth if they fail to reach a harmony with Nature" (Ji 81–82). In response to Ji's statement, Professor Fanren Zeng at Shandong University proposed an aesthetic perspective, coining the phrase "ecological aesthetics" in an attempt to shift from a mere ontological approach to one recognizing human aesthetic practices based on an ecological harmony between human beings and nature (Zeng, "Forward" 2–3).[3] All these efforts have advanced both the ecocritical movement in literary studies in China and China's nature writing.

Almost at the same time, ecocritical dimensions began to surface in Chinese literary studies. Scholars introduced many Western scholarly works in the field to systematize an ecocritical theory and frame out a new way of looking at literature. A glance at the major ecocritical statements since 1999 reveals a rapid development of Chinese ecocritical studies. Pioneering efforts in this respect may be attributed to Kongcao Si, who published a short introductory essay titled "Ecocriticism in Literary Studies" in response to the rise of Western ecocriticism and its major critics such as Cheryll Glotfelty, Harold Fromm, Jonathan Bate, John Elder, Robert Pogue Harrison, William Howarth, N. Katherine Hayles, and Glen A. Love (Si 134–35). His brief remarks on the ecocritical assumptions in both *The Ecocritical Reader: Landmarks in Literary Ecology* and the summer issue of *New Literary History* in 1999 are of paramount importance, drawing wide attention to these Western critics. Scholars in the field of comparative literature and foreign literary studies were then particularly keen on the subject.

Several leading scholars such as Ning Wang and Nuo Wang took an active role in introducing Western ecocritical studies, for the former edited a Chinese version of *New Literary History I*, which includes two translated articles from the summer issue of *New Literary History* in 1999.[4] The book was a success, bringing Chinese critics into a close encounter with ongoing overseas ecocritical theories and practices.

In a similar fashion, Nuo Wang published his introductory essays of which "Shengtai piping: fazhan yu yuanyuan" ("Development and Origin of Ecocriticism") and "Rachel Carson's Accomplishments in Eco-Literature" are very instructive. The former discusses how ecocriticism came into being and particularly focuses on "the importance of introducing the East Asian ecological ideas in ecocritical studies" (Wang, "Development" 54), while the latter highlights the contribution of Rachel Carson as an ecocritic in literary studies, claiming that "her *Silent Spring* and its ecological thought have reached a significant impact on our perception of nature (Wang, "Rachel Carson's Accomplishments" 96). Of equal merit and recognized as the first monograph on ecocriticism in mainland China is his *Oumei shengtai wenxue* (Ecoliterature in Europe and America), in which Nuo Wang has improved his understanding of both ecocritical theories and the notion of literary ecology, offering a panoramic view of European and American achievements in nature writing as well as in ecocritical studies. Here Wang not only corrects some of the assumptions in his previous research but also largely expands his scope of thought touching more broadly on notions such as ecological responsibility, the critique of civilization, ecological idealism, and warning against ecological degradation. He also addresses the seriousness of ongoing ecological problems that have affected China's development. He quotes widely to illustrate the immediate causes of China's rapid reduction of forestry, lack of fresh water, and endangered wildlife (Wang,"*Ecoliterature*" 231–32). It is a fascinating book, despite its lack of original scholarship, but the undertaking itself is noteworthy, for it served as an immediate reference for those who were interested in the subject. Many young scholars responded actively, turning out a variety of essays on ecocriticism. Among a cluster of introductory articles in recent Chinese journals, Xinfu Zhu's "A Survey of Ecocriticism in the United States" stands out, examining how American ecocriticism has developed. Here he emphasizes how theoretical perspectives of ecocriticism have enhanced ecopoetics and mentions the significances of "environmental ethics" and "environmental philosophy" (Zhu 137). Similarly, Maolin Chen discusses his own understanding of Western ecocritical studies, but he focuses mainly on when and why ecocriticism occurred, asserting that "critics should pay close attention to both cultural studies and ecocriticism" (Chen 114).

Another important circle of writers to the reception of ecocriticism in China is the group of young and promising scholars such as Qingqi Wei, who was then writing on the subject under the supervision of Professor Ning Wang. Wei began to conduct email interviews with American scholars such as Lawrence Buell and Scott Slovic. His paper based on an interview with Buell is very solid, not only arguing for significance of ecocriticism but for providing exemplary scholarly dialogues over green studies between scholars of both China and the United States. His translation of Scott Slovic's *Going Away to Think: Engagement, Retreat, and Ecocritical Responsibility* came out recently, and it will no doubt be of great interest to Chinese readers. Wei's newly released book *Lüxiuzi wuqilai: dui shengtai piping de chanfa yanjiu* (Green-Clad Scholarship: an Interpretive Study of Ecocriticism) is again monumental in its juxtaposition of the works of Western ecocritics and Chinese writers. Mapping the field of ecocriticism and its philosophical origins, Wei categorizes different types of greening cultures. His analysis of Chinese ways of ecological thinking is transnational, offering an engaging discussion of Chinese literature embedded in deep ecological thinking (Wei 216).

Introductory work on ecocriticism by Chinese scholars almost uniformly attempts to define in Chinese some terms used by Western critics, resulting in very similar remarks on the same topic. A case in point is Bei Liu's "Shengtai piping yanjiu kaoping" ("A Review of Ecocritical Studies"), which again deals with the rise of ecocriticism in the West giving a survey of the theory's origin, development, and major critical objectives. Liu translated Lawrence Buell's *The Future of Environmental Criticism: Environmental Crisis and Literary Imagination* into Chinese, and the book came out as a great success in May 2010.[5]

While exploring the critical mission and theoretical perspectives of ecocriticism, Chinese scholars have started to observe them critically.

Zhihong Hu at Sichuan Normal University is one such scholar who has tried to explicate Western ecocritical studies. In 2006, Hu published *Xifang shengtai piping yanjiu* (A Study of Western Ecocriticism), which closely examines the Western trend of ecocriticism and its major scholarship, incorporating feminist, cultural, and other theoretical perspectives framed by an attempt to reveal first its multidisciplinary features and second how literature is observed from an ecocritical perspective in the West. Hu opens his book with a richly contextualized chapter on the rise of Western ecocriticism and its preliminary theories, followed by a series of discussions over the impact of ecocriticism on literary studies, with a particular emphasis on the greening dimension in today's critical theories. The book is very relevant to current debates in the field and provides engaging and illuminating analyses.

In addition to books, many scholarly journals such as *Foreign Literature Review, Literature and Art Studies, Foreign Literatures Quarterly*, and *Contemporary Foreign Literature* have published articles on ecocriticism, playing a guiding role in drawing a wide attention to the theory. *Foreign Literature Studies*, in particular, published two special issues on ecocriticism in 2007 and 2008, respectively. Coedited by Scott Slovic and Lily Hong Chen, the first issue carried a cluster of ecocritical articles besides an editorial introduction. It was followed by a collection of essays named "Ecocriticism in Asia,"[6] which slightly preceded the conference on literature and environment at Central China Normal University in Wuhan in November 2008. Works published afterward are largely indebted to the pioneering studies carried in these journals.

A number of recent books and articles again suggest the promise of ecocriticism in China. What, then, are the major features that characterize ecocriticism in contemporary Chinese literary studies? Based on all of the work done in recent years, it is safe to say that there are four main stages characterizing Chinese ecocriticism: (1) reiteration, (2) comparative, cross-cultural theorization, (3) the study of the ecology of Chinese culture, and (4) the study of foreign literature.

CHINESE ECOCRITICISM AS A REITERATION OF WESTERN ECOCRITICISM

First, then, ecocriticism in China is currently a sort of follow-up of Western theories, despite its range of practices. Chinese scholars began to respond seriously to Western ecocritical theories in the late 1990s. Even so, there was immense ecological awareness that accompanied the Chinese preoccupation with economic and material pursuits in the 1980s. It was then the growing environmental deterioration that propelled the Chinese to examine what they were doing with nature. Alongside this awareness came Chinese environmental writing dedicated to revealing industrial pollution and various environmental issues. Writers at the time were astonished to see many parts of China endangered, and they called for environmental protection. Of the most representative were Qing Sha and Gang Xu, who wrote widely on environmental issues.

Qing Sha's "Beijing shiqu pingheng" ("Beijing Out of Balance", 1986) is an interrogative voice against humanity's acquisitive nature and stubbornness in overusing natural resources such as water. "There is not enough water in the city," Sha writes, "but its people are just crazy about producing iron, steel, foundry cokes, and plastics. In less than two years, half a billion tons of the city's water was used for the mere production of these materials." Gang Xu's *Famuzhe, xinglai* (Wake Up, Woodchoppers!; 1988), meanwhile, is a more subtle inward reflection on life and nature. Here Xu directly singles out human indifference toward the land as a serious problem and utters his deep concern for a deprived nature and ecological crisis that have affected the common Chinese. The book earned Xu a high reputation as a "Rachel Carson" in China. In such environmental writing there is always an urge to protect natural resources such as air, land, water, forest, and minerals. Herein lies the resonance of Al Gore's claim that "we must make the rescue of the environment the central organizing principle for civilization" (269).

With the importation of Western ecocritical theories, Chinese environmental writing changed its face from reportage to fiction and poetry in the 1990s. There appeared a group of writers who wrote in more conscious response to the rise of ecological studies. They no longer confined themselves merely to a call for environmental protection but began to probe into the causes of widespread ecological issues in China. Soon there occurred a challenge against the stubborn anthropocentric mode of thinking. At the core of this new wave of writing lies an author's thematic concerns in which one can not only read environmental imaginations but also discern obvious ecological emotions and thinking. Writers of this kind have tried to find a way to reach a harmonious relationship between humanity and nature and include such people as Qingsong Li, Yingsong Chen, Xuebo Guo, Fu Zhe, Wei Zhang, Pingwa Jia, and Rong Jiang. Criticism about these writers varies, largely revealing a disparity in merit. A case in point is Shudong Wang's *Shengtai yishi yu zhongguo dangdai wenxue*

(Ecological Consciousness and Contemporary Chinese Literature). It tries to explore the ecological concerns in contemporary Chinese literature and to offer a cluster of case studies in which it singles out environmental dimensions.

At a moment in the process of Chinese modernization when the status of the Chinese ecosystems is increasingly compromised, greatly needed are the kinds of articulations that address the relationship between humanity and nature. Despite its limitations, Wang's *Ecological Consciousness and Contemporary Chinese Literature* marks a successful and comprehensive step in opening our eyes to such environmental and ecological concerns in contemporary Chinese literature. Earlier in his *Zhongguo xiandai wenxue zhong de ziran jingshen yanjiu* (A Study of Natural Spirit in Modern Chinese Literature), Wang highlighted how a spirit of nature features modern Chinese literature, exhibiting a thorough explication of Chinese observation of nature in literature. To give voice to this new trend of exploration in its whole complexity, Wang draws wide attention to the narrative of nature and the natural ethos in modern Chinese literature. In so doing he has tried to demonstrate how Chinese writers mourn both the loss of natural tranquility and the increasing environmental deterioration in consequence of Chinese modernization. Still, in this study, Wang succeeds in raising important questions about Chinese modernization and the environmental endeavor before a blighted nature. A reformulation of studies of modernist Chinese literature alongside ecological concerns over nature would be a most welcome development, and hopefully the publication of *A Study of Natural Spirit in Modern Chinese Literature* will help to further influence the field toward that direction.

What is striking is that sporadic reviews and commentaries led to a boom of ecowriting in just a decade. Few critics were seriously ecocritical in their discussion, and most of them only focused on an individual author. Their critical remarks were mainly personal reflections on a particular work without much theoretical observation, for they used different expressions to mean ecoliterature such as "nature literature," "environmental literature," "environmental protection literature," and "green literature." Here critics seem to amplify the scope of nature writing, blurring the difference between a mere delineation of natural scenes and phenomena and what is of ecoliterature.

In fact, ecocriticism should not be random or borderless. It must have its own purpose and clearly defined objective. As Cheryll Glotfelty has argued, "Ecological literary criticism is the study of the relationship between literature and the physical world" (xviii). According to Glotfelty, ecocriticism is supposed to examine the relationship between the human mind and a literary text. Thus, it is important to distinguish ecoliterature from mere depictions of natural objects, and the major criterion for judging a piece of ecoliterature is to see whether its author holds an ecological stance and perceives nature as it is, devoid of human subjective dominance or anthropocentrism.

CHINESE ECOCRITICISM AS COMPARATIVE, CROSS-CULTURAL THEORIZATION

Studying Western ecocritical theories with a comparative perspective is the second dimension in today's Chinese literary humanities. Critics producing such work often explore the local significance of texts in terms of Chinese ecological thought. Many such critics search for the sources of Chinese ecology by reinterpreting Confucius and Mencius in the hope of turning them into critical practices. Enlightened by ecological philosophy, Chinese scholars tend to view literature and art as activities rooted in an ecological system composed of nature, human society, and culture. Thus their discussions often address human ecology, and the critical focus falls on a pursuit of ecological ethics. A case in point is Yongcheng Zeng's *WenYi de lüse zhisi— wenyi shengtaixue yinlun* (Green Reflections in Literary Studies—An Introduction to Literary Ecology). It explores how literature helps express a continuity of modern society and examines how literary ecology functions in a socialist market economy. "Literary and aesthetic activities have become part of ecological concerns" (Zeng 17). In his book, Zeng speaks highly of a greening culture identifying green as the color of life, hope, and harmony. He is strongly aware of the rising environmental issues that have provoked both Chinese artists and academics.

While speaking of environmental literacy, Yongcheng Zeng seems concerned about the future of Chinese environmental literature, for he is not sure if it can fare well. He quotes from Zhang Ren that contemporary Chinese environmental literature fails to realize the significance of human aptitude to save the earth from destruction. It is important to expose human hostility to nature, but it is more important to cultivate an ecological sense among human beings (332–33). Xiaohua Wang seems even more assertive when he speaks about the subjects of life in nature. He quotes from Tom Regan's animal rights theory, arguing that Regan's "inherent value" or "subject-of-a-life" status can help resume harmony between humanity and nature. In his opinion, nature, known for its inherent value and vital organisms, has a

vigorous life that should be respected for being "the subject-of-a-life."
Nature-oriented literature should therefore ascribe inherent value
to individual entities on earth. This is the true basis for holding an
ecological view, maintains Wang, for "there is no such thing as an
ecocriticism that fails to recognize nature's 'subject-of-a-life' status"
(Wang 19).

CHINESE ECOCRITICISM AND THE ECOLOGY OF CHINESE CULTURE

The third dimension of Chinese literary humanities is the turn
to studying the whole system of human civilization. This marks a
significant change in the perception of the bond between humanity
and nature. Human beings are responsible for the rising deterioration
of natural environment. Many critical assumptions interrogate human
behavior and biased value systems. How to protect endangered nature
and how to reconstruct human spirit have now become two major
objectives that contemporary Chinese seek to achieve. Many critics
such as Shuyuan Lu believe that literature should also be ecologically
concerned and should tell human beings how to get along with
nature, besides revealing human urges. In his *Shengtaiwenyixue*
(Ecological Research in Literature and Art), Lu quotes largely from
Alfred North Whitehead, with many critical arguments based on
readings of Whitehead's *The Concept of Nature* (1920) and *Science
and the Modern World* (1925).[7] Whitehead's wise and witty opinions
about a vast range of human endeavors and the role of science in the
rise of Western civilization have inspired Lu to observe the Chinese
literary environment and offer his insightful remarks on an ecological
approach to Chinese literature and art. His emphasis on a possible
combination of both human and natural spirits marks his own views
of literary ecology. Similar views are also obvious in Wenbo Li's *Dadi
shixue—shengtai wenxue yanjiu xulun* (Earth Poetics—A Critical
Survey of Ecoliterary Studies). Here Li observes closely how Chinese
literature has cultivated a poetic dwelling. He draws a deft comparison
between Chinese Taoist culture and Western perceptions of nature
(Li 86).

The return to ancient Chinese thoughts about nature has made it
possible for Chinese scholars to look into individual texts in classical
Chinese literature. Guided by various Western ecological theories,
Chinese literary critics started to read both traditional fiction writing
and landscape poetry in the hope of redefining their own ecological
poetics. Of outstanding merit are those articles about ancient Chinese

ecological ideas in literature. Xiang Gao, Qizhong Wang, and Rong Jiang were particularly active in this undertaking. A more detailed exploration is Hao Zhang's monograph *Zhongguo wenyi shengtai sixiang yanjiu* (A Study of Chinese Ecological Thought in Literature and Art), which digs for literary ecology in classical Chinese texts, highlighting some features of Chinese literary ecological discourse. The book is exemplary in opening up a new horizon for Chinese ecocriticism in literary studies. Many critics follow the fashion, and a cluster of books approaching contemporary Chinese literature from ecocritical perspectives have appeared. Especially noteworthy are two insightful books: *Shengtai piping shiyuxia de zhongguo xiandangdai wenxue* (An Ecocritical Perspective into Modern and Contemporary Chinese Literature) and *Shengtai Yishi Yu Zhongguo Dangdai Wenxue* (Ecological Consciousness in Contemporary Chinese Literature). The former is a joint work by Xirong Wang and her colleagues and students exploring the relationship between humanity and nature as one of the major themes in Chinese literature. It argues that this theme of literature is "the least tackled and even widely misread with regard to the study of twentieth-century Chinese literature" (Wang 126).

Authors of the book draw largely on ecocritical perspectives and try to revise the Chinese tradition of literary criticism by adding into it an ecological viewpoint. They examine closely such writers as Xin Bing, Moruo Guo, Ziqing Zhu, Congwen Shen, and Chengzhi Zhang from an ecocritical perspective. The book offers a fine interpretation of ecological implications in modern and contemporary Chinese literature integrated with an aesthetic view of nature. *Ecological Consciousness in Contemporary Chinese Literature* by Shudong Wang probes into the representation of nature in contemporary Chinese literature, interrogating modern civilization from an ecological perspective. It is divided into two sections. In the first part, Wang mainly examines the ecological consciousness in contemporary Chinese writing, while in the second part, he offers case studies in which he observes novels and short stories by Wei Zhang, Xuebo Guo, Zijian Chi, and Guangling Ye in addition to thoughtful analyses of Jian Yu's poems and many essays by Wei An, Gang Xu, and Cunbao Li. His discussion of Rong Jiang's *Lang Tuteng* (Wolf Totem) stands out, for it attempts to explore the novel's ecological thought. His *Zhongguo xiandai wenxue zhong de ziran jingshen yanjiu* (A Study of Natural Spirit in Modern Chinese Literature) also examines how Chinese writers perceive nature in modern Chinese literature, unveiling a rare treasure of Chinese natural spirit embodied in Taoist pursuits, mystification of the sea and forests, Dionysian and Bacchanal experience, and one that "returns to the wilderness" (121–32). It stands out for its thoughtful elaboration of modern Chinese literary representations of nature and for how it serves as an inspiring guide for those who have an interest in ecological perspectives toward modern Chinese literature.

CHINESE ECOCRITICISM AND FOREIGN LITERATURE

While using ecocritical approaches to analyze Chinese literature, many scholars in the field of foreign literary studies also reexamine foreign literature ecocritically marking the fourth dimension. For example, Professor Hong Cheng at Capital University of Economics and Business in Beijing belongs to this pioneering group of ecocritics in China, and she has published many articles on environmental literature in Chinese magazines. She turned out her first monograph on American nature writers entitled *Xungui huangye* (Return to the Wilderness) in 2001. She took similar efforts in her 2009 book entitled *Ningjing wujia: yingmei ziran wenxue sanlun* (Tranquility Is beyond Price: British and American Nature Writers), which explores both British and American writers such as Ralph Waldo Emerson, Henry David Thoreau, Mary Austin, Edward Thomas, and Thomas Hardy. Cheng views nature as the embodiment of spirit in Emerson's *Nature*, and in a similar fashion she examines further Thoreau's *Walden*, wilderness in Charles Frazier's *Cold Mountain*, and ecological awareness in Hardy's *The Woodlanders*. Cheng is also the translator of John Burroughs's *Wake-Robin*.

Some scholars of Russian literature also use an ecocritical approach. A case in point is the book *Eluosi shengtai wenxue lun* (On Ecoliterature in Russia), which reflects upon Russian notions of nature and offers a survey of how Russian literature integrates with ecological ideas and constructs a poetic dwelling. The book devotes a few pages to trace how the Russian ecological thought originated and asserts that there is an obvious voice of nature in Russian literature derived from its long nature-concerned oral tradition that outlasts all generations of human beings. Russian writers in the nineteenth century, according to Sumei Yang, a scholar of Russian literature, were particularly aware of human exploitation of nature and dedicated themselves to an exploration of harmony between human beings and nature. They have displayed their worries over human egoist impositions on earth in varying degrees (30–31).

Xianglu Zhou's *Eluosi Shengtai Wenxue* (Russian Ecoliterature) is another fine piece of Chinese scholarship on Russian literature from an ecocritical perspective. Zhou divides Russian literature into three different stages and focuses particularly on the ecological issues that many Soviet era writers had to face. Writers such as Viktor Astafiyev and Valentin Rasputin are, in Zhou's opinion, ecowriters who mourned the human hostility to nature. Here Zhou gives a critical survey of Russian ecoliterature (76–85, 173–96).

Two books of average merit on British literature are Meihua Li's *Yingguo shengtai wenxue* (Ecoliterature in England) and Chunfang Lu's *Shensheng ziran: yingguo langmanzhuyi shige de shengtai lunli sixiang* (Sacred Nature: The Ecological Ethics of the English Romantic Poetry), which show a different face of Chinese ecocriticism. *Ecoliterature in England* offers an ecocritical reading of British literature that explores its ecological themes in various literary works; while *Sacred Nature: The Ecological Ethics of the English Romantic Poetry* is mainly a close study of English romantic poetry, which handles in individual texts a current of ecological ethics. Both, however, discuss ecological sources in English literature, but neither has an explicitly ecocritical thrust: both might have benefited from a deeper reading in ecocriticism.

A more scholarly work of ecocriticism is Guangwu Xia's *Meiguo shengtai wenxue* (Ecoliterature in the United States), which sketches the development of American ecoliterature. In the first three chapters, Xia mainly discusses American nature writing from the colonial period to the nineteenth century. Many writers such as John de Crevecoeur, William Bartram, Washington Irving, James Fenimore Cooper, Ralph Waldo Emerson, Henry David Thoreau, Walt Whitman, John Burroughs, and John Muir are ecological in nature, for they all display their view of nature, though in varying degrees. Chapter four focuses on twentieth-century American ecoliterature, in which Xia discerns a sad voice sighing mournfully over human exploitation of land for economic purposes. He further scrutinizes E. B. White, Rachel Carson, and W. S. Merwin with reference to ecocriticism. Xia in his analyses of these authors unveils their awesome respect, love, and benevolence for nature. In doing so, he actually affirms that it is human indifference toward nature that causes environmental deterioration. The book is an important resource for studying American literature and a valuable addition to scholarship on ecocriticism.

In addition, Baisheng Zhao at Peking University and Lili Song at Tsinghua University are significant contemporary Chinese ecocritics who teach and write on the subject. Zhao is particularly active in organizing academic conferences on ecological discourse and has written numerous articles on environmental literature and Chinese life writing, while Song is the translator of Keith Thomas's *Man and the Natural World: Changing Attitudes in England, 1500–1800.*

Finally, a few words are necessary for a brief assessment of what has been achieved in terms of ecocriticism in contemporary Chinese literary studies. In general, ecocriticism has become favorable among Chinese literary critics, and the critical trend continues to grow. Chinese scholarship reached thereby will thus become more globally refined, but it is still necessary to further and improve Chinese scholarship on ecocriticism. First, we still do not know much about Western scholarship on ecocriticism, so it is extremely necessary for us to translate both monographs and essays by leading ecological scholars. Without knowing current ecocritical theories, we are only kept in the dark and confine ourselves to a narrow scope of knowledge. Second, a few Chinese critics are not quite aware of the distinct branches within the field of ecocriticism. This blurs the boundary between literary and cultural ecocriticism. Critics unaware of the distinct branches within ecocriticism don't seem to know what the aim of literary ecocriticism is. If ecocriticism studies the relationship between humanity and nature and aims at ecological protection, it can be defined as a type of "cultural criticism" in a very broad sense. Simon C. Estok is right when he argues that "ecocriticism embraces possibilities" (Estok 124). In his opinion, "ecocriticism is any theory that is committed to effecting change by analyzing the function—thematic, artistic, social, historical, ideological, theoretical, or otherwise—of the natural environment, or aspects of it, represented in documents (literary or other) that contribute to the practices we maintain in the present, in the material world" (124). Obviously, various perspectives such as the philosophical, the ethical, and the sociological have played respective roles in such criticism, but a true literary ecological perspective should go beyond such limits and explore how literature integrates an ecological concern as a discourse. Third, the ecological consciousness in contemporary Chinese literature is too limited, and critical practices are therefore a bit narrow-minded. The number of works that really both approach contemporary Chinese society from an ecological stance and stand out artistically is rather small. As some translations are of poor quality, misreading and sometimes farfetched interpretations of a text are a common practice in contemporary Chinese literary studies. This is especially the case with those that rely heavily on translations. Therefore, it is still necessary to encourage well-qualified translations of ecocritical theories to keep pace with academia outside China. Accordingly, we should find a voice for literary discussion and ecocriticism that does the highest kind of justice to the literary text, and at the same time reach outside the academy to include the world of writers, readers, and reviewers.

NOTES

I thank the peer readers of this chapter for their insightful ideas, and the present improved version is largely indebted to their instruction.

1. For a further understanding of Foucault's discussion of Friedrich Nietzsche's genealogy, argument on the end of anthropocentricism, and an antihumanist excavation of the human sciences, see Michel Foucault, *The Order of Things: an Archaeology of the Human Sciences.*
2. For further discussion, see Yongchen Wang, *Green Action in China* (29–30).
3. Similar views can be found in another book by Fanren Zeng titled *Shengtai cunzailun meixue lungao* (Critical Essays on Ecological Aesthetics). It is a collection of 39 essays focusing on the human existence and highlighting the importance of the natural environment which houses human beings. According to Zeng, natural environment is the origin of human health and happiness. He emphasizes that human beings should avoid their anthropocentric views when embracing nature.
4. The two translated articles are Jonathan Bate's "Culture and Environment: From Austen to Hardy" and Dana Phillips's "Ecocriticism, Literary Theory, and the Truth of Ecology" originally carried in *New Literary History*, Volume 30, Number 3, Summer 1999.
5. This translation, together with Qingqi Wei's translation of Scott Slovic's *Going Away to Think* and Zhihong Hu's Chinese version of Glen A. Love's *Practical Ecocriticism: Literature, Biology, and the Environment*, marks a new surge of ecocritical studies in China.
6. For details, see "Ecocriticism in Asia" in the special issue of *Foreign Literature Studies* 30.5 (2008): 1–42.
7. A Chinese version of *Science and the Modern World* came out in 1959 by the Commercial Press in Beijing.

WORKS CITED

Bate, Jonathan. "Culture and Environment: From Austen to Hardy." New Literary History 30.3 (Summer 1999): 541–60.
Buell, Lawrence. Huanjing piping de weilai: huanjing weiji yu wenxue xiangxiang (The Future of Environmental Criticism: Environmental Crisis and Literary Imagination). Trans. Bei Liu. Beijing: Peking UP, 2010.
Burroughs, John. Xinglai de senlin (Wake-Robin). Trans. Cheng Hong. Beijing: SDX Joint Publishing Company, 2004.
Chen, Maolin. "Prospects for Western Literary Theory in the New Century: Cultural Studies and Eco-criticism." Xueshu jiaoliu (Academic Exchange) 4 (2003): 114–119.

Cheng, Hong. *Xungui huangye* (*Return to the Wilderness*). Beijing: SDX Joint Publishing Company, 2001.

———. *Ningjing wujia: yingmei ziran wenxue sanlun* (*Tranquility Is beyond Price: British and American Nature Writers*). Shanghai: Shanghai People's Publishing House, 2009.

Estok, Simon C. *Ecocriticism and Shakespeare: Reading Ecophobia.* New York: Palgrave Macmillan, 2011.

Foucault, Michel. *The Order of Things: an Archaeology of the Human Sciences.* New York: Vintage Books, 1973.

Glotfelty, Cheryll and Harold Fromm, eds. *The Ecocriticism Reader: Landmarks in Literary Ecology.* Athens: University of Georgia Press, 1996.

Gore, Al. *Earth in the Balance: Ecology and the Human Spirit.* Boston: Houghton Mifflin, 1992.

Hu, Zhihong. *Xifang shengtai piping yanjiu* (*A Study of Western Ecocriticism*). Beijing: China Social Sciences Press, 2006.

Ji, Xianlin. "A New Interpretation of 'The Coexistence between Man and Nature'." *Dongxiwenhuayilunji* (*Essays on Cultures between East and West*) Vol. 1. Ed. Xianlin Ji and Guanglin Zhang. Beijing: The Economic Daily Press, 1997. 78–91.

Jiang, Rong. *Lang Tuteng* (*Wolf Totem*). Wuhan: Changjiang Literature & Art Press, 2004.

Li, Meihua. *Yingguo shengtai wenxue* (*Ecoliterature in England*). Shanghai: Xuelin Press, 2008.

Li, Wenbo. *Dadishixue—shengtaiwenxueyanjiuxulun* (*Earth Poetics—A Critical Survey of Ecoliterary Studies*). Xi'an: Shaanxi People's Publishing House, 2000.

Liu, Bei. "A Review of Ecocritical Studies." *Wenyi lilun yanjiu* (*Theoretical Studies in Literature and Art*) 2 (2004): 89–93.

Lu, Chunfang. *Shensheng ziran: Yingguo langmanzhuyi shige de shengtai lunli sixiang* (*Divine Nature: Ecological Ethics in British Romantic Poetry*). Hangzhou: Zhejiang UP, 2009.

Lu, Shuyuan. *Shengtai piping de kongjian* (*Space for Ecocriticism*). Shanghai: East China Normal UP, 2006.

———. *Shengtai wenyixue* (*Ecological Research in Literature and Art* [*Ecological Theory of Literature and Art*]). Xi'an: Shaanxi People's Education Press, 2000.

Phillips, Dana. "Ecocriticism, Literary Theory, and the Truth of Ecology." *New Literary History* 30.3 (Summer 1999):. 577–602.

Sha, Qing. "Beijingshiqupingheng" ("Beijing Out of Balance") January 1986. 28 August 2012. < http://baogaowenxue.xiusha.com/s/shaqing/001 /002.htm>

Si, Kongcao. "Ecocriticism in Literary Studies." *Foreign Literature Review* 4 (1999): 134–135.

Slovic, Scott. *Zouchuqu sikao: rushi, chushi ji shengtai piping de zhize* (*Going Away to Think: Engagement, Retreat, and Ecocritical Responsibility*). Trans. Qingqi Wei. Beijing: Peking UP, 2010.

———. and Lily Hong Chen, eds. "Ecoliterature and Ecocriticism." *Foreign Literature Studies* 29.1 (2007): 8–65.

Thomas, Keith. *Renlei yu ziran shijie* (*Man and the Natural World: Changing Attitudes in England, 1500–1800*). Trans. Lili Song. Nanjing: Yilin Press, 2008.

Wang, Ning, ed. *Xinwenxueshi yi* (*New Literary History, Vol. 1*). Beijing: Tsinghua UP, 2001.

Wang, Nuo. "Shengtai piping: fazhan yu yuanyuan" (Development and Origin of Ecocriticism). *Wenyi yanjiu* (*Literature & Art Studies*) 3 (2002): 48–55.

———. "Rachel Carson's Accomplishments in Eco-Literature." *Guowaiwenxue* (*Foreign Literatures Quarterly*) 2 (2002): 94–100.

———. *Oumei shengtai wenxue* (*Ecoliterature in Europe and America*). Beijing: Peking UP, 2003.

Wang, Shudong. *Shengtai yishi yu zhongguo dangdai wenxue* (*Ecological Consciousness in Contemporary Chinese Literature*). Beijing: China Social Sciences Press, 2008.

———. *Zhongguo xiandai wenxue zhong de ziran jingshen yanjiu* (*A Study of Natural Spirit in Modern Chinese Literature*). Harbin: Heilongjiang People's Publishing House, 2005.

Wang, Xiaohua. *Shengtai piping—zhutixing de liming* (*Ecocriticism: The Dawn of Constructing Intersubjectivity*). Ha'erbin: Heilongjiang People's Publishing House, 2007.

Wang, Xirong, et al. *Shengtai piping shiyuxia de zhongguo xiandangdai wenxue* (*An Ecocritical Perspective into Modern and Contemporary Chinese Literature*). Beijing: China Social Sciences Press, 2009.

Wang, Yongchen. *Green Action in China*. Beijing: Foreign Languages Press, 2006.

Wei, Qingqi. "Making a Dialogue on Chinese-American Ecocriticism: an Interview with Professor Lawrence Buell." *Wenyi yanjiu* (*Literature & Art Studies*) 1 (2004): 64–70.

———. *Lüxiuzi wuqilai: dui shengtai piping de chanfa yanjiu* (*Green-clad Scholarship: an Interpretive Study of Ecocriticism*). Nanjing: Nanjing Normal UP, 2010.

Whitehead, Alfred North. *The Concept of Nature*. Cambridge: Cambridge UP, 1971.

———. *Science and the Modern World*. New York: Free Press, 1967.

Xia, Guangwu. *Meiguo shengtai wenxue* (*Ecoliterature in the United States*). Shanghai: Xuelin Press, 2009.

Xu, Gang. *Famuzhe, xinglai* (*Wake Up, Woodchoppers!*).1988. Changchun: Jilin People's Publishing House, 1997.

Yang, Jincai. "Chinese Projections of Thoreau and His *Walden*'s Influence in China." *Neohelicon* 36 (2009): 355–64.

Yang, Sumei & Yan Jiqing. *Eluosishengtaiwenxuelun* (*Ecoliterature in Russia*). Beijing: People's Publishing House, 2006.

Zeng, Fanren. "Foreword." *Humanity and Nature: Literature and Aesthetics Observed from a Perspective of Contemporary Eco Civilization*.

Ed. Fanren Zeng. Zhengzhou: Henan People's Publishing House, 2006. 2–3.

———. *Shengtai cunzailun meixue lungao* (*Critical Essays on Ecological Aesthetics*). Changchun: Jilin People's Publising House, 2003.

Zeng, Yongcheng. *WenYi de lüse zhisi—wenyi shengtaixue yinlun* (*Green Reflections in Literary Studies—An Introduction to Literary Ecology*). Beijing: People's Literature Publishing House, 2000.

Zhang, Hao. *Zhongguo wenyi shengtai sixiang yanjiu* (*A Study of Chinese Ecological Thought in Literature and Art*). Wuhan: Wuhan Press, 2002.

Zhou, Xianglu. *Eluosi shengtai wenxue* (*Russian Ecoliterature*). Shanghai: Xuelin Press, 2009.

Zhu, Xinfu. "A Survey of Ecocriticism in the United States." *Contemporary Foreign Literature* 1 (2003): 135–140.

12

BETWEEN ANIMALIZING NATURE AND DEHUMANIZING CULTURE

READING YINGSONG CHEN'S SHENNONGJIA STORIES

Lily Hong Chen

A renowned writer who has won several top-level national awards in China since 2002, Yingsong Chen writes about the poverty-stricken people struggling in the great mountains of Shennongjia and about the people who leave these mountains and end up in neighboring cities such as Wuhan and Yichang.[1] His Shennongjia stories often strike readers with images of the desperate dehumanization facing characters who find themselves cornered into destitution in the country and anonymity in the city. Critics of his works tend to focus on human characters fighting for survival or on animal characters functioning as metaphors of human survival. This chapter attempts to show the close link between the fates of humans and animals in Chen's Shennongjia stories. Close readings of the texts produce the following observations: first, in the face of extreme material poverty, whether in the country or in the city, there is no ground for human superiority over animals; second, the most dehumanizing power is not poverty itself, but the pervasive industrial power that is fundamentally damaging to humanity as well as destructive to nonhuman animals. The chapter argues, therefore, that by denouncing human arrogance in a specific situation in contemporary China, the writer actually shows a posthumanist attitude. It goes on to argue that this attitude is also an ecological attitude, for it directly confronts the anthropocentric view that sees value only in humans and their activities.

Though philosophers and scholars in the West began to talk about "posthumanism" during the mid-1990s, they seem not to have reached an agreement about the meaning of the term. Nevertheless, we may still recognize the core of the term as always referring to changes or findings that challenge or even criticize human arrogance. One of the examples comes from Donna J. Haraway's observation in her essay "A Cyborg Manifesto," where she points out two fairly recent changes as contributing factors to posthumanism, one being "the border war" between organism and machine and the other "the thorough breach" of the boundary between human and animal (70, 72). Here the human connection with both machine and animal is what forms the basis for disrupting the long-cherished idea of human essence. The challenges posed by posthumanism is what Cary Wolfe has in mind when he describes posthumanism as "engaging directly the problem of anthropocentrism and speciesism and how practices of thinking and reading must change in light of their critique" (*What* xix). Wolfe specifically admits that "the animal problem" is "part of the larger question of posthumanism" (xxii). In his critical interrogation of major theorists such as Heidegger, Levinas, Agamben, and Derrida over their thoughts about the human-animal distinction, Matthew Calarco focuses on "the question of the animal" and explicitly defines his approach as posthumanist because of its challenge to "liberal humanism and [...] metaphysical anthropocentrism" (6). Whereas Haraway, Wolfe, and Calarco discuss "the animal problem" in relation to posthumanism in American or European contexts at the turn of the twenty-first century, Yingsong Chen explores the issue of the boundary confusion between human and animal as it unfolds in contemporary China in the space between the rural and urban areas. Here in Chen's works, we find very different causes of posthumanism from those described by the Western scholars. While an improved image of the animal based on new discoveries made about animal abilities such as language and consciousness contributes to the tightened connection between human and animal in the Western cases of posthumanism, it is the deterioration of the human state that leads to a disrupted confidence in the human distinction from animals in the Chinese cases. But the Chinese writer also shares a similar posthumanist attitude with some of the Western scholars in attacking violence toward animals and exposing it as a direct result of the unfounded belief in human-animal distinction. Among the stories discussed in this chapter, "Peace Dog" concentrates on the troubled relationship between human and animal in a dislocated situation and reveals connections with other texts where similar troubles exist in various situations.

Describing the story as "a sorrowful song of the drifting," critics of "Peace Dog" view it as a realistic narrative about the predicament of poor peasant workers in urban China, represented here by the protagonist of the story named Dazhong Cheng (Liu and Yu 60). Cheng is sensitive about threats to his human dignity following his arrival in the city of Wuhan: "In the city, one doesn't even want to piss. One has only a brain and a mouth, and the part below has lost all senses" (219). Later he makes an even more bitter remark: "One loses dignity as one comes to the city, and has to tear off one's cheek for others to stamp on as on the floor of a latrine" (219–20). In these two quotations, Cheng clearly associates his ill treatment with the city, a place of indifference and hostility as well as of the promise of prosperity. But whereas the man's first remark reflects on the oppressiveness of the city life that denies him his most basic animal needs, his second one emphasizes his need for respect as a human being, which, as the metaphorical expression hints to us, is based on a minimal requirement of sanitation that differentiates humans from animals in rural China. The lack of basic sanitary facilities, therefore, can be really humiliating and dehumanizing, as the descriptions of Cheng within his working environment reveal: "The work sheds where [the peasant workers] live stink to high heaven as they eat and piss and shit all inside behind the plastic cover, while on the other side of the cover is written the heartening slogan: 'I work to make the city shine'" (243). With words such as "piss" and "shit," the quotation clearly echoes the two previous ones by drawing attention to the workers' animal state of living and hence their hurt human dignity. The slogan is thus an ironic remark about the sharp contrast between the shiny surface of the city and the painful suffering hidden underneath.

Cheng's feeling of humiliation in the work shed arises from his fear of being confused with an animal, which in his view is much lower than a human being. His view of the dog Peace as his personal property, which he can dispose of at will, rather than as an independent life is actually rather common among the rural Chinese. A study of Chinese beliefs about and views of animals carried out by Ping Mang et al. is telling here. According to their observations, the idea of humanity's total harmony with nature is a main feature of ancient Chinese philosophies and has given rise to long-standing beliefs and practices among the ordinary people that regard animals as sentient and even moral beings not different from humans and that guard animals against deliberate harm or cruelty. Though Mang admits in his book that the idea of utilizing nature for human benefit exists in some philosophies such as Confucianism, it is not until the second half of the twentieth century that an abrupt change took place to replace the traditional respectful view of nature with a narrow anthropocentric view. The year 1978 is the point when the tension between human and animal that had already existed started to reach an unprecedented level. The Reform[2] brought not only rapid economic development and improved material life on a large scale but also corruption and moral crisis, and, as far as the animal issue is concerned, the deterioration or disappearance of natural habitats for wild animals as well as problems of maltreatment and cruelty for farm and pet animals.[3] Going back to the case in "Peace Dog," one may admit that when Cheng offers his dog as meat to his aunt just like any home-raised cattle, he is actually taking a utilitarian view of the animal that has long existed among the Chinese as part of the Confucian tradition. But when it comes to his heartless beatings of the dog and his selling of the dog to a notorious dog butcher, one can only understand his behaviors as a result of the recent changes in views and treatments of animals that are devoid of any moral considerations.

In the specific situation of Cheng as a poor country person in the city with an insecure life and identity, his wonton treatment of Peace cements his sense of superiority and mastery over the dog, and therefore assures him of his status as a member of the presumed higher human race. But the city refuses to give him such an assurance. In the city, the man himself is little better than the dog. When Peace appears on a bus with his master, the passengers are shocked and they shout angrily, "This is a country dog! This dog is so filthy! This dog must have rabies" (220). It is obvious that the dog is rejected on the bus simply because he is a country dog. The city people's curses reveal an attitude that combines speciesism with a deep-rooted prejudice against the country. Their association of Peace with filth and disease is in fact their attempt to deny the dog even the status of a real living creature by thinking of it in abstract terms, just as they used to think and are still thinking of the countryside in general. Cheng as a poor countryman is a victim of this biased view, just as his dog is. His problem is that he is unable to identify himself with his dog for their shared unfair treatment and misfortunes.

What happens to Cheng and between him and his dog following his move to the city is significant in terms of the transmuted cultural perspectives of the migrant peasant workers. In Jiewei Ma's ethnographic report about the migration of the Chinese rural population and its cultural effects, he points out that such a migration that happens on a mass level in contemporary China is driven by what he calls "the intriguing imagination about the modern city," which is caused in the first place by "huge internal economic gaps" (342). The economic power relations between the city and the country decide the power relations of their respective cultures. This is actually an underlying explanation for the process described by Ma in which the rural culture is affected or even replaced by the urban culture among the peasant workers. In the story, the rural cultural perspectives that Cheng originally takes is replaced by urban cultural perspectives when he comes to view his good hunting and reliable dog in terms of a few cash notes (216).

In the opinions of Jin Liu and Quanheng Yu, the tragedy of both Cheng and his dog Peace lies in their being defined "the Other" by the urban culture and having therefore lost the hope of acquiring their long-aspired urban cultural identity (61). Liu and Yu's remark is only partly right, as it ignores the fact that the dog does not share his master's aspiration and that it holds on to one single wish throughout the story: to go back to the mountains. In this regard, the dog is more fortunate as his othering is inflicted on him from outer forces and not from his own inner consciousness. What is ironic here is that whereas Cheng voluntarily others his dog by taking a different cultural perspective from his own, he is actually also othering himself, for no matter whether he likes it or not, he is judged by the city on the same level as his dog, as the poor and filthy thing from the country. Moreover, his maltreatment of his dog aggravates his othering by the city people. In fact, when his aunt confronts him on his savage deed to the dog with a rhetoric question, "Aren't you a man-beast from Shennongjia?" we see his othering being paralleled with his dehumanization (219).[4] The woman's denouncement of Cheng also reveals the prejudice held by her and other city people against Shennongjia. In their minds, the great mountains are associated with wilderness, barbarity, and poverty, all of which are valued lower than the civilized and prosperous life of the city. The woman's angry remark about Cheng's cruelty against the dog actually hides in it what Glen Elder et al. describe as "animal-linked racialization" (qtd in Huggan and Tiffin 137). Besides, the urban cultural perspective she uses to judge Cheng is essentially anthropocentric and therefore detrimental to all nonhuman animals as part of wild nature or rural culture.

The dehumanizing effect of the city and its cultural perspective is mainly evident so far in the protagonist's degradation to the state of an animal and, more important than that, in his own acute sense of a threatened human dignity. In my opinion, it is the character's self-conscious attempt to protect his human identity and pride, often built on an assumed human distinction from animals, and the failure of this attempt that eventually make the case a posthumanist one. The writer is critical of the two causes of Cheng's dehumanization: his brutal treatment of Peace, and the urban culture that treats him and his dog unfairly. The writer, however, shows a very different attitude toward the fates of humans and animals in the rural setting, as we see in some of the other Shennongjia stories.

In the stories where the characters stay on their native land among the big mountains of Shennongjia, humans are often forced into a situation in which the human-animal distinction no longer exists, and all have to compete on the same level with the wild mountain animals for a living. Of course, such competitions are not new or rare in either the real world or literature. What makes them worth mentioning in our concern about posthumanism is how the competitions affect the characters' sense of being human. In the story "Anecdotes about Balihuang," for example, the woman Jiarong Duan, who lives alone in a wasteland with her two little daughters, makes reflections on her condition by referring to animals in the forests. While lying in bed and listening to the beasts howling in the mountains and the birds chirping as if crying for their lost mothers, she feels she is "a little bit happy for being covered in this warm shed" and is comforted by the thought that "humans are more fortunate than beasts after all" (258). Though she regards her children and herself as the more fortunate ones at this moment, the use of the concessive expression "after all" seems to suggest that the gap between them and the beasts is not a big one. Like Cheng, Duan is eager to raise herself above animals, because only by doing so is she able to keep her already fragile belief in human superiority over the rest of nature.

It is this groundless belief of the woman that turns her into an invader of wild nature. Her attempt to open up the wasteland and change it to her own use also causes a hostile relationship between her and some of her animal neighbors. A major episode in the story is about the woman's relentless pursuit of a hungry old wolf who has eaten her four-year-old little daughter. Her moment of revenge is dramatic:

> Pressing her knee against the wolf's belly, Jiarong Duan opened up her mouth, howled and bit into the wolf's neck. She held it there, deeply and hard, and finally broke it. A stinking liquor spurted into her mouth. She heard approaching shouts for her and saw from the corner of her eyes a man limping towards her. It was Dashun Hong, coming with his hunting fork.
>
> She was still holding the wolf's throat tight in her mouth. (289)

It is obvious in this description that Duan is presented very much like a wild beast. The way she howls and bites into the wolf's throat and refuses to let the beast go until it is stone dead indicates one clear fact: the struggle for survival between the woman and the wolf has turned her into a beast. Though the wolf's death seems to have changed the power relations between her and the nonhuman creatures on the wasteland as she wished, the cost she pays for it is undoubtedly too high.

Critics point out the two dichotomies presented in Chen's Shennongjia series: the dichotomy between the city and the countryside, and that between the country and nature.[5] In the latter case, we come to realize that the conventional idea about the harmony between the natural person and the environment is false or at least inapplicable to the present reality that Chen's Shennongjia stories attempt to represent. In his reading of the story "The Last Dance of the Leopard," Xiangsheng Wang pays attention to an old hunter named Old Guan who never goes outside the big mountains and knows no other way of supporting himself but by hunting wild animals. In Wang's opinion, people like Old Guan tend to have "a very tense and bad relationship with nature and with animals" due to the pressure of hard living reality (38). His view is echoed by the writer, who seems to accept the competitive relationship between human and animal as part of the inevitable reality in such places as Shennongjia when he says, "Man has to kill animals in the end. Otherwise you cannot survive" (Zhou and Chen 45). Chen describes those living in the high mountains of Shennongjia as having nothing to rely on but their impulses and toughness and as being "the same as wild beasts" (Zhou and Chen 44). With this comment, he is actually showing more sympathy than contempt or criticism for the people and their survival instincts. Moreover, by comparing people to wild beasts, he is rejecting human superiority as an illusion.

Chen's egalitarian view of the human-animal relations in the wild explains why he chooses a neutral position before human and animal sufferings in nature. After declaring his position as an environmental protectionist, Chen emphasizes that he often has to avoid bringing his environmental ideas into his writings, which are supposed to be about the realities of Shennongjia (Zhou and Chen 45). What Chen means by the realities of Shennongjia may be better understood against the background of the economic development during the Reform era, whose effects have been felt in places as remote as Shennongjia. When facing fierce struggles for the limited natural resources between human and animal, Chen has to drop his environmentalist position, which would put him on the side of animals and would seem to him both hypocritical and unfair in this situation. The story "To Live Like White Clouds" is a good case in point. In the story, Laohe Qi tries to keep to his family the little water in a small shrinking waterlogged depression by driving away or killing those animals who come down from the mountain top to drink. Laohe regards himself fully justified in doing so because "if you live on such a high mountain, you cannot allow other beasts to stay here with you" (171). In his determination to kill the goat that refuses to leave, he says to himself, "[O]ne cannot share water with a wild beast as long as one lives on this mountain" (172). The use of free indirect thought that makes no clear distinction between the author's and the character's mind in these two quotations seems to indicate the author's understanding and acceptance of the character's attitude. In this regard, Chen is obviously taking an antiromantic view that puts him in alignment with writers both of the anti-Romantic tradition in modern Western literature and those of the so-called bottom narratives and suffering narratives in Chinese literature of the present age.[6] What he shares with these writers is the courage to face the dark aspects of nature and those of human society. And by deliberately avoiding any moral judgment about humanity in conflict with nature and showing him simply in his basic need for survival, Chen is expressing a view that is also akin to Darwinism.

Yingsong Chen's stories provide literary examples for the observation made by Graham Huggan and Helen Tiffin that in many contemporary instances in reality, "humans are pitted against animals in a competition over decreasing resources" (136). In Huggan and Tiffin's postcolonial study, the "apparently 'either/or' situations in contexts of land and resource scarcity or degradation" are the inevitable outcomes of both past and present cases of Western exploitation. In the Chinese situation, it also seems unavoidable to give priority to either human or animal over the other. In "Anecdotes about Balihuang," when Duan has finally settled down in Balihuang and begins to dream of her future life of abundance and security on her own farmed land, some officials of the local forestry station come and order her eviction because of her law-breaking farming attempt in the protected forests. In this case, where priority is given to nature with intervention from an external social power, the woman is deprived of her survival chances at the same time that her conflict with nature is stopped. Here is a case in which ecological protection clashes with social justice. From the woman's point of view, the external social power is much more compelling and dehumanizing than the power of nature, since it allows her not even the chance of living an animal's life on the land.

In his focused study on the archetypal image of land in Chen's Shennongjia stories, Chunmin Sun juxtaposes the fate of Dazhong Cheng in "Peace Dog" against that of Jiarong Duan in "Anecdotes about Balihuang." In his description of the former as "a misfortune from deserting the land" and the latter as "the frustration in clinging to the land," Sun has accurately captured the dilemma faced by the poor peasants in Chen's stories who find it hard to survive either in the remote city or on their native land (66, 67). It seems, therefore, that the writer views dehumanization as an inevitable outcome of an impoverished life, whether being located or dislocated. Now the questions are: how different is dehumanization in the country from that in the city? And what is the significance of the difference to the dislocated people's understanding of suffering and injustice and eventually to our grasp of the writer's posthumanist considerations?

Memories or dreams of those dislocated characters about their homelands turn out to be the points where the city and the country are interconnected and where the connection between the two different kinds of dehumanization is made available for observation. In "Peace Dog," when staying in a temporary shelter with other homeless people, both Cheng and his dog think of their remote home. In Cheng's memory about the fire-box room next to the kitchen, which shelters every living being of the family, human or animal, during the long cold winter, he is consciously opposing the warmth of home against the cold indifference of the city. The fire-box room also appears in the dog's dream, together with his fight with the cat inside the room and his hunting adventures with his master outside in the forests. What we observe here is the deep resentment felt by both the man and the dog toward their deprived state in the city, a realization that comes to them through the contrast between their life at home and that away from home.

Yet our understanding of life in the country from reading Chen's other Shennongjia stories makes us suspect: is the home of Cheng and Peace really as nice as they remember? The story itself does not give any clue to the answer, since their life at home exists only on the suppressed level in the characters' mind. But a partial answer is perhaps available in another story, "To Live Like White Clouds," where one finds a similar attachment to home in the character Ximan's[7] memory to that in Cheng's. What makes Ximan different from Cheng, though, is the former's self-consciousness of the representational effect of his memory, as is explained in the following:

> For the first time in his life, [Ximan] talks about his homeland to an outsider. He finds that the homeland in his narration is so beautiful, like a fairy land. It is from his own narration and from others' attentive listening that he realizes for the first time the beauty of his home, which is the extraordinary beauty of high mountains. (195)

What Ximan realizes at this moment is actually his subconscious attempt to romanticize his home in the presence of an "outsider" during his absence from home. He is also fully aware of the selectiveness of his narration or memory. Shortly after the passage quoted earlier, Ximan admits to himself the presence of many evils in the mountains, such as the blood-sucking leeches and the long unbearably cold and boring winter, things that "he didn't tell her" or "he has already forgot" (195). For readers of the story, Ximan's reflection on his narration about home is a reminder of the difficult life led by the family presented through the fight over water they have with their animal neighbors at the beginning of the story. In fact, if one reads "Peace Dog" and "To Live Like White Clouds" in the larger context of Chen's Shennongjia stories as a whole, one cannot possibly miss the romanticizing function of the memories and dreams about home in the two stories.

In the characters' thinking of home, what they themselves do not realize and what readers of the complete stories come to see is that their past life is better indeed in the sense that it is an autonomous one over which they may have some control. This is especially obvious in the case of Cheng. His home memory presents a life regulated only by the daily or annual patterns of nature. In stark contrast to the casual and peaceful life he remembers, his life in work sites is humiliating and even life-threatening. Ma's finding that the migrant peasant workers in southern China are often forced to work and live by "a mechanical rhythm rather than a physiological rhythm" certainly applies to the case of Cheng and makes us realize that Cheng is actually turned into a machine once the natural rhythm he used to follow is broken (344). In fact, the dehumanizing nature of modern industrial culture lies exactly in what Ma says about the regulation of the bodies of the peasant workers in their move "from casual labour to planned unit-labour" (345).

The significance of Cheng's change from a natural man to a machine might be better understood with a reference to Marx's theory of historical materialism as interpreted by Louis Althusser. According to Althusser, as soon as Marx defines the forces and relations of production as the determining base for the superstructure of the human society, he is actually building his theory on his rejection of the essence of man, which Althusser describes as Marx's "theoretical anti-humanism" (32). To go back to the story "Peace Dog" in light of Althusser's reading of Marx, one may say that what has caused Cheng's loss of humanness at the construction site and the toxic chemical plant is his involuntary involvement in the relations of production in which he plays the role of mere machines being owned and controlled by others. In the specific case of Cheng, his machine-like role in the production process is almost literal rather than metaphorical. His low status as a peasant worker without home and identity in the city decides that he may fall easy prey to exploitation and to the most deplorable situation without the basic protection and rights that any life would deserve. It is actually at this point (when Cheng loses all that would give him the sense of dignity as a human being) that Marx's antihumanism overlaps with posthumanism. In fact, the man in his machine-like role is even lower than an animal.

There is still one more important contributing factor to Cheng's extreme dehumanization in his lower-than-animal state, which the story demonstrates through the contrast between his and his dog's reactions to oppression. While Cheng shows neither desire nor power to rebel against whatever ills he suffers, Peace the dog is always full of fighting spirit, always ready to protect his master and himself with his sharp fangs. His short experience among the dogs in the slaughter cage is illustrative here. Being the only "wild" dog from the mountains among a host of stray dogs and sick dogs from the city, Peace is fearless. To get food and life and the chance to reunite with his master, he puts up fierce struggles against his competitors, which, however, bring him a painful realization: "It occurs to Peace suddenly that he has become senseless and ruthless. He has become a wild beast, not in the city, but in the wilderness. But he is in the city unmistakably" (233). In the dog's comparison between the wilderness and the city, both of which are cruel, it is the latter that both evokes and harbors more and greater cruelty. That Peace is humanized is evident in his self-realization quoted earlier. The dog in this way could be regarded as a metaphor, "an outbreak of the primitive wild power of Shennongjia, and a resistant warning to the city" (Liu and Yu 61). The dog is also a metaphor in the sense that he possesses all that his master as a human being is supposed to have but has lost once dislocated, the most important of which is his instinct for survival by all means, by fighting and struggling if necessary. The significance of Cheng's loss of his instinct is suggested in the following comment made by Huggan and Tiffin: "Contemporary humanity, having materially destroyed vast areas of wilderness—and many other animals—is now routinely configured as spiritually hollow, as lacking *the essence of the human* through the repression, withdrawal, destruction or absence, rather than latent threat, of the 'inner world'" (134; my italics). Huggan and Tiffin help us to see that Cheng's loss of his survival instinct, which is part of his inner wildness and which he as a complete and real human being must have, is a crucial factor in his dehumanization. The tragic fate of Cheng exposes the industrial power as most fundamentally destructive to humanity, for it brings threat not only to human existence but also, and more importantly, to the human spirit. It is clear by now that the industrial power of the city that has brought both physical and spiritual death to Cheng is the very target of the writer's posthumanist critique. In this critique, we hear a clear echo of the ecological idea that regards the natural power in preference to the industrial power as healthier to all humans and animals in its control.

There are also strong ecocritical and ethical implications in how we understand the dog Peace, whether we recognize it as a metaphorical or a real animal. Critics have commented extensively on both the advantages and disadvantages of thinking in terms of animal metaphors. To criticize the physical and cultural marginalization of animals in capitalist modernity, John Berger invokes, as Nicole Shukin has aptly described, a precapitalist relation of human and animal mediated by metaphor. It is a relationship that probably dates back to the very beginning of human language. While asserting that "the essential relation between man and animal was metaphoric," he thought it reasonable to suppose that "the first metaphor was animal" (16). Berger's attempt to trace "an ancient bloodline between metaphor and animal life" is praised by Nicole Shukin (Shukin 33). But Shukin also finds this attempt risky for it can obscure "how the rendering of animals, both metaphorically and materially, constitutes a politically and historically contingent, rather than a primal or universal, relationship" (33–34). Shukin is here warning against the tendency to see an unconditional connection between the reliance on animal metaphor and the importance of animal life in reality. In fact, she finds the animal figures in Derrida's works functioning in such a dangerous way as to "estrange every claim of presence" (34).

We may learn caution from Shukin in interpreting Peace's experiences in the slaughter cage. When Liu and Yu see the dog as a metaphor of "the primitive wild power of Shennongjia," they are apparently expressing an ecological value by celebrating the power of the wild. But there is actually a danger in reading the dog as a mere metaphor. If we interpret the slaughter cage episode as nothing but a metaphorical triumph of the wild power of nature over the hypocrisy of culture, we are downplaying the seriousness of one harsh reality, which the episode reflects: the actual lack of legislation to protect Peace and all the other caged dogs against their ill fate. The fact that the dogs in the cage ready for butchery are mostly strays and stolen pets is a truthful reflection of a serious problem in China, which has increasingly worsened in the last ten years or so and which has not yet been addressed. Compared with Peace's unbelievable good luck, what waits for the other dogs in the slaughter cage in the fictional world is what always happens in the real world. Besides, an exclusively metaphorical reading of Peace's fight against his human oppressors may prevent us from seeing the realistic significance of animal resistance to animal ethics. This is obviously what Calarco wants us to see by drawing our attention to "the unique ways in which animal themselves resist subjection and domination" (76).

In attacking the modern industrial slaughterhouse, Wolfe wisely recognizes "the humanist discourse of species" as the common underlying cause of the human exploitation of animals as well as that of other humans. He writes,

[A]s long as it is institutionally taken for granted that it is all right to systematically exploit and kill nonhuman animals simply because of their species, then the humanist discourse of species will always be available for use by some humans against other humans as well, to countenance violence against the social other of whatever species—or gender, or race, or class, or sexual difference. (*Animal Rites* 8)

When Liu and Yu comment on the "metaphorical co-construction" of the characters' miserable lives in the double narratives of Cheng and Peace, they are doing similar work to Wolfe's by emphasizing the inseparable fate of the man and the animal in their shared predicament (60). But the emphasis on the metaphorical feature of Peace's narration is problematic, for it denies such capacities as memory and reason to the dog. Those who raise the charge of anthropomorphism against the character of Peace should be told about those experiments in cognitive science that has proved a dog's possession of thinking ability (Wolfe, *What* 32–33). It is perhaps better to follow David Sztybel's example by regarding animals as "persons" with distinctive personality (Castricano, "Introduction" 21). With these scientific discoveries in mind, we may admit that the author's creation of the dog character by giving him a voice of his own is less a naïve act of anthropomorphism than an honest and posthumanist recognition of the animal and the human as not fundamentally different from each other. The author's concern for both humans and animals at the bottom of society and his view of them as connected take on a new significance against the following remark by Michael Allen Fox and Lesley Mclean: "We may be far from treating fellow human beings as true equals, but this shouldn't deter us from investigating the bonds that might be developed across species boundaries" (151). Chen's posthumanist view of the animal as the equal of humanity is his attempt to develop such cross-species bounds. Moreover, by setting up analogies between the abuse of human beings and violence toward animals, Chen diverges from the most common form of humanism that places more value and moral weight on human life and that would object to any comparison between human and animal suffering.

Yingsong Chen admits that in his value system, nature weighs over the country and the country over the city (Zhou and Chen 43). His Shennongjia stories express his values involving serious moral, social, and ecological considerations. Predating ecocriticism by decades, Raymond Williams writes about the country and the city and the implications of differing ideologies for human survival: "An insane over-confidence in the specialised powers of metropolitan industrialism has brought us to the point where however we precisely assess it the risk to human survival is becoming evident, or if we survive, as I think we shall, there is the clear impossibility of continuing as we are" (301). Williams comes to this conclusion through a historical study of the contrast of the country and city and their respective values in British society. By presenting the victimization of unprivileged humans and animals under the force of animalizing nature or dehumanizing culture in China and by exposing the latter as a greater evil, Chen's stories express a view compatible to William's. And his stories are good to listen to exactly because of the strong social, moral, and ecological obligations the author feels toward all that has fallen prey to the oppressive industrial power, the city and the country, humans and animals.

NOTES

1. The three places are all situated in Hubei province in central China. Shennongjia is a huge mountainous area (3,253 square kilometers) in the northwest of Hubei province. Being the only forest region in China

that has acquired the status of "administrative district," Shennongjia has a high forest coverage of up to 88 percent in the whole region and 96 percent in the protected area. Due to its relatively isolated location, the majority of the area remains undeveloped. Wuhan, in contrast, is the capital city of Hubei and the center of industry, commerce, and education as well as the largest city in central China. Yichang is a big city close to Shennongjia and ranks second after Wuhan in terms of economy within Hubei province.

2. The term refers to Chinese economic reform implemented throughout China since the late 1970s.

3. For the aforementioned observations made by Ping Mang et al., please refer to pp. 5, 7, 273–74 in particular.

4. There have been rumors about the possible existence of certain half man and half beast creature in Shennongjia, though no hard evidence has ever been provided.

5. Commentators on the issue of dichotomy include Xinmin Zhou (Zhou and Chen 42–43), Jin Liu and Quanheng Yu (61), and Yichen Fu, to name some.

6. Coming up in Chinese literature around the turn of the twenty-first century, "bottom narratives" and "suffering narratives" take as their subjects the misery and destitution of those living at the bottom of society, such as peasant workers and the urban poor.

7. Ximan is the character's pet name. As the character is only addressed in the story by his pet name, no family name is used here in this case.

WORKS CITED

Althusser, Louis. "Marxism and Humanism." In *Posthumanism*. Ed. Neil Badmington. New York and London: Palgrave Macmillan, 2000. 30–33.

Berger, John. *Why Look at Animals?* London: Penguin Books, 2009.

Calarco, Matthew. *Zoographies: The Question of the Animal from Heidegger to Derrida*. New York: Columbia UP, 2008.

Castricano, Jodey, ed. *Animal Subjects: An Ethical Reader in a Posthuman World*. Waterloo: Wilfrid Laurier UP, 2008.

———. "Introduction." In Castricano, *Animal Subjects*. 1–32.

Chen, Yingsong. "Anecdotes about Balihuang." In *Selected Works of Chen Yingsong*. 257–98.

———. "Peace Dog." In *Selected Works of Chen Yingsong*. 216–56.

———. *Selected Works of Chen Yingsong*. Wuhan: Yangtze Literature and Art Press, 2010.

———. "To Live Like White Clouds." In *Selected Works of Chen Yingsong*. 165–202.

Fox, Michael Allen and Lesley Mclean. "Animals in Moral Space." In Castricano, *Animal Subjects*. 145–76.

Fu, Yichen. "Looking into the Human Nature Caught in the City-Country Dichotomy: On Chen Yingsong's Shennongjia Series." *Fiction Review* 5 (2005): 50–54.

Haraway, Donna J. "A Cyborg Manifesto: Science, Technology, and Socialist-Feminism in the Late Twentieth Century." In Badmington, *Posthumanism.* 69–84.

Huggan, Graham and Helen Tiffin. *Postcolonial Ecocriticism: Literature, Animals, Environment.* London and New York: Routledge, 2010.

Li, Yunlei. "An Interview with Chen Yingsong." *Literary and Art Theory and Criticism* 5 (2007): 43–47.

Liu, Jin and Yu Quanheng. "A Sorrowful Song of the Drifting: Reading Chen Yingsong's Novelette 'Peace Dog'" *Modern Literary Magazine* 5 (2006): 60–61.

Ma, Jiewei. "Modern Bodies in the Making: Tales from a Factory and a Bar in Sourthern China." In *Empire, Cosmopolis and Modernity.* Ed. Luo Gang. Nanjing: Jiangsu People's Press, 2006. 339–65.

Mang, Ping, et al. *The World of the Interrelated Self and Other: Chinese Beliefs, Lives and Views of Animals.* Beijing: Chinese University of Politics and Laws Press, 2009.

Shukin, Nicole. *Animal Capital: Rendering Life in Biopolitical Times.* Minneapolis and London: U of Minnesota P, 2009.

Sun, Chunmin. "The Receding Figure of A God: An Archetypal Image in Chen Yingsong's 'Peace Dog' and 'Anecdotes about Balihuang.'" *Masterpiece Review* 6 (2008): 66–69.

Wang, Xiangsheng. "Exploration and Interrogation inside the Modern Predicament: On Three Pieces from Chen Yingsong's Shennongjia Series." *Anhui Literature* 10 (2008): 38–39.

Williams, Raymond. *The Country and the City.* New York: Oxford UP, 1973.

Wolfe, Cary. *Animal Rites: American Culture, the Discourse of Species, and Posthumanist Theory.* Chicago: U of Chicago P, 2003.

———. *What Is Posthumanism?* Minneapolis and London: U of Minnesota P, 2010.

Zhou, Xinmin and Chen Yingsong. "To Guard and Redeem the Soul: An Interview with Chen Yingsong." *Fiction Review* 5 (2007): 40–47.

13

ON THE FOUR KEYSTONES OF ECOLOGICAL AESTHETIC APPRECIATION

Xiangzhan Cheng

Since the initial publication of Joseph W. Meeker's paper "Notes Toward an Ecological Esthetic" in 1972 (4–15), ecological aesthetics (ecoaesthetics hereafter) has become one of the leading disciplines in the field of aesthetics. However, there is still some dissent among scholars about the exact object of ecoaesthetic study. Many scholars within and out of China confuse ecoaesthetics with environmental aesthetics, and some scholars still question the legitimacy of ecoaesthetics. We can consult the more mature discipline of environmental aesthetics to help define and develop ecoaesthetics. The objective of the study of environmental aesthetics is "environmental appreciation," which is clearly different from "art appreciation." It critiques and transcends the Hegelian philosophy of art, which views an artifact as an object of study. For scholars of environmental aesthetics, the main issue concerns the distinction and relationship between environmental appreciation and art appreciation. As for the study of ecoaesthetics, its object of study concerns how to appreciate aesthetically and ecologically. While it disapproves of traditional aesthetic appreciation that is not ecologically oriented (or without an ecological awareness), it does not necessarily oppose a form of aesthetic enjoyment based on artistic form, so to speak. In a nutshell, the argument of environmental aesthetics centers on the issue of the aesthetic object: is the object for the study of aesthetics artwork or the environment? By the same token, the argument of ecoaesthetics concentrates on the issue of the aesthetic way (or manner) and asks how to engage an aesthetic activity governed by an ecological awareness. In other words, it asks how to form an ecological aesthetic way (or manner) by letting ecological awareness play a leading role in human aesthetic activity and experience.

The major argument of this essay is that ecoaesthetics is different from nonecological-oriented aesthetics (or "traditional aesthetics" hereafter). It is a new type of aesthetic way and conception responding to global ecological crises, using ecological ethics as its theoretical foundation, relying on ecological knowledge to inspire imagination and elicit emotions, and aiming at conquering conventional, anthropocentric aesthetic preferences.

Moreover, there exist some fundamental differences between ecoaesthetics and traditional aesthetics, and the process of constructing an ecological aesthetic theory is one that elucidates such a difference.

The first keystone of ecological aesthetics is that it completely abandons a conventional aesthetics that is predicated on an opposition between humanity and the world. Subsequently it is replaced by the model of aesthetic engagement that promotes the idea of the unity of humans and the world.

In order to further analyze the theoretical fallacies of traditional aesthetics, it is useful to analyze the term "*shen-mei*" in Chinese and the context of the history of Sino-aesthetics in which the discourse shen-mei is situated. Influenced by Plato's philosophy on beauty, Sino-aestheticians have long deemed beauty as an objective entity, and the discussion has long been revolving around the issues of "the essence of beauty," "evaluating or judgment of beauty" (shen-mei), "sense of beauty" (perception of beauty), and artifacts (or the materialization of beauty). Henceforth, the trio of "beauty/judgment of art/art" became the dominant discourse of Sino-aesthetic theory.

While this chapter has no intention of criticizing this type of aesthetic model, it is, nevertheless, important to clarify the term "*shen-mei*" to see how this term has been misunderstood and misused. *The Contemporary Chinese Dictionary* [Chinese-English Edition] defines "*shen-mei*" as "comprehending the beauty of things or a work of art." In its English explanation, shen-mei refers to "aesthetics or appreciation of the beautiful." According to the dictionary, *shen* can be used as a verb and means "examining" or "interrogating." As a verb in a verb-object word group, *shen* can be linked with other words to denote the meaning of "reviewing manuscript" (*shen-gao*), "investigating a case" (*shen-an*), "examining the title of an article or questions before writing or answering" (*shen-ti*), and so on (Dictionary 1708–709). Due to such a convention, shen-mei thereby can also be understood as a verb-object word group, that is, "to review/judge/evaluate beauty," "to comprehend the beauty of things or a work of art"—in short, "to comprehend the beautiful." Here shen denotes the meaning of "comprehension" (but "appreciation" seems more appropriate), and "the beautiful" refers to the beauty of "things or a work of art." Briefly, then, the activity of shen-mei is that of "appreciating the beautiful." There are many similar verb-object word groups such as "appreciating a flower," "appreciating the Moon," and so forth.

This way of looking at the term *"shen-mei"* as a verb-object word group is prevalent among other Sino-aestheticians, like a form of "Sino-unconsciousness"—a powerful cultural habit and way of thinking. And when Sino-aestheticians notice that the aesthetic objects include not only beauty but also what is ugly, it naturally gives rise to other verb-object word groups such as "to judge/evaluate the ugly." According to such a logic and linguistic law, we can construct and explain other aesthetic-related verb-object word groups such as "to review/appreciate the comic," "to review/appreciate sublime," "to review/appreciate the absurd," and so on.

If we translate the verb-object word phrase, especially "review/appreciate beauty," into English, the fallacy becomes very obvious. The corresponding word for *"shen-mei"* in English is "aesthetic," which is not a verb but an adjective and denotes the meaning of the sensuous. When an "s" is added, it turns the adjective into a noun to denote the meaning of "aesthetic theory." Obviously *The Contemporary Chinese Dictionary* has noticed this, as is reflected in its first explanation of shen-mei as "aesthetics." Despite its inaccuracy, it nonetheless reveals a linguistic correlation between the Chinese term shen-mei and the English word "aesthetic." What is praiseworthy here is its second explanation: "appreciation of the beautiful" or "to appreciate beauty." The linguistic difference between Chinese and English resides in the fact that when a word changes from a verb or an adjective to a noun, it affects the word itself in English. For instance, "to appreciate" is a verb; as a noun, it is changed to "appreciation." In Chinese, the word used for the verb and the noun remains unchanged, and, as a result, it tends to create confusion.

To sum up, in Chinese aesthetic theory, shen-mei corresponds to the term "aesthetic" in English; however, in popular Chinese aesthetic theory, it is often construed as a verb-object word phrase to denote the meaning of "to appreciate of the beautiful" (*"shen"* here literally means "to appreciate" and *"mei"* literally means "the beautiful"). The confusing transformation in the process of translating the English term "aesthetic" as an adjective into a Chinese phrase shen-mei, a verb-object word group in Chinese language, typically reflects the difficulties and confusions in the communication between Chinese culture and Western cultures. What is more important here is that shen-mei as verb-object phrase in Chinese typically reflects the philosophical doctrine of objectifying the world in traditional aesthetics.

In traditional aesthetic theory, what is implied in such an aesthetic theory is exactly a "rational philosophical tradition" starting from Descartes onward. Renowned contemporary aesthetician Arnold Berleant criticizes the assumption that art is something that can be comprehended and controlled. He writes: "[T]his objectification of art is the predictable product of an intellectualist tradition, one that grasps the world by knowing it through objectifying it, and that controls the world by subduing it to the order of thought" (5). From this traditional philosophy of art, humans are the epistemological subjects apart from the world. Aesthetic activities are frequently understood as an aesthetic appreciation of an "aesthetic subject" toward an "aesthetic object." Sino-aestheticians tend to understand shen-mei as verb-object word group, unfortunately exemplifying such a Cartesian way of thinking. To attack such an aesthetic tradition, Berleant calls for "aesthetics of engagement," which is rooted in phenomenology. He thinks that the concept of "engagement" encapsulates the features of a contextual aesthetic:

> Aesthetic engagement renounces the traditional separations between the appreciator and the art object, between the artist and the viewer, and between the performer and these others. The psychological distance that traditional aesthetics imposes between the appreciator and the object of art is a barrier that obstructs the participatory involvement that art encourages…In contrast with this, boundaries fade away in aesthetic engagement and we experience continuity directly and intimately. (152)

Only through an aesthetics of engagement that transcends the subject-object opposition can an intimate relationship between humans and the world be established, through which to experience the interconnectedness of all life explained by ecology and deep ecology. And this is the fundamental contribution of aesthetic activity to ecological awareness.

The second keystone of ecological aesthetic appreciation is that ecological aesthetic appreciation is an aesthetic activity predicated on ecological ethics. It revises and strengthens the relationship between aesthetics and ethics in traditional aesthetics, and it takes ecological awareness as the premise of ecological appreciation. In this sense, the presupposition of ecological aesthetic appreciation is to have ecological consciousness.

In traditional aesthetic theory, the relation between aesthetics and ethics is an age-old and universal question. For example, Plato sees the ultimate goodness as the final ontology of beauty. Confucius's *jinshan jinmei* (literally, "perfect goodness and perfect beauty") connects goodness with beauty. These two famous examples demonstrate that ethics and aesthetics, or moral consciousness and aesthetic activity, are interrelated. The disruption between these two occurs in modern Western philosophy. For instance, when Western philosophy begins to divide knowledge, will, and feeling/emotions and correspond them, respectively, to epistemology, ethics, and aesthetics, it severs the internal connections among them. Kant's philosophical framework represented by his three famous *Critiques* (*Critique of Pure Reason, Critique of Practical Reason,* and *Critique of Judgment*) is the typical representation of the philosophical conception. However, Kant proposes the famous phrase: "The beautiful is the symbol of the morally good" (228), which directly illustrates the relationship between aesthetics and ethics. However, because post-Kantian philosophy of art (and art theory in general) is influenced by the prevalent notion of "the autonomy of art," it, to some degree, disconnects art from ethics.

Distinct from traditional aesthetic theory, ecological aesthetic appreciation strongly stresses the importance of moral awareness. There will be no ecological aesthetic appreciation without ecological ethical consciousness. Starting from the 1960s, with the global ecology movement, there also arose ecological ethical consciousness. It expanded the concept of "ethical community" to include all species and their dwelling places. Such an expanded version of ethical community recognizes the living rights for all species and their inner value. Here the main idea is "biosphere." According to the *Oxford Dictionary of Ecology*, the definition of biosphere is "[t]he part of the earth's environment in which living organisms are found, and with which they interact to produce a steady-state system, effectively a whole-planet ecosystem. Sometimes it is termed 'ecosphere' to emphasize the interconnection of the living and non-living components" (Allaby 52).

The fundamental difference between ecological and traditional ethics resides in the fact that the scope and objects of the ethical community are different. Here it begs an important question: within the biosphere, can nonhuman species become moral subjects? A deeper question to ask is this: do nonhuman species possess any intrinsic value independent from the benefits they provide to humans? The answer offered by American ecologist Aldo Leopold is positive, an answer based on the progress of "expanding concentric circles." Such a notion can be found through a brief glance at the history of Western ethics. In ancient Greece, for instance, the ethical community consists of only aristocrats. Both women and slaves were excluded and regarded as private property without any dignity. They, in other words, were not considered as ethical subjects. With the evolution of history, the slave system was abolished and women came to enjoy the same rights as men. Thus, in the era of global ecological crisis, shouldn't humans continue to expand it to include other nonhuman species?

Leopold's answer is positive and his land ethic serves as the foundation for modern ecological ethics (201–26). His "concentric circle theory" finds an echo in the Confucian concentric way of thinking. It begins with the self and expands outward through layers of widening groups, from family to community to nation and beyond, as exemplified in the opening chapter of *The Great Learning* that deals with the question of how to achieve world peace. It can be paraphrased in this way: if one wants to bring peace to the world, one should first begin with studying and understanding the underlying principles of things so as to become righteous and honest. Once one achieves this, one will be cultivated, and as a result, he or she can bring order to the family, and then the country can become organized. Eventually the whole world can become peaceful. From here we see a gradual progress of expansion from self to other in a concentric order. Ecological ethics is also based on a similar logic of layered expansion: the object of an ethical concern begins with self (self-cultivation), then expands to home (home-governance), then to society (the governance of the country), and eventually to the world (bring peace).

Similar concentric models can also be found in the ancient Chinese philosopher Zhang Zai (1020–1077), who came up with a philosophical notion of brotherhood and sisterhood: "All human beings are my brothers and sisters, and all creatures are my companions" (Shi 43). Also, the concept of "treating heaven and earth (or everything in the world) as one body" broached by the Ming Dynasty philosopher Wang Yangming (1472–1529), can serve as a prototype of Chinese ecological ethical theory. Finally, in his paper "The Ecological Turn in New Confucian Humanism," Tu Weiming points out that "[t]he idea of the unity of Heaven and humanity implies four inseparable dimensions of the human condition: self, community, nature, and Heaven. The full distinctiveness of each enhances, rather than impedes, a thorough integration of the others" (Tu 233–44). The following four salient features constitute the substance of the New Confucian ecological vision: (1) fruitful interaction between self and community; (2) a sustainable harmonious relationship between the human species and nature; (3) mutual responsiveness between the human heart-and-mind and the Way of Heaven; and (4) self-knowledge and cultivation to complete the triad (233–44).

If we synthesize the aforementioned Chinese and Western ecological theories, we can reach a conclusion that the core of ecological ethics is an outward concentric expansion of a benevolent heart, from a traditional ethics of human-to-human relations to an ecological ethics of "human-to-world." While one loves oneself, one loves fellow human beings, and, at the same time, one loves "ten thousand things" on earth—that is, loves all living beings within earth's living community or biosphere. One of the symptoms of ecological crises is the despoiling of nature, even war among some nations, due to the shortage of natural resources. It worsens interpersonal relationships. The second symptom is the creation of environmental injustice, that is, environmental degradation affects communities and further deepens a sense of ecological crisis. What it means is that ecological crises have resulted in the degradation of traditional human-to-human ethics: "loving your human fellows" is getting more difficult, let alone "loving ten thousand things" in biosphere. Therefore, to advocate "loving all things" as promoted in ecological ethics can be regarded as a way of improving the moral trait of human beings and human nature in times of ecological crisis. Considering this excellent practice of frugality (or "cherishing things" in Chinese) in Chinese traditional ethics, we might extend the practice to embrace "loving things" as advocated in ecological ethics. The key point lies in whether one has an all-encompassing benevolent heart (or whether one can develop an "ecological care"). And this is an example of how a connection between ecology and psychology, or natural ecology and spiritual ecology, can be established.

The ecological ethics I discuss here can be summarized as "humanism accentuating the holism of biosphere." It is similar to ecohumanism in Western academia. Ecohumanism is a synthesis of modernist humanism and radical ecology. While modern humanism criticizes religious superstition and stresses atheist rationalism, experience and human value, radical ecology excessively focuses on the independent value of the nonhuman species and the environment. According to Philip Regal, a professor of ecology at the University of Minnesota, "If knowledge of the human condition is a keystone of humanism, then it is important for humanists to understand the larger system in which we exist... 'Ecohumanism' implies insights into patterns of connectedness among individuals and between individuals and institutions and with the non-human environment" (Tapp 62). Here the "patterns of connectedness among individuals and between individuals and institutions and with the non-human environment" implies "loving non-human being/things."

To sum up, ecohumanism is a form of humanism that embraces the concept of ecoholism of biosphere. It includes two main points. The first one is the ecological vision of biospherical holism. Holism here does not refer to the entity of the solar system or the universe but only refers to the biosphere on this earth. Such a notion of holism does not sacrifice the ultimate or metaphysical dimension of ecology when developing the idea of "ecological love/care." Obviously, our ecological aesthetic experience may contain a holistic "universal or cosmic consciousness and experience." The reason why I limit the scope of holism to our planet is that human beings are by far still not capable of assessing whether the universe as a whole is in a state of balance. The second point is that while humanism disapproves of anthropocentrism, it announces humanity as its base, because human-kind is the merely species that can define the conception of biosphere and whose living quality and sustainability is the focus of humanis-tic research. The ethics of ecohumanism's "loving all things" can be short-handed as "ecological consciousness," and it is the foundation of ecological appreciation.

The third keystone of ecological aesthetic appreciation is that it is imperative for ecological aesthetic appreciation to rely on the ecologi-cal knowledge to refine taste and to enjoy the hidden rich aesthetic properties of the ordinary (even the trivial). Without basic ecological knowledge, it will be impossible to engage a full ecological aesthetic appreciation.

In traditional aesthetic theory, a series of questions concerns issues of the relationship between knowledge and the aesthetic (i.e., the conflict between beauty and truth, art and truth and art and science, art and knowledge and aesthetics and knowledge, and so forth). The "father of aesthetics," Alexander G. Baumgarten, once defined aes-thetics as "a science of sensitive knowing"; and the knowledge result-ing from such a science is autonomous, the nature of which is different from that of logic. Accordingly, the task of aesthetics is to transform vague information received by our senses into crisp clear objects of perception (Cooper 40–44). Baumgarten's goal is to theorize the way logical cognition is different from that of aesthetic cognition. After Baumgarten, Kant also viewed the aesthetic process differently from knowledge. Aesthetic judgment is distinct from logical judgment. In the "first moment of aesthetic judgment," Kant writes:

> If we wish to decide whether something is beautiful or not, we do not use understanding to refer the presentation to the object so as to give rise to cognition; rather, we use imagination (perhaps in connection with understanding) to refer the presentation to the subject and his feeling of pleasure or displeasure. Hence a judgment of taste is not a cognitive judgment as so is not a logical judgment but an aesthetic one, by which we mean a judgment whose determining basis cannot be other than subjective. (44)

Both Baumgarten and Kant elucidate a characteristic of aesthetic appreciation—that is, an aesthetic appreciation is not a cognitive activity: it aims at obtaining aesthetic experience, not knowledge. However, it does mean that it is appropriate to ignore the intimate relationship between aesthetic appreciation and knowledge. It would be a partial understanding if we did so. Here we can ask two follow-up questions: first, does an aesthetic appreciation require knowledge? Second, if yes, what function does knowledge play in the process of aesthetic appreciation?

With regard to the first question, an aesthetic appreciation requires knowledge in order to proceed. For instance, without basic knowledge of Chinese philosophy, one cannot fully appreciate ancient Chinese landscape painting; without understanding Christianity, one cannot properly appreciate the famous religious paintings in the West. At some level, one can say that the process of appreciating a famous religious painting is that of comprehending its thoughts and contents. To evaluate a work of art and its aesthetic value, one needs to compare it with other paintings. In other words, background knowledge, art history, and the like provide a basis for aesthetic appreciation and render a point of reference for artistic assessment. The same can be applied to the appreciation of nature. However, the knowledge required for nature appreciation is that of nature.

Why is ecological knowledge necessary for ecological aesthetic appreciation to make it different from traditional aesthetic appreciation? In other words, what are the crucial roles that ecological knowledge can play in ecological aesthetic appreciation? According to Leopold's "Land Aesthetic," summed up by Callicott, there are two fundamental roles that ecological knowledge can play: the first is to refine humanity's taste and the second is to appreciate the hidden rich aesthetic properties of the ordinary.

In his "Conservation Esthetic," Leopold emphasizes the importance of "the perception of the natural processes." Taking the swoop of a hawk as an example, he declares that only to those who have taken "nature study," the swoop of a hawk can be perceived as "the drama of evolution," which may thrill a hundred successive witnesses; to someone without ecological knowledge, it is only "a threat to the full frying-pan," and his response to it is nothing but a "shotgun." Leopold writes: "Daniel Boone's reaction depended not only on the quality of what he saw, but on the quality of the mental eye with which he saw it. Ecological science has wrought a change in the mental eye" (173–74). "The mental eye" is what Leopold calls "the perceptive faculty" (174). The logical consequence of his ideas is the statement as given: only appreciated by a changed perceptive faculty, can the "quality" of a thing be appreciated aesthetically and ecologically.[1] So Leopold thinks that "building receptivity into the still unlovely human mind" is much more important than "building roads into lovely country" (177). In another work, *Round River*, Leopold calls this kind of cultivation of sensibility "a refined taste in natural objects" (Callicott 161).

In order to appreciate the hidden rich aesthetic properties of the ordinary (even the trivial), ecological knowledge is also necessary. Traditionally speaking, aesthetic objects such as great artworks are always rich in aesthetic qualities (i.e., artistic quality) with high aesthetic value. Dominated by the philosophy of beauty, philosophers since Plato always concentrate on beauty. So it is safe to assert that traditional Western aesthetic theory never pays any attention to the ordinary, let alone to the trivial things. It is Leopold who changed the aesthetic tradition, and he was quite consciously aware of the profound revolution in general sensibility for which he was calling. He contemptuously disparaged "that under-aged brand of esthetics which limits the definition of 'scenery' to lakes and pine trees" (191). He declares that "a plain exterior often conceals hidden riches" (Callicott 163). As Callicott summarizes, ecology, history, paleontology, geology, biogeography—each a form of knowledge or cognition—penetrate the surface provided by direct sensory experience and supply "substance to scenery" (163).

As a loyal and outstanding successor to Leopold, Callicott takes his own environmental experience in a northern bog as convincing example to develop his ideas of ecological aesthetic appreciation. The plants in the bog he visits at least once each season "are not, by garden standards, beautiful." Wearing wet shoes and trousers, with his skin being bitten by mosquitoes, his experience in the mucky moat "is not particularly pleasant," "but it is always somehow satisfying aesthetically" (165). We may ask a question: why is unpleasant experience somehow satisfying aesthetically? I believe that this question penetrates the heart of ecological aesthetic appreciation. Callicott's answer is that, by his smell, touch, and feel, in his frequent visits to experience the changes (i.e., the rhythm) of the four seasons, he discovers that "there is a rare music in this place. It is orchestrated and deeply moving" (165). Although Callicott uses the phrase of "the beauty of the bog"—an expression clearly influenced by traditional "philosophy of beauty," which tends to describe some objects as "beautiful" or "ugly" and tends to think that only those "beautiful objects" are "aesthetic objects"[2]—he redefines the term "beauty" as "a function of the palpable organization and closure of the interconnected living components. There is a sensible fittingness, a unity there, not unlike that of a symphony or a tragedy. But these connections and relations are not directly sensed in the aesthetic moment, they are *known* and *projected*" (166–67). Based on his own rich environmental experience and his wide ecological knowledge, Callicott calls Leopold's "Land Aesthetic" a new natural aesthetics, which is first "informed by ecological and evolutionary natural history." This kind of aesthetic theory of nature "enables us to mine the hidden riches of the ordinary" and "ennobles the commonplace." The experience of a marsh or bog is "aesthetically satisfying" less for what is literally sensed than for "what is known or schematically imagined of its ecology" (Callicott 168). So it is ecology as a scientific discipline that reveals what I called "ecological aesthetic quality" in the natural world. With appreciating the ecological aesthetic quality displayed by the knowledge of ecology, we are in the process of ecological aesthetic appreciation, which is dramatically different from traditional appreciation of beauty in nature.

Fourth and finally, the two guiding principles of ecological value for ecological aesthetic appreciation are biodiversity and ecosystem health. Humanity must overcome and transcend anthropocentric value standards and human aesthetic preference, reflecting and criticizing anthropocentric aesthetic preferences and habits.

Generally speaking, human activities are values-based ones. So what are the right values in our ecological aesthetic activity? With regard to this question, it is easy for us to think of Leopold's legacy.

Leopold concludes his "Land Ethic" with a very strong statement: "A thing is right when it tends to preserve the integrity, stability, and beauty of the biotic community. It is wrong when it tends otherwise" (224–25). This "dictum" is strongly criticized by Canadian ecocritic

Simon Estok as "philosophically ungrounded and scientifically naïve."[3] On the other hand, some ecologists propose a kind of "global bioethics" that forthrightly accepts and seeks to build on Leopold's dictum. In contrast with the short-term view of future development of human society, ecologists hope to promote the long-term view based on fundamental ecological values, "with value placed on species survival and on maintaining healthy ecosystems worldwide. The logical consequences of extending ethics and law to the species, ecosystem, and landscape levels are reduced population growth and healthy life-support systems, leading to favorable survival for all people and for all life" (Odum 473). Very clearly, "species survival" means "biodiversity," and "healthy ecosystem" implies "ecosystem health." I argue that the two guiding principles of ecological value for ecological aesthetic appreciation are biodiversity and ecosystem health.

The notion of biodiversity gained popularity in late 1980s to describe all aspects of biological diversity, including in particular the richness of species, the complication of ecosystems, and the variety of genetic mutations (Allaby 49). Ecosystem health is advocated widely as a useful, perhaps essential, concept in ecological policy. The majority of ecological policy debates concern ecosystem "health" rather than ecosystem "integrity." "Such an emphasis on health (ecosystems altered by humans) is understandable because the vast majority of ecosystems are not pristine or even close to pristine" (Lackey 437–43). So "integrity" in Leopold's statement given earlier is replaced by "health" with the development of science of ecology since his time.[4]

Based on these two ecological standards, we will discover some fallacies committed in traditional aesthetic evaluation, ranging from an ignorance of a species' benefit or detriment to an ecosystem to "taking the detrimental view as beneficial." In other words, human aesthetic preference has resulted in countless ecological catastrophes. *Eichhornia* (or water hyacinth) is a case in point. This plant species, which originates from Venezuela in South America, was transported to the United States to be on display at the 1884 World Expo in New Orleans. People from all over the world were enchanted by the beauty of its flower and took it home. Ever since then, this aggressive species has become the number one threatening plant and is listed as one of the top ten most dangerous plants. The Ministry of Environmental Protection in China has listed it as one of the 16 most invasive species. Yesterday's beauty turns into today's econightmare! Here the moral lesson from the standpoint of ecological appreciation to be learned is this: humans should not blindly appreciate the beauty of *eichhornia* without taking into consideration its aggressive nature.

Compared to the example of *eichhornia*, the ecological disaster brought forth by traditional aesthetic preference embodied in "natural beauty" is less explicit, despite a bigger danger. The so-called natural beauty mainly refers to the aesthetic quality of natural things, including their pleasant colors and forms of things, enjoyable sound, seductive smells, and so on. The most typical example of this is the beauty of a natural landscape (i.e., scenic beauty). To enjoy a beautiful natural landscape is human nature, and normally one would not turn down an opportunity to do so, regardless of his or her virtue. Because of this, beautiful natural landscapes have been despoiled, especially in today's society where human population grows out of control, while the gap between the rich and the poor has widened. To own and to enjoy the view of beautiful natural landscape has become the privilege of the rich and powerful. Society's powerless class can only live in undesired, environmentally degraded areas. If we look around the world, all the beautiful natural places have been annexed into the operation of capitalism and co-opted into the logic of power. They are treated as "natural resources" to be developed and sold as real estate.[5] From the standpoint of social reality as such, the traditional appreciation of beauty cannot help harmonize human-nature relationship. On the contrary, it becomes the primal force of the destruction of nature. Therefore, the ecological aesthetics I am promoting here is a "critical aesthetics"—not only does it criticize the fallacies of traditional aesthetic theory as well as the various crimes against nature, but it also utilizes the viewpoint of nonhuman species to criticize and reflect humans' innate aesthetic preferences. It is true that everyone has a tendency to love and appreciate beautiful things. However, the love for the beautiful has to be founded on the respect for all things equally, too. That is, we have to appreciate the beautiful with an ecological awareness. Otherwise, if we continue to make the same mistake that we did with *eichhornia*, we will create more ecological disasters.

CONCLUSION

This chapter contends that ecological aesthetics is the theory of ecological aesthetic appreciation. It has a prominent distinction from traditional aesthetics. Four keystone points can be summarized and conceptualized as "one presupposition, three steps." The presupposition refers to the critique of a linguistic understanding of shen-mei as a "verb-object word group" and suggests replacing it with the conception of shen-mei as a form of "aesthetic engagement." The goal of this replacement helps deconstruct the dualistic conception of subject-object opposition in traditional aesthetic theory. Three steps evolve: (1) with ecological awareness, the traditional aesthetic appreciation begins to transform into ecological aesthetic appreciation; (2) with basic ecological knowledge, the ecological aesthetic appreciation begins to deepen; and (3) with the clear awareness of human aesthetic preference and the ecocatastrophe caused by it, we can reflect and criticize traditional aesthetic appreciation to achieve ecological aesthetic appreciation.

NOTES

The chapter's Chinese version was submitted to the International Conference on "Constructive Postmodernism and Ecoaesthetics" cosponsored by Shandong University Research Center for Literary Theory and Aesthetics, P.R. China, Shandong University Research Center for Ecoaesthetics and Ecoliterature, P.R. China, Institute for Postmodern Development of China, USA, and Center for Process Studies, USA, held on June 13–14, 2012, in Ji'nan, China. Upon my invitation, Dr. Chia-ju Chang translated it into English, and I revised her edition. I am deeply indebted to her kind help. The author also expresses appreciation to Dr. Simon C. Estok for valuable suggestions for improving it for this volume.

1. Based on the statement and the theory of "aesthetic quality" (i.e., aesthetic property) in aesthetics, I think it is proper to propose a new technical term to describe one of the focuses of ecoaesthetics in my mind, "ecological aesthetic properties." What I want to discuss briefly here is the connections and differences between the two phrases, "aesthetic quality" and "aesthetic property." Usually they are viewed as synonymic, such as in the Oxford's 1998 *Encyclopedia of Aesthetics*, the entries of "aesthetic qualities" and of "aesthetic properties" are designed as one entry. See Michael Kelly, ed., *Encyclopedia of Aesthetics* (vol. 4) (New York: Oxford University Press, 1998), 97–99, 556. But according to my understanding, most of the discussions about "aesthetic quality" appeared in the realm of philosophy of art proposed by analytical philosophers mainly in 1960s and 1970s, the phrase is the synonymic expression of "artistic quality." With regard to nature appreciation and environmental appreciation, which have transcended the limits of "art-centered" theories since 1970s, I think the phrase of "aesthetic property" is a much better choice to describe the rich aesthetic "properties" of nature and environment, although it enjoys smaller popularity than the phrase of "aesthetic quality" does.

2. For this important point, I am proposing an article entitled "Why 'Ecological Beauty' is a Misleading Conception," forthcoming.

3. Estok's criticism goes like this:
   This sounds good, but it is philosophically ungrounded and scientifically naive. It forces us to rehash the problems associated with the term "beauty." It suggests that biotic systems are static when, in fact, they are not. It compels us to believe that nature is kind and good, when, in fact, it is morally neutral. Nature actively disrupts the integrity and stability of biotic communities all of the time, and this is neither good nor bad. Leopold's dictum forces us to accept his anthropocentric notions of good and bad and to foist these notions of good and bad onto nature. (209)
   Estok's criticism sounds reasonable mostly, though his conclusion seems harsh. Even so, Estok's opinion is one shared by Harold Fromm, who states that
   Leopold's now almost Mosaic criteria, far from being inscribed on sacred tablets derived from the biota itself, are rooted in ultimately anthropocentric concepts that have been newly refurbished by environmental proselytes to serve as "revelatory" foundations for a contemporary ecotheology. Taken as absolutes lifted from the needs of Leopold's rhetorical context, however, these criteria pose serious problems. The notion of "wholeness" or "integrity," for example, has come in for a good deal of post-structuralist criticism, particularly in connection with the old "New Criticism's" touchstone of "organic unity," but it is also generally dismissed in other fields besides the literary. (. . .) As for "beauty," it is too obviously culturally determined and consciousness-generated to require comment. (81–2)
4. However, we must realize that there are some scholars who still insist on the conception of "integrity" and taking the "ecological integrity" as the theme and the conceptual foundation of their work. For example, during the past two decades, the Global Ecological Integrity Group (GEIG) has been undertaking a conceptual clarification of its central term, "ecological integrity." Its 2008 book, *Reconciling Human Existence with Ecological Integrity: Science, Ethics, Economics and Law*, explores approaches to the important attempt to develop and defend the concept of ecological integrity as a way of dealing with the impact of human activities on ecosystems and the growing threats to survival. See Laura Westra, Klaus Bosselmann, and Richard Westra, eds., *Reconciling Human Existence with Ecological Integrity: Science, Ethics, Economics and Law* (London, Earthscan: Routledge, 2008).
5. For example, in his paper entitled "On the Possibility of Quantifying Scenic Beauty," Canadian scholar Allen Carlson mentions that the aesthetic values of the natural environment are viewed as the most important "wilderness-recreation values." The US National Forest Service landscape management training document declares that "it has become appropriate to establish the 'visual landscape' as a basic resource, to be treated as an essential part of and receive equal consideration with the other basic resources of the land." With this quotation, Carlson discusses the issues of the recognition of the "visual landscape" as a "basic resource" (131–72).

236   XIANGZHAN CHENG

WORKS CITED

Allaby, Michael. *Oxford Dictionary of Ecology*. Oxford, UK: Oxford University Press, 1998. 52.

Berleant, Arnold. *Aesthetics and Environment, Variations on a Theme*. Aldershot: Ashgate, 2005.

Callicott, Baird. "The Land Aesthetic." In *Companion to A Sand County Almanac: Interpretive and Critical Essays*. Ed. J. Baird Callicott. Wisconsin: The University of Wisconsin Press, 1987.

Carlson, Allen. "On the Possibility of Quantifying Scenic Beauty." *Landscape Planning* 4 (1977): 131–72.

Cooper, David A., ed. *A Companion to Aesthetics*. Oxford: Blackwell Publisher, 1995.

Dictionary Editing Team of Linguistic Studies Institute of Chinese Academy of Social Sciences. *The Contemporary Chinese Dictionary [Chinese-English Edition]*. Beijing: Foreign Language Teaching and Research Press, 2002.

Estok, Simon. "Theorizing in a Space of Ambivalent Openness: Ecocriticism and Ecophobia." *Interdisciplinary Studies in Literature and Environment* 16.2 (2009): 203–225.

Fromm, Harold. *The Nature of Being Human: From Environmentalism to Consciousness*. Baltimore: Johns Hopkins UP, 2009.

Kant, Immanuel. *Critique of Judgment*. Translated by Werner S. Pluhar. Indianapolis: Hackett Publishing Company, 1987.228.

Lackey, Robert T. "Values, Policy, and Ecosystem Health." *BioScience* 51.6 (2001): 437–443.

Leopold, Aldo. *Round River*. New York: Oxford University Press, 1953. 32.

———. *A Sand County Almanac, and Sketches Here and There*. Oxford, UK: Oxford University Press, 1949.

Leopold, Aldo. *A Sand County Almanac, and Sketches Here and There*. Oxford, UK: Oxford University Press, 1949.

Meeker, Joseph W. "Notes Toward an Ecological Esthetic." *Canadian Fiction Magazine* 2 (1972): 4–15.

Odum, Eugene P. and Gary W. Barrett. *Fundamentals of Ecology*, 5 edition. Belmont: Brooks Cole, 2005.

Shi, Jun. *Selected Readings from Famous Chinese Philosophers* (Vol. 2). Beijing: People's University Press, 1995.

Tapp, Robert B., ed. *Ecohumanism*. Amherst: Prometheus Books, 2002.

Tu, Weiming. "The Ecological Turn in New Confucian Humanism: Implication for China and the World." *Daedalus* (*Special Issue* "Religion and Ecology: Can the Climate Change?") 130.4 (Fall, 2001): 243–264.

14

AFTERWORD

ECOCRITICAL AND LITERARY FUTURES

Karen Thornber

Human cultural products have negotiated—revealed, reinterpreted, and shaped—ecological changes since prehistoric times. Paleolithic cave paintings dating to well before 30,000 BCE give diverse perspectives on early human practices that altered environments. Human language has played an even more significant role in transforming and transformed ecosystems. It has been used to command, describe, justify, celebrate, condemn, encourage amelioration of, and both divert attention from and call attention to human treatment of environments. For thousands of years oral and written texts from around the world have probed not only how people are affected by their surroundings but also how and why they alter environments near and far. References in literature to constructing, inhabiting, and dismantling built environments as well as to hunting, agriculture, and eating all give insight into changed landscapes. Even creative texts that do not include human characters often at least mention human-induced transformation of environments. For its part, world literature—understood broadly as creative texts that have circulated beyond their culture(s) of origin—has since *The Epic of Gilgamesh* (second millennium BCE) depicted people as radically changing their surroundings.

In contrast, it is only since the 1990s that the study of the relationship between literature and the physical environment has been a defined intellectual movement.[1] To be sure, despite its recent beginnings, ecocriticism (environmentally oriented literature studies) has rapidly developed into a diverse, interdisciplinary field, an eclectic and pluriform initiative not bound to any single method of inquiry or to any one environmentalist doctrine or commitment.[2] In *The*

Cambridge Introduction to Literature and the Environment (2011) Timothy Clark observes that "ecocriticism makes up the arena of an exciting and imponderable intersection of issues, intellectual disciplines and politics. Its potential force is to be not just another subset of literary criticism, situated within its given institutional borders, but work engaged provocatively both with literary analysis and with issues that are simultaneously but obscurely matters of science, morality, politics, and aesthetics" (8). And in *Sense of Place and Sense of Planet* (2008), Ursula Heise argues that "[r]ather than focusing on the recuperation of a sense of place, environmentalism [including environmental criticism] needs to foster an understanding of how a wide variety of both natural and cultural places and processes are connected and shape each other around the world" (21). These statements point to some of the fundamental changes ecocriticism has undergone in the last two decades.

Early ecocritical scholarship, drawing in part from deep ecology, often adopted a biocentric or preservationist approach. It focused largely on nature writing and on the capacity of literature to model ecocentric values, as well as on literary depictions of the biological, psychological, and spiritual bonds joining humans and the natural world.[3] This ecocriticism was concerned with place-attachment at a local or regional scale, seen in writings by Wendell Berry (1934–), including *The Unsettling of America* (1977) and *Standing by Words* (1983), and Gary Snyder, including *The Practice of the Wild* (1990) and *A Place in Space* (1995). At the turn of the twenty-first century ecocriticism began adopting a more anthropocentric and sociocentric standpoint; this scholarship highlights literature of the city and industrialization, as well as environmental (in)justice and related social issues, particularly in the context of ethnic and minority concerns, indigeneity, postcolonialism, diaspora, and cosmopolitanism. It likewise moves place-attachment from the local to the transnational or global.

Not surprisingly, the two general trends have much in common. These include a sustained engagement with all expressive media, everything from printed texts to visual, musical, and cinematic performance, as well as legislative documents and NGO reports. Other ongoing interests include environmental rhetoric studies; environmental feminism (ecofeminism); enlisting scientific models, particularly from evolutionary biology, ecology, and information sciences; differences of environmental perception based on gender and heritage, such as indigeneity; and literary imagination of relations between people and animals.[4]

To date, both types of ecocriticism have made significant break-throughs, including foregrounding relatively neglected literary genres and subgenres such as nature writing, toxification narrative, ecopoetry, and ecodrama that are concerned with relationships among people and their environments; reinterpreting thematic configurations related to the environment such as the pastoral, environmental racism, and ecoapocalypticism; and uncovering environmental subtexts from a range of creative works. Most recently, the field has looked to diverse genres and media beyond the written text, including graphic novels, animated film, bioart and green architecture, and innovative digital data sources, transforming how scholars think about the ecocritical agenda.[5]

The environmental humanities have demonstrated especially clearly the many possibilities for humanistic intervention in local, regional, and global ecological distress. But substantial challenges remain, both *cultural* (linguistic and geographical) and *conceptual*.

Ecocriticism frequently is identified in broad terms. Scott Slovic, for instance, pegs it as "the scrutiny of ecological implications and human-nature relationships in *any* literary text, even texts that seem (at first glance) oblivious of the nonhuman world" (27).[6] The future of ecocriticism has been said to lie in demonstrating the place of environmentality (concern for environmental health) in literature, especially literature's posing environmentality as a "thought experiment...complicated by multiple agendas and refusal to take fixed positions."[7]

But despite such rhetoric of inclusiveness, since the early days of the field ecocritics have in fact limited themselves almost exclusively to creative texts written in Western languages, and English-language American literature in particular. Even in Asia discussions of the relationship between literature and damaged environments have focused disproportionately on Western, and primarily Anglophone examples.[8] To be sure, scholarship on environmentalism and post-colonialism has surged in recent years. Analyses of the ecological implications of texts from Africa, Latin America (including the Caribbean), the Pacific Islands, and South Asia, and comparisons of the "environmental imagination" of the relatively privileged north and the "environmentalism of the poor" found in the global south have contributed significantly to broadening perspectives of relations between people and the natural world, around the world.[9] The importance of this scholarship to the humanities and beyond cannot be underestimated. But it remains significantly hampered by its focus on Western-language writings, often returning to a few familiar favorites, to the near exclusion of texts from these regions written in other tongues. This scholarship also has not taken into consideration writings from East Asia, a region with a traumatic colonial history of its own, albeit one rarely acknowledged in postcolonial studies, a region, moreover, that is home to three of the world's largest economies and nearly one-fourth of its people.

East Asia has long been associated with belief systems advocating reverence for nature, especially Buddhism, Confucianism, Taoism, and Shinto as well as numerous indigenous philosophies and religions. These modes of thought have inspired the environmentality of numerous Asian as well as American, European, and to a lesser extent Middle Eastern and African intellectuals. Popular perceptions both within and outside East Asia often hold that environmental degradation in the region began in the late nineteenth century, when East Asian peoples, pressured by Western nations, assimilated the latter's technologies and industries. But actually, East Asian societies are heir to thousands of years of intense environmental degradation. Rhoades Murphey has gone so far as to argue:

> All Asian cultures in the areas east of Afghanistan and south of the former Soviet Union have long been noted for their admiring attitudes toward nature...All of this is contrasted with the Western view...The Asian record, however, makes it clear that, despite the professed values of the literate elite, people have altered or destroyed the Asian environment for longer and on a greater scale than anywhere else in the world, even in the twentieth-century West. ("Asian Perspectives" 36)[10]

Murphey perhaps overstates the case, since the changes early East Asian peoples made to environments did not have the reach of those instigated by societies in the twentieth-century West.

Nevertheless, the disjuncture between beliefs and behaviors is significant. As the historian Mark Elvin has observed concerning China:

> Through more than three thousand years, the Chinese refashioned China. They cleared the forests and the original vegetation cover, terraced its hill-slopes, and partitioned its valley floors into fields. They diked, dammed, and diverted its rivers and lakes. They hunted or domesticated its animals and birds; or else destroyed their habitats as a by-product of the pursuit of economic improvements. By late-imperial times there was little that could be called "natural" left untouched by this process of exploitation and adaptation...A paradox thus lay at the heart of Chinese attitudes to the landscape. On the one hand it

was seen...as a part of the supreme numinous power itself. Wisdom required that one put oneself into its rhythms and be conscious of one's inability to reshape it. On the other hand the landscape was in fact tamed, transformed, and exploited to a degree that had few parallels in the premodern world. (321, 323)

Heiner Roetz expands on this line of reasoning, boldly claiming that in early China, "a sympathetic feeling for nature, like that [expressed in] the *Zhuangzi*, was a simple reaction against [what was actually happening]" (85).[11]
Roetz stretches the point. Not all expressions of sympathy, much less celebrations of nature, even celebrations emanating from societies that are significantly transforming their environments, can be read as reactions against actual conditions. But most can be discussed as providing alternatives. East Asian peoples long have had a heightened consciousness of human-induced damage to environments, but despite the commitment of individuals, organizations, and governments to repairing extant damage and limiting further harm, overall environmental degradation in the region shows every sign of persisting. To be sure, many of East Asia's most obvious environmental problems have been ameliorated in the past few decades, including urban air and water pollution in Japan, South Korea, Taiwan, and to a lesser extent China. But as population sizes and distributions shift and lifestyles alter, the shape, rather than the scale of this degradation, changes. In many cases, for instance, pollution is simply being exported, not eradicated, creating multiple shadow ecologies.[12]
Likewise, East Asian literatures are famous for celebrating the beauties of nature and depicting people as intimately connected with the natural world. But analyzing Chinese, Japanese, Korean, and Taiwanese fiction and poetry of the past hundred years reveals these literatures as replete with discourse on ecodegradation to a degree that might surprise readers accustomed to conventional images of Asian ecological harmony. East Asian artists and philosophers have long idealized people's interactions with their nonhuman surroundings. Their representations have given the impression that East Asians, unlike Americans and Europeans, are inherently sensitive to the environment, that they love nature and intermingle peacefully with it. Yet romanticizing close relationships between people and their environments has more often defied than reflected empirical reality. More important, much modern and even some premodern East Asian fiction and poetry depict people damaging everything from small spaces to entire continents.

Researchers in the social and natural sciences both within and outside East Asia have written extensively on environmental problems in modern and premodern China, Japan, Korea, and Taiwan, on the many movements and organizations that have fought against ecodegradation, and on official responses at local, subnational, national, and regional levels. In contrast, most humanistic research on East Asian literary works that discuss interactions between people and nature has looked at creative manipulations of the latter: literary celebrations of nature; depictions of nature as a refuge, often imagined, from human society; portraits of relatively harmonious integration of people with nature; or, less frequently, episodes of people overpowered by calamities such as avalanches, earthquakes, and floods. Much less has been published on East Asian creative negotiations with environmental damage, despite its presence in thousands of years of Chinese-, Japanese-, and Korean-language literatures, and particularly in the region's twentieth- and early twenty-first-century creative corpuses.

Just as environmental conditions and responses to these conditions have differed greatly within the region and among different areas of China, Japan, Korea, and Taiwan, East Asian literary mediations of relationships among people and environments, particularly relationships that involve changes to the nonhuman, have also varied considerably across time and space. In the coming years, ecocritics will need to address a broader range of literatures.[13] As this present volume makes clear, East Asia's diverse literatures are fertile soil for twenty-first-century ecocritical research.

But even as the field of ecocriticism moves away from its disproportionate celebration of Western-language and particularly American texts and landscapes, East Asian literatures and other non-Western literatures ultimately cannot be examined in isolation. To be sure, the field will benefit greatly from more scholarship like *East Asian Ecocriticisms*, scholarship devoted to particular East Asian and other non-Western language texts. As Simon Estok rightly points out in the introduction, responses to environmental crises, even those of global scale, often are inevitably local, with varying cultural manifestations. It is imperative to probe these local contexts and literatures, not simply to counterbalance the plethora of scholarship on English-language writings but also to develop deeper understandings and appreciations of the world's many diverse cultural landscapes. And the present volume has expertly explored specific examples of ecocriticism within particular national and cultural contexts.

On the other hand, while cultures and environmental problems are distinctive, they are not unique, and the need to globalize ecocriticism remains acute. Precisely because damaged environments are a global phenomenon, literary treatments of ecodegradation regularly transcend their particular cultures of production and can be understood as together forming intercultural thematic and conceptual networks. Examining these networks will be an important part of our ecocritical, if not literary future. In fact, I would argue that literary systems ideally should be studied not only along cultural/national lines but also in terms of intercultural thematic and conceptual networks. The most significant networks address urgent matters of global significance, including poverty, disease, slavery, warfare, and environmental destruction. Spotlighting these networks reveals how readily literature traverses boundaries of all kinds: environmental, political and administrative, economic, demographic, and cultural and social.

Intercultural thematic networks are webs of creative texts from multiple cultures that focus on similar topics, whether or not the writers of these texts actively reconfigure one another's work. Werner Sollors calls attention to the importance of examining consistencies in theme:

> By making [a particular theme the constant], the persistence and scope of the literature can begin to be sketched; at the same time, many other variables are left open, inviting comparisons across literary genres and periods...What may seem intriguing or cryptic in an individual work may be clarified by considering other literary and nonliterary texts; what may appear radically innovative in one text may actually be widely shared by many earlier literary texts and other documents; what is praised as the accomplishment (or what the New Critics might call the "thematic unity") of a single text may be more fairly viewed as the nuanced refiguring of themes that are familiar from many other texts; what is regarded as the defining motif of a certain ethnic group may really be a shared feature of many other ethnic and national literatures; what is looked at as a startling and noteworthy "subversion" of a traditional element may actually be in itself a traditional commonplace. (25–26)

Likewise, Rob Nixon has rightly proposed that instead of automatically placing into national ecocanons creative texts on specific environmental issues such as land rights, nuclear testing, pollution, and oil, we instead reposition these works in international context and examine them comparatively. Doing so will allow us not only to diversify environmental literary canons but also to reconceptualize the prevailing paradigms of these canons. Examining literature on oil, for instance, allows us to uncover relationships among texts by writers as diverse as the American authors Edna Ferber (1885–1968), Linda Hogan (1947–), Joe Kane (1899–2002), and Upton Sinclair (1878–1968); the Nigerians Ken Saro-Wiwa (1941–1995), John Pepper Clark (1935–), and Tayo Olafioye; and the Jordanian Arabic-language novelist Abdelrah-man Munif (1933–2004).[14]

Going one step further in reconfiguring ecocritical paradigms involves focusing not on national networks or even on networks formed around a specific environmental problem (thematic networks) but instead on those formed around concepts (conceptual networks). Indeed, it is not enough simply to expand the linguistic and geographical range of the texts under analysis. The field also needs new conceptualizations and theoretical approaches, particularly those not confined to particular peoples or times. In *Ecocritical Explorations in Literature and Cultural Studies*, for instance, Patrick Murphy calls for developing "transnational ecocritical theory," by which he means "a theory that would transect, that is, cut across, the limitations of national perspectives and boundaries...Avoiding parochialism does not mean practicing universalism, but it also does not mean abandoning the idea that ecocriticism in whatever varied forms it may take is a crucial, relevant, and necessary literary and cultural practice to be promoted worldwide" (63).

As I discuss in *Ecoambiguity: Environmental Crises and East Asian Literatures* (2012), the concept of environmental ambiguity—the complex, contradictory interactions between people and the natural world—provides exciting new possibilities in this regard. Ecocritical scholarship has yet to give sustained attention to the complex ambiguities we face in responding to the vexed issues raised by rapid ecological change and degradation and the multiple ways fiction and poetry highlight the absence of simple answers and the paucity of facile solutions to environmental problems.

Every human action changes environments. Some changes are readily visible and accounted for, some are readily visible yet ignored or denied, some become apparent only after archaeological excavation or scientific examination, others are merely hypothesized, while countless remain unknown. Describing change to environments has long been a challenge: often new concepts must be developed and terms coined. Pinpointing agents of change has been no easier. Even the most obvious perpetrators can be wrapped in webs of disclaimers. Likewise, accurately predicting change has nearly always proved difficult. This is often because the nonhuman appears or is imagined to be inexhaustible, and signs of imminent depletion are easily ignored or are not readily apparent. Even more problematic has been evaluating change, whether past, present, or anticipated: what change can be understood as damage, what damage can be condoned, even encouraged? Simon Estok has characterized anthropogenic transformations of environments as stemming largely from ecophobia, understood as "an irrational and groundless fear or hatred of the natural world, as present and subtle in our daily lives and literature as homophobia and racism and sexism" (*Ecocriticism and Shakespeare* 4). Ecophobia, Estok writes, regularly "wins out" over its alleged opposites: biophilia, understood as "the innately emotional affiliation of human beings to other living organisms," and, more generally, ecophilia, or love of nature ("Theorizing in a Space" 219). To be sure, ecophobia can explain much of people's desire throughout history to control (parts of) the natural environment and engage in such massive destruction of nature as large-scale deforestation and species eradication. Likewise, ecophilia seems to propel people's embrace of nature, as well as promote environmental remediation and conservation, and, in fact, inspire the field of ecocriticism itself.

But as the cliche "love nature to death" suggests, environmental changes need not be symptoms of absolute ecophobia or ecophilia. A bias against the nonhuman that keeps someone inside a city apartment relatively cut off from nature surely alters the nonhuman less directly and potentially less substantially than a love of the natural world that leads someone to drive for hours to go hiking or canoeing.[15] And even when changes are motivated largely by ecophobia or ecophilia, the changes themselves often are less easily evaluated. The uncertainties suffusing relationships and interpretations of relationships between people and their environments suggest that ecoambiguity can be more prominent than ecophobia or ecophilia alone.

Creative discourse frequently capitalizes on environmental ambiguity. Literature's regular and often blatant defiance of logic, precision, and unity enables it to grapple more insistently and penetratingly than many other discourses with ambiguities in general and with those arising from interactions among people and ecosystems in particular. More specifically, literature's intrinsic multivalence allows it to highlight and negotiate the ambiguity that has long suffused interactions between people and environments, including those interactions that involve human damage to ecosystems. Ambiguity here emerges not primarily as an ethical or aesthetic value but as a symptom of epistemological uncertainty that is parsed both sympathetically and exactingly as a deficit of consciousness and/or implicit confession of the impotence of writers and literary characters.

Environmental ambiguity manifests itself in multiple, intertwined ways, including ambivalent attitudes toward nature; confusion about the actual condition of the nonhuman, often a consequence of ambiguous information; contradictory human behaviors toward ecosystems; and discrepancies among attitudes, conditions, and behaviors that lead to actively downplaying and acquiescing to nonhuman degradation, as well as to inadvertently harming the very environments one is attempting to protect. My research on hundreds of creative works from diverse cultures reveals these imbricated forms of ecoambiguity as fundamental attributes of literary works that discuss relationships between people and the nonhuman world. Most interesting is how creative works articulate the permutations and implications of these discrepancies vertically in time and horizontally in physical and social space—in other words, how they negotiate the ambiguities of ecocosmopolitanism.

Much literature that addresses harm to ecosystems, including many of the texts examined in this volume, is environmentally cosmopolitan, either explicitly or implicitly taking up ecodegradation beyond a single time or place. Analyzing how texts position themselves vis-à-vis environmental concerns of diverse types and scales, how they both open and close themselves to the wider world, can contribute significantly to our understandings of relationships among the local, regional, and global.

Patrick Hayden speaks of "world environmental citizenship":

> World environmental citizenship can be viewed as a component of the more general cosmopolitan conception of world citizenship...World environmental citizenship arises from an ethical concern for the social, political and economic problems associated with the environment and humanity's dependence upon it, and from a recognition of our global responsibilities for the human condition in light of humanity's interconnectedness with the environment. Thus the world environmental citizen is concerned about the common good of the human community and places particular emphasis on the fact that we are all citizens belonging to both local environments and a single global environment. (147)

Similarly, Ursula Heise coined the term "ecocosmopolitan" as:

> An attempt to envision individuals and groups as part of planetary 'imagined communities' of both human and nonhuman kinds...Ecocriticism has only begun to explore the cultural means by which ties to the natural world are produced and perpetuated,

and how the perception of such ties fosters or impedes regional, national, and transnational forms of identification...The point of an eco-cosmopolitan critical project...would be...to investigate by what means individuals and groups in specific cultural contexts have succeeded in envisioning themselves in similarly concrete fashion as part of the global biosphere, or by what means they might be enabled to do so. (*Sense of Place* 61–62)

My use of the term ecocosmopolitan resembles Heise's and draws from Hayden's conception of world environmental citizenship, but I focus less on human perceptions of ties to and identification with the natural world than on the state of the natural world itself, and especially the ranges of environmental devastation with which a text grapples both explicitly and implicitly.

Varying considerably among creative works are causes and types of ecodegradation; the range of species affected, including the presence or absence of notable human suffering; and the proportion of the text devoted to explicit discussion of environmental health or distress. Literature likewise discusses ecological damage of differing spatial and temporal scopes, including what can be regarded as situated damage—short-term injury to relatively small, isolated ecosystems; spatially pervasive damage—harm of relatively limited temporal scope that affects larger or multiple ecosystems; temporally pervasive damage—environmental degradation whose duration is greater than its spatial scope; and encompassing damage—environmental degradation that is both enduring and widespread.

The most obviously ecocosmopolitan texts are those that speak generally about degradation on a potentially global scale. These are frequently poems or other short texts that talk broadly of "human beings" destroying everything from small woodlands to the entire planet. More complex expressions of environmental cosmopolitanism are found in creative work that explicitly depicts particular types and instances of ecodegradation, regardless of scale, as encompassed in larger environmental problems or encompassing smaller ones. For instance, even a short poem that focuses on a single ailing animal might also speak explicitly of this animal's suffering as resulting from large-scale deforestation. Similarly, a lengthy novel on climate change or the eradication of multiple species worldwide is likely also to speak in detail on conditions in specific places. Other ecocosmopolitan texts depict problems in one space as analogous to those in others: a literary work focusing on a polluted field might speak of the resemblance between damage done to this tract of land and similar harm done to another at some distance. Many texts that concentrate on incidents that occur in a specific place and time both draw parallels with conditions in other places and times *and* speak of these instances as part of larger patterns of environmental distress or as encompassing smaller problems.

Although literary treatments of human relationships with damaged environments regularly exhibit strong local ties, on the whole they tend to be somewhat less culturally, nationally, or even regionally focused than discourse on other subjects, including celebrations of nature. This is not surprising considering that environmental globalization is the oldest form of globalization, predating its economic, political, social, and cultural counterparts.[16] In addition, many writers who take up environmental damage have spent substantial time abroad and have witnessed ecodegradation in multiple locales. Just as ecological globalization has arguably facilitated its literary counterpart, so too has literary globalization brought increased attention to its ecological counterpart.

Much ecocosmopolitanism is implicit and raises questions of environmental actuality and possibility. Environmental actuality refers to the ecological degradation that a text explicitly addresses or to which it clearly alludes. Environmental possibility indicates the human-induced environmental harm that a text more abstractly implicates. This can be damage a writer might mean to signify, but does so in a less-than-obvious manner; critical judgments of this form of environmental possibility can be based on the creative writer's knowledge, or at least on what is known of the writer's knowledge of environmental problems. More generally, environmental possibility refers to what can be deduced or extrapolated from a creative work, regardless of authorial intent and the specific social and environmental circumstances surrounding textual production. Numerous creative works focus on situated damage that could be read as a microcosm of spatially pervasive damage, temporally pervasive damage, or even encompassing damage. Thus in some cases a brief poem on a single ailing creature that contains no references to other animals can be read as addressing the plight of that species or of multiple species in multiple spaces. So too in some cases can a short story on animals suffering from pesticides used in a single field, with mere changes to place, personal, and species names (if these are given), increase understanding of the plight of animals in other spaces. In short, texts can be environmentally cosmopolitan without speaking explicitly of ecological degradation beyond a single time and place.

It is often difficult to determine whether a text's environmental possibilities can or should take precedence over its environmental actualities, especially when—as nearly always is the case—these possibilities are ambiguous. Indeed, even literature with a bioregionalist focus rarely specifies the precise spatial and temporal range of the environmental degradation it describes. But the extent of environmental degradation currently facing the planet requires that we look closely at these possibilities. This is not to deny the particularities of ecological distress in individual sites or the need to understand the specific circumstances of cultural production. The latter are especially important in cases where the writer is active in environmental or other political movements, or where the text focuses on ecological concerns seemingly distinctive to a single place. Moreover, the reader's own background and circumstances affect how a text's possibilities are grasped. Still, the analyst of literary works on environmental degradation must take seriously actualities, possibilities, and the myriad positions in between. Creative texts, as tangible cultural products, stand within, not outside, ecosystems from the local to the global, something that allows them to comment instructively on a variety of environments.

Insights from the field of world literature can be particularly useful to literature and environment studies. David Damrosch has identified world literature as

> all literary works that circulate beyond their culture of origin either in translation or in their original language...a work only has an *effective* life as world literature whenever, and wherever, it is actively present in a literary system beyond that of its original culture...World literature...is not a set canon of texts but a mode of reading: a form of detached engagement with worlds beyond our own place and time...[that helps us] appreciate the ways in which a literary work reaches out and away from its point of origin. (4, 281, 300)[17]

Many texts that address environmental degradation have been translated into at least one language, but few have had a truly active presence in literary systems beyond their original culture. They thus are not generally interpreted as works of world literature. On the other hand, almost all these texts address concerns that transcend those of their source cultures and are environmentally cosmopolitan, either explicitly or implicitly. Much can be gained by reading them *as* world literature, that is to say examining how they reach beyond their points of origin.

Proliferating worldwide crises impose an obligation on studies of literature not simply to expand their thematic scope but also to develop a keener planetary consciousness. One of the most effective means of increasing the planetary consciousness of textual scholarship is reading as world literature even those texts that might not be works of world literature in the conventional sense but that engage with important issues extending beyond single cultures. The worlds these texts discuss often are physically beyond our own place and time, but the concerns they address strike close to home.

Concepts of "planetary consciousness" have long been linked with imperialism. Discussing natural history in eighteenth-century Europe, Mary Louise Pratt aligns that era's "planetary consciousness" with disruption, (re)ordering, imperialism, and Eurocentrism: "The eighteenth-century systematizing of nature as a European knowledge-building project...created a new kind of Eurocentered planetary consciousness. Blanketing the surface of the globe, it specified plants and animals in visual terms as discrete entities, subsuming and reassembling them in a finite, totalizing order of European making" (30–31, 37). Racism, culturalism, and speciesism, which posit the superiority of people or particular groups of people, underlie quests for this form of planetary consciousness. Other intellectuals have argued that people are themselves the "planet's consciousness." But just as emphasizing "planetary consciousness" can strengthen local-, ethno-, anthro-, or other centrisms, it also can be used to counter prejudices. As Nelson Maldonado Torres observes: "Against the (imperial) 'planetary' perspective of European imperial eyes that became instrumental for bourgeois colonial adventures, Dussel deploys another 'planetary' perspective...Instead of serving imperialism, this 'planetary' perspective aims to overcome Eurocentrism" (210). This is precisely the objective of a number of contemporary imaginings of planetary consciousness.

In the past decade, critics such as Gayatri Chakravorty Spivak and Wai Chee Dimock have urged scholars of both comparative literature and national literatures to take a more planetary approach. By this they mean, in simplest terms, increasing both the scope and the cultural grounding of literature studies. Dimock proposes reading American literature as a subset, and by no means the most encompassing one, of "an infinite number of larger aggregates that take their measure from the durations and extensions of the human species itself, folding in American literature as one fold among others" ("Planet and America" 5, 10–11).[18] The perspective she advocates could easily be applied with modification to any number of other literatures, national or otherwise. Spivak argues somewhat controversially that

> as presumed collectivities cross borders under the auspices of a comparative literature supplemented by Area Studies, they might attempt to figure themselves—imagine themselves—as planetary rather than continental, global, or worldly...It is as an alternative...to the arrogance of the cartographic reading of world lit. in translation as the task of Comparative Literature, that I propose the planet. (72–73)[19]

Evocations of the planet enrich literature studies as they enrich human understanding more generally. Recent visions of planetary humanism and planetary consciousness stress the need to analyze creative and other discourse on urgent issues of actual or potential interregional and often planetary import. Paul Gilroy speaks of the importance of developing "a planetary humanism capable of comprehending the universality of our elemental vulnerability to the wrongs we visit upon each other," as well as "a planetary consciousness of the tragedy, fragility, and brevity of indivisible human existence" (4, 84).[20] Likewise, in her discussion of the value of adopting a more planetary research program, Dimock gives the example of slavery, which although "so often studied only within the geography and chronology of the United States, becomes a virtually unrecognizable phenomenon when it is taken outside these space and time coordinates." She rightly highlights the "conceptual broadening that comes with [the] broadening of the evidentiary ground" ("Planet and America" 6).[21] Although Dimock here speaks of broadening the evidentiary ground of historical research, literary criticism might follow a similar trajectory, examining more fully, for instance, intercultural networks on slavery and other human rights abuses. Such criticism would analyze creative works as products both of specific times and places and of shared human experience. But arguably even more vital to increasing the planetary consciousness of literature studies is identifying and analyzing intercultural networks that negotiate relationships between people and environments, particularly relationships involving ecological degradation.[22]

This approach is imperative for several reasons. First, such an orientation more accurately reflects its eponym: "planet," more than "globe" or "world," points at once to the planet Earth and to the diverse and interacting bodies—tangible and intangible, human and nonhuman, biotic and abiotic, massive and microscopic in size and impact—that form, inhabit, and move across this sphere.[23] Second, as recent environmental justice and ecofeminist scholarship suggests, examining how creative works articulate interactions between humans and environments in fact deepens appreciations not only of these relationships but also of those among people. Third, and most important, scholarship on literature can help us develop deeper, more nuanced understandings of human/nonhuman contacts; these understandings have the potential to speed the cultural changes necessary for remediating damaged ecosystems, limiting further ecological degradation, and preserving human health.

Ultimately, however, enhancing the planetary consciousness of literature goes beyond increasing the geographical breadth of scholarly research, and beyond moving the object of study from interactions among people to both these interactions and those between people and environments (i.e., intercultural networks of discourse on relationships between and among people and the nonhuman). It also involves assessing the environmental cosmopolitanism of these interactions: examining how individual literary works, even those that seem focused exclusively on very local environmental concerns, might increase consciousness of transnational and transcultural phenomena. Equally, it requires us to evaluate how literary treatments of widespread phenomena might increase awareness of concerns of smaller scope.[24]

Ecological degradation occurs everywhere on the planet, with a temporal and geographic scope unsurpassed by any other pressing global concern. More than other phenomena, environmental crises impel us to consider our lives and our responsibilities in planetary terms. Through cross-cultural analysis of literary works that confront damage to the nonhuman, we can gain new insights into some of our greatest challenges, regardless of specialization: how best to synthesize and to separate the dynamics of the local, the global, and everything in-between; how best to synthesize and to separate moments in human time from planetary time, and everything in-between.

Literature rarely offers comprehensive remedies, much less proposes official policies to prevent future or remediate current damage to landscapes; in some cases creative writing itself might even abet the ecodegradation it deplores. But drafting policies, not to mention implementing them, requires changes in consciousness—perceptions, understandings, and expectations—something literature is well placed to enhance. To be sure, celebrations of the wonders of nature, even those that make no mention of compromised environments, have moved readers greatly and done much to foster environmental consciousness. In addition, celebrations of nature, even those published by societies experiencing severe environmental degradation, are not necessarily products of ignorance or of active desire to conceal damaged ecosystems. They instead at times are protests against changes occurring in the experienced world.[25] Yet more explicit creative discourse on degraded environments—whether it describes actual conditions or imagines (im)possible scenarios, whether it is embedded in overt celebrations of nature or forms the center of a text—highlights especially clearly the immediate challenges confronting ecosystems of all kinds. Creative works that directly address environmental damage also indicate the difficulties in pinpointing precise causes and providing surefire solutions. And to varying degrees they address one of the greatest ambiguities of human changes to landscapes: to what extent these changes actually matter, morally and ecologically, across time and space. Literature that probes degraded ecosystems thus underlines the urgency of better understanding the complexities that pervade relationships among people and their environments, including human efforts to protect or repair the nonhuman.[26] This literature points directly to the consequences of failing to do so. At stake is less the loss of glorious, imagined wilderness than the loss of actual lives, both human and nonhuman.

NOTES

1. Clark 3–4.
2. Buell, Heise, and Thornber 418.
3. See Buell, *Future of Environmental Criticism* 21–28.
4. See Buell, Heise, and Thornber 419–20.
5. Buell, *Future of Environmental Criticism* 130; Heise, "Bloomington 2011."
6. See also Buell, *Future of Environmental Criticism* 138.
7. Buell, "Literature as Environmental(ist) Thought Experiment" 24–25.
8. See Thornber 451–52n70. On the other hand, East Asian literary scholarship has long discussed the place of nature in the region's creative output.
9. De Loughrey and Handley, "Introduction." See also De Loughrey and Handley; Ahuja; Bewell; DeLoughrey et al.; Nixon, "Environmentalism and Postcolonialism" and "Slow Violence"; Huggan and Tiffin; Husband; Mukherjee; Roos and Hunt; Tiffin; Vital; Volkmann et al.
10. See also Peter C. Perdue's comments in Hoffmann et al. 1437.
11. Cited by Elvin 324. For more on disjunctions between beliefs and behaviors, see Murphey, "Man and Nature in China"; Yi-Fu Tuan. The *Zhuangzi* is a foundational text of Daoism.
12. The term "shadow ecology" refers to "the aggregate environmental impact on resources outside [a nation's] territory of government practices,

especially official development assistance (ODA); corporate conduct, investment and technology transfers; and trade, including consumption, export and consumer prices, and import tariffs" (Dauvergne 2–3). Jim MacNeill et al. define the ecological shadow of a country as "the environmental resources it draws from other countries and the global commons" (58–59). MacNeill et al. cite Japan as an example of a nation with a substantial shadow ecology (59–61).

13. This issue was discussed at length at the February 2010 Officers' Retreat of the Association for the Study of Literature and Environment ("ASLE Officers' Retreat Summary"). See also Heise, "Species, Space, and the Imagination of the Global."

14. For additional examples of intercultural thematic networks involving specific environmental issues, see Nixon, "Environmentalism and Postcolonialism," 245–46.

15. As Martin W. Lewis argues in *Green Delusions*, indifference toward environments often contributes to their health.

16. Buell, "Ecoglobalist Affects" 227.

17. See also Dimock, "Literature for the Planet." The transculturations (e.g., adaptations, translations, intertextualizations) of creative texts that are circulated and read beyond their "original culture" should also be seen as part of world literature. In addition, the concept of "original culture" is somewhat problematic, since many works of literature, or at least their component parts, have "origins" in multiple spaces. Not surprisingly, understandings of what constitutes "world literature" vary both within and across cultures.

18. For cautions against the self-aggrandizing such approaches can foster, see Kadir, "Comparative Literature" 74–75, and "To World, To Globalize."

19. Spivak and Paul Gilroy both explain their preference for a "planetary" as opposed to "global" focus. See Gilroy xii; Spivak 72–73, 93. Vandana Shiva discusses differences between the "global" and "planetary consciousness" in "The Greening of the Global Reach" 53–66.

20. Gilroy draws from a variety of cultural forms, including creative texts. See 13, 18–19, 162.

21. Research on comparative slavery dates farther back than Dimock's reference to Philip Curtin's *The Rise and Fall of the Plantation Complex* (1990) suggests. Frank Tannenbaum (1893–1969) published *Slave and Citizen* in 1946. But Dimock's larger argument holds true.

22. Dimock in *Through Other Continents*, Gilroy in *After Empire*, and Spivak in *Death of a Discipline* acknowledge the importance of the nonhuman, but reconceptualizing relationships among people and environments is only marginally addressed in these works. Cf. Spivak's translations of the writings of Bengali environmental and social activist Mahasweta Devi (1926–) in *Imaginary Maps* and *Chotti Munda & His Arrow*, which are concerned with problems of environmental justice. Also noteworthy are efforts to combine world and environmental history. See Burke and Pomeranz; Tucker 1–3.

23. It is probable that planetary consciousness will need to be replaced by universal consciousness, as more becomes known about the impacts of human behaviors on spaces beyond the planet Earth. Much literature already exhibits this consciousness.

24. Transborder phenomena here are understood as both transculturated phenomena (those that actually cross borders) and phenomena that exist in multiple spaces but which have more local roots in each of these spaces.

25. As Mark Elvin asks, "Do our sources mainly reflect the dominant tendencies of an age, or are they more often *reactions*, by far-seeing and sensitive thinkers, *against* these dominant tendencies? And, if a mixture, where, and in what proportions?" (324).

26. This is part of what gives teachers of literature the opportunity to raise the environmental consciousness of society. Cheryll Glotfelty has gone so far as to argue that "as Literature professors, we may even have more of an impact in raising the environmental consciousness level of society than if we taught, say, Conservation Biology or Wildlife Management, for students in those courses are already ecologically inclined" (3).

WORKS CITED

Ahuja, Neel. "Postcolonial Critique in a Multispecies World." *PMLA* 124.2 (March 2009): 556–63.

Berry, Wendell. *Standing by Words: Essays.* San Francisco: North Point Press, 1983.

———. *The Unsettling of America: Culture and Agriculture.* San Francisco: Sierra Club Books, 1977.

Bewell, Alan. *Romanticism and Colonial Disease.* Baltimore: Johns Hopkins UP, 1999.

Buell, Lawrence. "Ecoglobalist Affects: The Emergence of U.S. Environmental Imagination on a Planetary Scale." In *Shades of the Planet: American Literature as World Literature.* Ed. Wai Chee Dimock and Lawrence Buell. Princeton: Princeton UP, 2007. 227–48.

———. *The Future of Environmental Criticism: Environmental Crisis and Literary Imagination.* Malden, MA: Blackwell, 2005.

———. "Literature as Environmental(ist) Thought Experiment." In *Ecology and the Environment: Perspectives from the Humanities.* Ed. Donald K. Swearer. Cambridge, MA: Harvard U Center for the Study of World Religions, 2009. 21–36.

Buell, Lawrence, Ursula K. Heise, and Karen Thornber. "Literature and Environment." *Annual Review of Environment and Resources* 36 (2011): 417–40.

Burke, Edmund III and Kenneth Pomeranz, eds. *The Environment and World History.* Berkeley: U of California P, 2009.

Clark, Timothy. *The Cambridge Introduction to Literature and the Environment.* New York: Cambridge UP, 2011.

Damrosch, David. *What Is World Literature?* Princeton: Princeton UP, 2003.

Dauvergne, Peter. *Shadows in the Forest: Japan and the Politics of Timber in Southeast Asia.* Cambridge, MA: MIT P, 1997.

De Loughrey, Elizabeth. *Routes and Roots: Navigating Caribbean and Pacific Island Literatures.* Honolulu: U of Hawai'i P, 2007.

——et al., eds. *Caribbean Literature and the Environment: Between Nature and Culture.* Charlottesville: U of Virginia P, 2005.

De Loughrey, Elizabeth and George B. Handley. "Introduction: Toward an Aesthetics of the Earth," in Elizabeth De Loughrey and George B. Handley, eds. *Postcolonial Ecologies: Literatures of the Environment.* New York: Oxford UP, 2011. 3–39.

De Loughrey, Elizabeth and George B., Handley, eds. *Postcolonial Ecologies: Literatures of the Environment.* New York: Oxford UP, 2011.

Devi, Mahasweta. *Imaginary Maps: Three Stories.* New York: Routledge, 1995.

——. *Chotti Munda & His Arrow.* Malden, MA: Blackwell Publishers, 2003.

Dimock, Wai Chee. "Literature for the Planet." *PMLA* 116 (January 2001): 173–88.

——. "Planet and America, Set and Subset." In *Shades of the Planet: American Literature as World Literature.* Ed. Wai Chee Dimock and Lawrence Buell. Princeton: Princeton UP, 2007. 1–16.

——. *Through Other Continents: American Literature across Deep Time.* Princeton: Princeton UP, 2006.

Elvin, Mark. *The Retreat of the Elephants: An Environmental History of China.* New Haven: Yale UP, 2004.

Estok, Simon C. *Ecocriticism and Shakespeare: Reading Ecophobia.* New York: Palgrave Macmillan, 2011.

——. "Theorizing in a Space of Ambivalent Openness: Ecocriticism and Ecophobia." *Interdisciplinary Studies in Literature and Environment* 16.2 (Spring 2009): 203–25.

Gilroy, Paul. *After Empire: Melancholia or Convivial Culture.* Abingdon, Oxfordshire: Routledge, 2004.

Glotfelty, Cheryll. "The Strong Green Thread." In *Essays in Ecocriticism.* Ed. Nirmal Selvamony et al. New Delhi: Sarup & Sons, 2007. 1–10.

Hayden, Patrick. *Cosmopolitan Global Politics.* Burlington, VT: Ashgate, 2005.

Heise, Ursula. "Bloomington 2011: New Adventures in Ecocriticism." *ASLE News* online (Spring 2011).

——. "Species, Space, and the Imagination of the Global," *ASLE News* online (Summer 2010).

——. *Sense of Place and Sense of Planet: The Environmental Imagination of the Global.* New York: Oxford UP, 2008.

Hoffmann, Richard C., et al. "AHR Conversation: Environmental Historians and Environmental Crisis." *American Historical Review* 113.5 (December 2008): 1431–65.

Huggan, Graham and Helen Tiffin. *Postcolonial Ecocriticism: Literature, Animals, Environment.* New York: Routledge, 2010.

Husband, Andrew. "Postcolonial 'Greenery': Surreal Garden Imagery in Nuruddin Farah's *Maps.*" *Interdisciplinary Studies in Literature and Environment* 17.1 (Winter 2010), 73–83.

Kadir, Djelal. "Comparative Literature in an Age of Terrorism." In *Comparative Literature in an Age of Globalization.* Ed. Haun Saussy. Baltimore: Johns Hopkins UP, 2006. 68–77.

———. "To World, to Globalize—Comparative Literature's Crossroads." *Comparative Literature Studies* 41.1 (2004): 1–9.

Lewis, Martin W. *Green Delusions: An Environmentalist Critique of Radical Environmentalism.* Durham: Duke UP, 1992.

MacNeill, Jim, et al. *Beyond Interdependence: The Meshing of the World's Economy and the Earth's Ecology.* New York: Oxford UP, 1991.

Mukherjee, Upamanyu Pablo. *Postcolonial Environments: Nature, Culture, and the Contemporary Indian Novel in English.* New York: Palgrave Macmillan, 2010.

Murphey, Rhoads. "Asian Perceptions of and Behavior toward the Natural Environment." In *Landscapes and Communities on the Pacific Rim: Cultural Perspectives from Asia to the Pacific Northwest.* Ed. Karen K. Gaul and Jackie Hiltz. Armonk, NY: M. E. Sharpe, 2000. 35–57.

———. "Man and Nature in China." *Modern Asian Studies* 1.4 (1967): 313–33.

Murphy, Patrick D. *Ecocritical Explorations in Literary and Cultural Studies: Fences, Boundaries, and Fields.* Lanham, MD: Lexington Books, 2009.

Nixon, Rob. "Environmentalism and Postcolonialism." In *Postcolonial Studies and Beyond.* Ed. Ania Loomba et al. Durham: Duke UP, 2005. 233–51.

———. "Slow Violence." *The Chronicle Review* (July 1, 2011), B10–13.

Pratt, Mary Louise. *Imperial Eyes: Travel Writing and Transculturation,* 2nd ed. New York: Routledge, 2008.

Roetz, Heiner. *Mensch und Natur im alten China: zum Subjekt-Objekt-Gegensatz in der klassischen chinesischen Philosophie, zugleich eine Kritik des Klischees vom chinesischen Universismus.* New York: Peter Lang, 1984.

Roos, Bonnie and Alex Hunt, eds. *Postcolonial Green: Environmental Politics and World Narratives.* Charlottesville: U of Virginia P, 2010.

Shiva, Vandana. "The Greening of the Global Reach." In *Global Visions: Beyond the New World Order.* Ed. Jeremy Brecher et al. Boston: South End Press, 1993. 53–66.

Slovic, Scott. *Going Away to Think: Engagement, Retreat, and Ecocritical Responsibility.* Reno: U of Nevada P, 2008.

Snyder, Gary. *A Place in Space: Ethics, Aesthetics, and Watersheds: New and Selected Prose.* Berkeley, CA: Counterpoint, 1995.

———. *The Practice of the Wild: Essays.* San Francisco: North Point Press, 1990.

Sollors, Werner. *Neither Black nor White Yet Both: Thematic Explorations of Interracial Literature.* Cambridge, MA: Harvard UP, 1997.

Spivak, Gayatri Chakravorty. *Death of a Discipline.* New York: Columbia UP, 2003.

Thornber, Karen Laura. *Ecoambiguity: Environmental Crises and East Asian Literatures.* Ann Arbor: U of Michigan P, 2012.

Tiffin, Helen, ed. *Five Emus to the King of Siam: Environment and Empire.* New York: Rodopi, 2007.

Torres, Nelson Maldonado. *Against War: Views from the Underside of Modernity.* Durham: Duke UP, 2008.

Tuan, Yi-Fu. "Discrepancies between Environmental Attitude and Behavior: Examples from Europe and China." In *Environmental History in the Pacific World.* Ed. J. R. McNeill. Burlington, VT: Ashgate, 2001. 235–50.

Tucker, Richard P. *Insatiable Appetite: The United States and the Ecological Degradation of the Tropical World.* Berkeley: U of California P, 2000.

Vital, Anthony. "Toward an African Ecocriticism: Postcolonialism, Ecology and *Life & Times of Michael K.*" *Research in African Literatures* 39.1 (Spring 2008): 87–121.

Volkmann, Laurenz, et al., eds. *Local Natures, Global Responsibilities: Ecocritical Perspectives on the New English Literatures.* New York: Rodopi, 2010.

CONTRIBUTORS

Bruce Allen is professor in the Department of English Language and Literature at Seisen University, Tokyo, Japan, where he teaches translation, comparative literature, and environmental literature. He has translated Ishimure Michiko's *Lake of Heaven* (Lexington Books, 2008) and is now working on a translation of the *Konjaku Monogatari*, a twelfth-century collection of Japanese folkloric and religious tales.

Kathryn Yalan Chang is an assistant professor in the Department of Foreign Languages and Literature in Huafan University in Taiwan. Her current interests include: ecocriticism, ecofeminism, food and environmental ethics, environmental justice and activism, and animal studies. Yalan Chang received her PhD in Western languages and literature in 2009 from Tamkang University, Taiwan. Her doctoral dissertation is entitled "Nature, Gender, and Risk: Margaret Atwood, Linda Hogan, and Karen Tei Yamashita." Her latest published article is "Greening the Everyday Barbara Kingsolver's Ecocritical Praxis and Sustainable Reinhabitation in *Animal, Vegetable, Miracle: A Year of Food Life*" (*Review of English and American Literature* 18 [2011]: 195–226).

Lily Hong Chen is a professor of English in the Research Center for Comparative Literature and World Literatures at Shanghai Normal University, where she specializes in English poetry since the Romantic period. She has presented a number of papers on animals and the concept of the wild in Chinese and English-language cultures. Her book *Bestiality, Animality, and Humanity: A Study of the Animal Poems by D.H. Lawrence and Ted Hughes in Their Historical and Cultural Contexts* was published by the Central China Normal University Press in 2005. Chen hosted the *Wuhan International Conference on Literature and the Environment* in 2008 and coedited (along with Zhenzhao Nie) the collected proceedings from this conference in a volume entitled *Ecocriticism from Wuhan* and published by Huashong Normal University Press in 2010.

Xiangzhan Cheng is a professor of aesthetics in the School of Literature and Communication at Shandong University, deputy director of Shandong University Research Center for Literary Theory and Aesthetics, executive editor of *Newsletter on Ecoaesthetics and Ecocriticism*, and a member of International Advisory Board of *Contemporary Aesthetics*. He has studied at Harvard University, and his fields of research include the history of Chinese aesthetics, environmental aesthetics, ecological aesthetics, and somaesthetics. His essays appear in prominent international journals including ISLE (*Interdisciplinary Studies in Literature and Environment*). He has published several books and has recently translated Richard Shusterman's *Body Consciousness* and Arnold Berleant's *Aesthetics and Environment* into Chinese.

Shiuhhuah Serena Chou received her PhD in comparative literature at the University of Southern California in 2007, and is assistant professor at National Sun Yat-sen University, Taiwan. Her teaching and research focus on American as well as Taiwanese/Japanese environmental literature. She is currently at work on organic farming narratives, Asian American agrarian experience, and geographical imaginings of Annie Proulx.

Simon C. Estok is a junior fellow (2011–2014) and professor of English and literary theory at Sungkyunkwan University (成均館大學校) in Seoul, South Korea. Estok has published extensively on ecocriticism and Shakespeare in such journals as *PMLA*, *Configurations*, *Mosaic*, *ISLE*, *English Studies in Canada*, *FLS*, *The Journal of Canadian Studies*, and others. His book, the award-winning *Ecocriticism and Shakespeare: Reading Ecophobia*, was published by Macmillan in 2011. His 2009 "Theorizing in a Space of Ambivalent Openness: Ecocriticism and Ecophobia," though initially controversial, has cemented the term "ecophobia" into ecocritical theory. Estok has several book collections currently in progress. His research involves the relationship between literary theory and everyday practice.

Peter I-min Huang is currently teaching in the English Department, Tamkang University, as associate professor. He received his PhD in English and comparative literatures from National Taiwan University in 2000. Recently, he has focused his interest and research on ecological literature, ecocriticism, and ecofeminism. His recent publications include "Feminine Writing and Naturalized Ethic of Mary Oliver" in *Foreign Literature Studies* 30.5 (October 2008): 10–19; "Ecocriticism in Taiwan" in *Ecozon@* 1.1 (April 2010): 185–88; "The Politics of Place in *Solar Storms, Lake of Heaven* and *Spider Lilies*" in *ASLE-Japan*

Journal 13 (September 2010): 37–45; "Ethics of Materiality and Commitment in Margaret Atwood's *The Handmaid's Tale*," *Indian Journal of Ecocritism* 3 (August 2010): 88–93; and "Virtuality, Globalization, and Neo-primitivism in Margaret Atwood's *Oryx and Crake*," *Foreign Literature Studies* 33.2 (April 2011): 7–17.

Won-Chung Kim is a professor of English literature at Sungkyunkwan University in Seoul, South Korea. He has published articles on American ecopoets including Gary Snyder, Wendell Berry, Robinson Jeffers, A. R. Ammons, Aldo Leopold, and W. S. Merwin. Kim has also translated ten books of Korean poetry into English, including *Cracking the Shell: Three Korean Ecopoets* and *Scale and Stairs: Selected Poems of Heeduk Ra* (finalist for 2010 Best Translated Book Award). As a founding member of Association for the Study of Literature and Environment (ASLE-Korea), Kim has served as the organization's president.

Keitaro Morita obtained an MA in Intercultural Communication, with a focus on environmental communication, and a DBA (Doctor of Business Administration) in Social Design Studies, with a focus on environmental sociology, both from Rikkyo University in Tokyo. His dissertation is entitled "Ecological Reflection Begets Ecological Identity Begets Ecological Reflexivity." He worked for WWF (World Wide Fund for Nature) Japan and the ESD (Education for Sustainable Development) Center at Rikkyo University, and is currently living in Princeton, New Jersey, surrounded by nature.

Dooho Shin is a professor of English at Kangwon National University in Korea, where he teaches courses on American culture and literature, nature writing, and literary theory. He has published numerous articles on both American and Korean environmental literature and theory and is currently working on a book project on American West places and nature writers. As a cofounder of the Korean Association for the Study of Literature and Environment (ASLE-Korea) and the former editor of the association's journal, *Literature and Environment*, he is now serving as the president.

Karen Thornber is Professor of Comparative Literature and Professor of East Asian Languages and Civilizations at Harvard University. Her research and teaching center on world literature and the literatures and cultures of East Asia. A 2006 Harvard PhD, she is the author of several books, including *Ecoambiguity: Environmental Crises and East Asian Literatures* (Michigan, 2012). She has published numerous articles and chapters on transculturation, postcolonialism, ecocriticism, trauma, and literature and medicine/global health. Thornber has recently begun studying Hindi and Urdu, and her current book project is titled *Global Health and World Literature: East Asia and the Indian Ocean Rim.*

Chan Je Wu is currently a professor of Korean literature at Sogang University in Seoul, Korea, teaching rhetoric and literary criticism. He served as the editor for such Korean literary journals as *Literature and Society, World Literature,* and *Novels of Today.* As literary critic he was awarded the Sochon Critique Award (2000), the Kim Hwantae Critique Award (2003), and the Palbong Critique Award (2010). Professor Wu also served as the president of ASLE-Korea. His publications include: *The Poetics of Desire* (1993), *Wound & Symbol* (1994), *Voices of Other: Temporality at the End of the Century & Literature of Otherness* (1996), *The Rhetoric of the Text* (2005), and *The Protean Flights* (2010).

Jincai Yang is currently professor of American studies and comparative literature and director of the Institute of Foreign Literature, vice dean of the School of Foreign Studies at Nanjing University, and the chief editor of the noted Chinese *Journal of Contemporary Foreign Literature.* He has studied at Harvard University, and was visiting scholar at the University of Hong Kong and Australian National University on several occasions. Professor Yang specializes in British and American literature, and has contributed to various journals a huge range of essays and articles. He has published many academic books and articles and has recently translated and edited *Typee, Omoo and Mardi* (Culture and Art Press, 2006).

Masami Yuki is associate professor at Kanazawa University. She received her doctoral degree in English with an emphasis on literature and environment from University of Nevada, Reno. She has been publishing books and articles on American and Japanese environmental literature with special focus on topics such as literary soundscapes and discourses on food and toxicity. She is also a translator and has worked on Japanese translations of American literature and scholarly articles as well as English translations of Japanese literature. Her most recent book, *Mizu no oto no kioku* [Remembering the Sound of Water: Essays in Ecocriticism], was published in 2010.

INDEX

abalone divers, 27, 32n4
Abbey, Edward, 80, 151
Abney Park Cemetery, 67
abortion, 27–28, 30–31
Academia Sinica (Taiwan), 139
activism, 137–139; Ishimure and, 37,
  39, 44, 54–55. *See also* environmental
  movement
actor-network theory (ANT), 99–100
Adams, Carol, 63, 179n8
aesthetic appreciation, 228–231,
  234n1. *See also* ecological aesthetics;
  ecological aesthetics, keystones of
  appreciation; traditional aesthetics
aesthetic judgment, 229
aesthetic property, 234n1
aesthetics of engagement, 224
aesthetic theory, 223
Africa, 239
Agamben, Giorgio, 206
Agenda 21 for culture (UCLG
  proposal), 95–96
agriculture: "Black Soil" and, 125,
  141–142; Farm Villages Revival Act
  (Taiwan) and, 138; in *Shafu*, 172
Alaimo, Stacy, 9, 125–126, 140–141
Allen, Bruce, 5
Althusser, Louis, 215
ambiguity, environmental, 12–13, 244,
  245–246, 249, 253
"Ambivalence toward the Mythic and
  the Modern, The: Wu, Mingyi's
  Short Stories" (Liou), 157–158
American ecocriticism, 167–162, 191
American literature, 198, 199, 250
American nature writing, 78, 239–240;
  Chinese scholarship on, 198, 199;
  translations of, 80, 151
An, Wei, 197
Anderson, Daniel Gustav, 106
"Anecdotes about Balihuang" (Chen,
  Yingsong), 210–211, 212–213

*Animal Geographies: Place, Politics
  and Identity in the Nature-Culture
  Borderlands* (Elder et al.), 209
animals/animality, 165, 180n9, 180n12,
  244; animals rights and, 195–196;
  association between women and,
  173–176, 179n8; bestiality and,
  65–65, 68, 70n7; butterflies, 148,
  153–148, 156–152, 159, 161n15;
  ethics and, 225–226; horse imagery
  in "Matsuri [Festival]" and, 61–65,
  65–69, 70n8; Ishimure and, 44–46;
  meat eating and, 61–62, 66–65, 68;
  "Peace Dog" and, 206–207, 208–209,
  213, 214, 215, 216–218; pigs and,
  170, 172–167, 175–171, 180n11;
  posthumanism and, 11, 205–206, 210,
  215–216, 218; in *Shafu*, 168, 169–178;
  Taiwanese writers and, 177–178; whale
  hunting and, 8, 9, 127–125, 134–129,
  136, 141. *See also* dehumanization;
  humans/nonhumans relationship
*Anthology of Taiwanese Nature Writing,
  An* (Wu, Mingyi), 151–152, 156
anthropocentrism, 93–94, 235n3;
  Chinese ecocriticism and, 193, 195;
  Chinese literature and, 187; Chinese
  people and, 208; early ecocriticism
  and, 238; ecological aesthetics and,
  222, 231; humanism and, 228;
  posthumanism and, 206; Shennongjia
  stories and, 205; Taiwanese nature
  writing and, 151, 152; Wu, Mingyi
  and, 158
anthropogenic transformations.
  See humans, transformation of
  ecosystems by
anti-Romantic tradition, 212
April 19 Revolution (Korea), 85, 89n4
art, 221–222; basic knowledge to
  appreciate, 229; objectification
  of, 224

"Rachel Carson's Accomplishments in Eco-Literature" (Wang, Nuo), 190
racism, 250
rape, 173, 176, 179n8
Rasputin, Valentin, 199
"Recent Critiques of Ecocriticism" (Gifford), 79
reconciliation, 5, 41–44, 52
reflective capacity of humans, 19
Regal, Philip, 227–228
Regan, Tom, 195
religion: Buddhism, 81, 89, 172, 177, 240; Tonghak, 86, 87, 89n5. *See also* Confucianism; Taoism
Ren, Zhang, 195
restoration, 103, 105–106, 108n5. *See also* Seoul Cheongyecheon Restoration project
"risk assessment" language, 139–141
Roetz, Heiner, 241
romance, 112
Roos, Bonnie, 146
Roszak, Theodore, 112
Rozin, Paul, 175
Rueckert, William, 165
Russian ecoliterature, 198–199

"sacred spaces," 128–129
salim culture (Korea), 86
Sand County Almanac and Sketches Here and There, A (Leopold), 80, 151
Sandilands, Catriona, 60, 70n7
Sang-yeon, Park, 8, 111
Saro-Wiwa, Ken, 244
scenic beauty, 233, 235n5
science, 158, 238, 242; ecological aesthetics and, 230–231; of ecology, 228–223, 234; nature writing and, 148, 152. *See also under ecology*
Science and the Modern World (Whitehead), 196
Sedgwick, Eve Kosofsky, 59
Seeking Spatial Justice (Soja), 105
Sense of Place and Sense of Planet: The Environmental Imagination of the Global (Heise), 51, 129, 238, 246–247
Sense of Wonder (Carson), 53
Seoul Cheongyecheon Restoration project, 7; cultural restoration and, 105–106; goals of, 94–95, 107n3; opponents of, 97; preservationism-development dichotomy and, 91–92,

92–94, 100, 102, 103, 104, 107; responses to, 100–107. *See also* "Clean Stream Novels"
Seoul Metropolitan Government, 94
sexism: *Shafu* and, 10, 170, 177; speciesism and, 180n9
sexuality: bestiality, 65–65, 68, 70n7; heterosexuality, 62–63, 67; homosexuality/queers, 59, 64–67, 69n2; in "Matsuri [Festival]," 65–67, 70n8; odor and, 68; patriarchal violence and, 173, 175, 178; prostitution and, 172, 173; queer ecofeminism and, 5–6; in *Shafu*, 170
"Sexual Politics and Environmental Justice: Lesbian Separatists in Rural Oregon" (Sandilands), 60
Sha, Qing, 193
Shafu. See Butcher's Wife, The (Shafu) (Li, Ang)
Shanghai wenxue (Shanghai literature) (magazine), 188
Shen, Congwen, 197
Shengtai piping de kongjian (Space for Ecocriticism) (Lu, Shuyuan), 189
"Shengtai piping: fazhan yu yuanyuan" ("Development and Origin of Ecocriticism" (Wang, Nuo), 190
Shengtai piping shiyuxia de zhongguo xiandangdai wenxue (An Ecocritical Perspective into Modern and Contemporary Chinese Literature) (Wang, Xirong et al.), 197
"Shengtai piping yanjiu kaoping" ("A Review of Ecocritical Studies") (Liu, Bei), 191
Shengtaiwenyixue (Ecological Research in Literature and Art) (Lu, Shuyuan), 196
Shengtai Yishi Yu Zhongguo Dangdai Wenxue (Ecological Consciousness in Contemporary Chinese Literature) (Wang, Shudong), 193–194, 197
"*shen-mei*" (evaluation or judgment of beauty), 222–224, 233
Shennongjia stories (Chen, Yingsong), 205–218; "Anecdotes about Balihuang," 210–211, 212–213; "Peace Dog," 206–207, 208–209, 213, 214, 215, 216–218; setting of, 219n1; "To Live Like White Clouds," 212, 213–214

Printed in the United States of America